Autumn Sunset

by

Daphne C. Murrell

Tate Publishing, LLC.

Published in the United States of America
by Tate Publishing, LLC
127 East Trade Center Terrace
Mustang, OK 73064
(888) 361–9473

ISBN: 1–5988628–8-X

Dedication

This book is dedicated in loving memory
to my father, Chaplain Warren B. Wall Sr.,
February 27, 1921 - August 21, 2003,

My biggest fan, who always believed I could do anything.

Acknowledgment

Many thanks to my family—Rick, Melody, Josh, Charis, and Mother—for allowing me the time off from dishes and laundry to do some creative stuff now and then. Also, I must thank Becky Lockhart, Jeannette Pearson, Gloria McKee, and Anita Hill for being the readers of my creations and the preliminary grammar police. Thank you for some lively discussion along the way and the subtle hints you graciously offered. Then, going way back, I would like to thank Bill and Mary Ann Bozeman for encouraging me right from the start to be willing to reach beyond the norm and boldly believe I could do anything I wanted; every person should have someone like you two to mentally lean back on. Special thanks to Richard and Becky Twilley for somehow knowing and always believing. And finally, heartfelt thanks to my four big brothers—Warren, Brooks, Bill, and Reid. You have influenced my writing both directly and indirectly. Thanks for all you have been in my life. But most of all, I must thank my Lord and Savior for placing in me a literal ooze of creativity. Because of Him, life is a never-ending adventure, and I pray that someday all this oozing will result in His ultimate glory.

Chapter One

Annie sighed deeply as she nervously drummed the pencil atop her desk. She glanced at the clock on the wall and silently mouthed the time, *4:57.* She hated procrastination. She was anything but a procrastinator. Yet today she had no motivation to complete anything, namely a project for Vivian McCall. The commercial jingle was due for review by Ms. McCall on Friday morning. It was Wednesday. Annie had nothing.

Two small taps on her door startled her, and she dropped her pencil to the floor.

"Knock, knock," came her secretary's soft voice from the other side.

"Come in, Terri," Annie said while leaning down to retrieve the wayward pencil. The point had stuck into the carpet. This one unusual thing actually brought a smile to Annie's otherwise glum face.

"I have got to get a life," she mumbled to herself, leaving the pencil in the carpet because it simply amused her.

"Anything?" Terri asked as she peeked inside the door.

"Nothing," Annie responded. "Not a note, a jot, or a tiddle."

"I've never seen you like this," Terri said as she came all the way inside the door. "You complete your work so early. Why the stall on this one? Writer's block or something?"

"Oh, let's call it McCall's block," Annie complained as she stood up, accidentally knocking over the stuck pencil. "Rats." She picked it up and placed it on the desk.

"What's the problem?" Terri wanted to know. This was not like Annie. Annie was always on time, in fact, always before time. Annie was a wellspring of talent and creativity. Annie was never *stuck.*

"The problem. Hmm . . . hard one to explain there. Are you familiar with Kelly McCall, Vivian's lovely daughter?" Annie began.

"Yes! Miss America?" Terri interrupted.

"*Former* Miss America," Annie corrected.

"Was she your age?" Terri asked excitedly.

Annie nodded.

"I bet you guys were great friends! She has a beautiful voice."

Annie thought back to high school, eight years ago. Annie was smart, talented, and athletic. She was the best in everything, and it was not by accident. She worked, studied, and practiced to make sure she stayed on top. Then there was Kelly McCall, always a step or two behind Annie. Annie never made much of it, but it ate Kelly up from the inside out. Their senior year, Kelly was captain of the cheerleaders and was homecoming queen. Annie was captain of the softball and basketball teams, drum majorette for the band, and prom queen. When Annie was pronounced valedictorian, Kelly literally burst into tears. Apparently, though, she was the only one surprised since Annie had made nothing lower than an "A" all four years of high school.

Annie secretly relished all the accomplishments, only because she knew it killed Kelly. However, when they went away to their prospective colleges, Kelly flourished. By her junior year, she was crowned Miss Alabama and went on to win the Miss America title. Suddenly, the town of Dockrey had a new darling, and Annie's flame was significantly snuffed out. To top it off, at the end of Annie's junior year in college, she was "asked" to leave the college where she, her parents, her two older sisters, and her younger brother had attended. Her "opinionated stubborn-headedness" had finally caught up with her. She had to leave a full, four-year scholarship behind, after already completing three years at Clarksville Christian College for the University of Alabama—Kelly's school.

"Kelly's a real sweetheart," Terri finally broke in.

"She's a doll," Annie muttered through barely clenched teeth.

"Did you know she had twins?"

"Yeah, her mother told me," Annie sighed. Then she silently thought, *Actually, her mother gloated.*

"Didn't you and Kelly go to the same college?" Terri continued.

"Uh huh," Annie said, deciding not to explain this to Terri, but hoping to scramble away from the office as soon as possible. Something would come to her tonight; she could play around on the keyboard at home. She reached up to turn off the power to all of her musical and recording equipment.

"You're leaving?" Terri exclaimed astounded.

Annie just looked at her and slightly grimaced.

"With *nothing* done? I mean—you've never done this!" Terri went on.

Yeah, rub it in, Terri. Let's just continue to make my day. "Yeah, I think I'm just tired—the wedding and all coming up," Annie lied.

"Next weekend!" Terri exclaimed. "Aren't you excited? I love weddings! Have you seen Megan's dress yet? She's so pretty and petite. She will look beautiful."

Well, no, she had not seen Megan's dress. There was her excuse.

"I'm headed over to see Megan right now," Annie tried to say with conviction. "We're going to look at *her* dress, at *my* dress, at *everybody's* dresses, and then talk about some last minute preparations."

"Have a good time!" Terri waved as she turned to leave. "I'll see you bright and early in the morning!"

Annie waited until the outer office door slammed then she sighed again and rolled her eyes. *I'm going to have to fire her. Too perky—and she likes Kelly McCall.*

Annie climbed into her blue VW Bug and cranked the engine. Immediately, the CD came on—Stephen Williams. She loved his music. *The Piano Album,* her favorite, gently wound around the inside of her soul, filling up all the empty spaces. She just sat quietly, closed her eyes, and then let the music melt away her tensions.

Genius. Musical genius. How does he write that? How does he touch the deepest part of me?

She let her mind wander for a moment and remembered his concert tour for this particular album. He normally used a band, but for this recording, it was only his fluid piano playing, not even an electric keyboard, and his gentle, flowing voice. The words of *Autumn Sunset,* his biggest hit, almost haunted her as she finally put the Bug into gear and backed out of the parking space.

Early November, gaze out my window
Watching the leaves barely hanging on
Pour me some coffee, pick up a novel
Ready to spend another evening alone
Never thought it would be this way
I simply played it safe
And somehow I never gave my heart away
So while I'm waiting for someone to love me
Someone who knows me through and through
I'll watch the Autumn Sunset from my single room apartment
And hope and pray that dreams can still come true
And long to hear the words, "I love you."

Annie drove through the town of Dockrey as she made her way to Megan's house. The song continued, and Annie wondered how one piece of music could describe her life so completely, one piece that she herself did not even write.

Cool, early morning, stretching and yawning
No reason to get up, but no reason to stay
Hear children playing, watch couples swaying
Down in the courtyard as they face the day
Never thought it would be this way
Just focused on other things
And somehow I let my time slip away
So while I'm waiting for someone to love me
Someone who knows me through and through
I'll watch the Autumn Sunset from my single room apartment
And hope and pray that dreams can still come true
And long to hear the words, "I love you."

Annie then found herself singing along as the bridge started:

Nobody warned me, nobody said,
"There's more to living than just success."
Nobody moved me, nobody dared, nobody showed me, nobody shared.
Nobody told me about the sunrise, nobody told me, nobody tried.
So, while I'm waiting for someone to love me
Someone who knows me through and through
I'll watch the Autumn Sunset from my single room apartment
And hope and pray that dreams can still come true
And long to hear the words, "I love you."

Annie turned the Bug into Megan's driveway. She was happy for Megan and her brother, Alex. They had dated for six years. They deserved happiness, but the haunting refrain of the Stephen Williams song had put her into such a melancholy mood that she was ready to pour cold water on anybody's happiness.

Could Stephen Williams possibly be as miserable as me? She thought on that for a moment. *Nope. He's rich, famous, and amazingly talented. He's just a good writer. This song couldn't have come from the heart.*

"I am so tired I could just die," Megan mourned as she plopped down on her bed after inviting Annie into her room. "I almost wish I would have taken Alex's advice and eloped."

"No, you don't," Annie smiled, actually happy to find someone more exhausted than she was. "When you walk down that aisle in that beautiful dress and see Alex all decked out in his tux, you'll be glad you went through all this hassle."

"I'm seriously beginning to doubt it. You won't believe what happened today."

"More surprises?" Annie giggled. She loved Megan. Having her marry Alex would be like gaining another sister. Megan was the sweetest woman in the entire world; no one would disagree with that.

"Kendra wants to be in the wedding," Megan said slowly.

Annie laughed this time.

"How? Are you going to have someone wheel her down the aisle?"

"No," Megan explained. "The doctor put some kind of cast on her leg and said she would actually be able to 'walk,' or more aptly hobble, down the aisle."

Annie fell down on the bed next to Megan and just continued laughing. Megan's expression of disgust was all the medicine Annie needed to pull her out of the melancholy blues.

"Well, just get her a dress and let her go!" Annie said.

"But now that means that we have to come up with another groomsman!"

"So? Come up with another one. There are plenty of guys to choose from."

"Not with Alex, there isn't!" Megan said in desperation. "I begged him to pick his own groomsmen. The only one he chose was Doug, your illustrious brother-in-law, who is liable to pull out a rubber chicken in the middle of the ceremony! I had to get all the others. It's like a list of Who's Who in *my* life! Not Alex's!"

"Well, *make* him pick someone for this. Don't give him a choice."

"Oh, yes, Mr. Decisive," Megan groaned. "I love your brother, but he can't even decide where to eat when the only available option is Burger King! If I ask him to pick another groomsmen, he may not even show! His brain might explode!"

"Okay, okay," Annie soothed as she reached over to caress Megan's face that was now beginning to redden as her eyes teared up. "I will talk to him. He *will* pick a groomsmen. You don't have to worry about this."

Megan let a small smile force its way to her lips. "Thanks," she managed.

"The least I can do," Annie smiled back. "Now, how about showing me that incredible dress you're planning to wear next Saturday?"

Annie gave Megan her full attention as she showed the dress. The two ladies were as opposite as could be. Megan was petite, a mere 5 feet 2, with pixied blonde hair and smiling hazel eyes. Annie, who never told anyone she was self-conscious about her height, was 5 feet 10, but she felt like she was 6 feet 3. Her dark brown hair fell halfway to her waist when she let it down, and her eyes were a deep brown, so brown you could only see her pupils in the bright light. Then there were her lips—the ones she and her older sisters, Angie and Andie, had inherited from their father. They were thick and full. As a child, those lips had been the brunt of sarcastic jokes. As a maturing teenager and woman, they became the brunt of suggestive jokes. Angie claimed the same treatment during her years of medical school, residency, and internship. Annie wasn't sure if they were a blessing or a curse, but she had given up on bright lipstick somewhere between college and graduate school, hoping the whole lip thing would be ignored. It didn't work.

After assuring Megan one more time that she would indeed get Alex to pick a groomsman, Annie headed home. Home. With her parents. Still. At 26. She rolled her eyes again. She envied Alex, even though he would be in a completely different situation if it had not been for her persistence in moving him along. He was an awesome bass guitarist. The only backbone he had ever shown in his life was declaring to their father that his goal was to play bass in a band; nothing else mattered. Of course, Jonathan Wright, pastor of First Baptist Church, Dockrey, felt that was too vague of a goal for his only son and youngest child. Alex said there was no room for discussion on this point. He was going to be a bass player when he grew up. End of discussion.

Annie and Alex were not very close because they were so different. Annie was driven, just like Angie. Alex was not. He did the minimal work required for the minimal passing needed. The girls were, in the words of Andie's husband, Doug, "beautiful, opinionated, and stubborn-headed." He would always follow his description of them with the phrase, "One out of three ain't bad." Nevertheless, because of this drastic difference between Alex and his older sisters, he never seemed to fit in. He slid through the cracks of their lives so easily because he never was *there* even when he was there. Annie once asked him if he enjoyed being a blob when he refused to comment on a heated political discussion one October. He just shrugged his shoulders and went to his room to play his guitar. The discussion continued as though he had never been there or left.

When Annie had to leave Clarksville College, Megan and Alex had just begun dating. Megan told her that Alex became a whole different person after Annie left. Annie took it the wrong way, thinking that Alex missed his older sister, but found out quickly it was quite the opposite. He suddenly became outspoken and a lot of fun on campus. His grades went up for the first time ever, and he was even on the homecoming court the next two years. Annie wondered if her shadow had been so big all those years that he never had room to be himself.

The clincher of her pushing him, however, had come this past year. She was still patting herself on the back, but had never received a genuine "thank you" from Alex yet. For a year and half he had been playing as a studio musician in Nashville. The pay was not all that great, and most of the music was country, definitely *not* Alex's style. Annie knew the talent he had, above and beyond anything she had ever heard before in a bass player. He was so good at it that he actually gave the bass almost a melody line, yet it could fit perfectly into any song. He was too good to pound out a monotonous *bum, bum, bum* for the rest of his life. Then in January, she happened upon a piece of information that literally brought her to her feet in a yelling fit when she read it on the Internet. Stephen Williams' bassist had been diagnosed with inoperable cancer and would be leaving the band for good. That meant Stephen Williams would need a new bass player, someone way beyond the average to take the empty space.

Annie spent three days on the phone trying to track down someone who would give her the time of day and listen to her plea.

"I am not an idiot!" she remembered yelling into the phone to an actual Stephen Williams representative, the first one she had managed to get through to. "I have a B.A. in music composition and a master's in music ed. Check my credentials if you must, but you have got to give Alex Wright an audition! You would be stupid not to!"

She was at the end of her rope, and her adjectives, as well as her composure, were waning fast.

"Let me get this straight," the representative said. "You believe your brother should be the next bassist for Stephen Williams? Do you understand the caliber of musician required to play with Mr. Williams?"

"Okay, apparently I sound like a total idiot to you." *Didn't I already use the word idiot?* "Yes, I am trying to explain to you that Alex Wright is a caliber above anything I have ever heard before. He is an awesome musician and an incredible bass player. It would be well worth your time," she slowed her words deliberately to make her point, "if you would at least audition him."

Silence and pause.

"And this *Alex* would be your brother, correct?" asked the man.

"Yes," she said with control.

"Why don't you send us a recording, then we will consider whether your brother is worth an audition."

"Okay, obviously you're not taking me seriously. I understand. You've probably had a million calls about this . . ."

"Actually, you're the first," the man interrupted. "All the calls we've had have been expressions of sympathy and loss over the illness and impending death of the present bassist, Jerry Carter."

Silence and pause again.

"Oh," she finally grunted. "I see."

"So I can honestly say that you are beating the bandwagon on this one," the man said sourly.

"Look," Annie tried to recover, "I am sorry about Jerry Carter. He was . . . *is* . . . a really talented musician. . . ."

"Glad you think so," the man said sarcastically. "I'll be sure to tell him. I mean, with your credentials and all, the B.A. and M.A. Sure it wasn't a B.S.?"

"Very funny," Annie muttered, embarrassed now. "All I'm asking is that you give Alex a shot. He is above and beyond any bass player I've ever heard . . ." she paused, and then added, "even Jerry Carter."

Silence.

"Well, it appears that you are either very sure of a good thing or a total lunatic," the man finally said. "Either way, I suppose we should give him a listen."

"Either way?" Annie was about to blow. "What do you mean either way?"

"If he's as good as you say, then by all means we should audition him," the man explained. "If you're merely a raving lunatic, then I would fear for the lives of all who work with Mr. Williams if we didn't audition him."

Silence again. She hoped he was only playing with her.

"I assure you, sir," trying to be controlled, "I am *not* a lunatic."

"Hmm," she could hear the smile in his voice, "they say that denial is the first step toward psychosis."

"Will you hear him?" She was afraid she had lost the fight, that this man was convinced she was crazy. If Alex got the job, she would make sure that someone talked with Stephen Williams about his representatives.

"I suppose. I must say I am extremely curious."

Annie whooped, then regained her composure and spoke calmly into the phone.

"How would you like the audition to take place? When, where and how?"

"Excuse me," said the man, "my ears are still ringing from the exclamation into the phone."

She rolled her eyes and began to giggle. "I'm sorry," she admitted sincerely, "but *you* won't be. I'm telling you, when you hear him play, you won't even listen to another bass player."

"Ooo, I'm sure," he teased. "Give me your number. Let me speak with Mr. Williams, and we'll set something up."

And that was that. Alex was flown to New York, and as Annie had predicted, his playing awed Stephen Williams. He was hired on the spot and moved to New York within two weeks to begin recording Stephen's 11th album. It was then that Alex finally proposed to poor Megan. After almost six years of sticking with him, she clung to his promise that when he "made it big" he would marry her. "Big," he had finally made. In fact, it did not get any bigger than this in the music business.

Annie dialed Alex's number and patiently waited past eight rings. Alex was not a phone talker or much of a talker, period. He would never answer the phone unless it was persistent. Nine rings. Ten rings. Eleven rings. Maybe he actually wasn't around the phone.

"Hello?"

"Alex? Hello! It's Annie."

"What's up?"

Haven't seen you since I got you that great job in New York playing for the most awesome musician in the world. What's up?

"I'm fine, and how are you?" she managed to say instead.

"Tired," he mumbled. "Stephen doesn't let up until it's perfect."

"Do you anticipate the album being good?"

"Definitely."

Ooo! A positive comment! It must be really good.

"Megan needs you to do something."

"Okay," he sighed. "What?"

"Kendra can walk and wants to be in the wedding. You need to get another groomsman."

Nothing.

"Just pick anybody, Alex. She won't care," Annie begged.

"I don't know anybody else," he complained. "I mean, Doug's the only guy I could come up with."

"For crying out loud, Alex, she picked the other four for you!" Annie chided. "Can't you come up with one more guy?"

"I don't know anybody else," he whined. "I mean, I don't want to ask some guy I don't know well to be in my wedding. Shoot, I just want to marry Megan and get through with all this stuff."

"I know, I know," Annie tried to calm him down. "Just . . . well . . . can't you think of anybody? What about one of the band members? I mean, you've been with them for four months now. Surely one of them could stand up with you."

"Aw, they're all married with kids and stuff," he griped even more. "I can't do that. It'd be embarrassing anyway."

"You gotta come up with just one guy, Alex. Come on. Buck up." She winced. She knew he hated it when she insinuated he was a wimp.

Complete quiet again.

"I'll do something," he replied curtly. Then "click." He hung up.

Good one, Annie. Just beat him up some more.

Chapter Two

The studio fell silent as everyone waited for the final note to fade and for the engineer to give the "all clear" sign. They sat in silence as the last waves of sound melted away inside the headphones. The engineer behind the glass window gave the thumbs up.

"Yes!" Stephen yelled as he jumped up from behind the baby grand. "Was that not unreal? We recorded an incredible album in four months!"

"An excellent album," came the producer's voice from the microphone in the sound room. "You guys outdid yourself on this one."

"That's an understatement," said Chip as he began to pack up his flute and saxophone. "Where did this stuff come from, Stevie? These songs were like a whole new step above anything you've done before."

Stephen once again ignored the "Stevie" nickname. He hated it, but he'd rather deal with it than belittle one of his musicians.

"It was inspiration, my friend, pure inspiration," Stephen smiled.

Alex laughed to himself as he pulled the bass guitar from around his neck. "What are you laughing at, Wright?" asked the guitar player, Jason, as he looked over toward Alex.

"Nothing really," he mumbled out. "It's just this guy, a college professor, used to say that writing music was 99 percent perspiration and 1 percent inspiration. He made any songwriter in that class feel, you know, 2 inches high—except my sister. She managed to put him in his place one day . . . got kicked out of college for it."

"Really?" said Stephen as he walked over to Alex. "Is this the same sister that got you auditioned?"

"One and the same," Alex blushed a little. He did not *even* want to know how Annie managed to get him an audition. He was glad, but he was sure it took more than a gentle phone call. "She tends to be—spirited," he searched for a good word.

You have no idea, Stephen thought to himself.

"Well, everyone, enjoy your vacations before tour time," Stephen said with sincerity. "You've earned them."

"When will the album be released?" asked Kurt, the brass player.

"We're actually shooting for early September," Stephen said.

"Early September . . . gaze out my window . . . ," teased Jason as he sang the altered line from *Autumn Sunset.*

"Which reminds me," Stephen said quickly while turning to Alex, "I'll need to give you the lead sheets and recordings of the old songs we'll do on tour that are not on this album. I hate to mess up your newlywed life having to learn songs."

"Hey, I'm still reeling from the fact that you'll actually pay me a salary even while out of the studio or not on tour," Alex responded quickly.

"Stephen takes care of his musicians," Sam added as he put his drumsticks into his back pocket. "Really well."

"You guys are my family," Stephen explained. "I wouldn't want to lose you for anything."

There was silence as everyone thought of Jerry Carter, the former bass player who had passed away three weeks ago. Alex had met him. He was a wonderful man, a great father, and a loving husband. He was an unprofessional comedian to boot. He had been the life of this band for eight years, and Alex felt extremely inferior taking his place. Alex knew he was good musically, but he would never fill the hole left when Jerry died. He had been more than a musician to these guys; he had been a devoted friend.

"Anyway," Stephen finally broke in, "enjoy your time off. September 11 we kick off in New York. Have a great summer everyone."

"Uh. . . ." Alex tried to be assertive. Everyone turned to him. "Well, I sort of need to ask a kind of favor, sort of."

Everyone stared, but Alex could not seem to get the words out. Where was the fire and forthrightness that his sisters seemed to be so blessed, *or cursed,* with?

"Spit it out, my boy," Stephen encouraged.

"Wow . . . um," Alex tried to talk. "You all . . . uh . . . well, you know I'm getting married next Saturday."

"Yes, sir," Jason smiled.

"Way to go," Kurt slapped him on the back. "Good looking girl too."

"Yeah, thanks," Alex tried to continue. "Uh . . . it seems that this cousin of hers, Kendra, well, you don't actually have to know her name. Anyway, she's gonna be in the wedding now. She broke her leg skiing. Well, actually *demolished* her leg, and she couldn't do it but now she can . . . this special cast or something." He felt his face getting hot. *Buck up.* "I need another groomsman."

The guys all stared at him, amazed at his self-consciousness.

"Why didn't you ask sooner?" Chip laughed.

"I didn't know until last night," Alex said. "My sister called, and well, this Kendra has kind of messed up the whole plan."

"Which sister?" Stephen wanted to know.

Which sister? The one that manages to run my life or ruin it? "Annie," he said softly. "The . . . uh . . . spirited one."

Stephen laughed aloud and slapped his knee. "I'm there!" he volunteered.

"What?" Alex said, startled at the idea of Stephen Williams being in his wedding, being in Dockrey, Alabama. "Are you serious?"

"I can't do it," Kurt chimed in. "Family plans already."

"Me either," said Chip. "The wife's got us taking a second honeymoon to the Caribbean. Ten years next week." Chip smiled big. He was looking forward to some time with his wife and no kids.

"Married life is great," Jason added. "You're gonna love it, kid. I'm headed to Colorado with my family. We're gonna do some camping and such."

"Got plans, man," Sam said as he shook his head.

Stephen put his arm around Alex and gave him a big smile. "Looks like you're stuck with me," he said to Alex as he stretched his arms first in the air and then down to touch his toes. "When do we leave for the Heart of Dixie?"

"Hey, Stephen," Chip laughed, "maybe you could write a song about Alabama? Has that been done before?"

Stephen began to sing, "Stars dropped down on Alabama . . ." He wrinkled his nose in confusion. "I don't think those are the right words."

"I don't think that's even a real song," Kurt doubted.

"Yes, I believe it's the state song, isn't it, Alex?" Stephen asked.

Alex just nodded. He could not bring himself to speak. He was still in shock that Stephen Williams was going to be in his wedding. The more he thought about it, the hotter his face felt. Stephen Williams meeting his family, talking with his sisters, it was too much to take.

"Then there's *Sweet Home Alabama,*" Chip brought up.

"Oh, yeah, I forgot about that one," Sam laughed.

"Wasn't there another one too?" Stephen asked them as they continued the Alabama music trivia game.

Alex was feeling warmer and warmer. "Excuse me," Alex said quickly. "I need a restroom break."

"This ought to be fun," Stephen said jovially.

"Do you think you'll be recognized in Alabama?" Jason asked.

"Maybe not," Stephen sighed. "Maybe I could actually go into a Wal-Mart or something!"

Alex was getting nauseous. He needed to leave the room quickly. How could he possibly entertain one of the world's greatest entertainers for an entire week?

No problem. My sisters will be there, all three of them. He couldn't get to the bathroom soon enough.

Annie sighed with relief as she hung up the phone. Alex had found one of the musicians agreeable to being in his wedding. Mark that one off. Now to write a jingle for McCall Ford, record it, and pitch it by 9:00 in the morning. How could she let herself put this off for so long?

The phone buzzed. "Yes, Terri," she said as she pressed the button.

"*Ms.* McCall is on line one."

Annie smiled because there was only one line and because of the way Terri had stressed the *Ms.* After her divorce, Vivian McCall insisted on being referred to as *Ms.*, something that wasn't really common in rural Alabama.

Annie picked up the phone. "*Mrs.* McCall," she answered on purpose.

"Vivian, please," came the syrupy response. "How is the jingle coming?"

Annie squirmed. She did finally have a melody, but finding something to rhyme with *Ford* just kept eluding her, other than hoard, bored, or gored.

"Oh, we're just plodding right along," she said cheerily.

"Well, look dear," Vivian started, "I just can't make the meeting in the morning. I hate to throw this on you because I know you work *so hard* with your *little* job."

Annie could hear the sarcasm shining through and imagined Vivian's peroxide head bobbing slightly to the side as she did when she was getting the best of someone.

"I've had an emergency phone call from Kelly in Hawaii."

Yes, rub it in, rub it in. Kelly's in Hawaii hosting a TV show; I'm in Dockrey, living with my parents, writing jingles for local TV and radio.

"I hope everything's all right," Annie lied. *Has she contracted a deadly disease and you need to be by her bedside as she slips away?*

"Oh, it's quite dreadful, I'm afraid," Vivian said with much drama. Annie perked up, feeling almost guilty for the smile spreading across her pale, thick lips.

"She's been asked to host a telethon, and with the twins still so young and her husband John at spring training camp for the Forty-Niners . . . you did know he played for them?"

"I seem to remember someone mentioning that to me." The smile faded. Okay, Vivian had won.

"Well, she needs me to come out and help the nanny with the girls for the next two weeks."

Thud. The emotional let down was almost too much for Annie to even pretend to be concerned.

"So when do you want to meet about the jingle? Or do you want me to run it by someone else at the dealership?"

"Oh, no, no, no," Vivian insisted. "I want to hear the sweet little thing with my own ears. You were always so good with that type of stuff."

That type of stuff? What on earth does that mean? I suppose it's a dig of some type.

"Well, when would you like to meet?" Annie asked, trying to sound as though she really cared.

"I hate to put you off like this, but from what I've heard, you probably have the whole thing finished by now. Everyone recommends you highly for this sort of thing." There it was again. She knew Vivian was digging in now. "I mean, who knows? If you keep it up, Annie, maybe you could go professional with it some day. Kelly says they're always looking for up-and-coming talent in the networks."

Dig. Dig. Dig.

"Well, I am putting on the finishing touches," she tried to sound sincere, "but it's not quite ready. I've had a lot on my plate with the wedding plans and all."

"Oh, that's right," Vivian was oozing again. "Your Alex is marrying that little orphan right?"

That was it. If Annie didn't get off the line soon, her mouth, fueled by her temper, would get the best of her.

"She's not really an orphan, *Mrs.* McCall. Her parents were killed, and she was raised by her aunt and uncle." She hoped the *Mrs.* stuck just a little.

"Yes. Poor dear." Ooze. "Lucky for her, though, really. With her uncle being a doctor and all, she's actually had it made, as opposed to what life could have been like had her parents survived the crash."

This woman was sick, eaten up with herself and her own bitterness.

God, help me not to give into this trap she is weaving. The prayer was genuine.

"You're right, Vivian. Lucky for her. Dr. Bob and Kim raised her like their own. She is truly blessed."

"And to be marrying your Alex. He is so handsome."

"Thank you, *Mrs.* McCall. I'll tell him you said so. Now, about the commercial, would you like to set another date?"

"Well, not really, dear," she finally admitted. "Let me spend some time with Kelly and the twins. When I get back, I'll get with you and we'll make some new plans. Just put my little tune on hold for now. You enjoy the wedding festivities with Alex and Megan. I'm sure it will be very *quaint.*"

Dig.

"Okay, then. You have a nice trip," Annie tried to conclude the conversation. "Tell Kelly I said 'hi'." Augh! She could kick herself for that one.

"How sweet of you," Vivian gushed again. "I'll be sure to do that."

Annie sprung from her chair in disgust. She hated being patronized, and Vivian McCall took great pleasure in doing just that. Well, at least the McCall Ford jingle was officially on hold. Annie grabbed her purse, pulled her keys out of the top drawer of her desk, and rushed out the door of her studio into the main office.

"Trouble?" Terri asked, startled by the burst into the room.

"No," Annie said as she tried to smile. "Vivian's going to Hawaii, and the McCall account isn't due in the morning after all."

"Super!" Terri said in her particularly upbeat way. "I bet you're really glad about that!"

"Well, to tell you the truth, it would have been nice to have it over."

Annie headed toward the door.

"Where are you going?" Terri questioned. "It's only 10:30."

"You know what?" Annie mused. "I'm taking the rest of the week off!"

"You're the boss, boss!" Terri perked.

I'm really gonna have to fire her. "Um, take it off too, if you want," Annie told her.

"No way," Terri countered. "You get too many phone calls as it is. I hate to deal with the answering machine when we close down. We're off all of next week anyway. You should hire some more people. This could really develop into a franchise!"

How about just a new secretary? "Maybe so, Terri," she conceded. "Maybe so. Have a great weekend if I don't see you."

"You too, Annie!" Terri called as Annie headed out the door.

Okay, I'm off. Now what do I do?

"Well, this is a welcome sight," came a voice from the doorway.

Annie leaned up from her reclining position on the couch to see her sister Angie standing in the front doorway with her luggage.

"Butter pecan?" Angie asked as she shut the door with her foot and moved over to the couch where Annie had an entire half-gallon box of ice cream sitting on her lap.

"Guilty," she smiled back. "Bryers."

Annie put the ice cream on the coffee table and stood up to give Angie a long, warm hug.

"How I have missed you," Annie said in full-blown melancholy again.

"Me too," Angie moaned as she fell back onto the couch. "I am so tired of going 99 percent of the time. I need a break."

"Then take one," Annie insisted. "Start seminary in the fall, not the summer."

Angie shook her head. Annie admired her older sister for many things, one being her incredible drive. Angie was beautiful, and the thick lips that Annie so despised on herself looked full and lush on her sister. Like Annie, Angie's hair was long, dark, and straight, but she had inherited the light green eyes from her father, the same eyes as Alex.

"No way," Angie continued as she talked about seminary classes. "I'm going to get this over with now. If I work hard enough and take full loads, I can get my seminary courses over with as soon as possible and be ready for Padawin."

"What's the rush?" Annie wondered.

"Rush? Hello? How many years have I already put into this? My life's plan is so close to being complete, yet it's still only the beginning. Become a doctor, then become a missionary to Padawin."

"I know," Annie stalled, "but you could really use a small break. Stay here with me for the summer, and let's pretend we have real lives again."

"Move back in with Mom and Dad? At 28? I don't think so," Angie said with condescension. "Not even for a summer."

"Well, I feel like a real winner now. You just described my life with great disdain."

"Hey, we all make our own choices," Angie scolded. "If this is what you want in life, then go for it, but this is not me. I've been in contact with an agricultural missionary in Padawin. He's dying for a doctor to come work with him in the villages. Now if I can only convince the mission board."

Annie was still reeling from the 'we all make our own choices' statement, but she managed a monosyllabic acknowledgment to her sister.

"I am so ready to do the whole missionary thing," Angie continued. "All this schooling, and I still have to go to seminary! Whatever. I promised to follow the rules, so off I go to school again. I mean, how hard can seminary be after med-school?"

"I'm guessing you will pass," Annie finally said.

"I'd better."

Dinner was wonderful. Annie enjoyed the evening with her parents, Jonathan and Barbara, and her two older sisters. Doug, Andie's husband, had taken the older boys to a baseball game so Andie had only brought two-year-old Ashley with her. She definitely had the Wright girls' curse—beautiful, opinionated and stubborn-headed, even for a two-year-old.

"Mom, we'll clean up," Annie offered for herself and her two sisters.

"Nonsense," her father quipped. "You girls are seldom together anymore, all three of you at least. Go talk, and your mother and I will do the dishes."

Barbara Wright gave her husband a look of unbelief. "You're helping me with the dishes?" she asked him.

"Of course," he smiled, "just reminding my girls of the type of men they should be looking for."

"Does that include me, Daddy?" Andie teased.

"No!" her mother chimed in quickly. "You'd better keep Doug! I don't know if anyone else could put up with you."

Andie pulled her long, wavy dark hair up with one hand as her brown eyes danced back at her mother.

"And that insinuates what?" Andie asked.

"You do the math," was the reply.

Angie and Annie laughed as the sisters headed out the back door.

"I believe mother likes Doug," Andie said as she pulled up a chair on the screened in back porch where her sisters had already sat down. "Even though he insists on calling us 'beautiful, opinionated, and stubborn-headed.' "

"Those three adjectives will be stuck with us for the rest of our lives," Angie complained. "Is it even possible to outlive them?"

"Or outgrow them?" Annie wondered.

"Well, all I know is that Doug certainly isn't complaining," Andie laughed. "He told me just this morning that he loves his stubborn baby more than ever!"

"You were lucky," Annie half mourned. "I'll never find anyone like Doug. I mean, it's as if he rolls with the punches. I've seen you literally yell at him with your face turning red and watched his smile just grow bigger and bigger."

"I know," Angie said with almost disgust. "How do you manage that?"

"Well, just because my voice volume isn't always the best doesn't mean I don't treat him well in other ways."

"Don't go there," Annie warned.

"There are a lot of perks to marriage," Andie teased.

"Okay, thank you," Angie said quickly. "I'm with Annie. No more secrets of your marriage."

"I wish one of you guys would get married so the whole bedroom thing wouldn't be off limits anymore," Andie explained.

"That's enough," Annie yelled with her hand over her ears. "Somebody change the subject, please."

"Okay, okay. Consider it changed," Andie gave in. "Seriously though, Dad's worried that the mission board won't appoint you, Angie, if you don't let up."

"Let up about what?" Angie bellowed. "What have I done?"

"Your insistence about going to Padawin. You can't go somewhere if there's not an opening or a need."

"A need?" Angie began. "These tribal villages have nothing but your basic witch doctors. This guy, Michael Collins, he works out there all by himself. He's been there for around ten years, and he's taught them how to grow stuff and eat healthy, but disease and sickness will come through and just wipe them out, dozens at a time. And it's not just because they can't fight the sickness! It's because these loony witch doctors give them crazy cures, sometimes even poisonous. Don't tell me about need! Need is there!"

"Okay, *I* understand," Andie explained, "but the board has to see the big picture."

"Yeah, yeah, I know. Sit back, trust God, and let Him work it all out."

"That's really the truth, Angie," Andie tried to console. "God will take care of it. I know we Wright sisters have a reputation for making things happen, but sometimes things are actually out of our hands."

Annie smiled. That pegged them pretty well.

"Why can't we be more like Moms?" Annie wondered aloud.

"Solid as a rock," Angie joined in.

"Calm in the eye of the storm," Andie agreed.

They sat in silence for a moment, and then started in again, each vying for control of the conversation. They never even noticed their father peeking through the back door windowpane, shaking his head in amusement. They were definitely his girls, but they had paid the price for their forthrightness. He stopped smiling. He hoped his influence hadn't cost the younger two hopes for better futures, futures that included sharing their lives with someone else. There was only one Doug, and he was more of a son to Jonathon than his own son, Alex.

ꕥ ꕥ

Annie and Angie leaned back in the hot tub and relaxed as the evening drew on. With Andie and Ashley gone, and their parents in bed, it gave them time to relax and wind down for the night. This was one of their favorite ways.

"This is awesome," Angie sighed. "This is what I needed after those endless days of residency. Home is nice."

Annie smiled. It was wonderful to have Angie with her, even if for only a little while. She had missed her sister so much during the past years. She dreaded the thought of Angie taking off to some foreign country for years on end, but thank goodness for the Internet. At least they could communicate as often as they wanted.

"So, no guys in your life either, I take it?" Angie asked, eyes closed as she leaned against the side of the tub.

"Never been a guy," Annie admitted. "It just seemed like a silly thing to pursue while I was getting an education."

"Yeah, I know. Dad even told me once to avoid anyone not considering the mission field. He was right, you know, but still, to have had a little fun while getting ready to go . . . definitely a *yes* on that." Her eyes looked over and twinkled at Annie.

Annie grinned.

"Yeah, and then you get a reputation that keeps you off the mission field," Annie warned. "You would have been smart to follow Dad's advice."

"I guess so," Angie mused, "but what if there really was someone out there for me and I missed it because I was too focused on the future."

"Well, you just described my life to a tee," Annie moaned.

That sat in silence for a moment until Angie broke through. "This is really pathetic, you know?"

Annie nodded. Angie began to smile her mischievous smile. "What?" Annie asked.

"Tell me your deepest fantasy about a guy," she whispered.

"You're worse than Andie!" Annie protested. "I will not!"

"Oh, come on," Angie urged. "It's a single sister thing."

"I have no fantasies." Annie wouldn't play.

"I'll go first," Angie teased.

Annie thought about that for a moment. It would be fun to hear

Angie tell.

"Hmm, I may have to take you up on that," Annie thought. "It might be worth it to hear your brain in gear."

"Okay, is it a deal?" Angie asked.

Annie thought for a moment, vacillated with embarrassment, and then agreed.

"But nothing . . . you know . . . weird or detailed," Annie insisted.

"For heaven's sake, I wouldn't tell you *that* anyway," Angie told her.

Annie set up and looked intently at Angie as she began. "I keep hoping that I'll go to seminary, and there will be this guy there—tall, good-looking—you know the type." Annie nodded. "And we'll sort of eye each other in classes for several days. Then one day he sees me in the cafeteria and comes over to officially introduce himself."

"What's his name?" Annie asked eagerly.

"What do you mean, 'What's his name?' I haven't met him yet."

"Yeah, but in your dreams surely he has a name," Annie insisted.

"No, he doesn't have a name."

"Well, you should definitely give him a name."

"Do you want me to continue?" Angie warned.

Annie rolled her eyes and sat back against the tub.

"Then we start talking, and he tells me he is hoping for an assignment in the Pacific. I, of course, immediately start telling him of the needs in Padawin. The more we talk, the more he's convinced that he needs to go there too. Before you know it, we're making all these plans, and the mission board has approved our appointments. Then before we leave, he proposes, saying that he adores me and doesn't want to be alone on an island with me if I can't be his wife."

Angie smiled off into the distance.

"Nice, but it'll never happen," Annie said, bringing reality back to the forefront.

"I know, but it's still a pleasant dream."

They sat in silence a bit longer when Angie turned to Annie and said, "Your turn."

Annie actually blushed. "I can't," she admitted. "Mine's way more personal than that.

"Oh, come on!" Angie blurted out. "That's not fair! I told you mine, and it was awfully silly."

"Yeah, but yours is some pretend guy in some far-fetched situation."

"You have a crush on a real guy?" Angie leaned forward. "Who?"

"Well, not a *real guy,* real guy," Annie tried to explain.

"That makes no sense. Either he's real or he's not."

"Well, he's real, but not in my world," Annie tried to dance around it.

"You have to tell me," Angie insisted.

"Yours didn't have a name," Annie protested.

"Okay, okay!" Angie gave up. "No names. Just tell me the scenario."

"Well, I imagine this incredible musician, you know, famous and talented, meets me. Then he hears me tell him about some ideas I have about his songs. When I play them for him, he is amazed and asks me to drop everything I'm doing and go on tour with him. Then, while playing in Paris, he realizes he can't live without me and asks me to make beautiful music with him for the rest of his life."

Angie looked over at her with eyes the size of quarters.

"What?" Annie asked, very embarrassed.

"Stephen Williams!" Angie yelled. "It has to be Stephen Williams!"

Annie shook her head.

"You'd better admit it!" Angie insisted. "There isn't anyone on this planet you admire more than Stephen Williams. Admit it."

Angie got up in her face and pointed her finger.

"Ad—mit—it!"

Annie's face was hot, and it wasn't because of the tub. She rolled her eyes.

"I knew it!" Angie laughed. "Why would you try to hide that from me? Who knows? Now that Alex works for him, maybe one day you guys will meet and the sparks will fly."

"Right," Annie mumbled. "I'm just what he's looking for. An opinionated, stubborn-headed, Alabama hick."

"You forgot beautiful," Angie giggled.

"I believe that's open for discussion."

"You're crazy. Why do you always do that?"

"Do what?" Annie asked.

"Downplay your beauty," Angie explained. "You're this incredibly attractive girl, and you always act like you're the scum of the earth."

"Oh, gee, could it be that I've never had a legitimate date in my entire life? Or perhaps the fact that no guy can carry on a single conversation with me without getting heated up over some statement I say off the top off my head. I just don't mesh well with the opposite sex."

"No, that's not it," Angie comforted her. "You just haven't met a man strong enough yet to deal with all that you are."

" 'Physician, heal thyself,' " Annie said with a smile.

Chapter Three

Annie fixed her cup of coffee with a large amount of cream and plenty of sugar. She wondered how late she and Angie had stayed up last night. Her father came shuffling in wearing a tattered old robe and monster feet slippers, a gift from his grandchildren one Father's Day. He was a good sport to wear them faithfully. Within a few seconds, Angie came bounding in.

"Mornin', everyone!" she said with a bounce.

Annie and Jonathan just stared at her.

"What's the problem?" she asked as she poured herself a cup of coffee.

"A bit early to be so—jovial, isn't it, dear?" her father explained.

"Well, that depends on your situation," Angie went on. "I slept an entire eight hours last night. No beeps, no calls, no sirens, no codes to respond to, and the cherry on top was that I slept in my old bedroom with the little blue night-light still glowing in all its glory. Life is good!"

The other two merely grunted as they each nabbed a piece of already cold cheese toast from a tray atop the stove.

"Who made these?" Angie wondered as she grabbed a piece too.

"Moms, I guess," Annie mumbled as she took a big bite. "What's she doing up so early?"

"Flowers at the church," Jonathan managed to say with his mouth full. "She wants to refresh the beds and trim things up so they will look nice for the wedding."

"How sweet of her," Angie said smiling. "That's so like her—being thoughtful in ways that no one else would consider. We should go help her, Annie, when we finish breakfast."

Annie choked on her toast. "No way!" she spit out. "I'm not digging in the dirt today. You and I are going shopping."

"For what?" Angie asked.

"Does it matter?" Annie replied. "We seldom get to even spend a day together anymore. Today is our day."

"Well, I suppose," Angie gave in. "Do you think Moms will mind?"

"Oh, I doubt it," Jonathan winked. "You girls out playing at the mall while she sweats over the flowers, *digging in the dirt.*"

"Guilt won't work with me, Daddy," Annie insisted.

"Well, it works with me!" Angie said. "Maybe we should stay and help her."

"Just kidding. Just kidding," Jonathan laughed. "Have a good time today."

"I'll tell you what we'll do," Annie said, offering a compromise. "We'll stop by and say *hello* on our way out."

True to her word, after the girls were ready, they climbed into the VW and Annie drove up the hill to the church. There was Barbara, on her hands and knees, with her curly hair sticking out from beneath the bandana in several directions. Barbara waved to them as they drove up.

"Hi, Moms," Angie offered as she bent down to kiss her cheek.

"Hey, girls," she replied. "Where are you headed off to?"

"Serious work, Mom," Annie teased. "We were going to help you up here, but duty calls." Her mom stared in question.

"Shopping," Angie smiled.

"Oh, I see," Barbara said nodding her head. "I should have expected it, but before you go, I want you to look at these." She pointed at a green plant in the middle of the bed. "There are three of these out here, and they are so unusual. At first I thought they were just weeds, but see how they are perfectly spaced? Someone must have planted them. At a second glance, they're really quite pretty. I can't think for the life of me who would have planted anything up here but me."

Annie and Angie stared at the plants in disbelief. "Moms, don't you know what that is?" Angie asked her. Barbara shook her head.

"It's cannabis," Angie said slowly.

"Really?" Barbara said, impressed that her daughter knew plants. "Will it bloom, or does it just stay green like this?

"Moms, you don't know what cannabis is?" Angie continued.

"Well, I believe its some type of lily, isn't it?" Barbara replied.

"Moms!" Annie interrupted, "It's marijuana!"

"Oh, my goodness, no!" Barbara screamed. "You can't be serious!"

"Moms, it is," Angie insisted. "It's a very unique plant that you can distinguish from anything else very easily."

"But who would do such a thing?" Barbara said with dread. "That's horrible! They weren't just accidentally put in here. Look! They're perfectly spaced!"

"This should make a great headline," Annie laughed. "Local pastor grows pot in church flower garden."

"That is *not* funny, Annie," her mother said soberly. "This is illegal, and here it is for all to see right in front of the church! How do we get rid of it? I don't want to touch it!"

"Well, you're gonna have to pull it up," Angie told her. "And make sure you get it by the roots."

"I am *not* going to pull it up!" Barbara re-emphasized. "I am *not* going to touch it!"

"Moms, it's not going to absorb through the skin," Angie explained. "Just pull it up and toss it in the garbage.

"I will not!" Barbara began to yell. "What if someone looks inside the garbage? I could be arrested for this!"

"Call the cops," Annie finally said. "This is a public place. Let them dispose of it. Plus, it gives you an opportunity to make an official report and perhaps gives them a chance to do some investigating."

"But then it will be in the newspaper!" Barbara blustered on. "Oh my, this is horrible. Horrible!"

"I'm sorry, Pastor Jon," the officer said as he finished taking down a few notes. "I can't think for the life of me why someone would pull a prank like this. However, not much surprises me anymore."

"Is there any chance of finding out who did this?" Jonathan asked.

"Not likely," replied the officer. "It could have been anybody. Maybe some kids thought it would be funny and did a little gardening in the middle of the night some time. Maybe some smart alecks threw some seeds out one day. There's really no way to pin this down."

"We could try," Annie suggested. "Whenever church meets, a couple of us could sort of nonchalantly hang out here in the front and see if anybody starts *really looking* in the flower bed, if you know what I mean. Watch their expressions and see if they act surprised that something's missing."

"That would only help *you* to know," the officer told her. "We couldn't do anything about it without some type of confession or hard evidence."

"Hey, if we found out who it was, I can guarantee we would employ our own means of vengeance," Annie grinned.

"Whatever," the officer smiled back. "I do feel badly about this. I mean, planting pot at the church. Do you think your wife will be all right, pastor? She looked awfully pale."

"She'll live," he sighed, "but I don't think she'll ever be as comfortable in the flower beds anymore."

"She feels like they've been desecrated," Angie explained.

Jonathan turned to his daughters after the officer pulled away and said, "Okay, you two have flower bed duty this Sunday. Park yourselves out here before and after Sunday school, and then after the worship. I think you had the right idea, Annie. Someone did this on purpose, planting them perfectly. Someone's been walking by here the past several weeks and having a good laugh on us. It's time to put the ball back in our court."

"What are you going to do if you find out who it is?" Angie asked him.

"That depends on who it is," he said thoughtfully.

"Sort of let the punishment match the crime?" Annie wondered.

"Exactly," Jonathan agreed. "You'd be surprised what a pastor can do from the pulpit when he has a little inside information."

Shopping with Angie was like a day ordered from Paradise. Annie had not laughed so hard in years, and it was wonderful to be with Angie again. Medical training had all but stolen Angie away from her, and she and Angie had always been very close. To be shopping with no assignments due for Annie, and no pending studies or reports due for Angie, was almost surreal for them both. They let the freedom go to their heads and took the opportunity to enjoy every moment.

"I can't believe we're at the mall, 50 miles from Dockrey, and you're eating a salad," Angie complained. "You need to live a little."

"Excuse me, but you can't get a salad like this in Dockrey."

"Yeah, I know, but a salad? You should have gotten the Bourbon Chicken," Angie chided.

"You know Moms won't touch that stuff," Annie said as she

removed a cracker from its package. "She's afraid someone from church might think she's an alcoholic or something."

Angie smiled. Barbara was always careful to do the right thing.

"You have explained that the alcohol cooks out of it," Angie questioned her.

"Oh, sure," Annie replied, "but she says not everyone would *know* that. She wouldn't want to be the cause of anyone stumbling.

"Are we related to her?" Angie laughed.

"Apparently, but I'm thinking the majority of our DNA crept in from Daddy."

Angie looked toward the glass doors that led into the food court from the outside. "It's raining," she said disappointed.

Annie turned back to look. "It's pouring," she corrected.

"Bummer. I really wanted to go riding this afternoon."

"We can still ride," Annie insisted. "There'll just be more mud to slide around in."

"Not me. I don't get out enough anymore to stay upright through that kind of mud. Maybe we can go tomorrow. It will still be a little muddy, but not downright slimy."

"Did you know Daddy bought Moms a four-wheeler?" Annie asked.

"No way!" Angie blurted out. "Does she ride it?"

"A little," Annie told her. "She won't go on the steep climbs or anything. Daddy usually takes a road around when we do power lines and such, but she sure enjoys riding through the creeks."

"I cannot imagine Moms on a four-wheeler," Angie laughed as she tried to envision Barbara riding through the back trails following the rest of them on motorcycles.

"I bought a bike," Annie said as she pushed her plate away and began to sip her Sprite.

"You're kidding?"

"I traded in the XR 100 for a 200."

"No way! You can ride one that big?"

"It's not all that big," Annie explained. "The seat's a lot bigger, though, a lot softer! I can ride all day without getting too sore."

"Yeah, but what if you fall? Can you pick it back up?"

"I wouldn't know," Annie said defensively. "I haven't fallen with it."

"I can't believe you traded in the 100," Angie pouted. "What am

I gonna ride now? I can't handle Dad's."

"Doug has a CR 150 he keeps at the house. I rode that for a little while and then decided I wanted a bigger bike."

"But why a 200?"

"Because," Annie said with a silly grin, "it was on sale! It was brand new, but a two-year-old floor model they had never sold. I got a *great* deal on it."

"Can I handle the 150?"

"Please," Annie scolded. "You could handle the 200 if you would just buck up."

"No, thank you," Angie warned. "I prefer the smaller and lighter versions."

Annie and Angie got soaked running from the mall to the car, the car to the ice cream parlor, the ice cream parlor back to the car, and then the run into the house. When they stepped inside, Jonathan and Barbara were sitting on the couch in the living room watching television. Their daughters were quite the sight.

"Are you two familiar with umbrellas?" Jonathan asked as Barbara jumped up immediately to retrieve a couple of towels.

"Never carried one," Angie said.

"You'd have to have one with you all the time to warrant actually owning one," Annie tried to vindicate. "You can't know when it's going to rain."

"Are you familiar with the Weather Channel?" he asked this time. "I was well aware that there would be periods of heavy rain and thunderstorms today."

"With 180 channels on satellite, you actually choose to watch the Weather Channel?" Annie said sarcastically as she took a towel from her mother.

"I like the home and garden channels," Barbara said quickly. Then she stopped for a moment with a look of confusion. "Who would plant marijuana at the church?"

"I don't know, Moms," Angie said as she hugged her mother. "But Annie and I are going to find out."

"You girls need to shower," Barbara said as she felt the coolness of Angie's damp skin. "You need to warm up."

"I know," Annie agreed. "This is very cool for the first week of June."

"One of you is welcome to use our shower," Barbara said.

"What?" Angie exclaimed. "The holy of holies?"

"Don't be sacrilegious, Angie," Barbara pleaded.

"Hey," Jonathan interrupted, "if we hadn't set boundaries for you guys, you'd have been in our room 24/7."

"That's okay," Angie grinned. "We would all pile in there on those rare occasions that you would leave us home alone for the night."

"Who would pile in?" Barbara asked.

"All four of us!"

"In our bed?" Jonathan questioned.

"In your bed, using your big ole' shower, watching TV until 4:00 in the morning," Annie continued the description.

"You did not," Barbara insisted. "You wouldn't have done that. Our bedroom was specifically forbidden."

The girls looked at each other and began to laugh. Barbara just stood silently with a look of unbelief on her face.

"Why would you be so deceptive?" she asked them.

"Because they were teenagers," Jonathan smiled. "If that's the worse of the mischief our children were involved with, we are blessed."

"But why would you all pile into our shower?" Barbara wanted to know.

"We didn't pile into your shower," Angie went on. "We would just use it to speed up all the showers so we could get into *your bed* quicker to watch TV all night."

Barbara shook her head, and Jonathan just continued to smile.

"I had already planned on using the shower in the garage apartment, Moms," Angie said.

"No, no, no!" Barbara exclaimed. "I just cleaned it this afternoon. Alex's guest will be staying there. Just use mine."

"He's staying here?" Annie asked with humiliation. "Why on earth would Alex have a professional New York musician stay at our house? For heaven's sake, Daddy, can't we put him up in a hotel . . . well, a motel if it's in Dockrey?"

"Alex said he offered that," Barbara explained, "but he insisted on staying here with the family if there was room. Alex told him we had a whole apartment up over the garage, and he seemed thrilled."

"Wonderful," Annie murmured. "He'll think we're the biggest hicks in the South by the time he leaves."

"I beg your pardon," her mother disagreed. "We are *not* hicks, Annie Wright! We are very educated and well-cultured people who happen to live in the South. There are just as many hicks in the North."

"Well, please don't tell *him* that," Annie replied. "This could very well turn out to be a disaster if we're not careful."

"Get over it, Annie," Angie said to lighten her up. "We will probably be very entertaining for this gentleman."

"Oh, very," Annie said as she took off for the shower upstairs. "I may hide in my room for the entire week."

"That wouldn't be a good idea," her father yelled up teasing her. "You're the most cultured of us all."

"But *not* the most educated," Angie insisted.

After dinner, the girls managed to get Barbara to let them clean the kitchen. Andie, Doug, and all three children came over to eat this time. In truth, Alex really was not missed because he seldom contributed to the conversation anyway. However, Annie did notice the considerable absence of Megan. She was full of life and always had a humorous outlook on the *serious* discussions of the Wright family. Alex was blessed to have her in his life.

The three sisters discussed everything imaginable from the time they cleared off the table to putting the last dish away. They each, as was the norm, had a differing opinion on everything discussed, with two occasionally agreeing thus teaming up against the other. It was a spirited session, which reminded each of them of days growing up in the Wright household. As older girls and teenagers, it had been their job to clean the kitchen after the evening meal. Barbara never made them do it during the day; she took care of that. But no matter what, with the exception of final exam week, it was their duty to make the kitchen spotless before carrying on with anything else for the rest of the evening.

"I miss this," Andie confessed. "Doing dishes alone is not near as much fun."

"Oh, this was fun?" Annie teased. "We didn't think that years ago."

"Who would have thought that the simple things, like washing dishes, would bring back such warm feelings?" Angie joined in.

"I wasn't going for sentimental," Andie said soberly as she looked over to Angie. "I just miss the company."

"Doug doesn't do dishes with you?" Annie said half-teasing as she dried another plate.

"Are you kidding?" Andie asked incredulously. "When the last bite is taken, he gets the kids in the bath and gets them ready for bed. By the time he's finished, I'm finished."

"At least you're working together," Angie said warmly.

Annie rolled her eyes. How was it possible to be this perky?

Stephen and Alex, well, mostly Stephen, negotiated with the car rental service about getting a blue convertible for the trip from the Huntsville airport to Dockrey. All they could come up with in all of Huntsville was either a red BMW or a yellow MG.

"We'll take the red," Stephen finally agreed. He turned aside to Alex and winked as he added, "I'm not riding around in a yellow convertible."

Alex wasn't sure why, but he did not really care to know. He was still nauseous at the though of Stephen Williams spending the next ten days with his family.

He'll fire me when Annie's finished with him.

Annie, always opinionated and never afraid to express it. Alex knew Annie loved Stephen's music, but he had also sat through her critical sessions during album releases and listened to her "I'd change that" and "Why would he do that there" monologue. Annie was thoroughly musically inclined, and no one knew it better than she did. Maybe Stephen wouldn't fire him based on that fact alone. Maybe he would have pity on Alex and keep him around out of the goodness of his heart.

"Here you go," said Stephen as he slid his sunglasses down over his eyes and handed out the keys to Alex.

"What?" Alex asked incredulously. "You want me to drive?"

"Hey, this is Alabama. I've been to Birmingham for concerts, and that was flying in. Yeah, I want *you* to drive. Can you drive a stick?"

Alex nodded and took the keys. *My first vehicle was a pickup. I can drive a stick just fine.* Annie would have said it aloud and punctuated it with a "moron" or "idiot." What a week this was going to be. At least at the end of it all was a life with Megan. He hoped with everything within him that she would be out of crying mode by now and just looking forward to the blessed event.

As they passed Decatur, Stephen seemed to enjoy taking in the fresh Alabama air. Every now and then, he would lean his blond head back, let his gentle curls flap in the wind, and take a deep breath, always following this with a "Nice, real nice" or something of that nature.

"So will this be like a family reunion?" Stephen asked him, finally breaking the silence.

"I guess so," said Alex, not wanting to offer more than a reply.

"Three sisters? Is that right?"

"Yeah. Three of them."

"Now, one is married?" Stephen questioned.

"Right. The oldest one, Andie." *Okay. Enough of the questions.*

"How old is she?"

"Thirty . . . well, maybe thirty-one. I can't remember exactly."

"And what does she do?"

Apparently a conversation about his family was inevitable, so Alex gave in and presented all the details. "She teaches music in the elementary school. She's got three kids. Her husband's a pretty neat guy—one of the groomsmen, by the way. You'll enjoy him."

"Is she the one that called about you?"

Alex shook his head and grinned. "No. That would be Annie."

"Ah, Annie," Stephen seemed to muse. "And she's the next sister?"

"No, Angie is next."

"Your parents had a thing for the letter 'A,' I presume?"

"I reckon," Alex replied, then immediately winced at using a Southern colloquialism rather than a more intelligent term. *I suppose. I imagine. Apparently. For crying out loud! I reckon?*

"Is Angie a musician too?" Stephen wondered.

"We don't know. She refused to do the music thing right from the beginning. She decided to be a doctor when she was in junior high, and that was that."

"And did she succeed?"

"Just got licensed. Finished med-school, did the whole intern and residency thing. I'm not really sure what it all entails."

"So, she's practicing medicine now?"

No, that would be too easy for a sister of mine. "No. She's headed to seminary now," Alex said shaking his head. How do you explain the most abnormal set of girls on the planet?

"Really? Astonishing!" Stephen simply said. "She's going to preach?"

That actually made Alex laugh. *She might as well.* "She wants to be a medical missionary. She's got some island picked out in the Pacific. It starts with a 'P.' "

"The Philippines?" Stephen asked.

"Are you kidding? That would too obvious and simple. No, it's somewhere in the middle of nowhere. It's a little island nation, independent—they change governments due to rebellions every couple of decades."

"Sounds dangerous," Stephen quipped as he threw a handful of sunflower seeds into his mouth. "I take it she's the adventurous type."

"I reckon." Alex winced again. He was going to strike that phrase from his mind.

"What about the other one, then? Annie? Is that right?"

Annie—my blot in life. "Right, Annie," Alex mumbled, knowing he couldn't be heard with the top down. He nodded though, so Stephen understood the answer.

"She's quite the musician, I suppose?"

"Yeah, she's heads and tails above the rest of us."

"Really? I find that hard to believe," Stephen said as he spit out a hull. "You're the most talented bass player I've ever met. You would put her ability above your own?"

Alex hated this. "In a heartbeat," he admitted. "No one can compete with her."

"What does she do? Teach?"

Alex laughed at this. *Annie teach? Hardly!* "No. She did not have the temperament for it. She writes jingles for commercials. Records them and all. She's sort of a one-woman band."

"Is that so? Doesn't she have an education degree?"

"Having the degree doesn't mean you should do it."

"I suppose not," Stephen agreed. "You know, I tried teaching music once."

"You did?" Alex was surprised. "In school? Private?"

"Private," he said, almost as though he were confessing. "I hated it." He spit out another hull. "I did not have the temperament for it either. I rather empathize with your sister."

Oh, please don't empathize with Annie. If there's one thing she does not need, it's empathy.

"I thought it would bring in some extra money while I was trying to break into the music business. I was in the middle of recording my first album when my former piano professor suggested I take on a few students," Stephen began to explain. "He thought teaching classical music would help me stay in touch with the 'higher form of the art' as he called it."

"It must have worked," Alex said. "You're the only rock star I know who mixes in a taste of classical music in every album."

This time it was Stephen who winced. "Eek," he grimaced. "Don't call me a rock star. It conjures up images of painted faces and laced-up leather. The *rock* stuff pays the bills. It's the pieces like *Autumn Sunset* that are the real me."

Alex nodded. That was easy to see and hear in his music. Stephen Williams was out to convert the world to a higher sound; he simply used rock music as a platform from which to dive.

"So is Annie the one who was kicked out of college?"

"That's the one."

"How?"

I guess it's inevitable. I might as well tell. "Annie is this musical genius," he began. "I don't really know how to describe what she seems to know about music. I mean, she had stuff figured out by the time she was in 9th grade that was just second nature to her—theory and stuff that somebody with a doctorate in music would have to sit and think about before he'd give an answer. She got a full scholarship to Clarksville College, where all of us ended up going, including Mom and Dad. That's where they met. Andie had gone there, Angie was a junior when Annie started, and then I came along two years later."

"All in the family, huh?" Stephen chuckled.

"Yeah, I suppose," Alex went on, really not wanting to recount the story. "She was a smart aleck, always has been. This one music professor, who even I will admit was a real jerk, did his best to humiliate every student who came through his theory classes. He would tear them apart, up one side and then down another. You'd do a composition, and he'd tell you how predictable it was, and then start playing something already published in the 15th century with the same chord progression or melody. It was a really miserable two years with him, taking freshmen and sophomore theory classes."

"Let me guess; he never pulled anything over on your Annie?" Stephen asked, taking in the story and all its details.

"Never," Alex said shaking his head. "He couldn't do it. In fact, her music would be unique yet within the bounds of whatever they were required to do that he couldn't take anything apart. This went on every week. It almost became this tug-of-war between Annie and Dr. Stanley. The students loved it because he never got to the point of classes just trying to one-up her."

"I had professors like that," Stephen added. "I think it's a prerequisite that every music department has at least one pompous idiot."

"Well, this guy was ours," Alex nodded. "And one day, after he had torn apart half of the class, failing them on their assignments, Annie had had enough. She asked him if it was his job to totally kill the gift of music in each person who came through this school, or was he so intimidated that someone might find out he didn't actually know everything that he felt it necessary to condemn those who didn't choose to think like he did."

"Bravo!" Stephen clapped. "They kicked her out for that?"

"No, not yet. She and this teacher sort of had a musical showdown in class. She challenged him to a bit of a *musical duel,* promising she would quit the music department if he could outwit her."

"No way! You're kidding?" Stephen was liking the spunk of this Annie more and more.

"She won. She totally baffled him with a minor seven diminished chord; totally threw him off. He called her some perverse name and left the room. Later that evening, the dean of the music school told her she would have to change her major or change schools; she could no longer study in the music department at Clarksville and that her scholarship would be revoked."

"Why? Because she was smart?" Stephen asked astonished.

"He didn't say. He just said it wasn't her place to do what she did."

"So they kicked her out for being really smart?"

"No, it's what she did next that got her kicked out."

"There's more?" Stephen was laughing now. Alex was a bit miffed that Stephen found it amusing, because it was the blight of humiliation that followed him there for the rest of his three years at Clarksville.

"When it was the final concert for the orchestra that year, she greased the director's baton, Dr. Stanley's, and the outer valves of all the brass instruments—and the percussion mallets."

Stephen stopped laughing and just stared over at Alex. "You're kidding." Alex shook his head. "No wonder she got kicked out," Stephen pondered. "I would have liked to have been there for that."

"It was just too over the top. I mean, she shouldn't have been made to leave the music department. I agree that was unfair, but when she did that to all those instruments, it was just too much."

"How did they know it was her? Did someone see her?" Stephen wondered.

"She left a note. She made it plain. She called them all idiots and said anybody who stayed in the hypocrisy of that department deserved all she had done and more."

Stephen was silent for a while. Alex could tell he was processing it all.

"Do you think she will do something vicious to me?" Stephen finally asked, looking over at Alex with a hint of uncertainty in his eyes.

"Honestly? She probably will," Alex confessed. "I try not to mess with her."

"I see," was all Stephen could say.

Suddenly a loud noise came from the front of the car as the hood began to smoke.

"I'm guessing we've got car trouble," Stephen managed to say. "I'll give someone a call."

He pulled out his cell phone as Alex pulled the car to the side of the road. When Alex turned off the engine, he looked over at Stephen who was staring skeptically at the phone's display.

"No service?" Alex asked. Stephen nodded. "Welcome to Alabama," Alex said as he started walking back down the road.

"Where are we going?" Stephen asked as he caught up with him.

"To the nearest working phone," he replied.

Barbara hung up the phone and turned to the rest of the family in the living room.

"Alex and his friend had car trouble," she began to explain. "They had to be towed back to Huntsville and then get a different car."

"Wonderful," Annie said with exasperation. "The trip to Hicksville has started properly, wouldn't you say?"

"Oh, stop it," Angie said, slapping Annie's knee. "Who knows? This New York fellow may have a great sense of humor and find all of us downright charming."

"And if he doesn't," Doug began to tease, "I'll take him out to the woodshed and show him a thing or two about us Alabama rednecks."

"By the way," Jonathan broke in, "since all four of my beautiful children will actually be here at the same time, I have a request."

"Anything you want, Daddy," Angie said with a big smile.

"I'm glad you said that, sweetheart," Jonathan mused, "because you may have the biggest problem with this. I want you all to sing together on Sunday morning."

The protests began, with Angie leading the way. "You've got to be kidding!"

"We'd only have one day to practice!"

"Alex will never do it!"

"So who would play the piano and who would sing?"

"It would be embarrassing!"

"We'd be like the Von-Trapp-Wright Family Singers or something!"

"Is this punishment for us using your bedroom when you were gone?"

Jonathan listened to all the complaints and then gently told them, "This may not happen again for many years. You all sing beautifully, and that includes you, Angie, and I want to hear you all sing together once more before I look back and kick myself for not making you do this."

"I get to play the piano!" Annie quickly volunteered.

"Oh, no you don't," Andie insisted. "I'm the church pianist. I *have* to play for the group."

Another argument began to ensue. After about a minute of tense discussion, Doug finally broke in. "As I see it," he began, "you're all nothing but a bunch of beautiful, opinionated, stubborn-headed women."

"Make your point, Doug," Andie warned him, "or shut up."

"Well," Doug said throwing up his arms, "that is my point. The three of you together cannot decide this point. Either appoint someone to referee this thing or draw straws, but don't attempt to *discuss* it."

"Well said, my boy," Jonathan said as he stood and gave Doug a slap on the back.

"When you've lived with one as long as I have, you learn to deal with it," Doug explained.

"And when you've lived with the three of them as long as I have, you learn to give up," Jonathan laughed.

"Ahhh," Angie sighed as she leaned back in the hot tub. "I want one of these."

"I don't think you'll find one in the seminary dorm," Annie told her.

"Nope, probably not. And I'm sure there won't be one in Padawin."

"You never know. Maybe one of those volcanic pools will be near your hut."

"Hut? You've got my place already picked out?"

"What are you expecting to live in?" Annie laughed. "A condo?"

"At this point, I don't care!" Angie blurted out. "I am just so ready to get on with my life! I have dreamed of this since, well, I don't know when!"

"Junior high," Annie said.

"That long? I believe it. This is all I've ever wanted to do."

That sat in silence for a while and enjoyed the moment. Then Angie cut in by asking Annie, "What did you dream of doing?"

Annie thought for a moment and slightly shook her head. "I don't really know," she finally responded. "For a long time I just wanted to get an education in music. Been there, done that. I guess I didn't know what I would do once I finished."

"Oh, come on," Angie said not believing her. "When you were in high school, weren't you going to be some great composer or singer or something?"

Annie smiled and weakly said, "Or something."

"What happened? What changed all that?"

"I don't know if I can really put my finger on it," Annie tried to reason. "When I got kicked out of Clarksville, it was because I was smart. In truth, that's what it really boiled down to. I mean, anybody else would have been suspended or punished in some way, but not kicked out. I butted heads with every professor in that music department, and a couple in other departments," she added. "But I was told, right smack at the beginning assembly for freshmen, 'Don't be afraid to ask and learn here. That's what college is about.' So I did. I thought I was supposed to. Some teacher would make a blanket statement, and I would question."

"Question or argue?" Angie asked her.

"I always started with a question," Annie grinned, "but it just seemed to always get blown out of proportion. Somewhere I realized that being good in music, being smart about life and other things, and always striving to be the best weren't impressive to others, but intimidating. I had no intentions of changing so I suppose I gave up on dreaming big."

Angie stared at her for a moment then said, "That's pathetic. No one can steal your dreams. You have to give them up."

"Then I guess I gave them up," Annie said flatly.

"Are you happy now?" Angie wanted to know. "I mean, living with Moms and Dad, writing commercials for other people? Is this what you want to do for the rest of your life?"

Annie sat quietly stone-faced for a while, and then a grin slowly grew across her face. "No," she said, smiling big now. "I want to be discovered by someone famous and be whisked off to impress the music world."

Angie shook her head. "It's either the pits of despair or your head in the clouds, isn't it? You can't find something somewhere in between."

"I am a little extreme, aren't I?" Annie said as she leaned back and closed her eyes. "Maybe I should just shoot for mediocre."

"Yeah, right," Angie mumbled sarcastically. "That'll be the day."

Chapter Four

Annie lay in bed for close to thirty minutes before finally deciding to get up. This was Saturday. She should linger and enjoy the moment. She thought of the line in *Autumn Sunset:*

Cool early morning, stretching and yawning
No reason to get up, but no reason to stay

She finally got up and pulled on the bottoms to the surgical scrubs that Angie had given her for Christmas over five years ago. Annie had made them her pajamas so that she would think of Angie every night and remember to say a special prayer for her during all of her medical training.

She moseyed down the stairs and began to measure out the coffee. While she was waiting, she unloaded the dishwasher and put in several dishes that had been snacked on before everyone had gone to bed the night before. When the coffee was finished, she retrieved a mug from the cabinet and went over to pour herself a cup.

"I was hoping this rattling around meant someone had made coffee," came a strange voice from the entrance to the kitchen.

Annie turned around to see who was there and stopped quickly in unbelief.

"Oh, my gosh," she whispered in a panic, followed by the dropping of her mug on the floor. It shattered into many pieces across the kitchen.

"Oh, I'm sorry," Stephen said quickly as he bent down and began to retrieve the broken pieces. "I guess it was a little startling to find a strange man walking into your kitchen asking for coffee."

"Uh . . . yes," Annie managed to get out as she got the broom and began to sweep up the pieces.

Stephen Williams is in my house. I broke my mug. I'm an idiot. What should I do? How do I act? Why didn't Alex tell us who he was bringing?

"I'm Stephen," he said as he put out his hand. "I came with Alex last night. I'm going to be in his wedding."

Annie shook his hand but could not say a word.

"Where's the dust pan?" he asked her. "At least I can help you get this cleaned up. It was really my fault."

"Between the refrigerator and the microwave," she managed to say, feeling as though her heart was stuck at the top of her throat.

Stephen placed the dustpan on the floor and Annie swept the remains of the shattered mug into it. He kept moving it slightly backward so she could sweep the lines formed at the edge of the dustpan.

"You would think someone could invent a dustpan that could eliminate those lines of dirt," he smiled. "We can send people to the moon, but we can't cure household nuisances."

Annie grinned. "You'd think," she finally said.

"Where's the garbage," he asked.

"Beneath the sink," she told him as she pointed to the cabinet.

She replaced the broom and washed her hands. "Let me get you that cup of coffee," she said as she dried her hands, finally beginning to gain control of her shakiness.

"That would be wonderful," he smiled. "I had a hard time sleeping."

"Was the bed uncomfortable?" she asked quickly, too quickly, trying to have some sense of composure.

"Oh, no," he reassured her. "It was just too quiet. At least the air-conditioner was a little noisy."

"Too quiet?"

"I've lived in New York over for ten years," he explained. "I see neon lights flashing through my windows and hear the rushing traffic constantly in the *city that never sleeps.* I've sort of become lulled by those things, I suppose."

"Do you take your coffee black?" she asked him as she poured the mug full.

"Ooo, yuck," he grimaced. "What would be the point? Three teaspoons of cream, three teaspoons of sugar."

"I just assumed. Most musicians I've known liked their coffee black," she said as she added the cream and sugar. "I like my well-diluted too, but not quite as much as you."

She must be the doctor. Hospital clothes. The thing about black coffee. Alex never mentioned his sister being so gorgeous. Do the others look like her?

"This is almost like an adventure for me," Stephen teased. "The whole rural Alabama thing is quite a different experience."

"Just be careful about the 'lions, tigers, and bears,' " Annie said as she took a sip from her steaming cup.

Stephen's eyes widened as he slowly asked, "Are you serious?"

Annie smiled back and answered, "No. Just teasing you a little. We don't get real city slickers like you around here often."

"Will this be the first of many jokes?" he wondered cautiously.

"Probably," Annie said as she reached up for the loaf of bread, "but not from me. I will protect you from the rest of them for the next week. Scout's honor."

"Are you a scout?"

"Nope," Annie said with a smile creeping up one corner of her mouth, "but that won't stop me from keeping my honor."

"I supposed I am relieved then," he said with a little doubt.

"Don't worry, we're nice folks around here."

Annie got a slab of cheddar cheese from the refrigerator and asked, "Would you like some cheese toast?"

He came over next to her to observe the process. "What exactly is *cheese toast?*" he wanted to know.

"Sort of like an open-faced grilled cheese sandwich. See, you slice up some bits of cheese and place them on the bread. Then you toast the bread. The cheese melts, the bread toasts, and voila' . . . you have cheese toast."

Stephen agreed to the breakfast and took great pleasure in watching Annie complete the process. As he stood next to her, he could swear her hair smelled like honey and found himself pretending to bend in closer to watch, when in fact all he wanted was a deeper breath. He watched her long fingers work carefully.

Those fingers should belong to a pianist, not a doctor. Those lips. My goodness! I must have a talk with Alex and explain his sister to him. This cannot be any of the girls he described to me.

"Morning, everyone!" greeted Angie as she bounced into the room.

Stephen quickly stepped away from Annie, slightly embarrassed at how close he had gotten, thankful that this was not a father coming in.

"Ah, you must be Alex's musician friend," Angie said as she put out her hand. "The stand-in groomsmen, I believe."

"Guilty," Stephen replied as he shook her hand. "And you must be another sister, well, assuming that," he nodded to Annie, "you are a sister."

"Guilty," Angie smiled. "We are his *sweet* sisters. Maybe you won't have to be subjected to the other one. I need coffee."

"She drinks it black," Annie whispered over toward Stephen.

"I see," he said nodding.

Stephen tried to concentrate on the conversation, but could not imagine how Alex had failed to mention how beautiful his sisters were. From the descriptions Alex had given, Stephen expected a couple of linebackers to attack him with verbal venom the moment he stepped foot inside the house. In truth, he had almost been dreading meeting the girls; how could he hold his own with three evil-hearted women? Now, however, he found himself staring back and forth as the two sets of identical lips, both thick and lush, made small talk. He felt like he was in a sitcom and two models had walked into the room. Was the camera focused on him waiting for the comedic reaction?

Wow! I wish I had known earlier that this was how they grew them in Alabama.

"I didn't even introduce myself," Angie said as she turned her attention back to Stephen. "I'm Angie," she said with a slight Southern drawl, less pronounced than her sister.

"Angie?" Stephen was confused. Wasn't Angie the doctor? "Then you are Annie?" Stephen asked, turning toward Annie who was staring into the oven.

"Right. Annie," Annie confirmed.

Stephen stared back and forth for a moment. "I thought Angie was the doctor," he said confused.

"I am," said Angie.

"But you drink your coffee black, and Annie is wearing doctor stuff," he tried to explain.

Annie laughed, understanding his confusion

"Hasn't anyone ever told you not to try and figure women out?" Angie giggled.

"My, I think I *am* confused," he said as he backed against the refrigerator. "So the one dressed like the doctor is really the musician, and the one who drinks her coffee black is a doctor?"

"What is he talking about with the coffee?" Angie asked.

"Never mind," Annie said shaking her head. "That's my fault. Don't ask. Everything's straight now."

"So what's your name?" Angie asked Stephen.

"Stephen."

"Oh, how cute," Angie said. "You have the same name as Stephen Williams, and you play in his band. Does anybody ever get confused and you both answer at the same time?"

Annie rolled her eyes; Angie had no clue that this was *the* Stephen Williams.

"Oh, frequently," Stephen replied. "Every time someone calls my name, I just assume they're referring to me."

"We do that a lot too," Angie went on. "You've got Andie, Angie, and Annie. When Moms would get really mad and start yelling, she'd get us all mixed up. To this day, when I'm on the phone with her, she calls me Andie or Annie more than my own name."

"Angie," Annie said slowly. "This *is* Stephen Williams."

Angie's mouth dropped open as she looked him over.

"Get out of here!" she exclaimed. "The real Stephen Williams is going to be in my brother's wedding?"

"Afraid so," he said smiling.

The timer dinged, and Annie opened the oven, taking a deep breath of her favorite morning smell, other than coffee—the smell of toasted cheese. She placed three pieces on individual plates and offered two of them to Stephen and Angie.

"Let's go to the porch," Angie suggested. "Maybe we can impress him enough with the beauty of our backyard that he'll forgive my not recognizing him."

"Actually, I found it rather charming," Stephen told them as he followed them to the back. "You can't imagine how frustrating it is to not be able to go anywhere in peace."

"Hmmm," Annie sighed thoughtfully as she held the door to the back open for him to walk through, "peace isn't a word often used to describe our household."

"So I've heard," he said as he raised his eyebrows.

What did you say to him, Alex? I don't even want to guess.

The conversation over breakfast consisted mainly of Angie. Annie tried to participate, but she could not get over being awestruck with their guest. She felt too self-conscious to attempt to be normal, and instead, began just nodding and smiling here and there. Stephen, however, appeared to be delighted with the whole situation. He listened attentively as Angie described every detail of the back porch, the house, the fireplace inside, the various flower beds around the house, her father's garden that was out of sight from the porch, the trails out in the hills, the occasional deer, raccoon and possum that found its way to the house, and the bonfire area where they spent many evenings with friends and family sitting around the crackling flames on split logs enjoying the cooler nights.

Annie was thankful that Angie's mouth seemed to be on a roll. She tried to stare at Stephen when he was preoccupied. It was he, complete with tousled blond curls, baby blue eyes, and a smile that could charm the hardest of hearts. She had fallen asleep many nights as a high school girl with that very face staring from inside her head or pinned up on her wall. During the turbulent years of college, his music has been the only soothing medicine she could find. And now, he had become a familiar habit that reminded her of better days. How could she just act *normal,* as though he were merely some guest Alex had brought home for the week?

The phone ringing popped Angie out of her seat. "Let me get that before it wakes anybody up," she said as she rushed to the door.

Stephen stood up and went to the screen of the porch, taking in the view. It truly was beautiful. The hills of northwest Alabama had a simple charm to them, and the creek running down the hill from the house could be heard over the chirping of birds and rustling of leaves in the wind.

"This is almost magical," Stephen said as he turned back toward her. "How did you manage to get such a beautiful place?"

Annie put down her mug and forced herself to get up and go next to him. She tried to appear as casual as possible.

"We've been here almost 25 years," she began, "not in this house, but at this church. We lived in the parsonage on Country Club Drive for four years, but that was *not* our family, if you get my drift."

Stephen nodded and smiled as he gave her his full attention. She felt her knees go weak as his blue eyes looked directly into hers. She turned her head.

"Daddy had done a lot of good things here in those four years. He's a good man, a good pastor, and just a good-all-around sort of guy." Annie winced at the sound of her Southern accent next to his very proper sounding inflection, but she continued. "This church had a lot of hurts and heartaches when he got here; he worked hard to keep it together and rebuild. The parsonage was old. It was beautiful, but it was old. Daddy's a real fixer-upper, and he put a lot of time into it, but he told the deacons that either they needed to overhaul the whole thing or sell it. I mean, in the winter, you could stand next to a window, and the breeze from the outside would blow your hair."

Stephen continued to look at her, smiling gently as she explained.

"They asked Daddy if he would consider buying a house; they wanted him here permanently, if possible. He teased them and said 'no way,' then told them he had always wanted to build his own. One of the deacons owned this land, right here next to the church. He offered Daddy this great deal, and well, you can see the handiwork."

Stephen surveyed the area again, nodding with approval.

"I have a country home also," he sighed, "in the Adirondacks, but I seldom go there. It's so, well, lonely. I have a staff out there year round, but no neighbors, no friends. Sometimes I'll go there to write for a couple of weeks, but that's as long as I can stand it."

He must think we're total hicks. I'll bet his house makes this one look like a trailer.

"It must be nice always having family around you," he said as he turned back toward her.

"It is," she agreed, letting herself gaze for a moment into his eyes. "But it has a few drawbacks."

"I can't imagine," he said as he went back to his seat. "How much land do you own?"

"Around 15 acres, but there are woods and trails that go way beyond ours. The same deacon owns all that land. We're free to have as much fun as we want on any of it. Most people around here are like that."

Stephen shook his head and said, "I can't imagine. No fences or anything?"

"Sure, but they all have gates—with no locks."

"I suppose that's a shining example of Southern hospitality?"

"Yes," Annie said as she walked back to her seat. "This is a small town. Everybody knows everybody. Sometimes that can be bad, but generally it binds you together."

"Morning," said Jonathan as he came through the door from the house.

Stephen immediately turned and offered his hand. "You must be the father," Stephen said.

"And you must be Alex's friend," Jonathan said as he shook Stephen's hand and sat down with his coffee and toast.

Annie rolled her eyes. Her father was clueless also. Was she the only one in this family who knew who this man was?

"This is Stephen Williams, Daddy."

"Nice to meet you, Stephen," Jonathan said. "It's nice out here this morning, isn't it? Slight breeze, creek rushing by—it doesn't get any better than this." He leaned back and sighed as he stretched his strong, defined arms above his broad shoulders. An easy smile spread over his lips, the same lips as his daughters, and his significantly graying hair was beginning to thin. He was also tall, the obvious contributor to the height of his girls.

"It is nice," Stephen agreed. "This is an awesome place."

Next Alex walked out. Annie noticed that his hair had grown quite a bit, but those sleepy eyes were unmistakable. She wanted to get up and hug him, ask him how the job was working out, and talk about New York, but she knew it would be awkward. As much as she admired her brother, she knew the feeling was not mutual.

"Good morning, baby brother," she managed to say cheerfully.

"Hey, ya'll," he said sleepily. "Did you get some breakfast, Stephen?"

"Yes, I'm fine. Thank you," Stephen told him.

"Okay, good," Alex said. "I'm gonna go call Megan then." He left.

"He's a man of few words," Stephen commented as he drained his mug. "Unlike the rest of you."

"That *he* is," Jonathan agreed, "and that *we* are."

Annie stood up and reached out for Stephen's mug. "Would you like another cup?" she asked him.

"Really? If you're offering, I'll definitely take another," he smiled.

"Three creams, three sugars," she affirmed. He nodded.

"That ain't coffee, boy," her father laughed. "That's cream with caffeine!"

Stephen just smiled and nodded as he said, "Yes, sir. That's how I like my caffeine!"

Annie took Stephen's mug and moved as if in a daze to the

kitchen. She still could not believe he was sitting on her back porch.

"Oh, my gosh! Oh, my gosh!" Angie said, rushing up to Annie as she walked into the kitchen. "Tell me this is not bizarre! I mean, just the other night you're talking about your deepest fantasy, and he shows up in your house!"

"Down, girl," Annie said with a furled brow as she sidestepped her sister. "Don't even think this is a possibility."

"Oh, come on," Angie said incredulously. "Only you would try to boil this down logically. This is so unreal, Annie! Don't roll over and let another dream die!"

"This is not a dream," Annie said forcefully, but barely above a whisper. "This is a nightmare. This is not Paris or New York. This is Podunk Dockrey, Alabama, the middle of redneck country, and there is no pretending beyond that."

"For someone who is so smart, you can be really stupid at times," Angie continued. "Get a grip and go after this! You are not small-town; you are big time. You know it too. Don't hide behind the little insecurity you actually possess! This is your chance!"

"And do what?" Annie said angrily, but still quietly, as she moved into Angie's face. "Tell him to hire *me?* Tell him to get *me* a real job? Tell him that I could go places if he would just give *me* a chance?"

"Why not?" Angie wanted to know. "You could blow Hollywood, New York, and Nashville out of the water if you were given half a chance. Shoot, then move on to Paris or wherever!"

"You think it's that easy?" Annie said as she turned away to pour the coffee.

"If you have Stephen Williams behind you, it is!"

Annie quietly finished Stephen's coffee, and then handed it to Angie. "Take this to Stephen, please. I'm going upstairs to get dressed."

Angie shook her head in disbelief. "You are too stubborn for you own good," she yelled after her.

ജ ഏ

Stephen showered and dressed comfortably. Alex suggested he wear something *old,* but Stephen wasn't quite sure what that meant. He looked around the garage apartment and found it quaint. There were many American Indian statuettes and artifacts around the room, as well as a few family photos on some of the shelves. There were books lining the walls, and then a sectional couch facing a television claimed one corner of the room. He picked up a frame and stared at a family portrait, obviously taken about ten years ago.

What a beautiful family. This must be the older girl. Same hair, although wavy, and the lips. She looks more like the mother. Brown eyes like Annie, though. Good-looking mom. Thin, beautiful smile . . . dark, styled short hair. I wonder why all the girls wear theirs long?

He stared at Annie. She must have been 15 or 16 in the picture. Her eyes were bright and mischievous. He wondered what could have subdued her so much over the years.

Life. Maturity. It can do that to all of us, I suppose. Reality is never as good as your dreams.

He placed the frame back on the shelf and went through the door to the open upstairs walkway that looked down onto the great room. Alex was cuddled on the couch with a girl Stephen had seen only in pictures, Megan. He watched in silence as Alex smiled and teased her. This was the first time he had ever seen Alex relaxed or even appearing to enjoy life. Alex whispered something to Megan, and she gently slapped him back. He pulled her close.

There is someone for everyone. I'm glad to see Alex can be happy.

Stephen started down the stairs and waved as he finally caught Alex's eye. Alex quickly jumped up from the couch, pulling Megan with him.

"Don't get up," Stephen insisted as he walked over to them.

"I want you to meet Megan," Alex said. "I mean, you're gonna be her boss too."

"I'm not your boss," Stephen tried to explain. "We're more like coworkers."

"You pay my salary," Alex said nervously. "You'll be paying hers too. You're our boss."

"Look at it how you want," Stephen said as he reached out to shake Alex's hand, "but for this week, I am your friend, a man who is going to be in your wedding and nothing more."

"We're going to Hawaii for our honeymoon because of your generosity," Megan said with a smile. "I'm afraid you'll have to settle for a little awe and respect."

"Nope," Stephen insisted again. "I am a friend. Nice to finally meet you, Megan. I am so glad to see the other half of Alex."

Megan actually hugged Stephen and sniffled as her eyes teared up.

"The only reason we're getting married in one week is because you gave him a chance. If he didn't have this job, I would still be crossing my fingers and pleading in prayers that he would find one."

"Well, I am glad to know I am an answer to prayer," he smiled. "And are you ready to start tutoring six very active kids around the world?"

"This is like a dream come true!" Megan insisted. "I will miss my junior highers here in Dockrey, but to travel the world with you guys and teach the crew's kids, plus," she took Alex's hand and leaned her head on his shoulder, "be with Alex every single day for the rest of my life. This is beyond incredible! I don't even know if I could possibly thank you adequately."

Stephen smiled at her enthusiasm and complete happiness and reached down to touch her cheek. "Trust me," he told her, "you have done a very adequate job."

Stephen left the two and headed toward the kitchen, curious if he could possibly rummage up another cup of caffeinated cream. The thought made him chuckle to himself. He liked Jonathan Wright. No wonder the man was loved as a pastor. He was down-to-earth and had a hearty laugh. *What's not to like?*

Stephen paused as he reached the door. Annie was carefully making sandwiches, meticulously placing everything in order like an assembly line. She was humming softly to herself as she worked. He could barely make out the melody because it was so low, but he finally recognized *Autumn Sunset.* He felt a twinge of something in the center of his stomach when he heard it. He seldom heard anyone else do his own music. She continued the process, shaking her long hair back now and then. She finally sighed in exasperation and went to a drawer next to the sink. She removed a rubber band, threw her head back, and swept her hair into a ponytail.

"I really ought to get this cut," she mumbled to herself. "I'm not 16 anymore."

She washed her hands and turned back to finish the sandwiches. That's when she noticed Stephen. She let out a small cry of surprise, and then put her hand up to her heart.

"You really need to stop doing that," she said as she tried to calm down.

"Not used to strange men spying on you in your own house, I suppose?" he teased.

"Not at all," she said, trying to be serious and trying to relax. She went back to her work.

"What are the sandwiches for?" he asked her as he came over to watch. There was that aroma again, honey or something sweet and delicious. "Is someone going on a picnic?"

She turned to look at him. "You don't know?" she asked him.

"I suppose not," he said, a little confused.

"Oh," was all she said.

"Am I going on this picnic?" he wondered.

"Alex says you are," she said as she began to place the sandwiches in small bags.

Stephen nodded, watching her complete the packing, and hoping for another brief scent of her hair. He was not disappointed. She whipped her head around when the phone rang, and her ponytail nearly hit him in the face.

"I'm sorry," she blushed. "Mom's not feeling well today, and we're trying to let her sleep."

"No problem," Stephen said, meaning it more than she could know.

She answered the phone and took down a few notes. Stephen could not believe this was the same sister that Alex had described so cruelly. He could not believe this was the woman who had insisted on getting Alex an audition. He watched her talk, smile, and take notes. She *was* animated, but she was poised, articulate, and well—beautiful. He stayed back by the sink, opposite of the entrance where the phone was located. She could not see him watch her. He had seen and known many incredible women around the world, but this one had something he had never seen before. He couldn't place it, like the feeling he got hearing her hum *Autumn Sunset.*

She hung up the phone and went into the great room. Stephen followed behind her.

"Megan," she said as she approached the couch, "you're not going to believe this."

"What now?" Megan sighed as she let her head fall back on the couch.

"That was the caterer," Annie explained. "She needs to meet with you this morning because her son's wife has gone into labor in

Birmingham. She wants to be there as soon as possible to 'witness the blessed event.' "

"Awww," Alex mourned. "You can't go with us?"

"You could go with *her,*" Annie suggested.

"Not a chance," Alex said quickly. "I haven't ridden in forever and won't get a chance to again for, shoot, probably a year. I'm riding."

"What kind of riding?" Stephen asked.

"He really didn't tell you?" Annie asked him again. Stephen shook his head. "Boy, are you in for a treat," Annie said with a smile. "Help me finish with the food, Mr. Williams, and I will show you personally in a minute."

"My pleasure, Miss Wright," he said continuing her formality. "Or is it *Ms.*?"

"It's *Miss,*" she confirmed. A vision of the peroxide-headed *Ms.* Vivian McCall popped into her mind. "Definitely *Miss,*" she reaffirmed.

After packing all the food, Annie had Stephen help her carry it to the large, closed-in building behind the house. With her elbow, she lifted the latch and the door swung wide open. She placed her container on a chair near the door and went over to turn on the light.

"Put yours right here," she told him as she pointed out another chair. "We'll strap them on after we get the cooler here."

Annie went over to a shelf and pulled down a couple of helmets. She tossed one to Stephen.

"Try this one," she suggested as she went over to a red motorcycle.

"Wait a minute," Stephen said cautiously. "Are we riding motorcycles?"

"Most of us are," she smiled back. "You'll probably be on the four-wheeler. Someone will ride with you. All you'll need to do is hold on."

"I've never done this before," he tried to explain, beginning to think he might ought to back out of this. "You probably don't want me along on this trip."

"Are you kidding? This will be the adventure of a lifetime."

"That's what I'm afraid of," he said as he put the helmet over his head.

"How does it fit?" Annie asked as she pushed the bike toward him.

"Okay . . . I guess. How should it fit?"

"Tight enough to save your brain; loose enough to not get a headache."

"Oh," he said as he shook his head around slightly. "Well, then, I *suppose* it fits."

"Let me see," Annie said as she gently jerked the helmet in several directions. Stephen caught a whiff of her hair again.

"It's fine," she concurred. "Take it off for now or you'll start to sweat."

He obeyed.

"Howdy, ya'll!" Angie yelled as she walked into the shed. "I haven't done this since last summer! Did you pack trail mix?"

"Check," Annie said with a thumb up. "This will be yours today," Annie told Angie as she moved toward the motorcycle she had walked out.

Angie stared at it for a moment a little uncomfortably.

"It's big," she finally declared. "A lot bigger than the 100."

"No, it's not," Annie said shaking her head. "Look, the suspension is a little high, but when you sit on it," she sat on it, "it goes down a bit. And you're gonna *love* the power. You know the really steep hill when we ride the power lines?" Angie nodded; Stephen gulped. "This 150 will take you up in five seconds with no faltering," Annie said proudly.

"How steep is this hill?" Stephen wanted to know. "Do I have to go up it?"

"Don't worry," Annie assured him with a warm smile. "All you have to do is hold on."

Alex and Megan walked in hand in hand.

"I gotta go," Megan announced with a wave. "Have a good time, and I'll see ya'll later."

"Good luck with the caterer," Annie called after her.

"I don't need luck," Megan grinned back. "I've got Alex here in Dockrey again. That's all I need. If the entire wedding is a complete disaster, but Alex and I walk out married, it will be the best day of my life!"

Alex kissed her cheek, and she ran her hand through his long, brown hair. She kissed him again and left.

"You're a lucky man," Stephen told him as he walked up.

"I know," Alex agreed.

"It's hard to find someone who will love you like that," he said as he looked toward the door.

"Tell me about it," Angie complained as she mounted the CR150. "Hey, you're right! It does compress quite a bit. Where's your 200, Annie?"

"Right over here," she replied proudly as she went over to another bike.

"I thought I was riding the 200," Alex said.

"If you want," Annie said turning toward him. "I can ride the 250 if I need too."

"No, you can't," Angie countered. "If you fall with that thing, you'll never get it back up."

"I just won't fall then," Annie said snidely.

"There's a chance of falling?" Stephen wanted to know.

"Only on a motorcycle," Annie grinned. "You just have to worry about falling *off* of a four-wheeler and getting pinned underneath."

Stephen gulped again.

"I'll ride the 250," Alex offered. "No problem."

"I'm riding the 250," came Jonathan's voice from the door. He walked in with a yellow cooler and placed it on the back of the four-wheeler.

"Well, what am I riding?" Alex wanted to know.

"The 200," Jonathan said.

"Then what am I riding?" Annie complained.

"The four-wheeler," Jonathan explained. "You're the best rider of the three. You should ride him so you can explain how he needs to take the curves and hills."

Alex smiled and Annie frowned. Stephen smiled too. This was the first hint that this trip might actually be enjoyable for him.

"So," Stephen said grinning, "all I have to do is hold on?"

"That's right," Jonathan said as he strapped on the cooler, "and look, the cooler will even give you a nice backrest. Annie, where's the food?"

Annie walked over to the chairs with a bit of an attitude growling inside. She hated the four-wheeler. She only rode the four-wheeler when Doug went with them and the boys had to ride too. She was the driver for the non-drivers.

"Why aren't you driving him?" she asked her father as she picked up the two containers. "You're the best driver of us all."

"Because I hate four-wheelers," he smiled.

Thanks, Daddy.

The trip was exhilarating. Stephen tried to remember anything he had ever experienced that could compare with this. The wooded hill-sides, even the steep power line hill, were a blast. Annie was a skillful rider indeed, as was her father. Angie took several falls, followed with a few comments by Annie concerning the new scratches on the 150. Of course, each comment brought on an argument between the sisters that Stephen found more amusing than alarming. Each time Angie would threaten to just "leave the pretty bike there and walk home," to which Annie would mutter under her breath, "if I could be so lucky." Alex did fairly well, but he had his share of spills also, at which Annie would always walk over to closely inspect her bike. The only vehicles that made the ride smoothly were the XR250 with Jonathan and the four-wheeler. However, this was the closest Stephen had been to a woman in five years. And the fact that he could breathe in the aroma of her hair for most of the trip, not to mention keeping his arms tightly around her waist, added a lot to the enjoyment of the ride.

After nearly two and a half hours of riding, the group made its way up a winding path to a precipice that jutted out over the valley below. There were no roads or power lines visible from any direction. When Stephen removed his helmet, the only sounds he heard were of the wind blowing and the soft talking of the rest of the riders. This had to be close to Heaven.

"Stephen!" called Jonathan. "Get yourself a drink and a sand-wich."

"Sure," Stephen said as his stomach growled again. "This stuff really takes it out of you."

"There's some fruit and trail mix in there too," Annie offered as she met him from the cooler on her way to the edge of the overlook.

"Any peanuts?" Alex asked.

"Roasted with no salt," Annie told him. "I remember what you like."

No response. Annie sighed as she sat down and opened her Sprite. She took several long swallows and then started on her sandwich.

Why does he hate me so? I know I've made some stupid mistakes in the past, but hasn't everyone? Why is it that I don't deserve forgiveness?

"Penny for your thoughts," Stephen whispered as he sat down next to her.

"Not for these thoughts," she mused.

"Bad?"

"More like sad," she said thoughtfully. "No matter how hard you try, you just can't change some things. How do you handle a situation like that?"

Stephen thought for a moment and said, "I wish I knew."

They sat quietly and ate while Angie argued with Jonathan over the fact that she would not have crashed any had she had the 100. Jonathan would insist over and over that she was too impulsive a rider, always had been, and would continue to be if she refused to stand up on the pegs during the rougher places.

"You don't want to get in on that conversation?" Stephen asked Annie.

She shook her head. "That's not my battle."

"What's your battle with Alex?" he asked her.

"Good question. If I could actually figure it out, I would make amends. But I don't know *exactly* what I've done."

"Exactly?"

"Yeah," she tried to explain. "I'm his sister. I've said and done a lot of things over the years that have probably not sat well with him. But heavens, I've done that with everybody and vice versa. Alex was no picnic as a brother either. I was always having to cover his tail for some mistake here or there."

"Has he always treated you like this?"

Annie shook her head. She thought back to happier times.

"We were closer in our junior high school years. We did a lot together. We laughed a lot together. Shoot, we rode a lot together. Remember the pit back there where we all took turns jumping?"

Stephen nodded. He knew the one. Everyone was rather impressive, except for Angie, who wouldn't even attempt it, claiming she might add another scratch to the bike. Annie, however, took the 200 and did several things Stephen wouldn't have the stomach to try.

"We would ride to the pit, do some fun stuff, then get off our bikes and lay on the hill watching the clouds roll by and talking."

"When did all that change?"

Annie shrugged her shoulders and took a bite of a banana. He knew that the topic had ended by the expression on her face.

"This is a pretty neat family hobby you guys have got here," he said, changing the subject. "Do all of you ride?"

"The three of us do, and so does Andie's husband, Doug. Doug used to have a street bike, and Andie would ride on the back with him when she was young and impulsive. She'll ride with him occasionally on the four-wheeler. Dad actually bought the four-wheeler for Moms. We would tell her about all these places we went to, but she was petrified to get on a bike. This past year he bought her this. She rides once in a blue moon."

"Is she feeling better?" Stephen wondered knowing that she had been a little sick earlier.

Annie smiled and then began to giggle.

"What's so funny?" he asked her.

"Oh, my," she said, still giggling. "You are not going to know what to think about us when you leave."

"What's wrong?" he asked again.

"Moms found marijuana plants in the church flower beds yesterday."

Stephen's eyes grew wide.

"She hasn't gotten over it yet," Annie went on. "She's *sick* over the fact that someone would do that."

"Maybe it was an accident," Stephen suggested.

"I wish," Annie now laughed. "They were all perfectly placed in beautiful symmetry to the rest of the plants."

"Who would do that?"

"I have no idea," she said as she gained control. "Angie and I are going to spy tomorrow and see if we *notice* anyone *noticing* the flower beds."

"That's pretty lame, wouldn't you say?" he offered.

"Very lame, especially for someone like my mother."

"I haven't had the privilege of meeting her yet. I've seen her picture, though. I love the big one over the fireplace. Alex and the other sister favor your mother."

"That was taken four Christmases ago," Annie said as she collected her trash. "There's quite a story behind that too. Rather tense situation."

"You're lucky, though, you know?" Stephen told her. "As tense as your family might be, it's great to have people like that in your life."

"I know," Annie agreed. "In fact, my family pretty much is my life."

They were quiet for a while as they listened to the gentle sounds of nature that echoed all around them. Annie loved this spot. She often rode out here on her own when she needed to think or pray or just get away. She could make it in 20 minutes if she rode straight with no meandering.

"Do you think that might be a rain cloud?" Stephen asked, breaking everyone's silence.

"Probably," Jonathan said, the only response.

There was more silence as everyone continued to relax, but Stephen was concerned about the growing thunderhead.

"If it is a rain cloud, which I feel like it might be," Stephen continued, a little more emphatic, "what will we do?"

"Get wet," was Annie's reply.

Stephen looked back at the cloud and then observed the lack of concern every one else displayed.

"Is that the plan?" he asked them.

"Plan for what?" Jonathan wanted to know.

"Is the plan that we just sort of sit here and let the rain come on us?"

"We don't plan when we ride," Annie said with a smile. "This is total freedom. No deadlines, no rushes, nobody demanding anything. We just come and go as the *spirit* moves us."

"Could I play the *spirit* right now and sort of get us heading out?" he said with a little more urgency.

"I suppose," Jonathan said as he stretched out on the ground one more time. "We probably should check on Barbara. Maybe she's gotten over the shock of the pot."

"I brought my cell phone," Stephen said holding it out. "You're welcome to use it." All four of the other riders just stared at him.

"What? I shouldn't have brought it?" he asked.

"Read your display," Jonathan said.

Stephen turned the phone around and looked at the words. *No Service.* Of course.

"How do you people survive?" he half laughed.

"You'd be surprised how well we survive," Jonathan smiled.

The trip home, though only 30 minutes, turned out to be what Jonathan called a "frog strangler." The rain poured, and everyone was soaked through and through. Stephen did take advantage to hold a little tighter to Annie, claiming the closer he held her, the less wet he got. She seemed to believe him and didn't complain. When the vehicles were all parked back in the huge shed, Stephen had to avoid the urge to say, "I told you so." It was good he kept his mouth shut, because what he had considered to be a miserable return appeared to be invigorating to the rest of them.

"Wooo!" Angie yelled.

"That was awesome!" Annie agreed. "I haven't been this drenched in years!"

"Great day for a ride," Alex commented as he pulled off his helmet and placed it on the shelf.

"You liked that?" Stephen finally asked them.

"Liked?" Jonathan said, turning to look at him. "Like doesn't even begin to describe what it feels like to ride in the rain."

"Well, my verdict is in," Stephen announced. "You are all crazy."

"I knew it," Annie said as she took Stephen's helmet from him and placed it on the shelf along with hers. "I knew you'd figure us out before the week was over. I didn't expect it to take just one day though."

Stephen tried to warm up by staying in the hot shower. He started to feel a little guilty as he thought of four others also needing the warm water. He changed his mind as he thought they purposely took their time when he had warned them of the impending rain. Chivalry got the best of him, however, and he decided to turn off the water as he thought of Angie and Annie and their long hair. They would need more water and more time. Then he thought of Annie's hair and how nice it always smelled.

Barbara got over her *sickness* of finding the marijuana and felt good enough to fry up several chickens for the entire family. Andie and her entire clan came over for dinner, and Megan was there with Alex. It was almost like a Wright family reunion. Andie recognized Stephen immediately and gave him a huge hug and "thank you" for hiring Alex.

Stephen could not remember a family gathering with so many animated people. He spent his time watching the dynamics and the way they all related to each other. He missed a family and found himself feeling more *alone* than a *part,* because this aspect of his life was no longer.

Stephen could not remember having eaten homemade fried chicken since he was 15. He normally would not have eaten so much, except that Barbara kept insisting she didn't want to deal with leftovers. Every time she mentioned this, he would grab another piece. He had also managed to sit next to Annie, which afforded him the opportunity to lean over and smell her freshly cleaned hair.

The cap of the evening, however, was when Andie announced that Jonathan wanted the entire family to sing the next morning in church. The protests were unbelievable! Andie and Annie argued about playing the piano and not singing. Alex insisted he was not a singer but an instrumentalist, and Angie complained that her *croaking* compared to their singing would stand out and be an embarrassment for the entire church. Stephen found it amusing for a while, then finally broke in.

"Excuse me!" he yelled above the griping. They all turned and stared at him. Doug started grinning. "I have a simple solution to the entire problem."

Doug looked around at the gaping mouths, looked back at Stephen and said, "Let's hear it, city boy. This ought to be good."

"Let *me* play," Stephen offered. "I play fairly well and shouldn't cause too much 'embarrassment' in the church." He looked at Angie after saying this. She fumed quietly.

"Also, since everyone tends to agree that Andie and Annie have the better of the four voices—I'm not making a judgment since I have heard none of you sing—they should sing so they can carry those of you who aren't true singers." He nodded toward Alex who grinned slightly.

"Then everyone will be equally miserable together. However, you can still honor your father by doing this one more time, and you can save yourselves the humiliation of being completely poor in your performance. I will cover all of your mistakes with pretty little interludes. Agreed?"

The group began to look around at each other nodding half-heartedly.

"Great idea!" Doug yelled. "Let's get started!"

"Okay, everyone up to my room," Annie moaned. "My piano is in tune; it's digital. This thing," she pointed to the old console in the great room, "should be used for timber or fuel."

"Bite your tongue!" Barbara snapped. "You and Andie learned to play on that piano, and here it will stay until the day I die!"

"We are not doing Southern Gospel," Angie mumbled as they started up the stairs.

"Nor anything Gaither," Andie added.

"No rap!" Jonathan yelled from the couch. "The older people can't understand it!"

Annie turned around and stared at him.

"Rap?" she said in unbelief. "When have any of us ever sung *rap?*"

"Never," he said quickly, "but with the attitudes I see walking up those stairs, I wouldn't put anything past any of you."

"This is one weird family," Stephen half whispered as he followed Annie into her room.

"You have no idea," she whispered back. "And remember, you've only been here one day."

Chapter Five

Annie awoke in a slightly lighter mood than was the norm. She pulled on her scrub bottoms and headed down to the kitchen to start coffee and some breakfast. She tried to convince herself that she was excited about Alex and Megan's wedding, or maybe that the entire family was here for the first time in so long. It could also be that the ride yesterday was so much fun with Angie and Alex along. Then, too, she did not have to worry about the McCall account for a while yet.

I'm an idiot. I am so starstruck over Stephen Williams that I can't even think straight. Any other man could have stepped into this house, and I wouldn't have given him a second thought. But Stephen Williams? I don't even remember what normal is anymore. He's been here one day, and all I can do is stare at him and wonder if he even knows I exist or if he's just being polite. Get a grip, Annie girl! Get over it!

"I just wanted to say that I, Stephen, am coming down the stairs," came a far away voice. "I am only wanting to get some coffee. I do not want to startle anyone or harm anyone who might be in the kitchen. I want to forewarn any persons rattling around down there that I am indeed coming in and to be prepared for my entrance."

He peeked inside the kitchen door, head only. "Was that ample warning?" Stephen asked with a grin.

"Very ample," Annie smiled back. "You didn't have to be *that* obvious."

"All I know is that I startled you twice yesterday, once ending with a broken mug. Today I intend to take all precautions so as not to make anyone uncomfortable with my presence."

Too late. Your presence has already upset my entire thought process.

"I don't believe that is 'cheese toast' that I smell," he said as he took a mug that Annie offered.

"Nope," Annie replied. "It's Sunday morning. We always have cinnamon rolls on Sundays."

"Homemade?" he wondered.

"No," she said as she picked up an empty can. "Home-baked, but not homemade. They're just as good, though, and way easier."

"I don't even know how to handle myself around here," Stephen confessed. "I can't remember the last home-cooked meal I had. I can't remember the last time I was even with a family."

"I bet you've never been with a family like ours," Annie said with sarcasm.

"No," he said shaking his head. "Do you guys make every day an adventure?"

"What?" she asked with a funny expression. "An adventure?"

"Yeah," he said, pausing to take a drink from his mug. "It's like you guys give 100 percent gusto all the time. High emotions, avid conversation, strong opinions are passed around like the fried chicken last night. And it doesn't seem to matter one bit that this total stranger is in your house observing the whole thing."

Annie felt her cheeks warm quickly. Yes, her family was pretty much like that all the time.

"I'm sorry," she apologized. "We haven't been together like this in so long, and there are so many changes taking place in our family. Angie's a doctor and heading to seminary, hoping she will get assigned to the Pacific some time soon. Alex has been away for what seems like forever doing all this music stuff. At least when he was in Nashville he could come home every couple of weeks. We tend to get high strung when . . . well . . . at times when . . . forget it! We are a rather *let-it-all-hang-out* type of family. We could have considered your presence here a little more thoughtfully."

"Are you kidding?" Stephen gawked at her. "This is the best time I've had in years! I do nothing! I have nobody! Jerry, the bass player, would sometimes invite me to spend some time with his family, but not often. They sort of took me as I was. That was the closest I came to being a real person. The other guys have had me over now and then, but it's like I'm the white elephant. 'Ooo, Stephen Williams is here. Tell us about yourself, Stephen. What's it like to be Stephen Williams? What's next on the Stephen Williams agenda?' Here, it's like I'm just a guy. I'm just somebody Alex brought home. I can't tell you how thrilled I was last night to have to actually *offer* to play the piano for you guys to sing today! That's unheard of . . . Stephen Williams in somebody's home and two girls are fighting over which one of *them* gets to play?"

"I am so sorry," Annie tried to apologize.

"No! Aren't you listening to me?" he continued. "I live alone. I order out food because it isn't worth it to have someone come in and cook and clean up for one person. I go to my country home, where a husband and wife live full-time; the husband keeps the grounds and repairs up, and the wife cleans the house and cooks for me when I'm there. They won't even eat with me! I can't go to Wal-Mart; I can't go to a movie. I haven't driven in over two years because people camp outside of my house, my apartment, my studio, and follow me relentlessly wherever I go. I can't go to Disney World! I could go on vacation, but who goes with me? What's the point?"

He looked at Annie, almost with tears, as he calmed down to add, "But here, *here* is the first place in probably ten years that I was invisible. And I am so scared that when I go into your church this morning, it will be like the last time I went to church. I had to leave because of disrupting the service. I can't even worship, Annie. I can barely breathe."

Annie felt even guiltier because she was so awestruck over him herself. She hoped she had hidden it well—apparently she had. She wished she could somehow comfort him and tell him she knew how he felt, but she was the wrong one to do that.

The oven beeper went off, and Annie was thankful for the interruption.

"Those smell so good," said Stephen as he drew in a big breath. "Can we get one and go out to the porch? That was so cool yesterday morning."

"It wouldn't be breakfast if we didn't," she tried to sound perky.

She iced the rolls and fixed a plate for both herself and Stephen. This time she followed him out to the back. They were silent for a long time. He smiled as he ate the rolls, drank the coffee, and took in the beautiful spring morning. Annie tried not to stare, but she could not help herself at times. Was he really that alone? How could someone with such success be as miserably alone as he claimed? She thought of the phrase in *Autumn Sunset:*

Never meant it to be this way
Just focused on other things
And somehow I let my time slip away

"I don't suppose you'd tell me your thoughts right now?" he asked.

She smiled and shook her head. "I don't verbalize everything," she teased. "There are actually a few secrets that we Wrights keep inside at times. Rarely, but occasionally."

"Wow," he drew out slowly. "I would pay a lot of money to know some of those thoughts."

"Well, Mr. Williams, your money couldn't pry those thoughts away."

"Why do you do that?" he asked her.

"Do what?"

"Start calling me 'Mr. Williams' all of sudden."

She thought for a moment. Perhaps it put some kind of distance there? Maybe she was afraid of becoming too familiar? She didn't know.

"Maybe I'm just being a polite Southern belle," she managed to say.

"Well, Miss Wright," he said with a mock accent, "I do declare that these are the finest rolls I have ever tasted in my enti-uhr life."

"Well, thank you, Mr. Williams," she teased back. "I shall have to make these for you more often."

"Wouldn't that be nice?" he whispered as he looked back out to the yard.

ꟸ ꟸ

"Here's the deal," Stephen told Annie and Angie as they approached the church. "If you girls stand out here by the flower beds and the culprits realize the plants are gone, they're going to put two and two together and know that the preacher's daughters are looking for someone. If, however, you stand under that big oak tree over there," he pointed, "and let me stand near the flower beds, I believe you'll have a better chance of finding them."

"Can you give us some kind of signal or something if you think you've pinned them?" Angie asked, really getting into the idea of being a type of private eye.

"Sure," he whispered. "I'll sort of nod my head towards them."

"Or," Annie said with slight sarcasm, "he could just come over and say, 'Those are the guys who planted the pot.' "

Stephen and Angie looked at her dauntingly.

"He could," Angie replied with her own bite of sarcasm, "and this whole thing could just be another boring Sunday morning."

"I'm gonna tell Daddy you called church boring," Annie grinned.

"And I'll tell Daddy how you used to preach in the pulpit when we would come over here to vacuum the church," Angie stuck her tongue out.

"And I'll tell him about you and Billy Marcum in the balcony," Annie said with triumph.

"Okay," Angie admitted defeat. "My lips are sealed. You win."

Stephen leaned in with wide eyes and a grin and said, "I'd like to know about Billy Marcum and the balcony."

"Not today, buster," Angie insisted and pushed his shoulder back. "I can't believe you brought that up, Annie! Even I had forgotten about that."

"How could you forget that?" Annie said dramatically.

"I'd pay," Stephen offered.

"I told you, city boy, you're money's no good around here," Annie reminded him.

Annie felt her heart skip a beat when he smiled at her. She knew what he was thinking; "These girls are treating me like a regular guy." The only thing now is that she was trying to do it for *his* sake. Add to that, trying to do it for her sanity, trying to keep herself from drooling all over him, and it made for one uptight Annie. She tried to shake the confusion out of her head.

"Back to the real point here, our stakeout," she redirected. "I think that's a good idea, Stephen. Head on over there and see what you can find. We'll stay by the tree and try to identify anyone that you think might be a suspect."

"Isn't this fun?" Angie whispered excitedly.

Stephen made his way nonchalantly toward the front flowerbed. *Billy Marcum in the balcony? Annie preaching in the pulpit? These girls had a life! How much of life did I miss pursuing what I thought real life was?*

Stephen smiled and was greeted by several members as they moved inside the church. No one, not a single person, recognized who he was. He couldn't believe it! Thank goodness this was Tammy Wynette country! For all they knew he was some dog food mill worker that had just moved to town. He looked back occasionally at Annie and Angie who would give him a thumbs-up and go back to their talking. He was wishing now that he were with them instead of standing guard over the flower garden.

"They're gone!" he heard a young male voice exclaim in a whisper.

"No way!" came a girl's reply.

"What?" asked a third voice.

"The pot, you moron!" came the first voice, a bit more panicked now.

Stephen moved slightly closer and pretended to be getting some lint off his shirt.

"Somebody finally found it!" said the girl. "Do you think they knew what it was?"

"You guys are freaking over nothing," said the second guy. "The only person who even digs around in here is that dufus preacher's wife. She wouldn't know a marijuana plant if it introduced itself to her. She probably thought it was some stupid weed and just pulled it up."

Stephen's blood began to boil slightly. Barbara Wright was a wonderful, caring, and hospitable woman. These kids, somewhere around 15 or 16, had no right to speak about her like that. He knew the plan was for him to just find the culprits, not do anything about it, but he wanted to see these kids squirm. They had defiled the church property, and as far as Barbara Wright was concerned, they had defiled her too.

"Do you think she found all of it?" asked the girl.

Stephen walked up to them and said, "Oh yeah. She found all of it."

They turned quickly, startled by the intrusion. The first boy whispered an expletive while the other two just stared at Stephen with their mouths agape.

"We don't know what you're talking about," the second boy immediately began to defend.

"Did you three know that growing marijuana is a felony?" Stephen asked them.

"Who the heck are you?" the second boy wanted to know.

"Perhaps a federal agent contacted by the staff of the church after finding pot growing in their flowers," Stephen put before them, "or not. Maybe I'm some guy just visiting the church who was admiring the dufus pastor's wife's handiwork."

Stephen now enjoyed watching them get antsy. The second boy's smart aleck, carefree attitude was fading, and his face was turning red. The first boy wouldn't even look up, and the girl's eyes were starting to water.

"Shouldn't you three be in Sunday school?" Stephen asked them.

"Yeah, right," the first boy managed to say. "We'd better get."

As they turned to go, Stephen stopped them short and added, "For the record, I've got my eye on you three."

"Yes, sir," the first boy said as they turned to go.

Not bad! Maybe I should go into acting now!

Stephen explained what had happened to the sisters. They could not believe the culprits. The two boys were deacons' kids, and the girl was the organist's daughter.

"What were they thinking?" Angie exclaimed. "Where did they get the seeds to begin with?"

"Well, I could give you a good guess on that one," Annie said to her. " 'The fruit doesn't fall too far from the tree,' you know?"

"Sort of like the whole Billy Marcum thing," Stephen added.

Angie stopped and stared at him for the moment, then hit his shoulder, fairly hard.

"Ow!" he said as he rubbed it gently.

"You deserved that," Angie said as she turned to head toward the church.

Stephen leaned over to Annie, catching the scent of her hair again, and whispered, "I've got to know that story."

"You don't know Angie. She would kill me if I told you," Annie tried to explain.

"I would never tell," he pleaded.

"Trust me, she would know," Annie said shaking her head. "Angie has this sixth sense about her."

"I don't suppose I could offer you any money?" he tried again.

"Mr. Williams!" she exclaimed. "Haven't you learned that I cannot be compromised with your money?"

He shook his head and smiled as he followed her to church.

Stephen had not sat in a Sunday school class since he was 15. His mom had always taken him and his sister to church. He had been asked to play offertories many Sundays and was always allowed to leave class early to run through them in the sanctuary before church started. It was impossible for him to go to church in New York City. It would require an entourage of bodyguards and escorts. He had found a nice country church out near his home in the Adirondacks, but he was a huge distraction from the service. He only attended once. He decided instead to read

Christian literature and listen to his favorite television pastors. The pastor of the country church would always call and visit him whenever Stephen was there, and he insisted that he could find a way to get Stephen in church, but it was more effort than Stephen was willing to give.

The Sunday service turned out to be refreshing and exciting. Stephen was impressed with how easily Jonathan filled the pulpit. He was charming, humorous, and compassionate all at once. And when the Wright quartet sang, he could not get over how incredibly well they blended. He had always heard that family voices were the ideal group because they would mesh so well. He could not pick out a single voice, not even Alex's. His tenor was so high or Annie's alto was so low that they continued to bump each other indistinguishably.

When the song was finished and the time for preaching began, Annie sat next to Stephen and whispered a soft "thanks" to him for playing.

"My pleasure," he winked at her.

She swirled her long hair back after retrieving her Bible, and Stephen inhaled that glorious aroma again.

Great, my first chance to be in church in five years, and I'm sitting next to Annie with dark brown hair . . . and big brown eyes . . . and lips . . . focus.

It ended up being easy to stay with the preaching. As the service went on, Stephen knew he would be receiving recordings of this man for the rest of his life. If they didn't tape the services yet, Stephen would see to it that they had all the equipment necessary to do it for every message Jonathan Wright gave. The thing that impressed him as much as his preaching was the fact that the day before he had ridden with him through the woods, through the rain, and been impressed with the man himself.

Following church was a covered dish dinner in honor of Alex and Megan, which included a church-wide shower for the couple. Stephen enjoyed himself as he carried on several unpretentious conversations with various people in the church.

"So, Alex works with you?" asked one man as he sat down next to Stephen.

"Yes, sir," Stephen replied. He stuck out his hand and introduced himself. "Stephen Williams."

“Oh, yeah,” the man smiled. “I think my son has one of your albums.”

“You’ve heard of me?” Stephen asked, a little timid that perhaps all was not as simple as he thought.

“Sure,” the man said as he bit into a piece of chocolate cake. “You’re the *Autumn Sunset* boy.”

“You’re familiar with my music?” Stephen wanted to know.

“Of course,” the man smiled. “Now, you ain’t no George Jones or Bill Gaither, but you write some pretty songs too.”

Stephen smiled and nodded his head. He liked Alabama. Never in his life had he been compared to George Jones! And Stephen was coming up on the short end of the comparison!

ꟾ ꟾ

After evening church, the entire family came back to the Wright house and popped popcorn and sat around the back porch. Stephen enjoyed the lively discussion, which, as he was learning, was to be expected in this house. He was always amused at Doug’s comments that would be interspersed throughout the conversation. Almost always one of the girls would yell a “shut up” at him and continue on. To this, he would almost always put up his hands in surrender and say something akin to, “Just trying to clarify the point.”

“Here’s another bag,” Annie announced as she came through the door with some more microwaved popcorn. She emptied the bag into various bowls and asked, “Do we need another one?”

Everyone said no, and she sat down on the floor at the opposite end of the porch from Stephen. Andie, Doug, and the kids got up to go; the kids needed to get in bed. They protested, especially Ashley, but Andie managed to round them out the door. Megan also needed to go. She had many things to do tomorrow so Alex walked her out.

“I guess now’s as good a time as any,” Angie announced when everyone had left.

“For what, dear?” Barbara asked.

“We know who planted the marijuana,” she told them.

Barbara’s face went pale.

“Who?” Jonathan questioned, looking more sober than Stephen had ever seen him.

“Brace yourselves,” Annie joined in as she moved up to take one of the empty seats.

"Oh my," Barbara whispered.

"It was Donny Deaton, Karie Adams, and Joey Cramer," Angie said slowly.

Jonathan sighed deeply and put his head back. Barbara put her hand up to her mouth.

"Are you sure?" Jonathan wanted to know.

"Positive," Annie affirmed. "Stephen heard the entire conversation, and Angie and I were there to identify them."

"Well," Jonathan thought aloud, "I'm going to have to deal with this creatively."

"Do *you* have to deal with it?" Barbara asked.

"You bet I do," Jonathan insisted. "But I can't just come out with it. It's our word against theirs."

"Honey, they could fire you," Barbara said.

"David Deaton and Jon Cramer have been against me from the moment I stepped foot in this church," Jonathan explained to Stephen. "They never wanted the former pastor to leave, regardless of the fact that he had stolen huge amounts of money from the church. Who knows, maybe they were in on it. Whatever the reason, they have fought me on every step made in this church. They made me their enemy from day one. I can't just walk up to them and say their kids planted pot in the church flower beds."

"What about the girl?" Stephen asked.

"Bad company corrupts good morals," Jonathan said shaking his head. "Karie and Donny have been a couple for several months now. Her mother isn't pleased, but doesn't seem to have what it takes to put a stop to it."

"What are you gonna do, Daddy?" Angie asked him.

He shook his head and replied, "I don't know yet. This is one of those situations where you spend a lot of time in prayer and ask God for the wisdom of Solomon."

"Can these guys actually throw you out?" Stephen wondered.

"Not actually," Jonathan tried to explain, "but they have enough power and money to cause huge problems, even split the church. They almost did it before, but the church would not allow the former pastor to stay. They tried some shenanigans shortly after I came, trying to tarnish my character, but I stood in the pulpit and declared that I was a man of God first. I told the church that if I ever found myself falling short of doing the right thing for the advancement of this church, I would resign before anyone would even know. I wouldn't gamble with the Body of Christ like that."

"They took your word for it?" Stephen asked him.

"Yes, and I intend to be a man of integrity in everything I do. I've made some mistakes in leading this church, but I've always confessed them before the church. I've made some mistakes in raising my family, but I've always admitted them publicly when I felt it was necessary. I've always been determined to stay accountable to the people of God here."

"Wow," Stephen said in admiration. "I'm not accountable to anybody. In fact, I haven't had to answer for a single thing I've done for probably ten years."

"Church?" Jonathan asked him.

"I can't do it. It's more trouble than it's worth."

"Do you know the Lord?" Jonathan asked, looking directly into his eyes.

"Actually, yes, I do," Stephen told him. "I was raised in church, but got away after some pretty severe family things happened. I went on with my goals, pursuing a career in music. Every goal I had was fulfilled. About five years ago, I realized that the lifestyle this whole music thing had created was totally destructive. I got on my knees and asked God to forgive me and cleanse me and help me start over again."

"And you've done all that without a church?" Jonathan wanted to know.

"Yes sir, but I had no choice."

"We always have choices, Stephen."

"You would think that," Stephen told him, "but I really don't. Me showing up at a church is like the president going to McDonalds. It's not just a matter of getting up and going. It's a major ordeal."

"You didn't have that problem here today," Jonathan stated.

"I know. It was unbelievable. I can't tell you how incredible this day has been."

"Then perhaps you have limited your choices," Jonathan smiled. "You say you can't go to church in New York, but there seems to be no problem with it in Alabama."

Annie could have curled up and died. Her father had no right to carry on like this with Stephen. He knew nothing of Stephen's life and the demands on him. When Jonathan, Barbara, and Angie left for bed, Annie found the courage to apologize, yet again.

"I'm sorry about my father," she began. "He likes to think there are solutions to every problem."

"Maybe there are," Stephen said thoughtfully. "Maybe he's right."

"Stephen, listen, my dad is a great guy, but he doesn't know what your life is like. He doesn't really comprehend who you are and what you do. He's been here nearly 25 years, and his concept of life is Dockrey, Alabama. Nothing more, nothing less."

"And you think *you* know what my life is about?" he asked her.

She paused, caught off guard. She was trying to defend him, to help him, not condemn him. But this question was almost rude.

"No, not exactly," she said cautiously, "but it's nothing like here."

Stephen stood up and walked to the screened wall of the porch. He ran the back of his finger against the screen and ran his other hand through his loose curls.

"Have I offended you?" she asked, going up next to him.

He shook his head unable to speak.

"Then what is it?" she asked gently.

He turned to her, and she could see small pools welling up in his blue eyes.

"I don't like my life much anymore," he simply said. "It's become so hard. I have nobody, and I do nothing except what's expected of me. You guys, all of you here, this is life. You have each other. You have memories. You have fun. Shoot! You have conversations. I have nothing."

Annie didn't know what to do. Had this been anyone else, a sister or a friend, she would have put her arms around him and held him close until the tears spilled or subsided. But again, this was Stephen Williams. How do you deal with Stephen Williams?

"I'm really sorry," she tried to comfort. "I had no idea, you know, that someone like you could actually be unhappy. I thought only people like me could be unhappy."

"Why are you unhappy?" he asked in confusion. "What do you not have?"

She glanced out to the yard and watched a moth fly into the light.

"I don't know," she tried to explain. "I guess I don't have any dreams, or maybe I'm afraid to dream. Or maybe I'll dream too big and they won't come true. So I just live life one day at a time, taking whatever comes, and I never try to do anything more."

"What's worse?" he asked her. "Not dreaming or having every one of them come true and then having nowhere else to go."

Annie found herself smiling. "We're being pretty pitiful, you know?" she said, looking back to him.

"You're right," he agreed. "How do we break out of this? I don't like feeling this way."

"Let's see if there's a good late movie on," she suggested.

"Escapism. Nice touch," he smiled as they headed inside.

Chapter Six

Annie awoke the next morning, 6:45 as usual, and considered the night before. She had left Stephen asleep on the couch and wondered if he had ever made it up to the apartment. She pulled on her scrub pants and left her room to peek over the balcony. He was still there sound asleep.

She quietly made her way down the stairs and into the kitchen to start the coffee. The kitchen was a bit of a mess with cups and bowls from the previous night. She started the coffee brewing and began to throw away empty popcorn bags. She unloaded the dishwasher as quietly as possible and began to place bowls and cups inside.

"Good morning," she heard faintly from the great room. "May I get up?"

She peeked out the kitchen entrance and saw Stephen sitting up on the couch with his hair looking like a tangled mess.

"I didn't want to startle you again," he smiled sleepily. "Is the coffee ready?"

"Almost," she told him. "I tried to be as quiet as I could. I'm sorry I woke you."

"I needed to get up," he said as he stood and stretched. "I think I've got a crick in my neck."

"I should have told you to get up last night and go on to bed."

"No, it was fine, but I haven't slept on a couch in years," he said as he rolled his neck around and around.

"Where does it hurt?" she asked him as she came over.

"Right here," he moaned as he pointed to the right side of his neck.

Annie reached up and touched his neck where he had pointed. "Right there?" she asked.

"Back to the left just a bit," he told her. She moved her hand back slightly.

"Right there," he said quickly.

Annie began to gently massage the side of his neck. She could feel the tightness beneath his skin.

"Oh, man," he sighed. "That's it. That feels good."

"Sometimes you can massage these out," she explained as she moved her other hand up to join the effort.

"You could just follow me around all day and keep it up," he grinned.

"Sure," she replied. "I've got nothing better to do."

She continued for a while and then stopped, asking him if it was any looser.

He rolled his shoulder and head around and said, "Yes, it is. That's wonderful! Who taught you that?"

She shrugged. "I don't know. Maybe nobody. You wake up with a crick, you try to rub it out," she said matter of factly.

"Marry me?" he asked innocently.

Annie was taken back by the joke. He still did not understand that he was *Stephen Williams* to her and not the normal guy she was pretending to let him be.

"Mr. Williams," she replied, reverting back to her Southern belle defense, "I believe you are still half asleep. You haven't had your coffee yet."

"I believe you are right, Miss Wright," he responded in like, exaggerated, Southern drawl. "Could you kindly lead me to the kitchen?"

One by one, the family joined Stephen and Annie on the back porch with their coffee and cheese toast. Annie was still trying to put together all that Stephen had said last night. How could someone with everything he ever wanted be unhappy? Millions of people waited expectantly to hear his next project, while she sat in an office in Dockrey, Alabama, writing and recording silly jingles to play on the radio and local TV. Maybe no one was really happy. No, her parents were happy. Andie and Doug were happy. Even Angie, with all the schooling and hours she had put in and still more to go, was happy. What made her and Stephen the exceptions? And what about Alex? He never seemed happy except maybe when he was with Megan. What was his problem?

"Annie," her mother interrupted her. "You need to go to Sam's today and get the stuff for the rehearsal dinner."

"Sure," Annie replied. "Do you have a list?"

"I'm working on it," Barbara replied. "Angie, do you want to go with her?"

"Nope," Angie said getting up. "Cindy Marcum is in town. I

promised to spend the day with her."

"What about me?" Annie protested. "I seldom get to see you anymore!"

"It's one day," Angie said as she opened the door to enter the house. "I haven't seen Cindy in years."

Annie was actually a bit hurt. She had envisioned spending the whole week with Angie.

Stephen leaned over and whispered to Annie, "Is this Cindy Marcum related in any way to the Billy Marcum of the balcony?"

"I told you already; I'm not discussing this with you," Annie said sternly.

"You should probably get going," Barbara said as she handed the list to Annie.

"Okay, I'll go alone," she moaned. She then yelled out adding, "Without my sister!"

"I'll go with you," Stephen volunteered. "Can we go to Wal-Mart?"

"Why?" she wondered.

"Because I can!"

"I guess," she agreed. "Whatever. If you're willing to keep me company, I'm willing to take you to Wal-Mart."

"Yee haw!" he yelled.

"Now," Barbara interrupted, "what about plates and such?"

"We'll just use the china in the fellowship hall," Annie told her.

"Annie, this is going to be huge. If we use the china and glasses and silverware, that means that we have to stay up half the night washing dishes before the wedding the next day."

"Mother, you invited everybody in both families!" Annie complained. "Do you know how many plates we'd have to buy? Not to mention cups, forks, and so on?"

"I know," Barbara sighed. "But honey, I want to be relaxed for the wedding."

"I doubt that will happen," Annie said negatively.

"Exactly," Barbara said rising. "Get the paper goods too. Please?"

"Okay," Annie agreed reluctantly. "Your Sam's bill is gonna be huge."

"I know, dear," Barbara said as she was leaving the porch, "but I will be happy on Saturday."

When Barbara was back inside the house, Stephen put his hand on Annie's shoulder and turned her toward him.

"Let me get it," he suggested.

"Get what?"

"All the paper plates and such."

"No way," Annie said shaking her head. "We're not going to let you do that."

"Why not?" he asked. "Look, I want to. It's the least I can contribute after all your family has done for me."

"Stephen, our family hasn't *done* anything for you," she tried to insist. "We can do this; it will just stretch the budget a bit. Moms wanted to go all out with this dinner and bring everybody in on it. Because of that, it got a little bigger than we had intended, well, a whole lot bigger. But we can do it. I'm always trying to cut corners; it's part of my nature."

"You don't understand, Annie," he said gently. He struggled to find the words to express himself. "I'm . . . well . . . worth more than your family can probably imagine. I mean, just on sales and residuals alone I literally make thousands of dollars a day at times. The cost of your plates and things wouldn't even make a dent in my daily income. Please, let me do this."

"Stephen, I can't. It wouldn't be right. We can't take your money," she insisted.

"Okay, have it your way," he said, "but I intend to fill my cart with every exact product that you put in yours, and I will check out before you do."

Annie grinned. He had no idea what a Sam's was.

"You can't," she told him.

"Why not? I'm going with you."

"Because," she explained, "you have to have a membership card in order to check out."

"Really?" he said puzzled. "Can't I get one?"

"Actually, you could," she said. "This is one place that would gladly take your money in exchange for a card."

"So do I win?" he asked with a smile.

"I haven't decided yet," she said as she stood, not wanting to give in. "Let's go trade my car for Dad's pickup. We're gonna need it."

Annie led Stephen to her blue VW and climbed in.

"Any reason for the blue?" he asked her as he got in.

"I like blue," she stated.

"You like blue as in *blue, blue, my world is blue?*" he asked.

"No. More like *blue, blue, I really like blue.*"

The last time Annie had been in the car was with Angie on Friday. When she turned on the engine, the CD immediately began to pound out "Autumn Sunset" from *The Piano Album.* Annie quickly turned off the sound system, embarrassed for some reason that she didn't know.

"Thank you," he said as he mockingly cleared his ears. "I didn't want to hear that guy anyway."

Annie didn't say anything. She just backed out of the drive and drove up toward the church.

"Were you embarrassed?" he asked. "I mean, I feel honored that you like my music enough to play it in your car."

"I really like *The Piano Album,*" she said, trying to act as if it were the *only* one she really liked. She was still nervous and slightly embarrassed.

"I do too," he said as he pulled on a Florida Marlins' cap he had seen in the back seat of her car. "Annie, it's okay that you listen to my music. You're this incredibly talented and knowledgeable lady. It's not like you're this google-eyed teenage girl crying over my songs. To me, you just have good taste."

He laughed at his comment, but Annie winced. No, she wasn't a google-eyed teenager at this moment, but 11 years ago when his first album came out, she most definitely was. And no matter how hard she tried, she could never shake *that* image of him, or that image of her.

The trip to Tupelo was lively to say the least. Stephen found it quaint eating at the mall and took great pleasure in buying a Stephen Williams CD from the music shop. He bought himself a hat, some shoes, and an inflatable chair. He insisted on buying something for Annie, but she kept refusing. He finally bought her a Stephen Williams calendar, signing each month, as punishment for not being more creative when he offered a favor. She took him to Elvis' birthplace and then to Wal-Mart. He bought gummy worms, M&M's, two softball gloves, and a softball to play catch with when they returned to Dockrey. They finished the shopping trip at Sam's. Stephen bought a laptop computer for himself, a food sealer for Barbara, and a huge block of cheese for Annie's breakfasts, along with all the paper items needed for the rehearsal dinner. He tried to pay for Annie's basket that contained the food, but she vehemently refused.

On the way home, Stephen talked constantly. It was almost as if he had been released from prison and couldn't get his thoughts out fast enough. He told Annie about the making of each album, the tours that followed, the musicians he had met and worked with over the years. He talked about his apartment in New York and his house in the mountains. He told her about France and Spain and Greece. He told her many details surrounding his life, but he never talked about his personal life. After spending six hours with him, she knew nothing more about him than she had learned from years of reading magazine articles and watching TV specials.

"Want to play catch?" Stephen asked Annie as he walked by the kitchen where she had just finished putting away the block of cheese.

"I guess," she replied.

"Here," he said as he tossed her one of the stiff, new gloves he had just bought.

She held up the glove and tried to bend it.

"Mind if I use my own?" she asked as she tossed the glove back.

"You have your own glove?" he asked wide-eyed.

"I play in a ladies' softball league," she said as she left the kitchen and started up the stairs. She found her glove at the top of her closet and came back out to the overlooking balcony.

"Am I going to be sorry I asked you to play catch?" Stephen yelled up at her.

"It depends," she answered as she came down the stairs.

"Depends on what?"

"Whether or not we just toss the ball or play *accuracy,*" she explained with a smile.

"Accuracy?" he questioned. "Is there actually a way to play a game when you're just playing catch?"

"In this family, there's a way to make a competition out of everything."

Annie led the way out to the back porch and then into the back yard.

"You stay here," she told him, "and I'll start about 20 feet away. Plant your feet comfortably."

Stephen placed his feet in the soft grass, looked up at her and asked, "What's next?"

"You're only allowed to move one foot per catch," she explained. "I throw the ball to you. You have to be able to catch it by only moving one foot. You can reach up; you can bend down. You can step right or left, back and forth, but you can't drop the ball."

"Okay," he said a little confused. "What if I drop it?"

"Then I get a point," she smiled. "However, if I throw and it's not legitimately catchable and you miss it, *you* get the point. Got it?"

Stephen nodded. Annie walked down the yard and then planted her feet.

Stephen yelled out, "Can we just toss a few times to warm up?"

"Suit yourself," she yelled back. "I'm ready when you are!"

"Smart aleck," he mumbled to himself.

"The first to ten wins!" she yelled again. "Then we usually do it two out of three times!"

"Got it!" he yelled back, and then mumbled again to himself, "I hope I don't totally embarrass myself here."

Annie was tricky. As soon as the actual game started, she would throw the ball in the most hard to get places. She beat him the first round hands down. But during the second game, he began to get the idea. She beat him again, but not as badly.

"How about seven out of ten?" he suggested. "I'm just getting the hang of this!"

"Are you sure?" she yelled back. "I wouldn't want to wear you out!"

"Hey!" he shouted to her, "I work out! Look at this physique!" He showed a muscle in his right arm. "I'm just getting warmed up!"

"Am I supposed to show you my muscles now?" she asked.

"No!" he yelled out quickly. "Yours might be bigger than mine, and then I'd have to kill you to protect my manhood!"

They never made it to the seven out of ten, but Stephen did manage to win a couple of rounds. He wasn't sure if it was done fairly or if Annie had pity on him. Either way, it had been a lot of fun. Annie sat in the bench swing beneath a large oak and Stephen joined her. He reached over and took her glove and began to turn it around and inspect it.

"This thing has seen a lot of action," he commented as it slumped in his hand.

"That's what makes it so good," she said as she leaned back in the swing, "well broken in."

"How do you do that?" he asked. "How do you make it floppy?"

"It's not floppy," she told him. "It's *seasoned.*"

"Okay," he complied, "how do you *season* it?"

"By playing," she replied.

Stephen nodded and handed her glove back. He held up his own glove and tried to flop it too. It was stiff as a board.

"Hmph," he muttered.

"What?"

"Sort of like me, isn't it?" he told her. "You guys are all laid back, easygoing, taking life as it comes. I'm stiff and always driving forward, barely taking enough time to see the roses, much less smell or plant them." He motioned toward Barbara's rose garden.

"Yeah, but you've got a lot of success to show for it," she said.

He nodded and then placed the glove in his lap. They were quiet for a while and took in the sights, sounds, and smells of the back yard.

"Are you happy with what you do?" he finally asked her breaking the pause.

She dropped her head to the side and thought seriously about it before answering.

"Hard question," she finally responded.

"No, it's not," he told her. "Either you're happy or you're not."

"It *is* a hard question," she said firmly as she looked at him. "You can be happy in some areas, but not quite as fulfilled in others."

"Interesting choice of words," he said knowingly. "I didn't say anything about being fulfilled. I asked about being happy."

"Oh, so this is a philosophical conversation," she said with slight sarcasm.

"What does that mean?" he asked defensively.

"It means we're not talking about *real* happiness. We're talking about some hypothetical situation. I happen to equate happiness with being fulfilled. Being happy doesn't mean you feel all gushy and mushy about life. It means you're doing something that fulfills a purpose and you find pleasure in what you do."

"I disagree," he said flatly.

"Really?" she asked a bit shocked. "How do you define happiness?"

"Happiness is making your dreams come true," he explained. "It means looking inside you, deciding the best place you could go, and then putting every ounce of energy you have into getting there."

Annie sat stone-cold for a moment. She had just had her view of happiness reduced to a rocky rubble of nothing.

"Not everyone has the privilege of making his or her dreams come true," she said flatly, hiding most of the emotion she was really feeling.

"Sure they do," he countered. "You can do anything you want."

"No. *You* can do anything you want. You're rich. You're famous. You don't have to bow to the demands of others. You don't have to lower yourself to fit into everyone else's expectations."

"Apparently, we're not hypothetical anymore," he said.

"What's that supposed to mean?" she asked a little angrily.

"How do you think I got where I am?" he asked her. "Do you think I signed a contract at 20 years old and walked into the studio and told everyone how it was going to be?" He shook his head and continued. "I didn't even want to do rock music! I hated it at that point. My songs were not designed to be flushed over with drums and heavy electric guitars. But they said, 'Boy, this is what sells. If you want to record with us, you'll do it our way.' I went with it. My dream was to make music for the world. If that meant compromising to get there, then I had to do it."

"But what about *The Piano Album?*" she insisted. "That wasn't rock! Far from it."

"Exactly!" he said turning back to her suddenly. "Album number seven. And you know what? It's my worst selling album. Do I care? No! Why? Because it's what I wanted to do! And you know why I could do it? Because I paid my dues with compromise. I listened to all those superiors who said to do it their way."

"So you're not even a little disappointed that your *real* music isn't appreciated as much?" she wondered.

"My compromised music made it possible for me to make my real music."

They sat without commenting for a time. Annie was actually quite miffed about the conversation.

"So you're happy then?" she finally asked.

"I should be," he replied doubtfully.

She was now angry. "So you tear apart my definition of happy?" she began to rant a little. "I say I'm fulfilled, but my dreams haven't come true. So then, according to you, I have to be miserable. But you're dreams have come true, and you're not really happy about that? Can you explain the irony here?"

"What are your dreams, Annie?" he asked.

"You're avoiding my question," she said soberly.

"No," he said slowly. "I just want to know what your dreams are."

"None of your business!" she shouted as she stood up. "I don't know what you're all about! You talk like you have a grip on the world, then you turn around and talk like life is falling apart at the seams. Figure out your own life before you start trying to *fix* someone else's."

She started to leave, and then turned around to grab her glove off the seat.

"You are stiff, Stephen Williams," she said coldly. "You are proud of your accomplishments, but you're afraid to open up. I may have given up on dreaming, content to live in a world of just so-so accomplishment, but I have people and family around me that give meaning, and yes, happiness to my life!"

Annie stormed back to the house, mumbling comments about Stephen and his audacity to question her life. Who did he think he was?

Stephen just sat in the swing and watched her stomp to the back porch. He didn't really mean to upset her apple cart. He just sensed that she was a miserable as he was and thought they could help each other out with a little friendly give and take. He was apparently very wrong.

As Annie reached the door, Alex was on his way out. She huffed past him.

"What's wrong with you?" he asked as she continued stomping toward the stairs.

"Shut up!" she yelled out without turning around.

Alex saw Stephen sitting on the swing and spied the glove. He assumed they had been together. He walked outside and joined Stephen on the swing.

"I see you met Attila the Hun," Alex said smiling.

"Is she always like that?" Stephen asked him.

"No," Alex replied. "Sometimes she worse."

Stephen laughed and picked up his glove again. She was spirited to say the least.

"I feel kind of guilty," Alex said to Stephen, not looking at him. "You came here with me to be in my wedding, and I haven't spent any time with you."

"Don't think twice about it," Stephen insisted. "Your family has kept me great company."

"Yeah, I can see that," Alex said sarcastically has he motioned toward the door that Annie had practically blasted through.

"I deserved that," Stephen told him. "I pried a bit too much."

Alex sighed, still not looking at Stephen.

"Is there something you need to tell me?" Stephen asked.

"Yeah," Alex nodded. "I wanted to take Megan out tonight. Just the two of us, you know? But I feel like I should do something with you."

"Don't even think about," Stephen said shaking his head. "I'm fine. I promise."

"Tomorrow we have this dinner thing with all our friends. Wednesday is church. Thursday we have to decorate the church and tie up all the loose ends. Friday is rehearsal. I mean, we don't have to go out, but I just wanted to spend one evening alone with her before the actual wedding."

"And I understand," Stephen told him again. "Please, don't think you have to entertain me. I am just fine."

"You're supposed to come with us tomorrow night. We're going to this sort of club place where you eat and dance and all," Alex tried to explain. "I don't really know what it is, but all the bridesmaids and groomsmen and other friends are supposed to go there and hang out or something. Megan says she's booked a banquet room. To be honest, I don't know what is going on."

"I'm there," Stephen told him as he patted Alex's back. "But tonight, spend some quiet time with your bride to be. I promise you that I'll be fine."

"So, you're not gonna fire me for neglecting you?" Alex smiled.

"I may fire you for letting your sister yell at me," Stephen teased.

"I warned you about her," Alex said seriously.

"Yes, you did," Stephen confessed. "But I have to confess, it was rather fun being yelled at for a change."

ꟹ ꟹ

Supper that night included only Barbara, Jonathan, Annie, and Stephen. Annie still wouldn't talk to him, but Barbara and Jonathan kept him good company. Barbara had made a chicken pie, and Stephen thought it was too delicious to be homemade. He could not remember the last time he had eaten so well. As suppertime began to linger, Barbara started to get up and clear the table.

"Let Annie and I clean up tonight, Mrs. Wright," Stephen offered. "You have done so much since I've been here. Please let us do this."

Annie stared at him with daggers in her eyes. Stephen just smiled.

"I think I'll take you up on that," Barbara sighed. "I would love to shower and go to bed."

"And I believe I'll join you," Jonathan said as he pushed away from the table.

"Daddy!" Annie exclaimed. "That's a bit more than we need to know, don't you think?"

"Not the shower," he winked. "It's just I think I'll retire for the evening myself."

Jonathan and Barbara left for their room while Annie and Stephen still sat at the table. Annie would not look at him. He just stared at her.

"You can't ignore me for the whole week," he finally said.

"No, but I can ignore you for the rest of the night," she stated.

"Not if you have to help me clean the kitchen."

"Who said I was helping?"

"I haven't cleaned a kitchen since I moved out of the house and into a college dorm," he said as he leaned down trying to catch her eye.

"Do you do things like this often?" she asked as she got up and began to stack plates. "Volunteer for things you have no idea how to complete?"

He began gathering glasses. "No," he replied. "I never volunteer for anything. I always get asked."

Annie continued to clear the table, but refused to look at him. They would pass each other in and out of the kitchen, but she always averted his eyes.

"You're funny," he finally said when the table was cleared and there was nowhere for her to hide as they began to work in the kitchen itself.

She finally looked up at him. "And why is that?" she asked exasperated. "Why do you seem to be enjoying this so much?"

"How long can you hold a grudge?" he wondered.

"You might be surprised," she said coldly.

"I don't know," he said shaking his head. "The way you've acted tonight, I feel like I might be on your blacklist for a long time."

She ignored him and began to load the dishwasher.

"I wondered when I would see this side of you," he finally quipped.

She stopped the loading, turned swiftly toward him and put her hands on her hips.

"Exactly what is *that* supposed to mean?" she asked, upset, but in control.

"Well, I mean, all I heard about you was that you were—*spirited.*"

She rolled her eyes. *Spirited. Great word.*

"I suppose Alex told you that," she wondered. "He has never had a lot of positive *expressions* about me."

"Well, he's not the only one," Stephen said nonchalantly as he handed her a plate.

"He's not?" she questioned. "Who else has talked to you about me?"

"If you'll remember," he continued, "there was a certain phone call you made several months ago to my offices concerning the auditioning of your brother."

Annie's face flushed. She wished she could control that. "Look," she defended, "that guy was a little rude! He said I was loony!"

"Well, now, you have to admit the whole situation was a little bizarre."

"You should do something about him," she said as she continued to load.

"What would you suggest?" he asked her.

"Fire him," was the reply.

"That would cause quite a problem with my company," he told her. "In fact, the whole thing would fall apart if I did."

"Then you should consider more carefully who you divulge responsibility to," she said huffily.

He chuckled to himself, but she heard him.

"You think that's funny?" she asked.

"Yes, because you are so mad you don't even know what you're saying."

"And you are so rude . . ." she couldn't continue. She put soap into the dishwasher, slammed the door, and turned it on. She walked out of the kitchen and started to head up the stairs when Stephen stopped her with his statement.

"That was me you talked to on the phone," he told her.

She slowly turned back toward him. He couldn't really read her expression.

"Why didn't you tell me?" she asked very seriously.

"Then or now?" he said with a grin.

"Then and now."

"Then, because I really did think you were crazy," he began. "Now, well, didn't I just tell you?"

"Now as in two days ago!" she yelled. "I bet you think I *am* a total lunatic, don't you? Do you know what an idiot I feel like?"

"It worked," he told her.

"What worked?" she half shouted as she threw her hands up in disarray.

"It got your brother an audition," he said. "My only disappointment was that you didn't come with him. I was really quite curious to meet you."

"Is that why you came this week?" she asked. "To spy on me and settle your curiosity."

"I must confess it was a huge part of my decision."

"Well, I hope you're satisfied," she said through clenched teeth.

This time she turned to the stairs and did not look back until she was in her room with the door shut. She turned toward her closed door and laid her head on it. She was humiliated. She was a freak show. Stephen Williams, the man she most admired in the world, had come here to do nothing more than gawk at her because he had nothing better to do. She felt tears begin to well up in her eyes.

I will not cry over this. My self-worth is not based on the opinion of some self-absorbed, egotistical maniac! I am better than this.

"What are your dreams, Annie?" she could still hear him ask.

He was toying with me. He was making fun of me. I can't believe I actually thought we were becoming friends.

The tears began to fall anyway. Annie lay on her bed and actually began to sob. The more she cried, however, the angrier she became. It was not fair for this man to come into her life and play emotional games with her like this. No, her life was not perfect. No, she wasn't doing anything close to what she had imagined years ago. But he, a total stranger, had no right to play around with either her dreams or her life. How dare he?

Chapter Seven

Annie was nowhere to be found when Stephen got up for breakfast. She was not in the kitchen; she was not on the back porch. Her bedroom door was open, but the light was off. He glanced out the front door. Her VW was gone.

I really ticked her off. I was mostly teasing. Alex was right; she's got a temper that can't be matched.

Stephen got his coffee, but avoided eating. That was his habit anyway. He never ate breakfast. It was too lonely. He would throw a premeasured coffee disk into the top of his coffee maker, add the water, and then check his e-mail as he finished his first cup. He would finish off the pot, rinse the coffee maker with hot water, and put it back together for the next batch later in the day. He would watch TV, read something, or make phone calls. He would do anything just to get through the next day. Being here with the Wrights had been like a release from the prison of monotony that ruled his life. He could not walk out his door without being followed or even attacked at times. He had become a recluse, not by choice, but by force.

Jonathan left close to 9:00 for the church. Alex left to go see Megan, and Barbara needed to cook lunch for a homebound elderly lady she had adopted from the church. Angie had gone to visit a few more friends while Annie was out of the house. Stephen took the opportunity to sneak around the house and get a closer look. He started downstairs with the parents' room. It was stacked with books and boxes. It was a large room, but seemed cramped because of all the stuff crammed in it. There were many framed photographs all around the room: on the walls, on the dressers, on the shelves. In fact, Stephen had not seen a single picture in the whole house that was not a photograph. There were no paintings and no fancy posters, only photographs.

He next headed up stairs. He went into Angie's room first. It was apparently kept just as it had been when she lived there as a teenager, with the only additions being stacks and stacks of textbooks. Alex's room was rather plain. No photos or posters on the walls. No diplomas or certificates displayed. It was almost sterile in its appearance. What had been Andie's room now held bunk beds and little boy items. He assumed it was used presently for the grandkids. He saved Annie's room for last.

Before going in, he walked to the edge of the balcony hallway and peeked out the window to make sure Annie had not returned. No sign of her. He walked in cautiously, afraid that if he put one object out of place or tripped over something, she would know and come after him. He had been in here before when the family had practiced, but he tried to concentrate on the music. Now he took time to really investigate.

The first thing that struck him was the number of awards. She had trophies, certificates, and plaques from piano and vocal competitions as far back as 15 years ago. Most of them were first place. There was a picture of her as a drum majorette. She was pictured with the high school softball team, and next to it, the basketball team. Framed on the wall was her diploma, and a valedictorian certificate was next to it.

My gosh, she was everything in high school. What happened in college?

The only evidences of college were two diplomas—her B.A. in music composition and her M.A. in music education.

Composition? I wonder if she's any good? Why didn't she do anything more than write jingles—in Dockrey? What's the future in that?

He peeked out the door again to make sure no one had arrived. When it looked safe, he went back to open her closet.

I can't believe I'm doing this. I wonder if I'm like some psychotic person obsessed with her. Good heavens! I would have someone jailed for what I'm doing!

He continued, however. Her closet was filled mostly with clothes. Blue was the predominant choice with her wardrobe. No high-heeled shoes.

I bet she's self-conscious about her height. She's not that tall, at least compared to a lot of the women I've known. She could be a model if she wanted to be.

He pulled the clothes to the side to look into the back. He was shocked. He now felt embarrassed. He had gone too far. Stuck on the back wall of her closet was a huge poster of him. It had come out ten years ago; he remembered it well. He tried to arrange her clothes back to normal and then exit the room quickly. He knew she would be humiliated if she found out that he had seen that. As he tried to leave, he tripped over her full-sized digital piano. The lamp fell off and broke in half on the floor.

Oh, man! What do I do? Do I pick it up? Do I leave it here? He heard a door slam outside. *Somebody's here! I've got to get out!*

He left the lamp where it was and ran out to the balcony. He was starting down the stairs when the front door opened. Annie walked in with a couple of garment bags and a sack full of groceries.

"Can I help you?" Stephen said as he rushed down the stairs.

She closed the door with her foot and just glanced up at him briefly. She put down the grocery bag and read the tags on the garment bags. She held one out to him.

"Yeah, try this on," she told him. "It's your tux."

"Okay," he said softly, still feeling horribly guilty for having gone into her closet.

"Make sure it fits okay," she continued speaking as she picked up the groceries and moved toward the kitchen. "The tailor will be in town on Thursday if anything needs to be altered."

"Thursday?" he asked following her. "Not at the shop every-day?"

"This is Dockrey," she reminded him. "Our tuxedo rental also happens to be a video rental store, a music store, a gift shop, and a pet food supply. The tailor comes on Thursdays."

"I see," was all he could manage. He hadn't felt this guilty in years, and he had the audacity to have called her "loony."

He held his garment bag as she put away the groceries. He just stood in the kitchen door and watched her. She didn't complain or fight, but she wasn't offering any conversation either.

"What's this thing we're supposed to go to tonight?" he finally gained the courage to ask.

"You're invited," was all she said.

"I know that," he said, still swallowing down the guilt, "but what should we wear? What are we supposed to do?"

"Wear clothes," she muttered as she passed by him on her way to the stairs.

"Could you be more specific?" he asked as he followed her.

"You're Alex's friend," she shot back. "Ask him. I'm going to take a shower."

I deserve this, and she doesn't even know why.

He cringed as she went into her room. He waited for the interrogation about her broken lamp. Time passed and nothing was said. He stayed at the bottom of the stairs and kept looking up, waiting for the response. Nothing. When she finally did appear, she was carrying a robe and heading for the bathroom. Still nothing.

Stephen went to his apartment room and laid the garment bag across the bed. He sat down next to it and rubbed his knees with his palms.

She knows. She wouldn't even look at me. Well, she hasn't looked at me on purpose since yesterday afternoon.

He turned on the TV to try and divert his attention. A man was standing next to a truck on a car lot yelling about the great deal he would offer if anyone would be smart enough to come to him first to buy a vehicle. The man jumped on the concrete and went berserk. In the background was a catchy tune played on a piano, ragtime, with a snappy saxophone and drum accompaniment. The man put his face right up to the camera and said with a sober look, "I won't do you wrong," to which the music grew louder and a voice sang out, "Howard Long won't do you wrong, won't do you wrong!"

Annie? That had to be Annie. Was that her piano playing? Man! That had to be her voice. B.A. in music composition.

Stephen flipped a few channels, watched a little local news, and kept flipping back to the first channel hoping to see the crazy guy jumping around his trucks again. There he was! Stephen turned up the volume and smiled as he recognized the jingle again. He totally ignored the man now and listened only for the music.

Unbelievable! How can she play like that?

He quickly tried to analyze the chord structure of the song. He couldn't totally pick it out.

What is that? One, five, seven? What is that chord? What is that rift? My goodness, how did she just play that? Digital overdubs, surely!

Then came the singing again, "Howard Long won't do you wrong, won't do you wrong!"

Stephen clicked off the TV. Was that her? Could she really be that good? It was definitely a local commercial. Everything about it spelled cheesy except for the music. He stood up and looked out the window, noticing her blue VW parked in the driveway. Did she actually write that music? No wonder she made good money here. He thought of the chunky guy jumping around yelling about his trucks and imagined Annie meeting with him over a jingle. He smiled at the image.

He walked over to the bed and began to undress, deciding to try on the tux so he could say he had complied with Annie's command when she got out of the shower. He really needed to make peace with her, but wondered if it were possible. He pulled on the pants and began to undo the shirt pins. He put on the shirt and got out the buttons to place in the holes. That's when he noticed the tear. He left the room to see if Annie was out of the shower yet.

"Annie!" he yelled as he came out onto the balcony.

She came running out of the hallway where the shower was.

"What?" she asked concerned.

She was wearing an old, faded baby blue terry-cloth robe, and her hair was soaking wet.

"Look at this," he said as he lifted up his right arm.

There was a long tear down the side seam.

"Great," she mumbled as she stuck her finger through it. "Only in Dockrey."

"The tailor will fix it," Stephen said. "We'll get it to him on Thursday."

"No," she responded. "I can do it. There's nothing to it. Just sew it up on the machine. It won't take two minutes."

She looked at Stephen and found a strange look on his face.

"What?" she asked, getting a little defensive again.

"You're hair's wet," he whispered.

"I just washed it."

"I know," he smiled. "I love the smell of your hair."

"You what?"

"I'm sorry," he said looking away as he tried top avert his eyes in awkwardness. "It's kind of embarrassing. Since the morning I met you I've been obsessed with the smell of your hair."

She just stared at him blankly.

"I keep trying to get near enough to you so I can catch the scent without your noticing. The four-wheeler ride was really nice."

She still stared at him, not changing expressions.

"I can smell it right now because it's been freshly washed," he said sheepishly. "If I didn't think you would slap me, I would actually lean over and bury my face in your hair and knock myself out."

Annie finally began to smile. She turned her head to the side to try and hide it.

"What?" he asked her.

"A couple of years ago I was in the dollar store getting something, don't remember what," she began. "I needed some shampoo and was pressed for time, so I decided to look through their options. Most of them were these off brands, so I didn't really know what to pick. I started smelling them. I got to this bottle of Organic Honey Shampoo. It smelled heavenly! So I bought it. I loved the smell so much that I couldn't bring myself to go back to the old expensive type I used before. It's only $2.50 a bottle."

Stephen smiled at her and remarked, "Good choice."

They stood there for a moment when Annie asked, "You really want to smell my hair?"

He nodded and blushed slightly.

"Go for it," she told him, then interjected, "but only this once."

"Really?" he asked. "You won't beat me up?"

She shook her head.

Stephen carefully leaned in and placed his face next to the left side of her head. He breathed deeply.

Annie did not know what she was doing. He had been so pathetic when she had returned that she began to feel guilty for lashing out at him. Maybe this could be a peace offering, letting him smell her hair. Now, however, she was beginning to feel silly. She had assumed he would take one smell and stop, but he now slightly buried his face into her hair. She felt his breath on her ear and her spine began to tingle. She put her hand up to his chest to push him away, but he moved closer. He took another breath and inched in a little closer.

He pulled his head back and was face to face with her.

"Thank you," he said with a gentle smile. "That's the biggest thrill I've had in a long time."

"You should get out more," she barely managed to whisper.

Stephen didn't move. He stood still and continued to gaze at her. She couldn't make herself pull away. Her whole body shivered, and now the pit of her stomach began to swirl. She could feel his breath breezing the top of her forehead. She tried to break her gaze, but she could not move any part of her body. She was 16 again, and this was a dream. Stephen stopped smiling and began to look down her face. He slowly leaned down and gently began to kiss her. Her head spun, and the swirling in her stomach began to deepen. She started to pull away, but found herself kissing him back. She didn't know what she was doing and hoped he couldn't tell. She felt herself losing her balance, but was afraid to move, afraid to break the moment.

Stop this, Annie. Don't let him do this to you. It's not real.

She finally found the strength to push him away.

"Stop," she whispered. Her eyes were still closed when he pulled away. "Please, don't," she said weakly.

"I'm sorry," he said softly. "I didn't intend to do that."

"I didn't think you did," she said quietly as turned to go.

"Annie, wait," he called after her. "I really didn't mean to do that. I don't know what came over me."

"No, I guess you don't," she said as she turned back with tears welling in her eyes.

"Annie, I'm sorry," he began to plead, not understanding the tears or what had just happened. "I didn't mean to hurt you. Is that what I did?"

"That was my first kiss," she managed to get out.

"What?" he asked in unbelief.

"I've never kissed anyone," she said looking away and trying to hide the tears. "I've never even dated anyone. By this time in my life, I figured that when I ever did kiss someone, it would be really special, not just some spontaneous, meaningless moment."

"I didn't know," he tried to apologize.

"No," she said as she wiped the tears that were now streaking down her face. "I'm just a google-eyed teenager that you could take advantage of."

"What?" he asked incredulously. "What are you talking about?"

"I realize now you were in my room," she faced him. "You were the one in my closet, weren't you? You left the door open. I probably wouldn't have thought too much about it had my lamp not been broken on the floor . . . and then of course, all *this*."

Stephen looked away. He was humiliated. Not just for going through her closet, but mostly for the fact that she really thought he was taking advantage of her.

"It's not like that, Annie," he tried to explain. "I don't even know how to talk to you about this."

"I'd rather you didn't try," she said turning back around to leave.

He grabbed her arm and turned her back around.

"Annie, please listen to me," he pleaded. "I haven't been with a woman in five years. I gave up on meaningless relationships. You are this incredibly beautiful person, and I just . . ."

"Stop!" Annie interrupted, putting her hand up in protest. "I've tried to be mature about you. I've tried to think you are just a normal person visiting with my brother, but you're not and you never will be to me. You are my dream, Stephen. There. Are you happy? You asked me about my dreams yesterday. Well there it is; I am 26 years old and I still have teenage crush on my teen idol from ten years ago."

He watched her face blush. He didn't know who was more disgraced. She thought he had kissed her because he could take advantage of a secret he had dishonestly discovered, and he knew it was more than that but couldn't find the words to tell her.

"Annie, I didn't take advantage of you," he promised. "If you would let me, I would kiss you again. It wasn't just a moment's weakness or anything."

"No, thank you," she said callously. "I've been violated enough for one day."

With that, she turned and left. Stephen just stood and stared after her. How could he make her understand what he was feeling when he couldn't name it himself?

Violated? Was that how she put it? The word made him shiver. He was headed back to his room when Angie came in the front door.

"Hey, good-lookin'!" she yelled up. "What you got cookin'?"

"Apparently not a whole lot," he managed to say glumly as he went to his door.

"Trouble in Paradise?" she asked.

"There's a rip in my shirt," he said as he lifted up his right arm.

"Annie or Moms can fix that," she called up. "Take it off and toss it down. I'll get it to the first one I see."

He pulled off his shirt and Angie whistled. He smiled and threw it down to her.

"I would be flattered except for the fact that you've probably seen many male torsos in your line of work," he smirked.

"Just trying to be polite," she said catching the shirt.

When Annie came down for lunch, Angie showed her the shirt.

"I'll get right to it," she said and took it to the utility room where the machine was, acting as though she had never seen it before.

"She'll have it fixed up in a jiffy," Angie said bubbly as she went into the kitchen to make some lunch. "Annie's good at everything."

"Is she?" Stephen replied, remembering all the awards and honors from high school. "Do you think she likes her job?"

Angie stopped what she was doing and looked straight at Stephen.

"Between the two of us? No," she said frankly, "she hates it, but she doesn't have enough fight in her anymore to try anything else."

"Why? Why doesn't she try to make more of herself?"

"You can only get knocked down so many times before you finally decide to just stay there," Angie said as she opened the refrigerator. "That's not characteristic of Annie, so whatever the final blow was, it obviously was too much."

"And you don't know?" he asked.

"Nope," Angie shrugged. "We're close, but she won't talk about it. Somehow she has cut this course out for her life, and she won't deviate from it. Kind of sad, isn't it? You have no idea how talented she is."

"Actually, I do," he offered. "At least, some idea."

"No, you don't" Angie countered him. "Hardly anybody does. She's not like one of these educated music people who can quote you some intellectual terms. She breathes music like the rest of us breathe air. I almost believe at times that if I took a blood sample, I would look in there and find music streaming through it. I know that's illogical, but that's how saturated she is with the whole music thing."

"But she won't do anything with it?"

Angie sadly shook her head.

"She won't even try," she told him. "She has cut her path in stone. I don't know why. Want a sandwich?"

He nodded. He really wasn't hungry. He was sick to his stomach, but perhaps something to eat would help to settle it. Annie had used the word "violate" to describe his kiss. To her that is exactly what it was. To him, it was so much more, but it was unlikely that she would ever believe that. If only she weren't so stubborn.

"Here's your shirt," Annie said as she came into the kitchen.

Stephen looked up at her, but she wouldn't meet his eyes.

"That was quick," he said faintly.

"Told you she was fast," Angie quipped with a smile. "Annie can do anything."

Annie looked up at him for just a moment, and then broke the gaze immediately. She was still reeling from the balcony. If only she could get over it and move on like everything was fine. He wasn't talking either. He was as uncomfortable as she was.

"Is everything all right here?" Angie wanted to know. "The tension is thick between the two of you."

"Stephen has felt the blow of my wrath," Annie said flatly.

"That's not true," he began to defend. "It was my fault."

Angie looked back and forth between the two of them.

"Oh my," she said slowly. "If I had only been a fly on that wall."

Annie walked out.

The party should have been exciting for Annie, but she found herself avoiding anyone that could make it lively. She sat in a dark corner while Megan and Alex laughed and joked with all their friends. Angie told the many gory horrors of medical school and training, and everyone seemed to enjoy the spirit of the evening—celebration. However, in another dark corner, Stephen also sulked, trying to avoid the few people who wanted to talk with him. Soon a band began to play, and people began to trickle onto the dance floor to continue the celebrating.

"What is the problem?" Angie insisted on knowing as she plopped down next to Annie. "Neither of you should have even shown up."

"Believe me, I wouldn't have if it wouldn't have been considered an insult," Annie moaned. "I'm too close to Megan to ditch the party."

"And Alex *is* your brother," Angie added.

"Like that matters," Annie whined.

Angie stared at her morose sister with a frown.

"You look so depressed right now that not even *I* know how to cheer you up," Angie complained. "And look at him," she said pointing at Stephen. "What's with that? He's been so happy since he's been here. What did you say to him?"

"What makes you think it's my fault?" Annie asked her irritably.

"Hello?" Angie said with wide eyes. "Open mouth, think later. Isn't that your motto?"

"Leave me alone," Annie said turning her back to her.

"Suit yourself, moody girl. But if you ask me, your dreams are sitting over there in the corner, and the only thing standing between you and them is some stupid prideful thing that you refuse to get over. Whatever happened or whatever was said isn't worth this chance."

"Leave," Annie repeated.

Angie threw her hands up in surrender, but put her head down in Annie's face one last time to say, "When you grow old and die alone and empty, I will put a note in your coffin that says, 'Too stupid for such a smart girl.' "

The comment stung Annie. What was she supposed to do? At this point, her feelings for Stephen were so juvenile and pitiful that she was mortified to even think about asking him for career advice. And if she did, how could she trust him? Would he use her again? Would he think of her as a groupie and string her along? Would it be a fun game for him, or would he be sincere? She did not even know who he was, not really.

She picked up a shrimp and dipped it into the cocktail sauce, biting off the meat and dropping the tail onto her plate. She wanted to leave and probably should. She was reaching down for her purse when she felt a hand on her shoulder.

"At least dance with me, and we could pretend, for Alex and Megan's sake, that we had a good time."

She looked up at Stephen. He could not know what it did to her to feel his hand on her shoulder.

"I'd rather not," she said as she removed his hand. "I think I'm gonna leave instead."

"Annie, please," he sat down next to her. "Just tell me what I can do to get you to forgive me. I'll do anything."

She tried to be cold. She didn't want him to catch her off guard again, but she couldn't. No matter how much she wanted to hate him, there was the simple fact that he was Stephen Williams. She would always have the schoolgirl crush on him, but she did not have to let him take advantage of her. She could be in control, even if she forgave him.

"Just don't hurt me," she said soberly as she looked up into his blue eyes. Those eyes, the same eyes that stared at her from the back of her closet. She closed her eyes and shook off the image. She was humiliated.

"Annie," he said softly as he leaned in closer to be heard above the band, "I have no desire to hurt you. Please, believe me. If you really knew me, you would know I'm not this monster that you thought you saw today."

"But that's just it," she said as she drew closer to him speaking loudly above the music, "I don't really know you. I know everything about you, but I know nothing of the real you. And you're never quick to expose yourself, though you're quick to ask others to."

"Touché'," he nodded. "Quid pro quo, huh?"

She didn't respond, but focused her attention on her dancing friends.

"Dance with me, and I'll make it worth your while," he promised as he held out his hand. Annie took it and followed him to the dance floor, thinking to herself during the entire walk that she was a complete fool.

"I should warn you," Annie said as he put his arm around her waist, "I have great rhythm, but I'm a horrible dancer."

"I thought you could do everything," he smiled as they began to sway.

"Don't believe everything you hear," she warned him.

"I won't," he affirmed as he moved her around the floor, "but take heart, you follow very well."

"Now that's something I don't hear often," she laughed.

"Just curious," he said as he pulled back from her for a moment, "is it just me, or is this band horrible?"

Annie laughed again and nodded her head.

"I try to be lenient," she said as she moved her lips to his ears to be heard above the music again, "but I will confess that this group has just about gotten on every single nerve I have."

"Wonderful," he laughed back. "I'm glad to know it's not just me."

They danced for several songs and had a few more laughs. Angie caught Annie's eye and wanted to know what happened. Annie just smiled and shrugged it off. It actually felt good to let go of the resentment. She would not think about what she was doing for now, and she would not hold the grudge.

When the song stopped, Stephen looked down at her and said, "Let's go somewhere and talk."

"Where?"

"I don't know. I'm not from here. Somewhere private where no one will interrupt us. We need a heart-to-heart."

Annie looked around and knew this wasn't the place. "Do you want to leave?" she asked him.

"That would probably be best," he agreed. "Let me tell Alex that I'm going with you."

Annie could only think of one place for privacy that she had access to: her office. Rain began to drizzle down about a mile before their arrival. She pulled into the parking lot and shut off the engine.

"I don't have an umbrella," she confessed.

"My hair will frizz," he said drearily.

"Do you want to just sit in here or go on up?" she asked.

"I want to see your studio," he said eagerly. "Promise me you won't take any pictures of my frazzled 'do' to sell to the tabloids, and we'll go on up, frizzy hair and all."

She pulled her Florida Marlins cap from the backseat and placed it on his head.

"That'll help a little," she said hopefully. "Kind of matches your eyes anyway."

She unbolted the front door then bolted it back behind them. She led him up a small flight of stairs to the glass outer office where Terri worked. She unbolted and re-bolted the glass door to the suite. She felt nervous as she began to unlock the soundproof metal door to her own office. It was almost as if she was revealing a part of herself to him with which she was uncomfortable. She hesitated.

"What's wrong now?" he asked.

"I don't know," she said uncertainly. "It's like I'm afraid to let you in here."

"You shouldn't be," he said seriously.

She looked up at him.

"What are we about to do?" she asked cautiously.

"Just trust me," was all he said.

She opened the door and turned on the lights. Stephen was immediately awed at all the equipment. Annie shut the blinds so no one would look in during their *talk.*

"I take it you like Roland equipment," he stated as he began to inspect each piece.

"They've proven themselves to be reliable for me, and they're easy to figure out."

"Once you've *figured* them out," he said looking back at her.

"I know, you like Korg," she said knowingly. "Not my personal favorite."

"Obviously," he continued as he ran his hand across the digital recording console. "You're serious about this stuff, aren't you? You didn't buy some mamby-pamby equipment when you started the jingle business."

Annie sighed and folded her arms.

"I didn't buy it for the jingle business," she admitted.

He turned around to face her.

"Why did you buy it?"

Annie ran her right hand through her long, damp hair and got her fingers stuck halfway through.

"I was hoping to do some demo work and then try to sell my music out."

"In what capacity?" he wanted to know.

She shook her head and said, "It doesn't matter now. I went a different direction."

"Quid pro quo, Annie," he said with a smile. "Quid pro quo."

"Yeah, well, you haven't *quidded* yet," she said firmly. "So I'm not *quo-ing*."

"Fair," he sighed.

He sat down on the bench behind the digital piano and lifted the lid.

"Play something for me," he requested. She quickly shook her head. "Please," he asked again. "Play that ragtime song from the commercial with the guy jumping up and down about his trucks. I know you overdubbed that."

At first she was shocked that he had seen the Howard Long commercial, but then she was defensive.

"I did not overdub that!" she said adamantly.

"Prove it," he said as he scooted over. "Prove to me you can play all those notes with only two hands at one time."

Annie felt her heart jump into her throat. Did she dare? What if he chided her or made fun of her? Then again, what if he didn't?

"Come on," he said patting the bench. "Play your little ragtime piece with only two hands."

She smiled a confident smile and sat down next to him.

"You need to scoot over a little bit," she told him. "It takes a lot of room to play this."

"Do I need to get up?"

"No, no, no," she teased. "You need to have first-hand view of this, one of my more complicated arrangements."

Annie turned on the piano and set the sound to honky-tonk. She jabbed a couple of keys to make sure the volume was appropriate and then gave Stephen a mischievous smile.

"I'm waiting," he said with anticipation.

Annie placed her fingers on the keyboard and gave herself a mental countdown. When she began, everything came back to her immediately. As her fingers flew up and down the keyboard, Stephen stared in astonishment. He watched the notes and once again tried to analyze the chord structure. He couldn't identify it! It was driving him crazy. Soon, however, he forgot he was a musician and just stared in awe as Annie continued, without missing a note, to dance her fingers across the keyboard. He glimpsed at her expression, and she was simply smiling, not concentrating, not biting her lip, and not furrowing her brow. This was a breeze for her, and she thoroughly enjoyed it. He shook his head in wonder. He had never seen anything like it in his life.

When she finished, Stephen jumped to his feet and applauded.

"Bravo!" he yelled out. "How on earth did you do that?"

"That?" she asked casually. "That was my college composition final."

"I assume you passed," he said sitting back down next to her.

She nodded and grinned. "A-plus," she said proudly. "They couldn't figure out the chord structure. It drove them crazy. I had to break it down for them before they would give me a grade."

"I couldn't figure it out either," he admitted. "I just couldn't. I didn't think it was possible to write anything unpredictable any more."

"That's what one of my professors said once," she said wearily. "I proved him wrong and got kicked out of college."

"You got kicked out for greasing the instruments," he corrected her.

She looked at him and said, "You know about that?" He nodded. "Actually," she clarified, "I got kicked out of the music department for the professor thing; I got kicked out of the school for the greasy thing. As I saw it, being kicked out of the music department was being kicked out of school. I had nothing else to lose."

Stephen shook his head. He still could not get over what he had just heard. This girl was incredibly talented, and she was writing jingles for small town businesses in Alabama.

"What?" she asked.

"Nope," he said shaking his head, "No more questions for you. I promised I'd go first."

"Okay, then go."

Stephen had never told anyone this story. He had never even mentioned it. He had not told his professors, he had not told the producers, and he had never told a single musician he had worked with. Somehow, he felt that if he had ever divulged his real life to anyone, he would have exposed a weakness. He kept his secrets to himself.

"All I ever wanted to do was play the piano," he began. "Mom started taking me to lessons when I was four. I literally spent hours practicing."

"It shows," Annie smiled.

"Yeah, and it showed back then too," he continued. "My father hated it. He thought I was this big sissy. He wanted his boy to play football or hockey or something, but *not* the piano, at least I guess that was the problem. It got so bad that Mom said I could only practice when he was at work. When he pulled up in the drive, I had to close the piano and do something else."

"I bet that was hard," Annie said softly.

"You have no idea," he said with regret. "He hated me, and I began to hate him, and as far as I know, it was all over image and preferences. When I was ten, Mom had another baby, Sandy. She was a doll. Blonde curls, big blue eyes that could melt your heart."

"Sort of like you in a feminine form?" Annie added.

"Sort of," he smiled, "but she was really adorable. I mean, this was the ideal little girl. She was bubbly and vivacious. She was always loving, and she was the apple of Dad's eye. My shortcomings kind of faded next to her, and though Dad and I never had a real relationship, I was tolerated a little better. He had the piano moved into my room so I could practice whenever I wanted."

"So I'm not the only one with a piano in my room," Annie giggled.

"No," he went on, "and I gave myself to the piano like crazy. Now, unlike you, that's all I did. My grades weren't top-notch, but I passed. I started entering competitions and cleaned up with them. Then

I started to be awarded money for the competitions. Things seemed to be doing fine until one night I had a competition five hours away on a Tuesday. Mom insisted on going because she went to every single one. She said she was my good luck charm. Dad had to work, so she would have to take Sandy with her. Well, he pitched a fit. No way was she dragging Sandy to one of these blasted piano things on a school night. He ranted and raved, but Mom wouldn't let up. She said she was going and that was final."

Stephen stood up and walked over to the window. He pulled down a slat of the blinds and peeked through to see that it was pouring down rain now. He pulled the hat off his head and placed it on top of the piano.

"I won again," he continued. "Mom and Sandy were so proud. Mom told me goodbye and headed on home because Dad had insisted Sandy be in kindergarten the next morning. On the way home, the group that I was riding with passed a wreck. I recognized the car."

"Stephen, no," Annie gasped as she stood and went to him.

He blinked hard and looked up at the ceiling. "They had Mom laid out on the road doing CPR. I jumped out of the car I was in and ran toward her. Then I saw Sandy's head through the car window. I yelled for them to get Sandy, but they didn't know who I was. Someone said, 'We saw her kid. She was dead before we even got here.' I couldn't move."

He went back to the window and peeked through the slat again. Annie didn't follow him. She held back her natural tendency to hold someone who would have hurt like this.

"One of the paramedics yelled out, 'She's gone. Load her up and let's get her to the morgue.' I screamed at them to save my mother. When they finally figured out who I was, they tried to help me understand the breadth of the injuries both of them had sustained, and that had they lived, it would have been bad."

Annie wanted to do something, but she just stood there.

"Of course, when Dad found out, I might as well have been dead too. He threw me in my room and beat the snot out of me. He took an axe and decimated my piano. He told me if I ever spoke another word to him, he would kill me. I didn't know what to do. I was 15. So I didn't speak."

"Stephen, I'm so sorry," was all Annie could get out.

"I then realized that my only chance in life was to place all my bets on music and give it my best shot. As a senior, still not having spoken a word to my Dad in three years, I auditioned for music scholarships at several schools."

"And Julliard accepted you," Annie interjected knowing where he had gone.

"Every single one of them did," he said turning toward her again. "I got the courage to show Dad my results, told him I could pick any school in the country if I wanted, and have them pay me to go. He slapped me, told me that was a good thing because he wasn't paying a penny for me to do anything. The only thing he wanted me to do was die."

"I entered Julliard that summer, didn't even wait for the fall," he went on. "Sometimes I think it was my father's hatred more than anything else that drove me to succeed, but I was determined to succeed. So, you see, Annie, when you ask me why I was so willing to compromise, it was because my dream was to succeed, not to have any standards or guidelines on that dream. So, I did."

"What does your father think now?" she asked him.

"He's a drunk. He still lives in the same house, but he doesn't do a thing. He just sits at home and watches TV and drinks himself blind."

"Do you ever see him?"

"Once a year," he sighed as he went back to the piano and sat down. "I see him for a couple of hours sometime during the winter holidays. I always send him some huge gift, just hoping for a response. I visit, and there it will be, plugged in or hooked up, but no word is ever mentioned about it. I'll bring in a bunch of groceries, fill his fridge and cabinets, and try to chat for a bit. Then I always leave emptier then when I came."

"Does he talk?" Annie questioned. "Does he say anything?"

"Oh yeah," he said mockingly. "He tells how the Bears are doing and talks about his favorite college teams. He gripes about the weather, the food, the neighbors, the commentators and the referees, but he never says a single word to me about my life."

"You still don't exist," Annie stated.

"Not in his world," Stephen said sadly as he began to pick out the tune to *Autumn Sunset.*

Annie sat down beside him at the piano.

"I'm really very sorry," she said sincerely as she turned his face toward her. "I imagined you had this perfect life and all was well in the world."

"I try to imagine that," he said with no expression, "but it doesn't work anymore."

He began to play and sing softly:

So while I'm waiting for someone to love me
Someone who knows me through and through
I'll watch the Autumn Sunset from my single room apartment
And hope and pray that dreams can still come true

Annie joined him for the last line:

And long to hear the words "I love you."

"Sing it for me," he asked.

"No way," she said steadfastly as she shook her head.

"Quid pro quo," he reminded her.

She looked up at him and continued to shake her head.

"I cannot sing *Autumn Sunset* for Stephen Williams," she said adamantly.

"Yes, you can," he told her. "And you can sing it for him in a way that no one else ever has."

"Stephen," she whispered, "I can't do this."

"Have you ever played and sang it before?" he asked.

She nodded.

"They didn't count, but this time it does," he appealed to her.

"I don't sing it like you do," she somewhat confessed.

"I hope not," he teased. "Your voice would have to be really low."

"I don't mean that," she hesitated. "I end each chorus with a deceptive cadence. Then I hit the four chord with a major seventh and finally resolve it with the five seven and back to tonic for the next phrase, except the end."

"And what do you do on the end?" he asked her, fascinated by the description she had already given.

"I end on the deceptive cadence," she said evenly.

"Let me hear it," he implored. "I'll never ask you to do anything else again."

"Really? You promise?"

"I'll *try* not to," he said as he crossed his heart. He then winked at her and added, "Scout's honor."

She moved her hands to the keyboard again and looked back up at him.

"I play it in D too," she explained. "A-flat is a bad key for my range."

"You're forgiven," he told her. "Now play."

Stephen did not quite know how to take the whole song. The deceptive cadence literally changed the entire mood. When she got to the bridge and began to sing it out, she pounded the keyboard with a pulsating rhythm that totally defined the hopelessness of the phrases:

Nobody warned me, nobody said
There's more to living than just success
Nobody moved me, nobody dared
Nobody showed me, nobody shared
Nobody told me about the Sunrise
Nobody told me, nobody tried

Next she changed keys as she went into the last chorus. Stephen began to sing harmony with her as she finished the song:

So while I'm waiting for someone to love me
Someone who knows me through and through
I'll watch the Autumn Sunset from my single room apartment
And hope and pray that dreams can still come true

He stopped to let her finish the song to hear how the deceptive cadence would affect the finale'.

And long to hear the words "I love you"
I long to hear the words, "I love you."

Annie was too nervous to move her hands. She just sat, silently frozen, feeling she may have taken too many liberties with his song. She half expected a scolding, but instead he took her hands in his. She turned to look at him and saw tears for the first time.

"Thank you," he said. "Thank you for listening to my story, and thank you for really hearing my song."

Annie looked at him confused.

"You knew that song well enough to know how it should really sound," he tried to clear up. "Why do you stay here? Why don't you reach higher?"

"Because I can't do it anymore," was all she said. "I can't do it. That's all."

Chapter Eight

Annie woke up Wednesday morning exactly at 6:45, same as always. However, she was still exhausted. She and Stephen had not returned home until sometime after 2:00 a.m. Annie's internal clock would never let her sleep late, regardless of the loss of hours. She tried closing her eyes for over 30 minutes, hoping to doze back off, but it didn't work. She finally dragged herself out of bed, pulled on her scrub bottoms, and headed for the kitchen.

Annie was typically the first one to the kitchen, but someone had beaten her up this morning. Annie could already smell coffee and breakfast. She smiled as her foot hit the bottom step because her head was practically swimming from exhaustion. Coffee already made would be wonderful.

"Good morning, sleepyhead," Angie said just a bit too energetically for Annie this morning.

"Back at'tcha," Annie managed to mumble out.

"Hmmm," Angie sounded as she handed Annie a mug.

"What's that about?" Annie asked. "What's *hmmm?*"

"Nothing really," she retorted. "You just got up a little later than usual. I suppose its because you got to bed a little later than usual."

"Good observation," Annie murmured. "You might want to consider that it could make me a little grumpier than usual."

Angie leaned into Annie's face and said, "You don't scare me."

Annie backed up and snarled, "I should."

Angie pulled a tray of sugar toast from the oven and fixed two small plates for them. She motioned toward the back porch, and Annie nodded. Annie still felt like a truck had hit her head as she took her seat. Angie was polite and remained silent, respecting Annie's sleepiness, and probably her potential grumpiness too. Several minutes passed before Annie broke the silence.

"I haven't had sugar toast in ages," she said with a little more energy.

"Me either," Angie told her. "It was always my favorite, you know?"

"I remember. Andie and I liked cheese toast; you and Alex liked sugar toast."

They were quiet again, enjoying the sounds of the morning. Angie finished her toast and leaned back against her chair, cradling her coffee with both hands. The birds were loud this morning, enjoying the warmth and the sunshine. Several pushed and shoved around the bird feeder hanging from a large hickory tree behind the house. Angie smiled at the simplicity of life at home. In some ways, she longed to be back here—relaxing, loving, and enjoying this life again. But her call to the mission field drove her harder than anything else in her life.

"Penny for your thoughts," Annie asked her.

A comfortable smile spread across Angie's face as she replied, "Just thinking about how nice it is here, how nice it is to be with family, to not be responsible for anything, actually relaxing for a change."

"And you *have* to jump right back in to school again?"

"Yes, I do," Angie persisted. "I really do, Annie. I don't think I could just sit here knowing that all that was standing between Padawin and me was seminary. I'm ready to go."

"But I'm not ready to lose you again," Annie confessed. "I miss you Angie. Sometimes I ache inside because I can't just look up and see you here anymore. You leave this huge hole in my life."

"I leave a hole in your life, Annie, because you don't fill it up with anything."

Annie rolled her eyes. She knew Angie was right. She had no social life, no fun life, and nobody with whom to share life. She and Megan spent a lot of time together, but they were not kindred spirits like she and Angie. Anyway, Megan would soon be gone. Andie's life was so busy with teaching and children that she seldom could get more than five minutes of uninterrupted discussion with her. Her parents were sweet, but they were her *parents.*

"Where did you go last night?" Angie asked trying to pretend she wasn't prying.

"How long have you been dying to ask that question?" Annie grinned.

"Since the two of you walked out last night," Angie admitted. "I suppose you're gonna tell me it's none of my business and to stick my nose somewhere else."

"Then why did you ask?"

"Oh, there's always hope," Angie lamented. "I guess maybe I dreamed you might be so tired you would just give in and not fight it."

"We went to my office," Annie divulged.

"Oooo," Angie raised her eyebrows. "And what did *we* do there?"

"Talked more than anything," Annie let her know.

"That doesn't sound very exciting."

"What were you expecting?" Annie asked defensively.

"Something more than that, I suppose," Angie sighed.

They made small talk for several minutes until Stephen came out to join them.

"What is this stuff?" he asked about the toast. "I know it's not cheese."

"Sugar toast," Angie informed him. "My personal favorite."

"Cool," he said as he pulled a chair up next to Annie. "What do you do? Just spoon sugar all over and it melts down like this?"

"Butter the bread first, then sprinkle sugar on it," Angie explained. "The sugar sort of melts into the butter."

"Yum," he smiled as he held up the toast. "Two of my favorites: processed carbohydrates and fat."

Annie and Angie gave each other a sour look. They then watched him take a bite, close his eyes to chew, and wash it down with a swig of coffee. He turned to them and smiled.

"Wow, I didn't realize how good unhealthy food could be," he conveyed, "but this is good."

"Do you not eat junk food?" Annie asked him.

"I try not to," he admitted. "I lived off of it for so many years that I'm now hoping to reverse the effects it probably had on my weary body."

Angie grinned up at him and said, "Then you'd probably better lay off the fried chicken."

He nodded and gave her a smirk saying, "You noticed that, I see. I was hoping it was oblivious to everyone."

"I need a shower," Angie said as she hopped up from the chair.

"Are you always this bouncy in the mornings?" Stephen asked.

Annie answered before Angie could even nod, "Always."

Angie left Stephen and Annie alone on the porch. Annie still found herself feeling uncomfortable with him. Even after he shared his life with her last night, she was still the 16-year-old adoring fan who could not get over the fact that the man of her fantasies was sitting here next to her on her back porch on a warm June morning.

"What's on the agenda today?" he asked her.

"Oh, well, I'm not totally sure," she managed to say. "There's church tonight, and I thought I might do a little work this afternoon."

"Really? Some composing of jingles?" he asked eagerly.

"Yeah," she said carefully. "Something like that."

"Can I come with you?" he pleaded. "We could do something really fun. What are you writing for?"

Now this could work! Vivian McCall would tear my stuff apart anyway. If I told her that Stephen Williams wrote it, she wouldn't give me near the hassle!

"You really want to lower yourself to help me with a commercial?" she wanted to make sure.

"Look, after listening to that ragtime piece you did, I'm not lowering nothing. What are we writing about?"

"Another car commercial. It's a Ford dealership. The owner is the mother of my nemesis in life, Kelly McCall. She was Miss America a few years ago and . . ."

"Kelly McCall of Hawaii?" Stephen asked her. "The talk show host over there?"

Annie's mouth dropped. He actually knew her?

"Yes," she said cautiously. "Kelly McCall of Hawaii."

"She's from Birmingham, isn't she? Her mother lives here?"

"Oh, she's from here," Annie stated flatly. "She just won't admit it. How do you know Kelly McCall?"

"I was on her show last year. She's really quite charming," Stephen said smiling.

Annie turned her head to stare out to the yard. *Great. Kelly's charmed Stephen. Apparently, I'm the only person in the world who finds her totally distasteful.*

"I'm sorry," he offered quickly. "I forgot, she's your *nemesis.*"

Annie waved it off and smiled at him.

"It's okay," she managed to say. "Obviously she has some wonderful qualities that I've never let myself see or she wouldn't have been Miss America and a world-renown talk show host."

"She's not world renown," he corrected quickly. "Just Hawaii renown. I was scheduled there for a benefit concert, and they booked me on her show too."

"Charming," Annie mumbled.

"But not near as charming as you," he beamed. "And I bet she couldn't touch your ragtime piece."

He got up and stretched his arms into the air and then leaned down to touch his toes. "I think I'm going to shower too," he informed her. "I am so tired that I can barely think straight."

"I know the feeling," Annie admitted. "We'll leave when you get through."

Annie sat still for a bit as she tried to overcome her total distaste for the discussion concerning Kelly McCall. It galled her more than she wanted to admit that Kelly had *charmed* Stephen. Now she was wishing she had not invited Stephen to help her with the jingle. Kelly would think it was all *her* doing that influenced Stephen to aid in the project.

Alex walked onto the screened-in porch and slammed the door, startling Annie from her revolting thoughts.

"What is going on?" he asked angrily. "What the heck are you doing?"

"Good morning to you too, Alex," she bit back sarcastically.

"Look, I don't know what kind of little game you're playing with Stephen, but it's to stop now!" he demanded.

"I don't have the slightest idea what you're talking about," she defended.

"You've managed to occupy most of his time, you've yelled at him, you danced with him last night, and you leave my party with him—to go who knows where—and then you show up back home in the middle of the night! That kind of game!"

Annie stuck her finger in his face and declared, "*You* are the one who has deserted him, *little brother*. I didn't invite him to ride my back on Saturday, and he volunteered to go to Tupelo with me on Monday. As for my yelling at him, he asked me some questions that were a bit too personal and were none of his business. *He* asked me to dance last night, and it was *he* that suggested we leave the party. If you want to know who's playing games, you take it up with him!"

"I didn't bring him here to be wooed by you into some kind of . . . of . . . tryst!"

"Tryst?" she said, completely offended now.

"You'd do anything to get out of Dockrey, wouldn't you?" he said shaking his head. "Let me make one thing clear: if you talk him into some kind of deal, I'll never forgive you for as long as I live!"

"Excuse me," Annie said in shock, "I don't even know what you're suggesting, but I would never dream of trying to edge myself into something by way of Stephen Williams! You are way out of line!"

"You look," Alex demanded, red-faced and obviously out of control, "my life is good. In fact, my life is great. And in a matter of days, my life will be perfect. *You* stay out of my life!"

Annie wanted to remind him that the only reason his life was so good was because of the calls *she* had made to get him where he was. He didn't have the backbone or fortitude to do anything on his own. Had she not rammed open the doors, he would still be sitting in Nashville studios with no plans for a future and no impending wedding with Megan.

"You're welcome," was all she could manage to spit out as she rushed toward the door.

"I mean it, Annie!" he yelled back at her.

I know. Why do you hate me? Why?

Stephen suggested they take the yellow convertible he had rented instead of the VW; he also insisted that Annie drive. At first she was nervous, but she soon found herself enjoying the ride. She took a few back roads to her office and tried to let the anger fly away. Alex's demands almost sounded like an ultimatum. What did he think she was doing? What exactly was he accusing her of? What was the "tryst" she was trying to form? When she finally pulled into the drive of her office building, she had managed to work through some of the emotions, but her mind was still not freed from the plaguing thoughts.

Great. Terri's car is here. She must have come in to work anyway. Why can't she just take the week off as I asked?

The doors were all open, so Stephen and Annie walked right into the front office.

"What brings you here, Terri?" Annie asked as they walked in.

Terri jumped up unexpectedly.

"Annie!" she half-shouted. "What are you doing here?"

"I work here," Annie said mockingly.

"But you were taking the week off," Terri reminded her.

"And so were you."

Terri just stared, almost looking like the cat that caught the canary.

"We're here," Annie pointed to Stephen, "to work on the McCall project."

Terri's jaw dropped.

"Stephen Williams," she whispered. "Oh—my—gosh!"

Stephen held out his hand, "I see an introduction isn't necessary."

Terri held out her hand and barely shook his. Her face turned red as she reached down for her purse.

"I forgot, um, some—things, and now I've got them," Terri went on nervously. "I need to get going and all. It was nice to meet you, Mr. Williams; I love your music. I really need to go. Good luck on the thing you're doing."

And then she left very, very quickly.

"I wonder what that was all about?" Annie muttered as she unlocked her office door, only to find it had been left unlocked. "I must have left this open last night."

Stephen followed her in and looked around with a strange expression.

"What is it?" she asked him.

"I'm pretty sure you locked the door," he told her. "In fact, I remember you locking it then deliberately trying to open it to make sure. I was impressed with your double-checking."

"Well, I usually do that," Annie said as she turned on her equipment. "I just thought maybe I was tired because it was so late."

"No, it was definitely locked when we left last night," he affirmed. "Don't you think your secretary was a bit jumpy?"

"Terri?" Annie asked skeptically. "She always jumpy. Besides, she doesn't have a key to my studio. I have the only one."

"You're not worried?" Stephen wondered.

Annie shook her head and laughed, "This is Dockrey. What could happen in Dockrey, Alabama, to a small-time jingle writer?"

"If you're not worried, then I'm not," he finally concluded.

Annie spent the morning in pure heaven; she was writing music with Stephen Williams. Most of it started out totally silly. She gave him all her ridiculous rhyming words for Ford, and they came up with several inane verses before finally getting down to the meat of it. By afternoon, they were starving, not realizing that lunch had already passed. He suggested they order takeout somewhere, at which she reminded him they were in Dockrey, and there was not a single place that delivered anything. They drove to a Chinese restaurant and had the buffet. Several people recognized Stephen, and he graciously chatted with them and signed autographs.

After returning to the studio, they began to work on actually recording the jingle.

"We have to keep it right at 30 seconds," she explained. "It shouldn't be a problem, but we need three seconds up front for the announcer, and ten seconds for Ms. Vivian McCall to come on the screen and tell everybody why they need to buy from her."

"On my first album, I had to keep every song under three and a half minutes," he told her. "No room for interludes there."

"Except for *Under the Sun,*" she reminded him. "You had a nice little piano solo there."

"I cut the bridge out," he clarified.

"There was a bridge?" she said excitedly. "How did it go?"

"Doesn't matter," he said despondently. "It's copyrighted and forever written in recording without the bridge. It will never exist."

"I played that one time as an offertory," Annie confessed. "I started with the hymn *Blessed Be the Name,* then segued into the *Under the Sun* interlude, and closed with the chorus to *Blessed Be the Name* again. I was a junior in high school. Mom thought it was beautiful."

"That's not really a church type song," Stephen chided.

"I know, but no one else knew, except Andie. She thought it was funny."

They continued their work until the entire project was finished. It was nearly 4:30.

"I can't believe we wrote, arranged and recorded an entire piece in one day," Stephen said incredulously. "How much will you get for this?"

She told him.

"You're kidding?" he said astonished. "I guess you do pretty well then."

"It didn't start out like that," she elucidated. "But when people all over northwest Alabama began humming the tune for a hot dog restaurant and its sales sky rocketed, I became very popular; I could name my price."

Stephen smiled at her and nodded his head.

"This was fun," he grinned.

"Yes," she agreed. "It really was."

"I've never cared much for collaboration," he owned up. "I've done it for a couple of projects, and it was always so laborious. Everybody wanted to make sure *their* mark was on it. It was so drawn out."

"I've always preferred to do everything alone," Annie agreed with him. "I hated doing group projects in high school and college. It usually ended up that I did all the work and the group just presented it."

"I assume they were all well-graded?" Stephen asked.

"Of course," Annie nodded with a grin. "But I agree; this was fun. Not only that," she continued, "but I have finished the McCall account! That monkey is off my back."

"Nothing else we can do?" Stephen asked.

Annie thought for a moment. She opened her calendar on her desk and thumbed through the book. Nothing was due immediately; she would have plenty of time to work on the next projects. Then a thought came to her.

"Well, not any jingles," she began to explain, "but there is something coming up you could do."

"Anything!" he agreed eagerly.

"I'm supposed to sing *I Knew It Was Love* for Alex and Megan's wedding."

"I can't wait," he said readily. "It ought to be beautiful."

"No," she quickly interrupted. "You should sing it."

"I can't do that," he said as he shook his head. "You're the sister and the friend. They asked you. Besides, I would much rather hear your rendition of yet another of my songs."

"But they had no idea *you* would be at their wedding!" Annie persisted. "This would be perfect! Stephen Williams singing *I Knew It Was Love* in their wedding."

"No," he said point-blank. "That would not be right."

"Okay," she said thinking, "how about a duet? You sing and I harmonize?"

He thought for a moment and slightly cocked his head to the side. It still didn't seem right to him.

"Alternate plan," he offered. "You sing lead, in your key, and you play. I harmonize with you."

Annie rolled her eyes.

"That would be stupid," she countered. "*Me* singing *your* song in another key, while *you* follow along behind me? I don't think so."

"Well, that's the only deal I'm offering," he said firmly. "Take it or leave it."

Annie shut her calendar and heaved a deep sigh.

"Why do you do this?" she asked him seriously. "Why do you insist on making me do this? Play *your* music *my* way. I have to confess—it was really hard to sing *Autumn Sunset* for you last night. And now this?"

Stephen pulled her down next to him on the bench and smiled gently at her. He reached up and softly ran his hand down her long, flowing hair.

"Because you are good," he told her. "I have to confess that in my eleven years of professional music making, I have never come across someone quite like you. And frankly, I don't exactly know what to do with you."

Annie had been here before. It was like being on the balcony with him back home. He was too close and too personal. She could see his blue eyes so clearly that she noticed the green flecks speckled throughout them. She could feel his breath on her face, and every breath sent chills through her body again. Her stomach began to swirl, and she felt her face flushing. She had to stop this moment or she would not be able to talk coherently.

"Okay," she sputtered out weakly.

"Okay what?" he asked in a whisper.

"You can sing with me," she said as she gained control.

She forced herself to turn to the keyboard and begin playing the intro to *I Knew It Was Love.* She let her fingers glide and closed her eyes to concentrate on the music rather than the man sitting next to her. She tried to keep her voice steady as she began to sing.

When I look in your eyes all I can see
Is all that life has promised to me
When I look in your eyes, I see my heart
And I leave behind what pulled me apart
And others have asked how I can be sure
That what I have found is true and is pure
I knew it was love when you found my soul
I knew it was love when you made me whole
I knew it was love when my hand touched your face
I knew that I wanted to live life this way
I knew it was love.

"Feel free to join in any time," she said looking up at him as she continued to play. "This is supposed to be a duet."

"I will," he whispered. "Keep going."

Throughout all my life all I could do
Was stand on the side and just make it through

Throughout all my life I tried hard to be
All of the things I thought others should see
But then you found me and suddenly now
I can lift up my head and say clear and loud.

This time on the chorus, Stephen did join her. His harmony melded with her voice, and he modeled each inflection to match hers.

I knew it was love when you found my soul
I knew it was love when you made me whole
I knew it was love when my hand touched your face
I knew that I wanted to live life this way
I knew it was love.

"That was really nice," she said smiling as she continued on.

"We work well together," he agreed as he leaned his head next to hers, barely touching her.

Why should I wait to call you my own?
Why leave it to fate or take chances unknown?
All that I knew before I found you
Has faded away as all things are new.

Annie changed the key, dramatically increasing the volume and deliberately slowing the rate.

I knew it was love when you found my soul
I knew it was love when you made me whole
I knew it was love when my hand touched your face
I knew that I wanted to live life this way
I knew it was love.

༄

Annie finished the song and looked up for his response. Once again, his face was so close to hers that she felt extremely uncomfortable. He only smiled and slightly shook his head.

"Where have you been all my life?" he asked feebly.

Annie, determined to change the mood, stood up from the bench and said with a lively response, "In Dockrey, Mr. Williams. Dockrey, Alabama."

Stephen got up, still shaking his head.

"Does that meet your acceptance for a duet, then," he asked her.

"Absolutely," she said confidently. "Now I have to decide whether to tell them or keep it a surprise."

"Hmmm, that's a thought. Do you think they'll be upset about it? Do you think you should ask first?"

"Who knows?" Annie declared. "Megan would be thrilled. Alex, I have no idea. It's a fifty-fifty shot with him no matter what you do."

Stephen enjoyed the mid-week service at church that evening. The church furnished a fellowship supper, and he had the opportunity to meet more people. Once again, his stardom didn't seem to affect anyone in Dockrey. Most people admired his fame, but not overbearingly. He gave a few autographs, but no one hung on his every word. Most just smiled when he was introduced as "the musician that Alex works with" and then went on about their business.

He really enjoyed seeing Annie dressed up. He didn't mind her jeans, but her black slacks and vivid red shirt tonight seemed to accentuate all that was beautiful about her. Then, of course, sitting next to her during the service, he could breathe in the scent of her hair by inadvertently leaning near her.

"I know what you're doing," she told him once.

"What?" he asked innocently.

"I'm gonna send you back to New York with a case of that shampoo," she whispered to him.

"It won't be the same," he avowed. "Smelling a bottle won't bring quite the same pleasure."

"Should I move?" she finally asked.

"No. I'll behave."

He lied. During church, he would lean in occasionally and breathe deeply. Annie refused to look at him, but he could see her face begin to flush, and she would always bite her cheeks attempting not to smile. As a last resort, she wrote a note on her prayer list that said, *I'm going to tell my Daddy if you don't stop.* He wrote back, *I promise to be a good boy.*

"Hot tub?" Angie asked Annie as they walked into the house after church.

"I don't know," Annie hesitated. "What about Stephen?"

"Invite him," Angie said simply, as though there were nothing complicated about it.

Annie stopped for a moment and scrunched up her nose. She wasn't comfortable with that at all. Angie looked back at her.

"Or don't invite him," Angie stated. "Either way, he'll probably end up out there with us anyway because, whether you have noticed it or not, he seems to go wherever you are."

"No, he doesn't," Annie said very guarded. "Why would you say that?"

"All I know is that you've complained about not spending time with *me* this week, but you don't seem to be complaining about who you *have* been spending time with."

"It's not on purpose," Annie tried to declare.

"I'm not complaining," Angie said as she put her hand on her shoulder. She then leaned over to whisper, "Go for it."

"Go for what?" Annie wanted to know.

Angie refused to continue the conversation. She turned around and began to head up the stairs as she said, "I'm changing. Join me if you want!"

Stephen had stayed around the church to talk with the men who ran the sound equipment. He learned that their recording equipment was rather old and the best they could do was try and get him a tape each week, if the recorder was working that day. Some days it wouldn't budge. Stephen told them he would be sending some equipment in the mail. He went on further to explain how they could use the equipment to mass-produce CD's or tapes to give out as a ministry for the church. In return, he only asked that they send him recordings of all three services each week. They were thrilled to oblige. In thanks for their willingness, he said he would include a new soundboard also as well as a professional DVD camera.

When he made it back down to the Wright house, all was quiet. Jonathan had fixed a snack and was going to the bedroom as Stephen came in.

"Hungry?" he asked Stephen.

"Not really," he responded.

"Okay then," Jonathan said with a smile. "Make yourself at home, son."

"Thank you, but I believe I already have."

"That's how we like it around here," Jonathan confirmed. "See you in the morning."

"Good night, sir," Stephen waved.

Where is everybody? Alex was probably with Megan, but where are Angie and Annie. Perhaps the back porch.

He walked to the back door and heard the familiar laughing that seemed to accompany the two sisters whenever they were together. He opened the door and went on out. It was hard to determine who was more shocked at the situation.

"We are dressed," Angie told him as she interpreted the look on his face.

Annie felt extremely self-conscious. Apparently, Stephen did too.

"I wondered if you ever used this old tub," he finally managed to say. He didn't know if he should leave or stay, but it didn't seem to bother Angie a bit, so he pulled a chair up next to the tub and decided to enjoy the conversation with them. He could tell, however, that Annie was nowhere near comfortable. Too bad.

"We actually use it a lot," Angie informed him. "We've just been busy this week."

"I have one at my estate," he began to explain, "but would you believe I've never been in it? My staff has. They say it's wonderful in the winter. They actually go outside and sit around in it while it's snowing."

"We use this a lot in the winter too," Angie told him as she moved her head around trying to relieve the tension in her neck. "This is probably the biggest luxury I've missed while in school."

"I'm going to have to give it a try," Stephen said as he leaned over to touch the water.

Annie's eyes grew big. Stephen saw her reaction and quickly clarified, "When I get home."

"You can join us now, if you like," Angie insisted.

He actually thought it would be exciting, but he could tell it made Annie nervous so he offered an excuse.

"Don't you think it's a bit too hot to be wallowing around in there?" he suggested.

"For a New York boy, maybe," Angie told him, "but not for me. I won't speak for my sister, who apparently is *not* speaking for herself at the moment anyway."

Annie knew she was blushing and rolled her eyes, hoping her cheeks were already flushed from the heat of the tub and no one could tell.

As the conversation carried on, Annie began to wonder who would out-sit whom. She wasn't about to stand up in a bikini in front of Stephen, but he didn't seem in any hurry to rush off. She hated feeling so self-conscious around him, but he didn't help by always smelling her hair and leaning in too close for her comfort. She was thankful he hadn't joined them. She had put her hair up, but the very bottom of her neck had gotten her hair wet and she could smell the honey shampoo herself.

After what seemed like an eternity to Annie, Angie finally asked Stephen to hand her a towel. Undaunted, she stood up, bikini and all, and took Stephen's hand to get out of the tub. He didn't appear phased by the act in any way.

"I'm too hot to stay in any longer," she said as she dried herself off. "I'll see ya'll in the morning. Can't wait to decorate that church."

Annie smiled because she knew Angie hated anything like that. She was most definitely not the homemaking, home-decorating type. They said their goodbyes and Angie left. The porch was noticeably quiet. Stephen leaned back in his chair, and Annie tried to act calmly. The truth was, she was so hot that she felt she would pass out if she didn't get up soon. But as long as Stephen sat there by the tub, she was not going to budge.

"How long are you planning on staying in there?" he finally asked her.

"As long as I have to," she replied with a sigh.

"Meaning?"

"Meaning I'm not getting up until you leave," she said, looking him squarely in the eye. This time he blushed and stood immediately.

"I'm sorry," he said, slightly flustered. "I didn't realize you . . . well . . . never mind."

Now Annie was embarrassed again.

"This is not a swimsuit I would wear in public," she tried to explain without making the situation more awkward. "I only wear it in here because it is so easy to dry out. Angie obviously has no trouble with it."

"Obviously," he replied, determined to keep his eyes averted.

She has no reason to be ashamed, he thought to himself, and then closed his eyes in a grimace. *That's exactly what Annie is worried about now.*

"Yes, I should have been more thoughtful about all of this," he managed to say. "I was just enjoying your company so much it never occurred to me that this might be inappropriate."

Annie now rolled her eyes again and felt pity for poor Stephen. She had embarrassed him probably beyond making amends for it, but she could try.

"I've always been more modest than Angie," she tried to make clear. "I'm not very fond of even swimming with guys, you know? It's just . . . I don't know. Maybe because she's seen so many bodies in her line of work—it's just a part of normalcy or something."

It wasn't working. The tension was getting thicker.

"You know," he began as he started toward the door, "perhaps I should just leave and let you get out. I'll see you in the morning, and we'll all have slept through this, and it will be like nothing ever happened."

Annie nodded and managed to say, "Well, okay. That sounds good."

Just as Stephen got to the door, however, he turned back to say, "I will confess to being just a little disappointed. I'm afraid I may have been waiting you out."

Then he left. Annie dropped her head back to the tub and closed her eyes in humiliation.

Just when I thought he was being decent, why did he have to say that?

As Stephen walked through the great room toward the stairs, he thought to himself, *You just couldn't leave well enough alone, could you? You had to say that last statement.*

Chapter Nine

Six forty-five a.m.—there was no sense staying in bed. Annie slept horribly, even though she had fallen in bed the night before so tired that her head ached. Two nights with little sleep didn't help her attitude about decorating the church. She might as well get up and get started. She pulled on her scrubs and brushed out her hair. It was rather tangled from the hot tub. She hadn't felt like grooming anything last night when she finally got to her room; she didn't even let down her hair. She just dropped, hoping to sleep, but instead kept replaying images and scenes of her past five days with Stephen.

I've got to stop this. I cannot be obsessed with this man. Oh, my gosh, I don't know if I can stop! At least I will have a reprieve from him today.

As she thought about the reprieve, she sighed. *I don't want a reprieve. I'm really pitiful. I need some coffee.*

Annie was the first in the kitchen again. That fact actually comforted her because it was normal and familiar. She started the coffee and instinctively began the cheese toast. She paused for just a moment and remembered how well Stephen had liked the sugar toast. Maybe she should make sugar toast.

Get it together, Annie-girl! Make the stupid cheese toast and go decorate the church!

She continued with the plan. However, when she removed the big block of cheese that Stephen had bought her while at Sam's, the funny feelings and mushy thoughts started all over again. She threw her head back in disgust as she dropped the cheese onto the counter.

"Having a rough day, already?" her mother teased as she walked into the kitchen.

"Just a rough night," Annie told her.

"Anything I can help with?" Barbara asked as she gave her a tiny, warm hug.

"No, Moms, as usual, this appears to be a beast of my own creation."

"I wouldn't be so sure about that," her mother smiled.

Annie stopped slicing cheese and looked over at Barbara with a confused look.

"What do you mean by that?" Annie wondered aloud.

"I watch. I have eyes and," Barbara looked at her tenderly with her dark brown eyes, "I know my daughter."

Annie could feel the tears pushing inside her eyes. She knew if she closed them, the tears would fall.

"Moms, I don't know what is happening here," she confessed. "I don't know if I like it or if I don't like it. I don't know if all this is just a—a—game or a dream. I don't really know what I'm doing."

Barbara came over and embraced Annie in a firm hug this time. Annie had not been hugged like that in years. It helped to wash away some of the confusion. Barbara broke the hug and pulled away to look Annie in the face again.

"Annie, you're a good girl and a smart girl. You're not perfect," she smiled slightly and then continued, "but you're a godly person. Take this to the Lord. Ask Him for wisdom. This could very well be a game. All this could be a taunt. That would be evil, and it would be wrong. However," he voice trailed off slightly as she slanted her head to the side, "it is possible for some dreams to come true."

"But Moms, I don't even know what I'm hoping to get out of all of this. I don't know what I want to happen."

Suddenly Angie burst in on the scene. "Sorry for eavesdropping," she beamed as she joined them. "However, I think you know exactly what you want to happen, but you're scared to death its gonna be like everything else in your life: high hopes, deep falls. You gotta take a chance, Annie. You gotta go for some things. You've just got to."

"Why?" Angie asked in exasperation. "Why do I have to take chances? Why can't life just be simple? Why couldn't I be a doctor like you? Or a great wife and mother like Moms and Andie? Why am I like this?"

"Because God made you unique," her mother put out plainly. "You're not like me or Angie or Andie. And honey, even if you tried, you would be miserable. I don't know what God has planned for you, but somehow I don't feel like you've found it yet. Be patient, walk with God, and keep your eyes open. People don't often fall into God's will by accident."

"Way to go, Moms," Angie said as she hugged her mother. "Set her straight!"

"Should I start in on you, now?" her mother raised her eyebrows in question.

"Me?" Angie asked incredulously. "I know where I'm headed!"

"Yes, we all know *you* know," Barbara agreed, "but do you know that's where *God* wants you?"

Angie's jaw dropped and she shook her head at her mother's question.

"Go Moms," Annie smiled, glad not to be the only one under the spotlight at the moment.

"What are you saying?" Angie asked. "You think I've run ahead of God or something in all of this?"

"I am saying," Barbara laid out calmly, "that you have had these ideals about your life and your pursuits, but I have never heard you once say, 'Thy will be done.' "

Angie looked up and sincerely said, "Thy will be done! Please."

"Don't be sacrilegious," he mother scolded.

"Moms, I'm not," Angie said soberly. "If this isn't God's plan for my life, then God help me."

All was quiet for the moment. This discussion had been way too serious to start the morning. As the coffee finished, each one quietly poured a cup and began to doctor it up. The oven dinged, and Annie pulled out the cheese toast.

"Hello, ladies," came the now familiar voice through the kitchen entrance. All three turned to look at Stephen who was grinning widely at the sight.

"Now *this* is a great way to start the morning off," he said as he came on in. "Three beautiful ladies milling around in the kitchen, and the coffee's already made. It doesn't get any better than this."

"You need to get a life," Annie mumbled as she grabbed some small plates from the cabinet.

Angie came up behind her and whispered in her ear, "Physician, heal thyself."

Decorating the church was about as uneventful as both Angie and Annie had predicted. Kim, Megan's aunt who had raised her, along with Megan, Andie, Barbara, and a couple of ladies from the church rounded out the decorating crew. Andie was actually rather good with this kind of stuff. Annie and Angie mainly followed orders and did whatever was suggested, careful not to make any of their own suggestions in the process.

"Remind me to elope," Annie murmured to Angie as they hung garland above the baptistery.

"Oh, you're planning on getting married?" was Angie's response. "Anyone I know?"

"Don't get smart," Annie snapped. "I was just making a point."

"So was I," Angie said curtly.

"Look," Annie wouldn't let up, "you're about as close to *never* getting married as I am."

"Actually," Angie said a little mournfully, "I'm probably closer to *never* than you are. You'll still be in America, at least. I'll be on some Pacific island with a bunch of tribesmen. I feel the odds are more in your favor."

"Maybe you can marry a chief or something," Annie suggested. "Take your bikini with you. It may help."

A voice from the choir loft interrupted them.

"I rather liked her bikini myself," said Stephen grinning impishly. "Is it okay to talk about bikinis in church?"

"Did you come to help decorate or to shower us with flattering compliments concerning our hot tub attire?" Angie asked, never missing a beat.

Annie admired her ability to stay calm and never seem flustered about anything.

"Well, actually neither," he said sadly, and then perked up as he added, "but if you would like to continue the discussion on *bikinis,* I am more than willing to oblige."

"Okay," Annie said, halting the direction of the conversation. "We are not continuing on about bikinis. Why are you here?"

"I wanted to talk with you for a moment, if Angie doesn't mind."

"Here," Angie said as she handed him the tape and pins. "You can finish putting up this green stuff with her as you talk. I'll find another productive and artistic thing to do—ha!"

As she started to leave the choir loft, she turned back to Stephen and asked, "You can do two things at one time, can't you? Talk and hand out pins or tape?"

"I will try," he said cordially.

"Well, don't let her mess up, and make sure it's straight," Angie said as she walked out.

Annie placed another section of the garland across the top and asked for a pin. Stephen obliged. She then asked for two strips of tape. He tore them off and handed them up to her on the ladder. He kept quiet as he watched her work, enjoying the view probably more than he should. He felt slightly guilty about thinking as he did in a church.

They continued on until the garland was completed. Annie climbed down the ladder and took the tape and pins from him.

"What did you want to talk about?" she asked him, still trying to act normal, but feeling far from it.

"Can we go outside?" he asked.

She gave him a strange expression and then nodded. He followed her out the front door.

"Is something wrong?" she asked as they sat down on one of the front steps.

"Oh, no, nothing like that," he said quickly. "I was just with Alex."

Wonderful, Annie thought to herself. *I suppose you hate me now too and will be flying out as soon as the wedding is over on Saturday.*

"He and I were going to do something tonight. I can't quite remember what it entailed, a crying bridge or something," he began, "but Megan needs him to help her with something and he had to bow out gracefully."

"Cry Baby Bridge," Annie said with a smile.

"Yes, that was it," he remembered.

"It's not that big of a deal," she told him, "unless you're superstitious."

"Well, the truth is, I had really wanted to do something with *you* tonight."

"You didn't tell Alex that, did you?" she asked hastily.

He looked at her peculiarly and shook his head.

"Good," she sighed. "He wouldn't approve, you know?"

"I'll be honest, I don't really care what Alex thinks about us," he affirmed. "This is between you and me; Alex is not a part of this."

"But he is," Annie said somberly. "He doesn't really *approve* of me spending time with you."

"As I see it, you have been polite to me, where as I have been a bit overbearing in my insistence on hanging around you."

Annie nodded. That was sort of how she had seen it too. In fact, she had tried to avoid him on many occasions.

"What I'd like," he continued, "is to take you out to dinner somewhere. Somewhere away from here and somewhere nice."

"Why?" she said out of curiosity, and then added with a bit mischievousness, "You don't like our dining faire in Dockrey?"

He smiled and explained, "I want to take you *away* from here for the evening. You name the place, and I'll make the reservations. When will you be through with all the decorating?"

"I'll never be through here," she said annoyed. "I'll be doing this stuff in my sleep tonight."

He stared with a questioned look.

"Okay," she tried to analyze when she would be through. "Surely we'll be through by 3:00. I'll have to shower because . . ."

"And wash your hair?" he interjected.

"With *Head and Shoulders,*" she said sternly. "I could be ready to leave around 4:30, if everything goes as planned here."

"Great! Where do we eat?"

"Do you like Italian?" she asked. He nodded.

"Riccatoni's," she replied. "It's in Florence. They have great lasagna and this little saucer of oil and spices that you dip your bread into."

"It's a date then?" he asked her.

"Is it?" she asked back.

"Yes," he said, nodding slightly. "Dinner tonight, you and I."

As he walked off, Annie tried to contain her heartbeat. She knew he had to have seen it rising up through her throat. What was this? Was it a *date* date, or just a date?

"There you are," Angie said bursting out the front door. "We have to put the candelabras together."

Annie turned around and Angie gave her a funny look. "You look like you've seen a ghost," Angie said. "What happened?

"It really isn't a big deal," Annie tried to downplay it. "We're going to Riccatoni's tonight."

"We? Who is *we?*"

"We, as in *he* and *I,*" Annie said pointing her thumb back at Stephen as he walked down the hill to the house.

"I don't guess I'm invited," Angie smiled.

"I don't think so."

ℬ ℬ

The church was not decorated by 3:00, but Angie insisted that Annie go ahead and leave. She was more thankful to be through with the tedious task of embellishing the church than she was about going out to dinner with Stephen. In fact, the longer the day went on, the more nervous she became about the evening. Alex would be fuming if he knew. Then there was the fact that she was not exactly sure why she was going out with Stephen. Surely he didn't actually mean a real *date.* If so, this would be her first.

She talked to herself in the shower, making sure she did not over anticipate the evening.

There is nothing going on here. He is being polite and taking me out as a way to say "thank you" for spending time with him this week. What should I wear? What will he wear? He's thinking nice; Riccatoni's could be either. Oh, my gosh! I should have picked somewhere really nice! He's probably wearing a suit, and I was gonna come down in jeans! This is already a disaster!

She opted for her black dress slacks and a blue silk button-down shirt. Then she began to wonder if that was a bad choice. If she were to sweat a lot, it would come right through the blouse. But if he took the convertible, she would dry out.

Come on! Get it together! Okay, pull my hair back in a braid. If we take the convertible, it shouldn't blow around too much. But would he put the top down if this is supposed to be a nice evening? Aughhh!!!

When Annie finally managed to leave the room, Stephen was patiently waiting on the couch. He heard her shut her door and stood up immediately to greet her. He smiled warmly and held out his hand as she came near the bottom.

"You look absolutely gorgeous," he told her.

"So do you," she smiled, knowing she had blushed, but only slightly. He was wearing black denim pants with a blue dress shirt and black tie.

Casual, but dressy. You're a smart man, Stephen Williams.

"We'll take the MG, if you don't mind," Stephen suggested. "It's hardly been used. We can keep the roof up if you prefer."

Annie pulled up her braid.

"Good girl," he smiled as he held the keys out to her.

"I'm not driving," she said plainly.

"Well, I'm not driving," he insisted.

"I don't believe there's room for a third party in here," she said as she moved her hand over the seats of the car. "So who else could be driving?"

"Annie, I haven't driven in forever, besides you know the way," he said smoothly.

"You have a license, do you not?" she asked.

He nodded.

"It's an easy drive, Stephen," she assured him. "It's a beautiful back road for most of the way. You'll be glad we left during the daylight. Then a four-lane highway takes us into Florence. You don't even have to drive on any back streets."

"I had planned for this evening to be non-stressful," he said as he opened her door.

"Really?" she laughed. "Hasn't anyone told you? There's no such thing as spending non-stressful time with me. I won't allow it."

"I'm beginning to agree," he moped as he climbed behind the wheel.

It didn't take long for Stephen to begin enjoying the drive. It truly was a beautiful road running by wooded forests and hills, lovely country homes, and huge rock precipices that jutted out from the hills on occasion. By the time they reached Riccatoni's, the driving, the scenery, the countryside, the open air, and the company had invigorated him.

"No valet parking?" he asked doubtfully as they drove up to the restaurant that was located along a main street.

"No," she confirmed. "We may need to park on a side street."

"I don't parallel park," he warned her.

"Neither do I. Take a left on this next street."

He parked, and they walked on to the restaurant. Annie could sense nervousness in him.

"What's wrong?" she asked him.

"This is a little too public," he said as he surveyed the area. "If we have to leave, we may not be able to get out fast enough."

"You're with me tonight," she smiled. "No one will mess with you with me around."

"That's almost reassuring," he said as he opened the restaurant door.

The host greeted them and asked if they had a reservation. Stephen nodded and gave them his name.

"Yes, Mr. Williams," said the man. "Follow me, please."

They followed the host up a metal staircase and to a table in the far corner overlooking the street. He placed their menus on their placemats and informed them their server would be with them shortly.

"He knows," Annie said shortly.

"What?" Stephen asked.

"He knows who you are," she said with caution.

"I thought so too," he winced. "I'll see what I can do."

When the server came, she was markedly nervous.

"Jessica?" Stephen said to her as he read her nametag. "Is that your name?"

She nodded.

"Do you know who I am, Jessica?" he asked her.

"Yes, Mr. Williams," she replied.

"Jessica," he continued to use her name, "it is very important that we settle a few things in order for me to continue dining here. Do you understand?"

She nodded.

"There is a huge tip in this for you if we can take care of all these little issues."

She nodded again.

"First, please do not tell anyone that I am here until I have left, okay?"

She continued her nodding.

"Next, I will need to speak with the working manager tonight concerning a back exit if necessary. Is there a way to leave this building other than the front door?"

"Yes, Mr. Williams," she said quickly. "You can even exit from up here."

"Very good," he smiled. "Would you please go and tell the host right now that he is not to inform anyone else that I am here and then ask your manager to come?"

"Right away, sir. Can I get you something to drink on my way back?"

"I'll have a diet soda, whatever kind you have," he said flatly, and then glanced over at Annie.

"Sweet tea," she said softly, afraid to draw any attention.

The waitress left immediately, and Stephen breathed a sigh.

"Is this a bad idea?" Annie wanted to know.

"I don't think so," Stephen reassured her. "We should be fine. As long as we have a place to hide for a moment or two, we'll be all right."

The waitress returned with their drinks, some bread and oil dip, and the manager.

"Mr. Williams, what can I do for you?" he asked with a slight Italian accent.

Stephen explained the situation, and the manager understood. They laid out a plan in case anything was to happen. Two of the busboys were relatives who had just moved here from the *old country,* and they were rather intimidating in size. The manager placed them at a table next to Stephen and Annie, and then told them to be prepared to escort the guests out through the back door if necessary.

Stephen began to genuinely relax.

"I think our bases are covered now," he said as he took a deep breath. "We can get down to business."

"So this is a business dinner," she mused, finally starting to relax herself.

"Serious business," he said as he tore off a piece of bread and dipped into the oily, spicy mixture.

"Well, you've got me curious," she said as she prepared her own bread. "What's going on?"

He sighed a bit as he chewed his bread, and then put his hands in his lap to give her his full attention.

"Annie, I don't even know how to start with all of this," he began. "The whole reason I even came here this week was you."

Annie's eyes grew wide.

"It's true," he confessed. "When you didn't come with Alex to the audition, I was floored. I just assumed you would be there. Alex is good, no question there, but it was *you* that I wanted to meet. I didn't really seriously consider hiring him until I actually heard him play. And then when he played, I realized several things. First, you knew what you were talking about. Second, you didn't show up so you weren't some star-seeking lunatic looking for a way to meet Stephen Williams. I put two and two together and realized you were exactly who you said you were."

"I can see how you thought I might have been misleading you," she said sheepishly. "I didn't know what else to do."

"Anyway, when Alex needed a volunteer for his wedding, I was thrilled! Perfect opportunity!"

"And here you are," she said, a little taken back by his admission. "And here I am." She paused for a moment then asked, "Disappointed?"

"Not by a mile," he admitted. "Annie, you're like no one I've ever met. I can't even describe what I've discovered in you. First, there's the whole music thing; you are above and beyond anything I've ever seen."

"Please," Annie said as she rolled eyes. "Now you're being kind."

He took her hand and redirected her attention back to him.

"I'm serious, Annie," he said almost severely. "I don't even know what to do with what I've discovered here, but I have to do something."

"What are you saying?"

"You have got to get out of here," he tried to explain. "You are literally wasting your life away and tossing around your talents like you would pennies in a fountain. I can open doors for you like you would not believe."

She jerked her hand back and stared at him in a daze.

"Annie, listen to me," he became more urgent. "I went on and on about your piano playing and your composing, and it was all sincere, but then there's your voice. I mean, it's like the passion of Celine Dion with the soul of Karen Carpenter."

"My gosh," she mused, "what an odd description."

"Exactly!" he snapped at her. "That's you! You're like nothing this world has ever seen. You have got to come back with me. You have got to start doing something, and I'm talking something really big."

Annie leaned forward and asked, "What *are* you talking about here?"

He leaned in to answer, "I'm talking about pushing you and your music to the world. Listen to me; I've had people beg me for the past 11 years to make them a star. I've listened to countless songs and singers, and I finally gave up on even *trying* to be polite. They're all the same; they're just a different version of someone who's already out there. Nobody wants that! The world already had Elton and Billy; it didn't need another piano man. And I wasn't that. I was a new thing. And I'm telling you, Annie, that's what you are."

Annie could not seem to absorb what he was saying. She understood the words, but were they really about her?

"What are you suggesting?" she asked, trying to gain some kind of emotional footing for all she was having to process.

"I have a plan," he told her. He practically leaned over the table to say, "Come on tour with me."

Annie took a deep breath and looked up to the ceiling. This was the moment she had dreamed of her entire life. She literally began to feel faint as she felt the blood leave her head and drain to wherever it goes when these things happen. And the punctuation mark was that it was Stephen Williams asking her, not some indifferent person out to make a buck off of her music. She almost couldn't breathe. She forced herself—inhale, exhale, breathe in, breathe out.

"Are you okay?" he asked as he stood up and came over to kneel down beside her. "Do you need a drink?"

She nodded. Stephen handed her the glass of tea, and Annie drank a few swallows.

"I'm okay," she finally spoke. "Sit back down."

He went back to his seat and looked at her with great concern.

"Surely you knew this day would come," he said to her. "You have to understand the talent you've got. You can't be that ignorant about it."

"I gave up," she said as her shaking hand reached for the tea again. "I just got to the point that I believed I was somehow being punished for what I could do. That's all that's happened since I left high school."

"Listen, music is an intimidating business," he explained, "and it's extremely subjective. Those that enjoy classical think country is an insult, and those who like rock find classical boring and predictable. I mean there is no standard for what is really good and what is crap. Musicians are at the mercy of someone else to determine if they are actually good or not. You, however, broke the mold."

"How?" she questioned him as she shook her head in disbelief.

"Because music is so ingrained in you that you just know it!" he tried to clarify. "Hardly anybody is like that! It's like Mozart. He appalled his peers because he was so good at what he did. Yet when they tried to create, it wasn't even close to his throw away stuff. You are the Mozart of this day."

The server came up to take their order. Annie couldn't even begin to think of ordering food. Her whole life was about to change, and she could not imagine trying to do something as simple as ordering a meal.

"We'll both have the lasagna and the house salad," Stephen told the waitress. "Ranch dressing for both."

"Yes, Mr. Williams," she said politely, although somewhat concerned about Annie's listlessness.

"Come with me," he asked her again. "You can even bring a Roland," he winked. "You play in the band, and then we feature you on a few of my songs. For starters, *Autumn Sunset* and *I Knew it was Love.* I'll back you up, and the band will play in your key. We'll eventually write something together and add that in. Then we let you do something that is all yours. You play, you sing, you wow the world."

"I can't sing your songs," she said emphatically. "No way! Your audiences would hate me!"

"Trust me, Annie," he said warmly, "when you open your mouth and let those songs go, everyone will be dumfounded. I promise you that."

Stephen continued to talk about the tour, the cities, and the countries. Annie was still trying to put all of this together in her mind. Was it possible? She had commitments to keep. She had things to do. She couldn't just stop her whole life and jump on board with Stephen Williams! Or could she? Then the biggest jerk reality could give suddenly slammed in her face. Alex. Annie grimaced and threw her head back.

"What?" Stephen asked. "What is it?"

"I can't," she said with tears forming.

"Why not?" he demanded. "I'm offering you the chance of a lifetime!"

"Don't you think I know that?" she said, almost grieving. "But I can't do this!"

"Annie? You *have* to do this!"

"I can't do it," she reemphasized, slowly and deliberately.

"Give me one good reason," he said angrily. "And it had better be good."

"Alex," was all she said.

Stephen nodded in understanding. He took another bite of lasagna and put down his fork as he thought. There had to be an answer. Annie now had her face in her hands. She couldn't believe this—her one chance of a lifetime and her brother would literally loathe her if she took it.

"Annie," Stephen said as he turned up her face, "this is *not* about Alex. This is about you, and it's about me too. I *want* to do this. I *want* this to happen."

"He'll never forgive me," she lamented. "I might as well wrap up his life in one neat little package and throw it in the fire to burn. I can't do this to him."

"Annie, what about *us* in all of this?" he wanted to know.

"What do you mean *us?* Why are you saying *us?*"

He looked at her tenderly and his blue eyes twinkled in the candle-light.

"That kiss hasn't left my mind for more than a minute."

Annie looked up quickly. What was he saying now?

"Stuff like that doesn't just happen. Annie, I can't stop thinking about you. All I do is try and figure out some way to be with you, but I'm scared to death to tell you because then you might think that what I think about your music is just concocted to get you to stay with me."

"Is it?" she asked. "You wouldn't toy with me, would you?"

He took her hand again and held it up to his mouth.

"Annie, I will put your music before my feelings," he promised. "If you come with me, and you say there is nothing between us, I will honor that. If you insist that nothing could happen with us, I won't even go there. It will be hard because I can't stop thinking about you, but I promise you, I won't *violate* you again."

"That was a bad word," she apologized. "I shouldn't have said it, but I tend to use words rather harshly."

"I know," he smiled. "That's one of those things I love about you."

"How could you like that? Alex despises me for that."

"And I am *not* Alex," he reminded her.

"Can we get out of here?" she asked almost in desperation. "I'm starting to feel all closed in, and I don't know . . . can we go?"

"Absolutely," he said quickly.

He pulled out five 100-dollar bills and placed them on the table, and then held out his hand to help Annie up.

"It didn't cost near that much," Annie told him.

"Trust me," he said as he led her toward the stairs. "It was worth every penny if it gets you in my life."

Their waitress was coming up the stairs as they were about to head down.

"Keep the change," he said as they passed her.

Annie waited for the scream when the server found the money. It came just as they headed out the door.

"We'd better hurry," Stephen told her as he handed her the keys. "You know the streets. Just get us out of here quickly. I'll take over when we make it out of town."

She opened her door, but Stephen just jumped in through the open top. Right before she cranked the car, a crowd appeared around the corner screaming Stephen's name.

"Step on it!" he yelled. She obliged.

"So this is Cry Baby Bridge?" he half chuckled as they walked out onto the deserted trestle in the middle of nowhere. "I suppose there is a legend behind this."

"I don't really know it," Annie confessed. "But if you stand still and listen quietly, you're supposed to hear the faint cry of a dead baby or something. I know it's tragic, but the story never had any staying power in my mind."

"So you've been out here often," he asked.

"Actually, no," she admitted. "I came out with some friends once on Halloween, and they all totally freaked out. I had to insist they were all nuts and then drive them home."

"I bet this is a great make out spot," he teased her.

"I wouldn't know."

"That's right," he nodded. "Was that really your first kiss? The other day, on the balcony?"

"Yes," she hated to admit it.

"I'm sorry. I could have been more selective with that. I don't know what came over me," he paused. "Well, that's a lie. I *do* know what came over me. *You* did. You still do."

"Stephen, I can't do this with you," she said as she closed her eyes and tried to shake the memory out of her head. "I can't think clearly or feel clearly about you. I don't think I can ever see you as anything other than Stephen Williams the superstar. I'm no different than any other google-eyed girl who listens to your music—or hangs your poster in her closet."

Stephen hung his head. How could he make her understand what he felt? He couldn't. He would have to show her, if she would just give him the chance.

"Will you come with me?" he asked. "Do the tour."

"I can't answer you right now," she finally said. "Let me think on it."

"I'll give you until after the wedding Saturday night," he agreed.

"When are you leaving?" she wanted to know.

"The car is due back Sunday afternoon," he said as he took her hand.

She pulled it back and pleaded, "Don't do that anymore. I can't think clearly when you do that."

"Humor me," he said as he turned her face to his and studied it in the moonlight. "Has anyone ever told you that you have the most inviting lips in the world?"

"Actually, yes," she said seriously, "and I slapped him."

Stephen held her hand tighter and then reached for her other hand.

"But you won't slap me, will you?" he asked her.

"Apparently not," she smiled as she wiggled her hands in his.

"I'm going to kiss you again," he said softly, "and I want you to know that it has been long considered, is not spur of the moment, and is in no way meant to violate you."

"I really don't think you should," she began to protest. "I don't know how I feel, and I don't really think . . ."

"Shut up," he whispered back. "Sometimes your brother is right; you can talk too much."

This time when he kissed her, Annie did not resist. She slowly moved her hands from his and placed them around his neck. She touched his soft curls and realized she had always wondered how they felt. As he pulled her close, she felt her knees weaken again, but he pulled her even nearer, almost holding her up. She tried not to give into the passion, but she could not find enough protest left in her to stop. This was wonderful.

"Wow," Stephen whispered as he looked down into her eyes in the bright moonlight. "Trust me on this; that is not a normal kiss."

"I wouldn't know," she blushed. "What kind was it?"

"On a scale of one to ten, it was a million," he smiled at her. He gently ran his hand down the side of her face and continued to gaze at her. "Please come with me, Annie. Please."

"Saturday night," she reminded him.

He kissed her again and again. Annie was totally lost, and anything she had ever thought of as fact began to disappear, even the thoughts of Alex's retribution if she accepted Stephen's offer.

Chapter Ten

Annie awoke with a start the next morning and almost screamed out as she noticed someone sitting on the edge of the bed.

"What the heck are you doing?" she shrieked at Angie who continued to sit calmly while smiling down at her.

"And good morning to you too," Angie said with her typical morning enthusiasm.

Annie sat up and tried to collect her thoughts and clear her head. She looked at her clock; it was 7:30.

"Wow," Annie thought aloud, "I actually slept in this morning."

"Yeah," Angie agreed, "I was starting to get worried. So tell me about last night."

Annie stared for a moment at her sister.

"Will you teach me how to be as subtle as you one day?" Annie said sarcastically as she still tried to gain her bearings. "Let's get some coffee and I'll try to ferret it out for you."

"No!" Angie said firmly. "Stephen's already up. He's smiling and whistling around the house. I want to hear it all from you, uninterrupted."

Annie shuffled her back to the headboard for support and tried to imagine how to piece together last night in a presentable way. She did not want to share everything, only what was pertinent. But how did she decide?

"For crying out loud!" Angie exclaimed. "Don't sit there and analyze every point! Just tell me what's going on! Something big happened. I can tell."

Annie stared at the ceiling, still processing everything herself. She sighed and tried to make it as concise as possible.

"He wants me to go on tour with him," Annie got out.

Angie wrinkled her nose and cocked her head.

"For what purpose?" Angie asked.

"Play in his band and actually sing a couple of songs."

"Awesome!" Angie shouted. "I knew it! All he had to do was

hear you play and sing! This is so cool! When do you leave?"

"Are you kidding me?" Annie questioned her. "Do you think it's just that simple—he asks and I go?"

"Do *not* tell me that you are weighing options here," Angie said sternly. "This is the chance of a lifetime! You're not actually trying to figure out if you *should* do it or not?"

"What about Alex?" Annie asked her. "He is going to explode when he finds out. Somehow, this will all be my fault. He will accuse me of being manipulative and deceptive and having arranged the whole thing myself."

Angie stared at her wide-eyed and said, "So what? Alex is a big boy! He can get over it. And if he can't, I would say that it's his problem. Annie, don't even think about throwing this away to try and win Alex's approval."

"But he despises me so much, and I have no clue why!" Annie said exasperated. "What have I ever done to him that deserves all this hate?"

"You're a tough act to follow," Angie guessed. "You were Miss Perfect. You did everything right. You were the straight-A student, you were the athlete, and you were the musician. Alex was two years behind you. Everybody expected the same. However, he did not have your drive or ambition."

"Wouldn't you say that's his fault, not mine?"

"Absolutely," Angie agreed. "I figure that rather than try to rise to the occasion, Alex chose to rebel against it. You became the target of his frustration."

"Do you know that he's never said one thing to me about getting him the audition with Stephen," Annie told her. "Not a thank you, not a word of appreciation, not even an acknowledgment that I had anything to do with it."

"Hmmm. His resentment runs deep. But you can't let that hold *you* back from pursuing this, Annie. You have got to go; you have got to take this offer from Stephen."

"But what if Alex quits?"

"Then Alex makes a stupid decision to mess up his life. That is not *your* responsibility. Like you said, you got him the job in the first place! If he can't stand the heat, then he'd better get out of the fire."

Annie slammed her fists on the bed in frustration.

"Why does this have to be so hard?" she shouted out. "Why does there have to be an obstacle, a big obstacle, standing right here in the way?"

"Annie, let me tell you this," Angie said as she took Annie's hand. "If you don't make the right choice here, you are going to force Stephen to choose between you and Alex. And I get this feeling that Stephen wouldn't pick Alex. If that happens, then Alex will hate you more than ever. Your best bet is to go on, go with Stephen, and if Alex chooses to leave the best thing that has ever happened to him, then it all lies on his shoulders."

Annie nodded slightly. That was certainly a good point, but the thought of dealing with Alex's resentment throughout the entire tour was unsettling. Would it be worth it?

"I really need some coffee," Annie finally said. "Maybe it will clear my head a little."

"First," Angie took her hand, "let's pray."

"Yes," Annie agreed. She looked Angie in the eyes and soberly added, "You know this could change my life drastically."

"Thank God," Angie replied, "and I'm *not* being sacrilegious."

Annie smiled and bowed her head as Angie began to pray.

After a hearty *amen* and a long, warm, embrace, Annie and Angie joined their mother in the kitchen. Annie immediately began to fix her coffee while Angie kissed Barbara on the cheek.

"Morning, Moms," Angie said merrily. "Ready for the big night?"

"I don't know," replied Barbara shakily. "Tonight the rehearsal dinner, tomorrow the wedding, and I am in my usual fog."

"What?" asked Annie turning around. Her mother was generally in a fog, but Annie never imagined that she knew it.

"Oh, goodness," Barbara sighed. "When I have so much to do like this, the moments that I am supposed to enjoy just tend to pass me right by."

"It shouldn't be that bad," Angie consoled. "You've got the ladies at the church preparing the dinner; the sanctuary and fellowship hall are all decorated. What else is there to do?"

"Get through the rehearsal," her mother moaned.

"I'm sure Megan's got it all planned out," Annie said as she passed by with her toast and coffee. "She's fairly organized."

"Megan? Organized?" Barbara laughed nervously. "Oh, I feel so much better now!"

Angie squeezed her mother again in a hug and told her, "Moms, sarcasm doesn't wear well on you. Stick with the fog."

They joined Alex, Jonathan, and Stephen on the back porch with their breakfasts. Conversation was somewhat lagging until the ladies joined in. Annie deliberately avoided Stephen's eyes for fear of revealing more than she wanted anyone to know. When he did manage to catch her gaze, he just gave a warm smile, nothing overt to give away what had happened between them. She was thankful for his discretion. She still did not know how to interpret their relationship.

"Alex," Jonathan said as he stood up and stretched, "let's go cut some wood."

"Dad, it's the day of my rehearsal," Alex complained. "Tomorrow's my wedding."

"Your point being?" Jonathan replied with raised eyebrows.

Alex took a deep breath, exhaled and said, "Let's go cut some wood."

They left the porch to change clothes, and no one spoke for a moment. Stephen, unsure of what had transpired let his curiosity get the best of him.

"Is Alex in trouble?" he asked them.

Angie laughed.

"You'd think he is," she admitted, "but no. They're just gonna have a 'heart-to-heart.' "

"Daddy always does this when we hit milestones in our lives," Annie explained. "Somehow if both are busy working while these deep conversations are going on, it eases the tension and makes the whole thing more comfortable."

Stephen just nodded.

"I've had several of these," Angie confessed. "Probably will get another one before I leave for seminary."

"Wow," Stephen said in admiration. "I think it's great. I wish someone had given me a few 'heart-to-hearts' over the years."

Annie cringed. She alone knew Stephen's past, and she knew he had probably longed for advice with all the decisions he had been required to make on his own.

"My dad doesn't think too highly of me," Stephen acknowledged to Angie and Barbara.

"My," Barbara said softly, "I'm so sorry. I can't imagine why."

"Me either," Stephen agreed. "He just never cared much for me, especially when it came to music."

"What about your mother?" Barbara asked.

"She was wonderful," Stephen said quickly, his eyes twinkling again. "She was the biggest support any one could ever have. She died when I was 15."

"Oh, Stephen," Barbara said as she put her hand on his shoulder, "how horrible for you. You have done well for yourself to be alone."

"Was your mom a musician?" Angie asked him. "Did she play the piano as well?"

"Hmmm," Stephen began, as he looked slightly confused, "she read music wonderfully, so I know she had been trained somehow. But she was handicapped."

Annie looked up now. This was new information.

"Her hands were gnarled," he told them. "They were knotted and twisted. I suppose she loved music, but just couldn't play anything. She had a pretty voice and sang in the choir at church, but she struggled to do anything with her hands."

"No wonder she encouraged you so much," Barbara said smiling. "You were her hands."

Stephen smiled and nodded. He remembered how she would always sit and listen to him practice, even if it were nothing more than running scales up and down the keyboard. Sometimes she would even cry. When a piece would be too difficult, she would always tell him nothing was too hard for him because his fingers were perfect. He would always continue, feeling ashamed for even complaining.

"Oh, my gosh!" Annie yelled suddenly.

"What?" asked Barbara, totally shocked by the outburst.

Annie ran to the radio that sat on a table at the back of the porch. It generally stayed on all the time with gentle music playing in the background. Annie turned up the volume and told everyone to be quiet.

When the commercial finished, she turned to everyone, face red in anger and announced, "That was *my* music!"

Everyone just stared at her, not understanding her reaction.

"Bravo," Angie finally said. "A new one, I suppose?"

"You don't understand!" Annie continued to rant. "That is *not* my commercial! I did not write that advertisement, but I guarantee you I wrote that music!"

"Honey, are you sure? You do so many," Barbara said calmingly.

"Mother, I know every commercial I've written!" Annie seethed. "I could sing them to you by heart. I did not write that; I have never written anything for Carl Couples, CPA! I would know!"

"Maybe it's just a variation of something you wrote, not exactly it," Stephen joined in.

"I know what I wrote," Annie chided. "I've tried to use that tune several times, but it never fit anything. I keep it filed away in an *Unused Songs* file. I pull them out when I get a new account and need some direction. Sometimes I'll be riding in the car and a tune will come into my head. I write them all out so I can pull from them later."

"Resourceful, aren't you?" Stephen commented.

"Yes," Annie said with a little scorn in her response. "I can guarantee you that's my song."

"Is it copyrighted?" Stephen wondered.

Annie rolled her eyes and shut the radio off.

"No," she regretted. "I don't bother trying to protect something unfinished."

"Neither do I," Stephen told her. "Who has access to that file?"

"Nobody," she said, still fuming. "I have the only keys. You'd have to get into my office, which remains locked, and then into my filing cabinet, which also remains locked."

"Your secretary?" Stephen asked. "She was awfully jumpy the other day."

Annie shook her head and said, "Not even she has a key. No one does. I'm it."

"Well, if what you're claiming is true," Angie began to allege, "then somebody else obviously has a key to your office and your file."

Annie, Angie, and Stephen left for Annie's office to check for some kind of clue. Annie unlocked the outside door, the office door, and then her studio door. Everything was as she left it. She unlocked her filing cabinet and pulled out her *Unused Tunes* file. It was thick.

"Good heavens," Angie exclaimed, "that thing's huge."

"Sure is," Stephen agreed. "How prolific are you?"

Annie ignored them and began to thumb through the file until she found the piece she was looking for. She removed it from the folder and sat down at the piano. She didn't play; she simply stared at it.

"Is that it?" Angie asked her.

Annie turned on the piano and pecked out the tune with her right hand.

"That's it," Stephen recognized immediately. "No question."

"What is going on?" Annie wondered aloud. "How could any one get into this file? How could any one even know it was here?"

"*Why* would anyone do it?" Angie added.

"That's easy," Stephen said.

Both girls looked up at him.

"She's got the market cornered," he clarified. "Nobody does what she does in this little area. She can name her price and nobody can complain. It's lucrative and it's unique. So someone else decides they want in on this, wants to make the market a little competitive, but doesn't quite know where to start. They manage to get into your studio here, start rummaging a little bit, and find a hidden gold mine—your file."

"I doubt that," Annie disagreed. "Who else in Dockrey would want to write commercial jingles?"

"Maybe they're not from Dockrey?" Stephen suggested. "There are tons of these little small towns dotted all around here."

"Because it doesn't make sense," Annie continued. "In this area, if someone wanted to start another business like this, they're more likely to pay me a visit and say, 'I'd like to do this too. How do I get started?' Southern hospitality still runs deep."

"Then what's another option?" Angie asked her. "Why steal your music?"

"That's what I wonder," Annie sighed. "Whoever did it is doing more than just looking into the commercial market. Somebody wants me to know they've got my music."

"Do you have any enemies?" Stephen questioned.

Angie snickered. Annie gave her a harsh look.

"Well, you *do* have enemies," Angie said point-blank.

"I know," Annie acknowledged.

Annie and Angie prepared a simple lunch for the family—potato soup with ham sandwiches. Stephen enjoyed the idea of family life. It had been a long time since he had been exposed to a normal American family, especially for an extended period. He enjoyed all the dynamics that were expressed. There was a lot of teasing and a bit of sarcasm, but the undercurrent was always love and unconditional acceptance. Alex was not there, so the tension that seemed to accompany him was also absent. Stephen was going to miss this when he left. He almost found himself fighting depression as he considered it.

"Do you write any music about the Lord, Stephen?" Jonathan asked him as he changed the direction of conversation.

"Yes, I do," Stephen told him, slightly stunned by the sudden inclusion in the family conversation. "I've put a Christian song on each of my last five albums."

"Why don't you do a whole album like that?" Jonathan questioned.

"I can't,' Stephen sighed. "I was 20 years old when I entered a contest for Rhythm Records. They were a new company and looking for new talent. I won. They wanted me to sign a contract for 15 years. They said they had to own me if they were going to promote me."

"That's not fair," Angie protested.

"I was 20," Stephen continued. "I had nothing and no one. There was no one to turn to and ask for suggestions. It never occurred to me to talk with a lawyer. They handed me a check for $5000 and said more would come, but I had to do everything they told me to do. I didn't care!"

"So, you're in a 15-year contract?" Jonathan asked.

"Actually, 14," Stephen smiled. "My mother was big about numbers, and she always did everything in sevens because she said seven was the perfect number. To honor her, I asked for 14 years. They didn't know why, but they figured it was no big deal."

"And they won't allow a Christian album?" Jonathan continued probing.

"They won't even allow me to do an instrumental album," Stephen lamented. "I've begged them to let me do one album that's pure music, no singing. They said it wouldn't sell."

"What about *The Piano Album?*" Jonathan queried.

Annie's face contorted at her father's question.

"What do you know about *The Piano Album?*" she asked him quickly.

"I have ears," her father said as he looked toward her. "I know an awful lot about Stephen and his music. We went through your reviews of every album and every song at the dinner table. When something means so much to my kids, I make it my habit to look into it."

Everyone, except Barbara, stared in disbelief.

"What?" Jonathan asked defensively. "Did you think I let you do whatever you wanted? Listen to whatever you wanted?"

"I never thought about it," Annie admitted. "You've listened to my Stephen Williams albums?"

"Yes," Jonathan disclosed, "and they're all quite good."

"Thank you, sir," Stephen said slightly stunned.

"Can't you do an album with another label? Just one?" Jonathan continued the questioning.

"No way," Stephen said shaking his head. "Breach of contract. They could literally sue me for millions of dollars."

"How many years left on your contract?" Jonathan asked.

"Three," Stephen sighed.

Everyone was quiet as Jonathan appeared to be mulling over the information. Stephen glanced over at Annie and gave her a quizzical look. She just smiled and gently shrugged her shoulders.

"Are you accountable to anybody, Stephen?" Jonathan finally asked.

"No sir," he answered honestly. "I just play life as it comes."

"Everyone needs to be mentored in some ways," Jonathan said soberly. "You don't go to church, but you claim Christ as your Lord."

"I know. I'm not comfortable with that, but I don't know how to remedy it."

"How many people do you pay salaries to?" Jonathan asked.

"Oh, jeeze, I don't know exactly. Probably close to 50," Stephen estimated.

"Why?" Jonathan probed.

"I guess because I need them to carry out all the responsibilities that go along with what I do."

Jonathan nodded, and you could tell by his expression that his was thinking hard about all of this. Annie was beginning to grow uncomfortable with the conversation. She felt her father was prying too much into Stephen's personal life. Stephen, however, seemed intent on whatever the man had to say.

"You hire your staff because you feel there are priorities in your life that need to be handled, that not having extra hands would neglect some needful things. Is that right?" Jonathan asked Stephen.

"Right," Stephen agreed.

"But you do not consider your spiritual life, your needs to be discipled and taught as high priority," Jonathan said more as a statement rather than a question.

Annie could feel her face flushing. Her father had stepped over the line.

"Well, I want them to be," Stephen said earnestly, "but I don't know how to go about it. Do you suggest I hire someone to travel with me and teach me how to grow in Christ?"

Jonathan's expression was one of uncertainty.

"I don't know. All I'm saying is that you hire people to take care of those priorities that you place value on. However, you claim to place value on your spiritual convictions, but you don't place them at a high enough priority to actually ensure that anything is done about them."

"Daddy!" Annie finally called out. "I think that's enough!"

Everyone turned to look at Annie this time.

"I mean, come on," she pleaded. "I think you've made your point."

"Have I?" Jonathan asked as he looked back to Stephen.

Stephen smiled and nodded.

"Yes, sir," he replied, "and you're right. I've been totally on my own with this. I will give this some thought and try to come up with some kind of solution."

"Good boy," Jonathan said as he pushed his chair back and stood up. "I'd like to know your plan before you leave."

"Daddy!" Annie exclaimed again.

"Annie," her father said firmly, "let's go cut some wood."

Annie set up a heavy round log of red oak onto the hard ground. Her father lifted the axe above his head and came down on the center of the log. It cracked. He lifted the axe again, and this time when it fell, the log split into three pieces. Although she was still in a foul mood for being "brought to the woodshed," the strong, familiar smell of the red oak gave her a sense of comfort and belonging. Annie collected the wood, placed it onto the woodpile, and set up another log.

"You want to tell me why we're doing this?" Annie finally asked him.

Jonathan placed the axe head on the ground and leaned against the handle as he looked at her.

"I've raised you for 26 years, Annie," he said seriously. "I know you better than you probably know yourself. You might find that hard to believe, but I do."

"What does this have to do with Stephen?" she asked him, still perturbed with his hounding questions.

"I know you won't admit this to me, or your mother, and probably not even Angie, although I know you two are close and that might be a fifty-fifty call," he said cautiously, "but you are quite taken with Stephen."

"Daddy!" she protested. "He's like my . . . my teen idol! Of course, I'm taken with him! It would be like Marilyn Monroe to you! I mean, if she spent a week at our house, you would probably walk around a little star struck yourself!"

"You know it's more than that," he insisted as he lifted the axe again, "and I know he returns your feelings. I see how he looks at you. I can tell he admires you."

"It's not like that," Annie tried tell him, although she knew what Stephen had said and knew that Stephen had claimed to want something more.

"Annie, don't kid me, but more importantly, don't kid yourself. I want to make it clear to anyone who has designs on my daughters: they need to be men of God who know Him and walk with Him. I think Stephen has a good heart and wants to do the right thing, but he is in a business that will tempt him in every possible way. Before he can ever be anything to you, he needs to settle some things with God."

"He's not going to be *anything* to me," Annie said resolutely. "I've already decided against that."

Jonathan put the axe back down and smiled in exasperation as he looked over at Annie.

"You can control a lot of things, Annie dear, but the heart is beyond anyone's control. Especially when it's your own."

"I'm not . . ." she searched for the words, "I'm . . . not . . ."

"Falling in love with him?" Jonathan volunteered.

"No!" she nearly yelled. "I am not doing *that!*"

"I fear the lady protesteth too much," he finally stated. He then grinned slightly as he added, "And by the way, Marilyn Monroe was slightly *before* my time. I'm not *that* old."

The rehearsal was turning out to be much as Barbara had feared. Megan had definite ideas about what she wanted, but the wedding director, Mrs. Rhiner, was struggling with how to *translate* the unique ideas to everyone else.

"Okay," Mrs. Rhiner clapped her hands several times, "let's have the bridesmaids line up and practice coming down the aisle."

"Oh, no," Megan said quickly. "They don't come down alone. They're escorted by the groomsmen."

"They walk down together?" Mrs. Rhiner asked her. Megan nodded. Mrs. Rhiner scribbled out something on her note pad and added something else.

"Okay then," she continued, "let's line everyone up at the back and start coming in."

Annie was lined up with Megan's cousin, Nick, from Florida. She had worn the heels Megan had insisted went *perfectly* with the bridesmaids' dresses. The only problem: Annie was not naturally graceful in heels. She hoped practicing in them during the rehearsal would make for a perfect promenade down the aisle. Annie was a good two inches taller than Nick to begin with, and then the extra two-inch heels made them look ridiculous.

"You're very tall," Nick said looking up at her. "Are you a model?"

"It's the heels," Annie tried to convince him.

Angie, who was standing in front of them, began to shake with laughter. Annie thumped her head.

"Stop it," Annie insisted. "You're almost taller than George."

Angie turned around and grinned saying, "Almost, but not quite."

Angie and George walked down the aisle and took their place. Megan did not want the bridesmaids nor groomsmen separated so they stood with the gentlemen behind the ladies, arms on their waists, alternating the couples as they came in, one couple to the groom's side, the next to the bride's side.

Annie and Nick were next. She could see Angie still giggling in the front of the church. Annie knew her face was red from embarrassment or from anger at Angie. They continued up the aisle and took their place on the groom's side opposite Angie and George, next to Stephen and Kendra, the bridesmaid with the huge contraption on her leg.

Next came Andie and Doug, the maid of honor and best man.

Perfect couple, Annie thought.

They smiled happily as they gently glided down the aisle. They stood next to Angie and George on the bride's side. When Doug got behind Andie and managed his hands on her waist, he began to nuzzle her neck. Angie slapped him and told him to behave. He responded with a look of innocence. Andie only grinned.

Next came Megan on her Uncle Bob's arm. She beamed as she walked down the aisle, eyes on Alex alone. Then she began to look at all the attendants, one couple then another. Suddenly she stopped and yelled for the music to halt.

"What's wrong now?" Mrs. Rhiner asked, running up to Megan mid-aisle.

"That looks horrible?" Megan exclaimed.

"I thought it looked darling," Mrs. Rhiner said in confusion. "The couples look so sweet standing together."

"Most of them do," Megan startled to laugh, "but look at Annie and Nick!"

Everyone looked over, and slowly laughter began to rise amidst the entire group. Annie felt her whole body go warm now. She smiled at the attention, but inside she was seething. She looked over at Stephen and found the only sympathetic look in the whole church. Saying nothing, Stephen removed his hands from Kendra's waist, stepped over to Nick and moved him behind Kendra. He placed Nick's hands on Kendra's waist then stood behind Annie, gently wrapping his arms all the way around her. The church burst into applause.

"Much better," Megan sighed loudly. "You can start the music up again."

The music started and Megan continued down the aisle. Angie, however, gave Annie the most unusual look. Annie looked back in wonder, trying to interpret her expression. Angie just continued with her *look,* and then began to shake her head slightly.

"What?" Annie mouthed.

Stephen, who whispered in her ear, "Do I get points for chivalry on that one?" interrupted her communication.

Annie looked back at him and said, "Big points. Thank you for being 6 feet 2."

"Actually," he whispered again, "I'm only 6 feet 1¾."

"That's not what the magazines say," she informed him.

"Well, by the time I put on shoes, I'm easily the full 6 feet 2. How tall are you?"

"I think about 9 feet," she half-teased. She felt that way right now.

Jonathan looked over at Annie and Stephen and cleared his throat. Annie immediately turned around and mumbled an apology. Angie, however, was still giving her *the look.* Annie cocked her head to communicate her confusion. Angie shook her head again. Stephen, however, gently began to caress her waist with his hands. Annie was blushing again. Angie continued to shake her head.

As the ceremony rehearsal continued, it came time for the song. Jonathan mentioned that Annie would step out to the piano and begin singing as the lighting of the unity candle began.

"Stephen's singing with me," she said timidly.

"He is?" Alex blurted out. "Since when?"

"I don't have to," Stephen quickly added. "We just thought it would be a good idea."

"I'm not complaining," Alex tried to amend, "I just didn't know."

"That's incredible!" Megan exclaimed. "Stephen Williams is singing at my wedding!"

"No," Alex said as his jaw began to twitch. "Stephen is singing with Annie. Imagine that."

"I didn't realize this was a problem," Stephen said soberly as the crowd quieted in the tension. "Annie can sing the song herself."

"Only my sister would have the nerve to suggest a duet with Stephen Williams on a song he himself composed and recorded," Alex continued.

"Actually," Stephen said firmly as he stepped from behind Annie and looked Alex squarely in the eye, "she suggested I do it alone. I'm the one who insisted we do it together. I felt it would be inappropriate for me to sing seeing that I have very little connection with the two of you, whereas Annie has spent a lifetime with you."

Alex's face was red. Annie was not sure if it were anger or humiliation. All she knew was that at some point in time she would hear from Alex concerning this. She closed her eyes at the thought.

"Alex," Megan said as she took his hand, "I think it's a wonderful gesture. It will be beautiful."

"Of course," Alex conceded. "I was just surprised, that's all."

As the wedding group and everyone else who had been invited made their way to the fellowship hall for the dinner, Angie grabbed Annie by the arm and drug her outside and around the corner of the church.

"What is your problem?" Annie wanted to know.

"Why didn't you tell me?" Angie said in frustration. "Did you think I wouldn't know?"

"I don't have the slightest idea what you're talking about!" Annie said totally disturbed.

"What is going on between you and Stephen? I'm standing over there watching what I assumed to be a friendly exchange, when suddenly the lights came on!"

"You are out of line," Annie said firmly.

"Oh really?" Angie said with disgust. "Well, now I know why Daddy took you to the woodshed."

"What is it with this family?" Annie cried out. "There is nothing between Stephen and me! How do I convince you all of that?"

"Start by convincing yourself," Angie said emphatically. "You can't tell me that you don't feel anything for him. I know you! I stood there tonight and saw something in you that I've never seen before, and you won't even own up to it."

Annie threw her hands in the air and suppressed a scream.

"Of course I feel *something,*" Annie blurted out. "Who doesn't? Stephen Williams, a legend, yes, a good-looking one, has been in my home for an entire week! Yes, I'm awed! I'm impressed! I'm overcome! But I am *not* whatever it is everyone is accusing me of!"

"In love?" Angie asked blankly.

"You can't tell me his being here hasn't affected you," Annie insisted. "You listen to his music too."

"I *can* tell you that his being here has *not* affected me. Not in the least. Nice guy, glad to meet him, that's it."

"Well, why should he affect you?" Annie reasoned away with the wave of her hand. "You're headed to the mission field! He wouldn't follow you out there anyway!"

"He doesn't affect me," Angie said slowly and deliberately, "because I don't have feelings for him, mission field or not."

Annie gritted her teeth and moved right into to Angie's face as she insisted, "And neither do I."

Angie stepped away and shook her head in disbelief.

"You've always told me everything," she said sadly. "I never thought the day would come when you would shut me out like this. I know what I saw. I don't know what Stephen feels for you, but your feelings are written all over your face. And as far as your decision about the tour is concerned, if I were you, I wouldn't worry about sorting through Alex's feelings; I think he's pretty clear. You need to sort out your own, *little* sister."

Angie rushed toward the building, leaving Annie alone and still fuming. Annie wanted to just leave, go back to the house, and avoid anybody's company for the rest of the night, well, maybe the rest her life. Megan came running out, however, flagging her down.

"Annie! Annie!" she called.

Megan caught up with her and hugged her tightly.

"I can't thank you enough!" Megan said out of breath. "I can't wait to hear the duet! That's the best wedding gift you could give me! How sweet! And I'm sorry about you and Nick. I forgot how tall you were when I put you two together in my mind. I need to thank Stephen for the old *switcheroo* he pulled in there. That was a life saver."

Megan linked her arm in Annie's and started pulling her toward the fellowship hall.

"I'm gonna miss you so much, Annie," she said tearfully. "It's like you've become my best friend these past months."

Annie resigned herself to going on to dinner. She leaned her head down on top of Megan's and smiled. She would miss Megan too, unless she joined the tour. However, she seriously began to doubt if she would even go. She grimaced at the thought of turning down such an opportunity. She was still far from a decision.

As the dinner began, laughter and talking ensued. Annie found herself avoiding everyone's eyes. She did not want to see Alex, and she did not enjoy the looks of hurt that Angie continued to give. She tried not to look at her father, and then realized her mother had to know everything her father knew. And most of all, she did not want to make any contact with Stephen. If everyone but she seemed to think her feelings were so obvious, no wonder Stephen had been so forward with her. He wasn't initiating anything on his own; he was merely responding to something he had already seen.

Please, don't let him be using all of this to get something out of me that I'm not willing to give. God, give me wisdom.

Annie excused herself and walked outside to the small deck behind the fellowship hall her father had built to overlook the wooded valley and stream below. The sudden peace and quiet did not help the unsettling in her heart. The thing that hurt her most is that Angie somehow felt Annie had deliberately deceived her. She would never do that.

Angie was closer to her than any other person on earth.

Annie leaned her arms against the railing and shook her hair behind her as though she could shake the dooming thoughts from her head.

I don't love him. I am infatuated with who he is and who he has always been to me. Of course I shudder when he touches me. Of course I melt when he looks at me. How could I not? Every time I've listened to him sing, it's always been to me, at least in my mind. That was fantasy. So is this. How do I make this decision clear-headed? God, you have to show me what to do here! Moms said people don't just fall into Your will by accident. This is no accident! Stephen Williams? For heaven's sake, what do I do? Couldn't you maybe give me some kind of sign?

"Please tell me I am not the cause of all this doom and gloom you're parading around," came Stephen's voice from behind.

Annie swung around quickly, hoping she had been thinking all those thoughts inside her head and not speaking them aloud.

"Actually, you are," she confessed, turning back to face the valley.

He came up beside her and leaned his hand on the railing.

"Can I help?" he asked. "I rather like the spirited Annie as opposed to the defeated one."

Annie dropped her head between her shoulders and sighed. "Count your blessings," she mumbled.

Stephen reached over and stroked her hair. She melted, again.

"I count finding you as a blessing," he said softly.

Annie jerked up and moved away from him. She could not think clearly when he was near. Why did he have to follow her out?

"You have to stop doing this to me," she somehow choked out. "I can't take all that's happening right now and make a clear decision."

"About the tour?" he asked. Annie could only nod. "I meant what I said," he assured her. "If you want the tour, but you don't want me, I would never force you to do that."

He walked over to her and made her look him in the face.

"Annie, I care for you," he said sincerely, "and I would never overstep anything. I want to see you *fulfill* your dreams, and I know I can bring that about. But if your dreams don't include me, I won't insist on that. I'm not that kind of man."

Annie reached up and ran her fingers through the top of her hair. She closed her eyes, trying to shut him out. He wouldn't let her. He took her hands again and leaned in.

"I mean that," he said tenderly. "I want you on this tour, first and foremost, to show yourself to the world. *That* is my ulterior motive. I would love it to be more, but that will never be an issue if you choose it not to be."

Annie had become too familiar with his being near her. His hands, his breath, his eyes. She might as well throw her hands up in surrender when he was this close. The breeze blew behind her, tossing her hair toward him, and she knew he was breathing in the honey shampoo. She let a small smile work through the side of her mouth. He touched his forehead to hers and held her gently.

"You didn't use *Head and Shoulders,* did you?" he whispered. She slightly shook her head. "Thank-you," he said as he wrapped his arms around her.

She laid her head on his shoulder and put her arms around his waist. This was not getting easier. She had until tomorrow to deliver a verdict, and she was no closer to knowing what she would do than last night.

"Interrupting anything?" came Angie's voice from the edge of the deck.

Annie jerked her head up as Stephen turned around, still holding Annie, though somewhat loosely now.

"I missed you guys," she said smiling as she came over to them. "I supposed I might find you together. They've brought out the banana pudding, and I knew that was Annie's favorite."

Annie detached herself from Stephen and straightened her blown hair. Stephen, however, took Annie's hand and suggested they go eat; he loved banana pudding also.

"Go on in," Annie told him. "Angie and I will join you in a minute."

"Suit yourself," he smiled, "but I should warn you, I can eat as much banana pudding as I can fried chicken."

He left the sisters alone on the deck.

"It's not what you think," Annie tried to defend. "Nothing was going on."

Angie nodded slightly and walked over to the edge of the deck. Annie followed, knowing Angie still did not believe her.

"I swear," Annie added.

"Then you are stupid," Angie said as she looked at her, shaking her head.

"Why are you doing this?" Annie asked in frustration. "Why don't you believe me?"

"Because I'm not blind. Explain what I just saw."

Annie turned to face the wind coming across the valley. She never wanted to be at odds with Angie. She had no answer.

"I can't explain it," she finally responded.

"Too bad, because if you could, you could end the whole thing with *happily ever after.* The end."

Chapter Eleven

Annie did not want to get out of bed. She stopped looking at the clock because she did not want to know how late it was getting. She heard milling around downstairs, but all she wanted to do was avoid everyone presently staying in the house for the rest of the day. Now laughter was sounding along with the clanking of plates, and she knew that the breakfast dishes were being loaded into the dishwasher. She tried to imagine some way to escape her room and leave with no one finding out. She had done it as a teenager; Angie had joined her, but that really seemed too juvenile at this age in her life.

She managed to force herself up, but she still would not get out of bed. It was D-Day, decision day, and she was more confused now than when she had awakened yesterday. She reached to her nightstand and picked up the CD cover of Stephen's last album. She leaned back in her bed and looked over the songs. Several of them brought a smile to her face as she recalled the melodies or the lyrics. She felt a twinge of excitement at the thought of a brand new album coming out by the end of the summer.

She finally put the CD case down and forced herself to get up from the bed. She pulled on her scrubs and sat down at her piano. After opening the piano's cover and turning it on, she leaned on the top with her head in her left hand and her right hand picking out a melody on the keyboard. It was *Autumn Sunset.*

Unreal. Even when I am not thinking about him, I still play his music. If everyone could understand that I adore him as Stephen Williams the musician, not Stephen Williams the man, they would leave me alone. Yes, I think he's wonderful, but I thought that long before he ever stepped into this house. I feel about him like any other girl that was raised on his music; I love him for what he is, not who he is.

Annie slammed her hand on the keyboard in frustration.

I cannot allow myself to drop into this fantasy! I will end up hurt, broken, and weary from trying to make myself believe something that is unbelievable. I can't do this! I can't. I can't.

"Knock, knock?" came Angie's voice outside her door. "May I come in?"

Annie heaved a deep sigh and seriously considered telling her *no*. However, she couldn't bring herself to follow through just for sheer meanness, so she said nothing. Predictably, Angie opened the door and peeked in.

"Lovely song," Angie grinned referring to the bang. "Something new you're working on?"

Annie wouldn't play the game. Angie had accused her of too much last night, and Annie was not ready to put it all behind her.

Angie came inside the room and closed the door. She looked at Annie with a slightly sheepish expression and put her hands up in surrender.

"Okay, I give up," she said softly. "I was out of line last night."

Annie would not respond, not even to look at her. She turned off the keyboard, closed the top, and stared toward her gabled window.

"Annie, you've got to forgive me," Angie said lightly, trying to tease her. "We're sisters, the closest that any two people can be. We always have been. Let's talk this out, clear the air, and then enjoy another week together, alone, with no extra men hanging around the house. What do you say?"

Annie nodded, but wouldn't smile. She was still intensely troubled by all that was hanging over her. The fact that her family had projected feelings about her toward Stephen only complicated the process. With everything inside of her, she wanted to take this chance and do the tour. When Alex was the only obstacle, the decision was hard. With these unrealistic expectations that she was being swept off her feet in a fairy tale romance, the decision was impossible. Should she set everyone down, including Stephen, and lay out the guidelines? Or should she just forget everything? She could just stay in Dockrey for the rest of her life and bemoan the fact that she threw away her biggest chance to do something great with her abilities.

"It's not a hard thing to do," Angie said as she came to the piano and set next to her sister. "You just say, 'I forgive you,' and we start all over again. We've done it many times."

Annie laid her head on Angie's shoulder and finally said, "You know I forgive you, but it's not you alone."

"I've seen you in every situation imaginable," Angie began explaining. "I've seen you relishing in winning, and I've seen you suffering in failure. I've seen you happy at life and miserable with luck. I've seen you soar in the heights and drown in the depths. The one thing I had never seen was you in love. It really looked like that last night. I was only hurt because you didn't tell me."

Annie started to chastise her again, but Angie stopped her by admitting, "However, I realize that I misinterpreted the whole thing. Okay? Peace?"

"I wish I could somehow explain this to everyone," Annie said as she stood up from the piano and went over to her gabled window. "It's not that the idea of falling in love with Stephen is so unpleasant. It would be wonderful! But the reality is: he is the man of my *dreams,* and one day I would wake up or he would wake up and one of us, or both of us, would realize that I simply *adored* him, not *loved* him."

"My gosh, Annie!" Angie exclaimed. "You are *so* unbelievable!"

"I am not unbelievable," Annie countered. "I am realistic."

"Do you not remember what Daddy used to say to us all the time about reality?"

Annie nodded. Of course she remembered. "You make your own reality," Annie repeated in a mumble.

"Yes!" Angie bellowed. "How do you think I made it through everything I've done? My reality was to be a medical missionary. Do you know how many times I've been told I'm stupid for doing that? Stupid for spending all that time and money on school so I can go somewhere and practice medicine for pennies a day? It didn't matter! My reality was not taking money for offering healing; my reality was giving healing and the Gospel to those who had neither."

"Yes, I agree, you're very admirable," Annie smarted off, "but this is *not* the same thing."

"I'm not looking for your admiration," Angie said with hurt as she got up and headed toward the door. "I'm just trying to help you see beyond that ignorant shell you've managed to concoct."

"Wait, wait, wait," Annie said going after her. "I'm sorry. I don't want to do this again. I just need you to know that this is not what you're wanting to believe it is."

"Whatever," Angie sighed out. "But for the record, there's no way you can hide in this room all day."

Annie smiled. Angie knew her inside out.

"I'll get dressed and see if I can just remain invisible or something."

When Annie made it down the stairs, only Angie was in sight. She was sitting on the couch in the great room watching television. As soon as Annie entered the kitchen, she noticed the coffee pot was on with enough coffee in it for one more cup. She breathed a thankful sigh and retrieved a mug from the cabinet. As she reached for the creamer, the ceramic container was accidentally knocked to the floor and shattered into pieces.

"You okay?" Angie yelled from the other room.

"Fine!" Annie shouted back. "The creamer, however, has bit the dust!"

"Need any help?" Angie wanted to know.

"I've got it!"

Annie grabbed the broom and began to sweep up the mess. As usual, she began to hum as she swept, not paying attention to the melody. When she turned around, Stephen was standing next to the refrigerator, having gotten the dustpan. He knelt down and waited for her to sweep the remnants into the pan.

"This is sort of where we started, isn't it?" he asked her as he moved the dustpan back so she could finish the job.

"Yeah," Annie said softly. "Apparently this is becoming a bad habit of mine."

"You must really like *Autumn Sunset,*" Stephen commented as he emptied the trash. "You were humming it again."

"Another habit, I guess," Annie muttered.

"Are you humming my version or yours?" Stephen wondered.

Annie thought on that for a moment. Who was she hearing when she was humming that melody?

"I actually think it was mine," she said as she turned back around.

Stephen nodded in slight defeat and said, "And I believe that is what everyone else will be humming when they hear you sing it on tour."

Annie rolled her eyes and took a swig of her coffee.

"I am *not* singing *Autumn Sunset* on tour with you," she said determinedly. "Don't even consider it."

"You don't understand the response you will get," he clarified. "They've heard it my way a million times. When the music starts, you'll be all by yourself, of course—just you and your piano. Immediately the crowd will start cheering; they always anticipate this song in the concerts. Then the light focuses on you. Everyone gets quiet as you start singing. They're wondering what's going on. You get through the verse and the first chorus starts. Another light pops on me, singing with you. You know what happens next?"

"They start throwing vegetables?" Annie suggested derisively.

"No," he whispered. "They start screaming. It's never been done before. I've never done a duet with a girl and never done a duet on one of my own songs. The audience will then hush, overcome by your voice, the uniqueness of the situation, and will listen in anticipation for what comes next. We end with your deceptive cadence, and you go on to the next verse, only you step away from the piano. We'll digitalize the remainder of the performance. You step front and center stage. On the next chorus, I join you front and center and we sing to each *other* this time. They will scream so loudly that it will be hard to hear ourselves. Then comes the bridge. We sing to the audience as though each of us were in torment, '*Nobody warned me, nobody said, there's more to living than just success.*' We go on until the last line, when we look at each other, hold hands and softly sing, '*Nobody told me about the sunrise. Nobody told me, nobody tried.*' Then total silence, no instruments, nothing. We close our eyes, give a silent count of seven, then belt out in a new key, '*So while I'm waiting for someone to love me, someone who knows me through and through.*' "

Annie was slightly overcome by the description. By the time he had finished, she had seen it as clearly as though it had actually happened.

"You've put some thought into this," she said slowly.

"This is going to be the most awesome tour ever," he was convinced. "By the time that first concert is over in New York City, your name will be plastered over every entertainment network available. People will be wondering who you are and where you came from. When we leave that night for the airport, you will be dodging reporters *and* fans."

"Fans?" she said incredulously. "I don't have fans."

"You will," he said with certainty. "I've got some more ideas too."

"I haven't said I'm going," she said with prudence.

"A man can dream, can't he?"

Annie just shrugged and went out to join Angie on the couch. Stephen followed and sat in the faded leather recliner next to them.

Angie was flipping channels as most stations were airing commercials between shows.

"Stop!" Annie yelled suddenly. "Go back!"

Angie recovered from the starling yell and turned to the previous channel.

"One more!" Annie shouted as she moved up to the television screen.

Angie turned back one more channel.

"That's it!" Annie cried as she knelt down in front of the TV. "I don't believe it!"

"What is wrong with you?" Angie said in irritation.

"Shut up!" Annie yelled back.

Angie and Stephen looked at each other in total bewilderment. They shrugged and turned their attention back to Annie whose face was now clearly red with anger. When the commercial finished, Annie shut off the television and folded her arms.

"That was my song, again, but *not* my commercial," she said barely controlled.

"Same song?" Angie asked.

"No," Annie said fuming. "Another song. Another song from my unused song file. Somebody is ripping off my music, and I don't even know where to start looking for them!"

"I still say you start with your secretary," Stephen suggested.

"My secretary is an idiot!" Annie said adamantly. "I have the only keys to my office and my file cabinet. For her to have gotten copies of them somehow would be totally impossible! First, she would have to get my keys without my knowing it. Next, she would somehow have to make copies of them and then return them to wherever she picked them up, all this taking place with me never missing them. That can't happen!"

"It *could* happen," Stephen kept insisting. "In fact, what you are accusing *someone* of doing means that *someone* did exactly that. Those songs didn't magically appear in someone else's studio. Someone was handed your music because *someone* got into your office and your filing cabinet. So you need to take the word *impossible* out of this equation and start eliminating your suspects down to *possibles*."

Annie plopped down on the couch next to Angie with her arms folded in despair. Who would do this to her? But more dumfounding, how could someone do this to her?

"I really had a special request of you ladies today," Stephen said hesitantly, "but I'm beginning to think maybe I ought to just forget it."

Annie and Angie both looked over to him.

"Spit it out," Angie said with a curious look.

Annie nodded. A request? This may be more interesting than her stolen music.

"Well, this is my last full day here," he said sadly. "I really wanted to do that ride to the overlook like we did last Saturday. I've never done anything like that in my entire life, and I just wanted that experience again."

Angie smiled and said, "We got you hooked, didn't we?"

Annie, however, immediately began with demands. "You're riding by yourself this time. I am not driving you around on that four-wheeler. I am riding my 200. Angie will drive you this time if you insist on being chauffeured again."

"Oh, no, Angie won't," Angie said as she shook her finger toward Annie, "because Angie's not going."

"Please," Stephen pleaded. "This has been a week to remember, and another ride today, it can be very short, would absolutely cap it off."

"It's not a matter of *want,*" Angie explained. "I'm having my hair trimmed at 11:00 this morning. A decent ride cannot be worked within the time frame. Annie will take you, I'm sure."

Stephen looked to Annie with his blue eyes pleading and said, "I'll ride that thing by myself if you insist, but I'll admit to being scared to death of it."

Annie dropped her head to the back of the couch and confessed, "Stephen, a ride today would be so unrelaxing. We have a wedding tonight. Showers, hair, dresses, heels, not to mention needing to go over our song again."

Stephen nodded in defeat, but Angie simply gave Annie a look that basically said, *You selfish, unthinking pig.* Annie nodded and rolled her eyes. At least she could send the city boy off with a bang.

"Okay," Annie agreed in vexation, "but this can't be a marathon."

"Yea!" Stephen yelled in delight. "Can we picnic too?"

"Of course you can," Angie said joining him with the delight. "I'll even pack your lunches while you both go change."

"Yes!" he yelled out again. "Yes, yes!" He pumped one fist into the air. "I'll be back down in five minutes."

He ran toward the stairs then stopped abruptly and turned back to the girls.

"Do I really have to drive it myself?" he asked timidly.

Annie stared at him for a moment still trying to collect her thoughts from the whirlwind decision.

"No," she finally gave in. "I'll ride you on the four-wheeler."

"All right!" he shouted as he headed up the stairs, and then added, "I won't even complain if it rains!"

When his door slammed, Annie turned to Angie and said dryly, "Thanks. That's just what I was hoping for today: stress and being pressed for time."

"Glad to help," came the bubbly reply.

Annie and Stephen rode for about two hours through mostly mild trails. She took him up a few steep climbs and then began to show him some of the basics of riding. He actually drove for a little while on one of the easier roads through a shaded vale with only mud holes and no major hills. As they reached the trail to the overlook, Annie returned to the driver's seat and maneuvered her way along the cliff until they reached the end.

"This place is truly awesome," Stephen sighed as he pulled a sandwich Angie had made from the plastic bag. "Have you ever written a song from out here?"

"Probably," Annie commented as she sat down next to him with her own lunch. "At times like this, maybe a tune will come into my head, but I don't dwell on it too much. Since music is my work and this is my escape from work, I don't generally see this place as inspiration. It's more like recreation."

Stephen nodded in understanding as he took another bite. The breeze always seemed to be blowing lightly up here, and he enjoyed the coolness it brought to his heated head after hours inside a helmet. He observed a hawk soaring out in front of them and realized he had only seen hawks from below before. He watched it ride the different currents, seldom flapping its wings. Occasionally it would give a cry, which Stephen believed to be of delight, as it soared gracefully over the pristine valley below. It finally began to rise on a thermal, round and round, until it was totally out of sight above.

"I can't thank you enough for bringing me back out here," he told her as started on a banana.

"You're right," she mocked while laying back on the rock behind her. "You can't think me enough. I hate being pressed for time."

"You're not pressed for time," he corrected her. "It's only 12:15."

"Anything like this could have unexpected errors," she went on to explain. "Something could happen and then we could be stuck out here. That would be pressing us for time."

He looked at her perplexingly.

"Don't borrow trouble," he suggested with a furled brow. "So far, so good. Besides, don't you function just a little better under stress? Doesn't it get the adrenaline flowing?"

"No," Annie said firmly. "I do not like stress in any way, shape, or form. I avoid it. Life is stressful enough without creating added reasons to worry."

"Hmmm," he sighed with a hint of question.

"Well, what does that mean?" she asked defensively.

"I don't know you all that well, but you sure seem to add a lot of unnecessary stress to your life anyway. You're a bit of a worrier, you know," he told her.

"I am not," she was insistent. "I just like things in order; I like things to fit where they belong. I like organization."

"Yeah, you do," he laughed, "but the rest of the world could care less. So you spend your days bemoaning the fact that every one is not like you."

"I do not!" she said a little louder.

"There you go," he said in defense. "You're starting it now. Can't you just agree to disagree with anybody?"

Annie closed her eyes and shook her head. She knew he wasn't making any point; he was toying with her again and enjoying getting a reaction from her.

"Whatever," she mumbled.

"Wow," he half-whispered. "Did you just give up an argument?"

"No," she said with her eyes still closed. "I just gave up a worthless exchange of hot air."

Stephen laughed and laid back on the rock himself. Annie was fun.

"What was your mother's name?" Annie asked as she changed the subject.

"Ellen," he replied.

"What did she look like?"

"Blonde hair," he described. "It wasn't quite as curly as mine."

"Does your dad have curly hair?" she wondered.

"No, straight as a board. And mom had these big, beautiful brown eyes, just like yours. And she was very kind, but very insistent."

"What's your Dad's name?"

"Edrew."

"What?" she asked him again.

"Edrew," he grinned. "Weird name, huh? I am so thankful I wasn't named after *him!* I can guarantee he's the only Edrew Williams in the city of Chicago."

"Where did they come up with a name like that?" Annie questioned.

"Dad had an uncle who died in World War II named Edrew. He would have been my only uncle had he lived. He was Dad's father's brother."

"So what about other family? Grandparents? Aunts or cousins?"

"I know this is hard to believe, but I literally have no close living relatives other than Dad," Stephen said as he put his hand up to shield his face from the sun. "Mother had no siblings, and both of her parents died before she even met Dad. Dad's father died when he six, his mother died when he was 19, and like I said, his only uncle was killed in the war."

"I can't imagine that," Annie said sorrowfully. "My family is the biggest part of my life. I don't know how you go on with no one to lean on or to share with."

"For the most part, I stay really busy," he explained. "I mean, I've put out an album every year for the past eleven years. That's almost unheard of. I write on and off during the year, record the albums from February through April. June, July and August I don't do much of anything. I might write a little, but most of the summer is spent doing interviews and making appearances preparing for the album release in late August. I tour from September through November, then start the whole process again."

"So you like that?" she asked looking over to him.

"At first I loved it. I thrived on it. Now I pretty much endure it. Until my contract is up, I can't try anything new or different. I'd rather just keep pumping out the albums and doing the tours to bide my time."

"Gol-lee," she scowled, "you make it all sound so mundane."

"It is," he confessed. "Annie, this week with your family has been the best time I've had in years. I love your parents. They are like these caring and wise people who tenderly watch out after their kids and their community. All of you guys are adults, and they somehow manage to treat you like that while still offering wisdom and support. Andie and Doug are this perfect couple with three beautiful kids. When they swing into the house, it's like a breath of life rushing through. They laugh, they yell a little, but all the while they enrich who your family is and give the hope of a future generation. Then there's the whole dynamic between you and Angie. I have laid in bed at night laughing myself to sleep over some of the exchanges you guys have delivered this week. It's almost like you are twins in your connection. You are so much alike, yet so different in other ways that there is never a dull moment between the two of you. And of course, there is the fact they you're both incredibly beautiful, so the discussions are twice as interesting as they might normally be."

Annie reached over and slapped him playfully.

"That was a warm description of our family," she said sweetly. "Thank you. It reminds me of why I love them so much."

"I have been fighting depression the past two days because I know I am leaving all of this tomorrow. I wonder if I can bear the loneliness that awaits me back in New York," he lamented.

"You know you're welcome here any time," Annie said seriously.

Stephen sat up and nodded. He knew, but that did not mean he would ever get to come back. As much as he loved this family, it was not his family. And sometimes being reminded of what you don't have is worse than pretending to have it for a short while because when the pretending is over, the emptiness just grows larger.

Annie still thought the idea of all the bridesmaids, along with the bride, getting dressed in one tiny room at the church was a ridiculous notion. She could have dressed herself, done her own hair and makeup, all in the comfort of her own house with elbowroom to spare. Yet here she was, trying desperately to remove hot curlers while being bumped and knocked as another girl tried to slide by.

Megan was a nervous wreck. Andie, serving as matron of honor, did her best to live up to the position by calming Megan and assuring her that everything was perfect and in order. Angie was trying to help Kendra and her rather cumbersome cast get into her bridesmaid dress. It was turning out to be almost impossible, and Kendra's complaining was only adding to the circus in the room. Another cousin of Megan's, Emily, was pregnant and hot. She had been trying to curl her hair with a curling iron while looking into a compact mirror. It was not working. Annie offered to curl her hair when she finished with her own. Emily told her not to bother because her head would be wet with sweat by the time the wedding started. Occasionally, Mrs. Rhiner or Barbara or Kim would stick their heads inside the room and ask how things were coming, to which someone would always scream because they would have been knocked over from standing in front of the door.

At one point, when Angie was passing by, Annie grabbed her arm and pulled her head down to whisper in Angie's ear, "I am eloping. I swear."

"As long as I am invited," Angie replied with a smile.

"Nope," Annie shook her head. "Just me and the groom, and *no* bridesmaids."

Angie just laughed and went on to help someone else.

Alex and the groomsmen had been ready long ago. The photographer took a few shots and then left to get some photos in the bride's room. When he opened the door, screams flew out immediately. All the groomsmen looked at each other in mystification. What was taking so long? Doug gave Alex a few words of sage advice, which really amounted to more of a comic routine than anything genuinely helpful.

Stephen was trying to be happy, but he found himself slipping deeper into the depression that had already begun to plague him. He was leaving tomorrow. He would go back to his empty apartment. No more breakfasts of cheese toast with the family. No more family dinners where arguments and laughter ensued. No more rides to the overlook. No more fatherly or motherly figure to show concern about his life. But most of all, no more Annie. Even if she went on the tour, he knew it would only be to sing and play; she was not interested in anything else. His heart literally ached.

I find the girl of my dreams after years of evading everybody, and she doesn't return the feelings. How ironic is that?

"Snap out of it, Mr. Williams," Doug said sharply as he slapped Stephen on the back. "You're not the one getting the old ball and chain today!"

Stephen smiled, but did not share Doug's enthusiasm over the joke.

"Is that really what it is?" he asked Doug.

"Absolutely," Doug told him, but then quickly added, "and the best prison I've ever had the pleasure to know."

The moment had arrived. All the bridesmaids and groomsmen gathered at the back of the church as the wedding music began. Stephen found Annie immediately and tried not to let her know that she took his breath away. Her hair had been curled and pulled back on the sides with small sprigs of baby's breath pinned around in a wreath. He took her arm and immediately caught the scent of honey. Emily, still sweating and miserable, took her husband's arm and began down the aisle, wobbling slightly in all her eight-month glory. When they reached the front, Kendra and Nick started down. It was a long walk as Kendra hobbled in the huge cast.

"Stephen," Annie whispered nervously to him.

He bent down his head to hear what she had to say.

"I cannot walk in these heels," she complained. "If I trip, just hold on tight and act like nothing happened."

"I'll do my best," he assured her.

Finally, Kendra and Nick made it to the front, and then it was time for Angie and George. Angie walked down in full confidence, occasionally waving at someone she had not seen during her week home. She blew a kiss at one gentlemen sitting on the edge of the aisle who Annie quickly pointed out to Stephen as being Billy Marcum.

"Billy Marcum of the balcony?" he asked with heightened interest.

"That's the one," she replied with a mischievous grin. "And the blonde next to him is his twin sister, Cindy."

When Angie and George had reached the front, Stephen and Annie started down. Stephen actually felt nervous walking down the aisle in front of a group of total strangers with beautiful Annie on his arm.

I can perform songs on a stage in front of thousands I have never met without blinking an eye, but a wedding gives me the willies. "I'm nervous," he whispered down to Annie.

"You're kidding?" she said discreetly as she continued her smile and walk.

"No, I'm really nervous," he affirmed.

"Then be glad *you* are not in *heels,*" she said as she tightened her grip on his arm.

They stood next to Kendra and Nick and looked back the aisle as Andie and Doug started down. Annie glanced over at Angie who gave her a wink. Stephen gently settled his arms on her waist, and her stomach felt a small swirl again.

Down girl, she thought to herself. *It's just the wedding.*

When Andie and Doug took their place, the music swelled, Kim stood, and the congregation rose to their feet. Megan beamed on her Uncle Bob's arm, and she kept her entire focus on Alex. Annie glanced at her brother who was wearing an unusually soft smile. She hoped he knew how lucky he was to have Megan adore him so.

As Jonathan performed the opening ceremony and came to the giving away of the bride, Annie was constantly aware of Stephen's hands on her waste and his breath on the back of her neck. With each breath, a new set of tingles spread down her spine. She almost found herself giggling until Angie caught her eye with a puzzled look. It immediately snapped Annie back to reality.

When it came time for the duet, Annie and Stephen stepped away together to the piano. Annie sat down and immediately began to play. She could hear the whispers of the congregation when Stephen picked up a microphone also. She smiled. No wedding in this church, not even Kelly McCall's, could surpass this one. Stephen Williams was singing at Megan and Alex's wedding.

Top that, Kelly, she thought quietly as she continued the intro. She finally lifted her mouth to the mic and began to sing:

When I look in your eyes all I can see
Is all that life has promised to me
When I look in your eyes, I see my heart
And I leave behind what pulled me apart
And others have asked how I can be sure
That what I have found is true and is pure

When she got to the chorus, Stephen lifted his microphone and began to sing with her in a harmony that melted together perfectly.

I knew it was love when you found my soul
I knew it was love when you made me whole
I knew it was love when my hand touched your face
I knew that I wanted to live life this way
I knew it was love.

They continued through the song until the last note faded, and something that Annie had never seen occur before in a wedding happened—applause. She and Stephen quickly made their way back to their place and prepared for the wedding's closing. Jonathan said a prayer of blessing and then told Alex to kiss his bride. Annie felt the tears begin to stream down her face now. They had started with Andie and Angie long ago, but she had controlled hers because of nervousness over the impending song that was to come. With the song over, however, her emotions let loose.

Megan and Alex were presented to the congregation and immediately headed back down the aisle. Andie and Doug followed with Annie and Stephen right behind. When everyone had made it to the foyer of the church, tears and hugs followed. Stephen actually felt tears beginning to burn his eyes. He wanted to walk out, but more pictures were to be taken. He bit his lip as he watched Annie hug everyone in sight, everyone but him. Angie hugged him, Megan hugged him, and Andie hugged him, but Annie deliberately kept her distance. He sighed.

Annie had long since removed her shoes during the reception. Her dress slightly drug on the floor, but she didn't care. She felt released from high-heel torture, and found herself nearly gliding around the room. The reception went on and on. Music played, people laughed, and the food was wonderful. Annie gave Angie a quizzical look when she saw her sitting with Billy Marcum at one table. Angie responded with a look that inferred, *Don't go there.*

Annie tried to avoid Stephen, but he plagued her thoughts during the entire evening. Tonight she had to give him a decision. She could not believe she was still weighing the whole thing. Stephen was pretty much occupied with people for the evening so he never noticed when she would stare at him. She admired his graciousness. He smiled, nodded, shook hands, and gave autographs continuously. If she went with him, she would have the opportunity to learn from a master in many ways.

She finally found herself becoming so flustered that she left the building for the deck behind. The moon was up and the stars were bright. She was glad for Megan's sake that it had not rained. She leaned against the rail and breathed in the country air deeply. This was her life and her home. She knew that saying *yes* to what Stephen was offering meant leaving this behind. However, no matter how happy she might be here in some ways, it was always tinged with huge disappointment and failure. She knew she should be doing more with her life, but she had lost the drive to push herself any longer. Leaving Alabama would be leaving one kind of fulfillment to try for another. Was it a fair trade-off, or would she end up like Stephen, alone and miserable? Was it worth the try?

"I know you're avoiding me," she heard Stephen say as he joined her at the railing. "We might as well have this talk and get it over with."

Her heart suddenly got faster. She wasn't ready yet. She still did not have an answer.

"I'm trying not to push you either way, Annie," he said tiredly. "I love life here. If I could, I would run away from everything, buy some land here, and throw up a log cabin."

He paused and turned around to lean his back against the railing. He crossed his arms and looked into her eyes.

"I can't do that," he said somberly. "Now you, you have options. You can stay here and relish in the love and shelter that this place offers. I will tell you this: If you leave here and go with the tour, this life will never be the same. I promise that you will become an overnight sensation. By the end of the tour, you will have people knocking down the walls to get to you, begging you to sign with them, go with them, sell yourself out to them. This," he said gesturing around the church and the valley, "will never be like this again. Do you understand what I'm saying?"

Annie swallowed and nodded.

"I know exactly," she confirmed. "Had I not gotten to know you this week, I don't think I would have understood it so clearly. I'm so torn, Stephen. I still don't have an answer."

Stephen chuckled as he turned back around.

"I would gripe and complain that you were making this harder than it should be," he told her, "but it is a big decision. It really boils down to one thing, Annie. What are your dreams? What do you really want in this life? What is it in the deepest part of you that you long to do more than anything else? When you can answer that question, then you'll have your answer to my question."

Annie sighed. Simple, but impossible.

"Then again," he continued, "sometimes it's not always about us."

"Where are you going with this now?" she asked.

"God," he said simply as he shrugged his shoulders. "God gifted you in an unusually abundant way. Why? To write commercials? To make a few people here in north Alabama happy with hearing your little jingles on TV and radio? I think you need to consider *that* in your decision."

"So, are you saying that *God* wants me to do this tour?"

"I am here. I know your gifts. I am making an offer that could take you anywhere in the world, literally. This tour can open any door you want. Dockrey can't. That's all I'm saying."

"Aughhh!" Annie screamed out. "Why can't someone just tell me what to do and it be as simple as that?"

Stephen held her arm and turned her body to face him.

"I'm telling you what to do. Come with me," he said simply.

Annie smiled and shook her head. Maybe so. There was no way to reason this out in some rational order. No, she did not want to be stuck in Dockrey for the rest of her life writing commercials at the beckoned call of every business in the area. No, she did not want to live with her parents until they passed on and she inherited the house. No, she did not want to look back at her life and always wonder about the *what if's* had she gone on with Stephen.

She turned back to the valley and lifted her head up to the moon. She took a deep breath and tried to calm herself with the decision. If she said *yes,* it would be *yes* and there would be no turning back.

She looked back at Stephen. He was totally bewildered. She found herself smiling at his reaction. Did he know what he was getting into having her and Alex on the same trip? What if he was wrong and his fans despised someone sharing the stage with him. She knew *she* would. What if she couldn't handle the pressure?

She faced him squarely and nervously smiled. "I'll go with you," she finally managed to drag out.

"What?" he said in surprise, taking a step toward her.

"I'll go," she repeated, taking a step back, "but only for the tour."

"You'll go? You're serious?" he said still in shock. "I actually thought you had talked yourself out of it! I can't believe it!"

He jumped up and clapped his hands in the air.

"Calm down," she warned him. "People will start coming out to see what's going on. However, I'm only coming for the tour. This whole *exchange* that has happened on and off between us during your week here is not going to happen on the tour. You said you would agree to that."

He nodded and agreed, "I know. I can't say that I'm not disappointed, a lot. But if you don't have feelings toward me, they can't be forced. I've been in your place too many times. I wouldn't want to put you through that."

"Stephen, don't be upset by this," she consoled. "It's just not meant to be. You and I are, well, maybe more like colleagues. Or maybe you'll be like a mentor. It's not that I'm not totally flattered by your suggestion. Trust me, I am. But until I can figure out who I am and where I'm going, we need to just, well, not go there."

"Are you saying there might be a chance someday?" he asked hopefully.

This time she took his hands and pulled him to her.

"I'd be stupid to totally rule it out," she acknowledged. "But right now, for some reason, I can't think clearly where you are concerned. Let's just do this *tour* thing and let the other part of *us* stay on the back burner."

He pulled her closer and held her tenderly.

"No problem," he said with relief.

He did nothing more than hold her. Annie finally felt the relief over having made the decision, and Stephen's hug did not even seem threatening. She let herself lean into him and took comfort in his embrace. He was about to change her life, and she had three months to get ready for it.

All would have ended fine had she not glanced up and seen Angie shaking her head at them both. Annie chose to close her eyes and ignore her sister this time. Life was good and simple for the moment. She would deal with the complexities it offered later, and that included Angie.

Chapter Twelve

After a wonderful Sunday dinner of roast beef with potatoes and carrots, Stephen pleaded with someone to drive him back to Huntsville. Barbara insisted Annie and Angie go with him, so after a rather tearful goodbye on his part, Stephen managed to have Annie drive him in the MG while Angie followed behind. He took the opportunity to tell Annie all that she needed to do over the next three months to prepare for the tour.

"I'll send you a copy of the new album along with keyboard parts for you to practice with," he began. "Decide what keyboard you want and I'll make sure it is delivered and ready to go when you get to New York. As soon as you can, send me your arrangements to *Autumn Sunset* and *I Knew it Was Love.* Plus, pick out a few of your own compositions and send them too. You can write out the arrangements if you want, or you can leave it up to me. Personally, I think you ought to do them yourself. It should be all you when you're actually performing."

"I am not singing *Autumn Sunset* or *I Knew it Was Love,*" she argued.

Stephen threw up his hands in exasperation.

"Must you always be so contrary?" he practically yelled. "This is my tour. Please let me do with it what I want!"

"I don't want to sing those songs!" she insisted firmly.

"Yes, I know," he said annoyed. "However, if you will just trust me on this one thing, it will prove to be remarkable. And another thing, when that tailor comes in town on Thursday, have him take all your measurements, top to bottom. Include your shoe size too. E-mail them to me."

"Why do you need my measurements?" she wondered.

"Clothes for the tour," he told her. "You need to match me on stage.

"Why? All your other musicians just wear ratty old jeans and t-shirts."

"That's my point," he tried to make clear. "I don't want anyone in the audiences or any reporter or any reviewer confusing you with just one of the *other musicians*. You are going to be a *featured artist* on this tour, a surprise that will blow the minds of all who see and hear you."

"You sure are holding high expectations for me," she said nervously. "And about the shoes, *no* heels."

"Don't worry," he said knowingly. "I would like for you to be the full four inches shorter than me on stage. Any heel you wear, I would have to match."

Stephen continued with the directions, reminding her that many of the cities would be farther north than she was used to. She needed to be sure to pack warm clothes for them, cooler clothes for the warmer states. September and October were months for extreme weather variations in the US.

"Make sure your luggage is light and easy to carry around," he continued. "Sometimes we will stay on the plane. Other times we will hotel it. It all depends on how long the flight is to the next city. Since you are the only single woman on the tour, I'll try to get you your own room on the jet. They can probably do some switching around with furniture this summer."

"Wait a minute," she stopped him. "What do you mean my *own room?* On a *jet?*"

"On *my* jet," he informed her. "Most of the crew is single while the musicians are all married. The crew shares rooms with bunk beds. I try to give each family their own room. When we can make it to the hotels, we put the families in suites so the parents can have a little quiet time away from the children if you know what I mean."

"How big is your jet?" she wanted to know.

"A Boeing 747," he said plainly. "It's big. We have a kitchen, a big dining area, a lounge, two television rooms, several restrooms, and several showers. We also have a rather nice dance floor, and I'm still not sure why I did that."

"Why the hotel at all?" she wondered aloud.

"Trust me, you get tired of being cooped up in that tube of tin after a while. Now, you've got my home phone numbers, both at my apartment in the city and at my home in the Adirondacks. You've got my personal cell number also. You've got my e-mail address and both mailing addresses. There is no reason for us to lose touch during the summer months. You don't need to show up in New York a week before the tour and have us feeling like total strangers. Call me, write me, talk to me. Give me any ideas you come up with, and I'll do the same."

It was fun for Annie to suddenly watch Stephen revert to his element. He had become all business as they discussed the tour. In Dockrey, he had been a fish out of water. However, when she saw him next, she would be the proverbial fish and would have to rely on him completely to get her through. She hoped she would not let him down.

Annie pulled into the Huntsville airport with her head spinning from information. She told Stephen he had better e-mail her with all the things to do because she was bound to forget more than one between now and then. He agreed. They returned the car and transferred his luggage to the VW. When they got in with Angie, country music was blaring through the stereo.

"For crying out loud," Annie grumbled as she turned off the radio. "What the heck are you listening to?"

Angie just smiled and replied, "I'm sorry, but you must face the fact that your sister likes country music."

"Please tell me no," Annie moaned.

"I'm caught," Angie said simply with a wide grin.

As they stood by the gate watching the other passengers board, Stephen continued with his instructions to Annie.

A young lady walked over to them and gently interrupted them.

"Excuse me," she said shyly, "but aren't you Stephen Williams?"

Stephen immediately shook his head and replied, "No, Adam Andrews. But thank you for the comparison. He's one of my favorites."

"Mine too," she said slightly embarrassed. "I'm sorry. You look so much like him. Have you been told that before?"

"I don't believe so," he said calmly, "but I will consider it a compliment."

As she walked off, Annie and Angie just stared at him in unbelief.

"Just consider it a white lie," he said to calm them down. "I don't have time right now to do the whole celebrity thing."

The loudspeaker gave the last boarding call for his flight. He turned quickly to the sisters and smiled sadly. He reached for Angie first and gave her a long, warm hug.

"I will miss you," he said as he pulled back to look her in the eyes. "I will see you on the tour in New Orleans. As soon as we land, we'll call you and send a car for you. It will either bring you to the jet or to the hotel, depending on where we're staying. You'll have a backstage pass and hopefully can stay with us until we leave."

"I can't wait," Angie said sincerely. "I'm really gonna miss you."

"No, you won't," he said resolutely. "You'll be so busy studying that you won't give me a second thought."

"No," she said with a smile, "I will miss you."

"Thanks."

He then turned to Annie and fought with how to say goodbye to her. He put his hand up to her face and gently caressed her cheek.

"You, I will see in three months," he began. "Remember, keep in touch."

Annie took his hand from her face and pulled him into a hug. He closed his eyes and buried his face in her hair. As usual, it was heavenly.

"I will keep in touch," she promised as she spoke softly in his ear.

He pulled away and smiled as he said, "And bring your shampoo, please?"

Annie nodded and smiled warmly. "You'd better go," she insisted.

"Goodbye, ladies," he said as he began to walk backwards slowly toward the gate. "I will see you both when the time comes."

He turned around and walked into the entrance. Annie felt a huge twinge of loss, almost to the point of tears. They stayed until the jet lifted into the air, and then they turned to go. Annie was still on the verge of tears and was very thankful that Angie chose not to make an issue of it.

"I'll miss him too," Angie finally confessed as they got into the VW to leave the airport. "He's really a rather nice guy."

"He is, isn't he?" Annie mused. "I think I was starting to get used to having him around."

"The tour should be fun," Angie suggested. "I'm glad you're going."

"I'm hungry," Annie said, changing the subject suddenly. "What about you?"

"Well, yes I am. But if we stop to eat, we will miss church. Do you want to just drive through for some fast food?"

"Are you kidding?" Annie asked in amazement. "We're in Huntsville! I was thinking maybe Olive Garden or Japanese."

"I'm assuming you're paying, because I do not have the funds for either."

"Absolutely," Annie said with a wave of her hand. "I am independently wealthy! I have a lucrative business that everyone wants to contribute to, and I live at home. What else do I have to do with my money? I'm voting Japanese."

"Daddy will be disappointed in our decision to skip church," Angie warned.

"Oh, and that will be a first," Annie replied sarcastically.

ℵ ℵ

They enjoyed the restaurant and had a lot of fun flirting with the Korean chef. The other people at their table consisted of three couples out for the evening. By the end of the night, everyone knew Annie and Angie well, and all wished Annie good luck with the tour. Angie had disclosed everything. Annie left a large tip and Angie winked at the chef as she passed the table where he was now cooking. They giggled and laughed for a long time on the trip back, recalling the many adventures they had experienced over the years.

"This may be the last time we get to do anything like this," Angie said seriously as her mood began to change. "I'm going to seminary, then hopefully on to Padawin. You'll be going on tour with Stephen, and who knows what will happen next?"

"Don't be so gloomy," Annie said with a frown. "We've got this week, and then we'll have Christmas."

"I know, but that's not much anymore. I used to always think that somehow we would get large chunks of time to reminisce over the years. We would vacation together and bring our kids to the beach together. Our husbands would be best buddies, and perhaps we would even live next to each other. The permanence of us being separated never really sunk in until this visit."

"Angie, you certainly didn't think I would pack up my family and follow you to Padawin and build a house next to yours, did you?"

Angie smiled and shrugged her shoulders.

"I don't know," she admitted. "I just never imagined my life without you always being there."

"Can you say *medical training?*" Annie reminded her. "I haven't been with you for years now!"

"I know, but that was just temporary," Angie tried to tell her. "I just assumed when I finished there would be all this time for us."

"Enough," Annie managed to say. "Let's take one day at a time, starting with this week. Let's squeeze the life out of it and enjoy every second we have together. Agreed?"

"Absolutely," Angie said as she perked back up. "I will just take life as it comes from now on. Now let's change the subject. Did you tell Stephen about Billy Marcum and the balcony."

"No," Annie said definitely, "but he sure did beg to know."

"Good girl," Angie said with relief. "My future on the mission field may depend on nobody ever finding out about that. Does Andie know?"

"I never said a word."

Angie nodded with satisfaction and reprieve.

"Is that what you discussed with Mr. Marcum at the wedding reception?" Annie asked in curiosity.

"Not exactly," Angie grinned, "but he *did* suggest a repeat performance."

"Okay, I do *not* want to know any more than that, thank you—no more."

ꕥ ꕥ

Annie decided that since business had been going so well, coupled with the fact that she had completed the McCall account with Stephen, why not take the next week off and spend it with Angie. She called Terri on Monday morning before she would have left for work to let her know there was no need to come in.

"But Annie," Terri protested, "the answering machine will be full of messages. I need to sort them all out and begin scheduling meetings. If I don't, we will be so swamped when we return that it will be impossible to catch up."

"We won't be taking on any new accounts," Annie told her. "Come September, I will be taking a leave of absence."

There was a long silence before Terri finally said, "Will I be losing my job?"

"Probably," Annie said plainly. "We will finish all the accounts still on the calendar, and then close up shop when they are completed. You need to start looking for other work. If you find something good immediately, you're welcome to go ahead and resign. I don't want to keep you from moving on as soon as you can."

There was more silence as Annie allowed Terri to process it all.

"But I don't want to work for anyone else," Terri told her.

"But you'll have to if you want to work," Annie explained. "I'm closing up at least until after Christmas."

"Where are you going, Annie?"

"All over," was the only reply she gave. "It's time for me to do some traveling."

"I don't want to work for anyone else until you're gone," Terri said. "I would feel like I am cheating somehow."

"Do whatever seems best for you, Terri, but don't go to work this week. It will be a paid vacation, though, okay?"

"Sure, Annie. Bye."

What a fruitcake. There is no way she can be behind the stealing of my music files. She probably has to take notes every morning to remember how to spell her name.

Annie and Angie did not waste the week. They went on three rides, two of which their father accompanied them. They went shopping again, this time with their mother and Andie, with Annie insisting on buying some pieces toward a new wardrobe for Angie's seminary experience. Angie went with her to the tailor on Thursday to get all the measurements that Stephen had asked for, and while there, they rented five movies for an all-night movie watching sleepover pajama party. They invited Andie and were thoroughly delighted when she agreed.

They set up the sleepover in the garage apartment where Stephen had spent the week. With popcorn, brownies, an air mattress, and all the movies ready, they began the first one. It wasn't long, however, before the movie was totally forgotten and the girls were just talking.

"Thank you for inviting me over for this," Andie said warmly. "Do you know how long it has been since I've done anything like this?"

"I'm guessing since before you married Doug," Angie answered.

"That's exactly right," Andie admitted. "In fact, it was the night before we married. Sherry Montgomery had all the bridesmaids over, the older ones," she clarified since neither Annie nor Angie had been invited, "to sleep at her house. It was a blast. I hardly slept, and could barely keep my eyes open during the wedding!"

"Yeah, but don't you and Doug have pajama parties all the time?" Angie teased.

"Wouldn't you like to know," Andie smiled as she lay back on the couch.

"Actually, no," Annie said quickly.

"I'm pregnant again," Andie told them without warning. Her sisters looked up at her totally baffled by the announcement.

"What?" Angie asked in unbelief. "Four kids? Do we need to have a talk about how this happens?"

"Mom and Dad had four kids," Andie quickly reminded them, "and that seemed to be just fine."

"Did you want another child?" Annie asked. "You were just settling back into a normal routine of teaching school."

"I know," Andie said, but not with reservation. "Doug is doing really well with his construction business. He believes I could stop working all together and stay home if I wanted."

Annie and Angie just stared in unbelief. This was not like Andie. She had a drive that matched their own.

"Do you want to stop working?" Annie asked her. "I thought you loved it."

"I did love it," Andie confessed, "but I actually enjoy being a mom more than that. I've even thought about home schooling all the kids."

"That might be fun," Angie volunteered. "I've talked with a lot of couples who home school because I knew that's what I would have to do if I had kids on the mission field."

"Are you planning on adopting?" Annie asked sarcastically. "Because if not, then you'd better start working on the husband end of that."

"I'm not worried about that," Angie said lightly. "God can provide anything He wants for me. If He has a man in mind, I guarantee *I* won't miss him, unlike *other* girls in this room whom I won't choose to *name* out loud."

"Oh, very subtle," Annie groaned as she rolled her eyes. "We are *not* going to talk about Stephen Williams again."

"What?" Andie asked immediately. "Stephen and Annie have a thing going?"

Both Annie and Angie responded at the same time; Annie gave a *no* while Angie gave a *yes*.

"We do *not* have a *thing* going," Annie jumped in. "It's just a little fantasy that Angie has created in her mind."

"Excuse me," Angie butted in, "but I believe that was *your* fantasy."

Suddenly Annie's cell phone interrupted the conversation, and she was thankful for the distraction. She got up and went over to the counter to answer it.

"Hello?"

"Annie? Annie, it's Stephen."

"Hey! How are you?" she said quietly, not wanting to reveal to her sisters who was on the phone.

"Really lonely," he confessed. "I have been absolutely miserable since I left. I kept wanting to call, but didn't want to bombard you too soon after leaving. You might think I'm smothering you or something."

"No, not at all," she told him as she went into the bathroom to have privacy from her very curious sisters. "I thought about calling you too, but . . . well . . . ditto. That, and the fact that Angie and I have stayed pretty busy."

"Did you ride any?"

"Three times."

"Man. . . ." She could hear the longing in his voice. "Maybe I can get some four-wheelers or motorcycles and ride them up at my house. You could give me some more lessons. Which would you suggest? A two-wheeler or a four-wheeler?"

"I much prefer the bikes. They're easier to maneuver, and they're just a lot of fun."

"They kind of scare me," he divulged. "I never even rode a bicycle very much."

The talk went on, and before Annie realized it, an entire hour had passed. She could tell Stephen did not want to hang up. She hated to mention the fact that she was spending the night with her sisters, but if she did not get off the phone soon, she would never live down the fact that he had called and talked so long.

"Andie and Angie are over, and we are sort of having a final sister pajama party."

"Oh man," he moaned. "I interrupted."

"It's okay," she reassured him. "I'm glad you called. Don't ever hesitate to call me."

"Yeah, all right," he said in embarrassment. "I'd better let you go."

"I meant that, Stephen," she tried to convince him. "Please call any time."

"Okay," he said trying to sound lively. "I will. E-mail me some time."

E-mail. She hadn't even looked at her e-mail in two weeks. She winced as she thought he may have written to her and she never responded.

"Gee," she tried to get around the heaviness of the situation, "I haven't even been on the computer in forever. I'll send you the measurements from the tailor tomorrow."

"Well, okay, and . . . bye then," he said slowly.

"Goodbye, Stephen."

Click. She sat still for a moment and collected her thoughts and emotions. If she were on his end, this call would have seemed rude and invasive. That was far from what she was trying to convey. He still did not understand that she could not just be *normal* with him. He was going on and on about his mundane existence, and she was so star struck that she hung on his every word. Yet when she did talk, it was about things that insinuated he was intruding on her life. Would she ever relax around him enough to just be herself?

When she opened the bathroom door, her sisters' conversation came to an abrupt halt. They stared with curious expressions, and she knew there would be no easy escape from the questions they would ask. It would be easier to just come clean straight out.

"It was Stephen," she told them as she laid her phone back on the counter and began to put a bag of popcorn into the microwave. "He was lonely and missing the family and decided to give me a call. The conversation consisted mainly of reminding me about all the things I need to do to get ready for the tour.

Well, she lied there, but perhaps it would deter any questions.

"I think he's cute," Andie volunteered.

"And he's rich too," Angie added.

Annie rolled her eyes and reached in the fridge for a Sprite. It was going to be a long night.

The girls were just too old for the pajama party business anymore. They could not even make it through an entire movie, and by 2:00, Andie could not keep her eyes open. She lay back on the couch and dropped off to sleep immediately while Angie and Annie shared the blow up mattress. They talked for another 30 minutes or so, but soon found themselves drifting also. However, when 6:45 rolled around the next morning,

Annie's eyes popped open, and regardless of how exhausted she was, she knew it was senseless to try and go back to sleep.

She started the coffee and opted for sugar toast this morning. Angie would be leaving on Sunday, and Annie wanted her last two days to be wonderful.

After fixing her coffee, she made her way to the computer to check her e-mail. As she pulled up her inbox, she cringed—171 messages. She sat back to enjoy her breakfast while everything downloaded. As it neared the end, she had guessed right, Stephen had sent her several messages.

Sunday Night Mail:

Hey Annie.

Just wanted to let you know that I made it home fine. The trip on the plane was uneventful, and I am about to go to bed. Thanks for the great week! I can't wait for the tour to begin. I will try to get the album and music together for you so I can mail them by the end of the week. I find myself missing your entire family and the noise and hustle of the Wright household.

Enjoy your week with Angie!
Yours, Stephen

Monday Afternoon:

Annie,

You asked me to remind you about the things you needed to do to prepare for the tour. Following is the list:

Annie smiled as she read through the list. He was thorough, to say the least, a quality she admired in anybody.

If I've left out anything, I will send it on later. Tell Angie I said hi and that I am still curious about the Billy Marcum/balcony situation.

Yours, Stephen

Tuesday Evening Mail:

Dear Annie,

I wanted to let you know that I will be on CNN Thursday morning for about a three-minute interview. It will just be a brief thing announcing the upcoming release of my album in late August and the tour. I am going to begin telling everyone now to expect an exciting surprise for the tour. That would be YOU!

Hope all is well in Alabama.

Stephen

Thursday Evening Mail:

Hey,

I just hung up after talking to you. I apologize for crashing the sisters' slumber party. You should have just told me right away what was going on. I would never want to do anything to interfere with your family. Do you know how lucky you are? It is amazing how you all relate to each other. I can't decide what I miss the most about being there: talking with all of you or watching you all talk! Anyway, I hope the movies were good, although, I must confess, I cannot imagine the three of you actually being quiet long enough to sit and watch a movie! I'm sorry, but I really think that would be an impossible feat for the stubborn-headed, opinionated, beautiful Wright girls! I think I'm going to end up watching a movie myself . . . just not sleepy at all.

Take Care, Stephen

Annie was right; she had made him feel like a heel for calling. At least he seemed to get over it. She knew she needed to write him something significant to make up for apparently ignoring him the whole week. She felt horrible for missing him on CNN, and wished she had at least known so she could have watched and then joked with him about it. How should she start?

Stephen,

You cannot imagine how busy my week has been! I gave Terri the week off and decided to spend it with Angie instead. We have managed to cram at least a month's worth of activities into the past four days. She leaves for seminary on Sunday, and my heart is already breaking. She is the closest person in the world to me, and even though we haven't spent much time together the past few years, I know this is the last step before the mission field for her. I am trying to forget that for the moment and, as you told me on Saturday, "not borrow trouble." At least the tour will keep me busy. However, I do not know how I am going to get through the next three months . . . with no Angie . . . and no tour . . . just back to me, myself alone.

That wasn't enough. She needed to write more to make up for all he had written, plus the phone call last night that she had ended before she knew he was ready to hang up.

Daddy had the three teenage "felons" help him do some work around the church this week. Sunday morning in Youth Sunday School he asked for three volunteers to contribute some work time with a few odd jobs. He called out their names, and to the surprise of everyone in the department, they agreed! Hmmm? Wonder why? Like we told you, Daddy has a way of getting deep into heart-to-heart talks while you're deep into work. I heard two more of my songs on TV this week, stolen songs, that is. I have decided to record the commercials and do a little investigating to see if I can discover who is behind it. At least that will give me something to do over the summer.

That seemed pretty good. She didn't want to write too much and appear guilty or anything. She just wanted a friendly letter. She added the tailor's measurements, along with her shoe size, 10B. She cringed as she typed it down; "boat feet" she had always called them. In fact, if her memory was correct, it was Kelly McCall who had coined the term for her.

Lovely. I'm now thinking about Kelly McCall. I hope that's not an omen for the rest of my day.

"Why did the armadillo cross the road?" Angie asked Annie as they sat in the hot tub on Saturday evening.

"What?" Annie asked bewildered. "What does an armadillo have to do with our present discussion?"

"It's a joke," Angie told her. "The pediatrician I worked for this spring told it to me when he found out I was a 'country girl.' "

"Country? As in music or as in raised in the country?"

"Does it matter?" Angie asked flustered at how something so simple could become so difficult with Annie involved. "Can I not just tell you a joke without being questioned to death? You should have been a lawyer."

"You're probably right."

"Why did the armadillo cross the road?" Angie asked again.

"To wage war with the chicken," Annie said rigidly.

Angie stared at her in amusement.

"Only you would try to answer a joke that you didn't know," Angie grumbled.

"If you don't want an answer then don't phrase it as a question," Annie scolded. "You ask me a question and, regardless of how stupid it might be, I will give you an answer."

Angie started to laugh as she said, "You are in such a bad mood that it's actually funny!"

Annie splashed Angie's face with water and insisted, "Just tell me the answer to your stupid riddle, please."

"Okay, why did the armadillo cross the road?" Angie began again, and then suddenly she stopped and started laughing wildly.

"What? Is it really that funny?"

"I messed it up!" Angie yelled. "I blew the punch line!"

Annie rolled her eyes and tried to suppress her own laugh. How typical. Angie could manage to make it through medical school but still could not remember how to tell a joke without ruining it.

"Let me start again," Angie said trying to calm down.

"I'm gonna take a wild guess here and say that the answer has something to do with an armadillo," Annie said with no smile.

"Here we go," Angie regained her composure. "Why did the chicken cross the road?"

"To wage war with the armadillo?" Annie replied.

"Annie, stop answering!" Angie shouted at her.

"Then stop asking me a question!" she laughed back. "Please, tell me why the proverbial chicken had to cross the road!"

"To show the armadillo and the possum that it could be done!"

Angie laughed heartily again. Annie managed a smile, but the gnawing in her heart knowing that her sister was leaving tomorrow was too much to overcome. The more she watched Angie, amused at her silly joke, the thicker the tears grew in her eyes. She tried to blink them back but realized it was of no use. Slowly one began to make its way down her face, then another.

"What's wrong, Annie?" Angie asked suddenly.

Annie took a deep breath and choked out, "I am really going to miss you."

Angie smiled and nodded in agreement, then told her, "Thank goodness. I was afraid you didn't like my joke."

Annie simply splashed her again.

"I'm getting really hot," Annie began to complain. "I'm afraid I'm gonna have to get out."

"If Stephen Williams were sitting out here with us, you wouldn't get out until your skin melted off."

"You're right," Annie said definitely. "I didn't think he would ever leave. I was about to die of the heat and he just sat right there, talking away about whatever."

"You should have given him a thrill and stood up!"

"Oh, I think you took care of that. I just wanted to pull him under for not leaving us alone."

They sat quietly for a few moments and merely stared at each other, both knowing that moments like this may never come for them again.

"I hope the tour goes well for you, and that great things happen as a result," Angie said seriously.

"Stephen seems to think I'm just going to take off like crazy," Annie told her.

"Well, I'm guessing he knows what he's talking about. He's the expert in that area."

There were a few more moments of silence before Annie burst out of the tub.

"I can't stay in here any longer," she announced. "I'm gonna shower and get ready for bed."

"I'll stop by and say goodnight," Angie promised.

Annie nodded and smiled as she stepped out of the tub.

"Thanks."

As Annie watched Angie drive away the next morning, tears burned her eyes. She knew this was the end of one segment in their lives and the beginning of another. Why did Angie have to be a missionary? Why couldn't she settle for just doing community service somewhere close by? She admired Angie because of her certainty in her call and future, but she despised her for leaving. After two weeks of wonderful highs, Annie had hit a low, and this one seemed like a horrible, endless pit.

She went inside to her room and shut the door. No, she did not *want* to be alone; she just was. Life was now back to its normal lull, and the emptiness and loneliness almost suffocated her. She wondered if this was how Stephen felt. Stephen. She picked up her cell and dialed his number.

"Williams," was the answer he gave.

"Stephen?" she wondered.

"Annie!" he recognized her voice immediately. "Hey! Glad you called!"

"Hey yourself," she mumbled back. "How's New York?"

"Starting to get busy. How's Dockrey?"

"Back to its boring, usual self."

"Oh, yeah," he remembered, "Angie left today, didn't she?"

Annie was crying now. She was embarrassed to be crying over the phone to Stephen.

"I'm sorry," she strangled out. "I didn't mean to do this. I just felt so alone and needed to talk to somebody."

"It's okay," he assured her. "I'm glad you called. If there's anyone who understands lonely, it's me."

Annie sniffed a bit, trying to pull herself together, and then asked him, "Is this how you feel, Stephen? Is this the aloneness you told me about?"

"I'm sure mine's different. I don't have anyone to miss or long for. I'm just, well, empty, I guess. You miss someone who adds energy and love to your life."

"Which one of us is the most miserable?"

"Right now, you are," he laughed. "I'm really glad you called. It's nice to know that there are actually other people in this world who ache now and then too."

They talked for 30 minutes when Annie realized she needed to get ready for church. Stephen had cheered her up, and she was grateful for the friendship. For the first time since having met him, she actually looked on him as a friend, as a *normal* relationship in her life, and not the super star that hung on the back of her closet wall.

"Thanks for talking," she told him as she prepared to go.

"Anytime," he replied, and she could actually hear the smile in his voice. "And by the way, thanks for the e-mail."

"I'm bad about writing," she confessed. "I'll try to do better."

"Don't worry about it," he told her. "I just had a lot of time on my hands this past week. Things will start kicking in now. I'll be on Letterman Wednesday night if you get a chance to watch."

"I'll be watching for sure," she promised him. "Goodbye."

Annie put her phone down and went to the closet. She shoved all the clothes to the side and knelt down to see the poster of Stephen clearly. Her heart began to ache again. No Angie, no Stephen. How was she ever going to make it through this summer?

Chapter Thirteen

Annie leaned back in the chair at her desk as she fingered through the phone messages Terri had copied from the answering machine. She decided to take a couple of the accounts anyway because of friendships, but the rest she would have to call and inform that her office would be closing down for a few months. She separated the two accounts she would acquire and placed their messages in her top drawer. The others would receive personal calls from her today.

The intercom buzzed and Annie pressed the button to see what Terri needed now. She had buzzed in all morning with menial problems from a possible mouse sighting to low toner in the copier, all of which could have been solved with a little creativity on Terri's part and no needed input from Annie.

"Yes, Terri? What now?"

"Vivian McCall is on line one," Terri announced.

We only have one line, Annie thought as she shook her head, half in unbelief and half in perturbation.

"Thank you, Terri," she replied instead. "I'll take it now."

This should be fun, she thought as she picked up the receiver and tried to prepare herself for whatever bashing Vivian may have in store. At least Annie had her ace in the hole this time—a jingle co-written by Stephen Williams.

"Hello, *Mrs.* McCall," she said cheerfully with a mocking smile to match.

"It's Vivian, dear," she insisted again. "Must I remind you of that every time we speak?"

"I'm sorry," Annie replied unconvincingly. "I was always taught to never call older people by their first names. It's just a habit I can't seem to break."

"Oh, my," Vivian called out, "I'm not that much older than you, dear!"

Only old enough to be my mother." I'm glad you called," Annie continued. "I actually found the time to work on your commercial, and it is finished."

"Oh, did you?" she sounded surprised. "I wish you would have waited. If you'll remember, I told you not to worry with it until I returned from Hawaii."

"I try to keep my clients happy," Annie said, now trying to sound sincere.

"Well, dear, you may have been wasting your time," Vivian started oozing again.

What is it this time?

"You see, Annie," she began to explain with a touch of condescension in her voice, "there is another company that has started producing commercials in the area. I thought I would try and give them some business to help them sort of get off on the right foot."

Oh, really? Imagine that! I wonder if you would have anything to do with pilfering my songs and sending them off to another supposed company?

"That's fine, *Mrs.* McCall," she said in complete control, knowing that Vivian was hoping for a big letdown on Annie's part. "I have actually heard some of the commercials, and I must say, the composer is a genius! Good luck to you."

"Well, I appreciate you being so understanding about this," Vivian oozed again. "I just believe in good business competition. You have had this market cornered for a couple of years now."

"I agree, *Mrs.* McCall. I just had a little extra time, and I'm sure you heard that Stephen Williams was down for the week of Alex's wedding. Well, he and I were sort of fooling around in my studio, and he actually helped me write *your* jingle."

Stone-cold silence followed.

Yes! I zinged her! Wahoo!

"Excuse me?" Vivian questioned. "Stephen Williams, *the* Stephen Williams helped you on my commercial?"

"Yes, ma'am. But it's no big deal. I have several other accounts in the workings right now, and I'll just change a few words and stick it with one of them."

Now the silence was golden. Vivian was having to think about this one. Should she stop the insulting removal of her account from Annie, or did she go for the impressive honor of having Stephen Williams write her commercial? Annie was smiling for the first time since Angie had left, and she was enjoying the upper hand with Vivian McCall for the first time in her life.

"Well, dear," Vivian tried to regain her composure, "I haven't actually signed a contract with the other firm yet. I would love to hear what *Stephen* wrote for *me*. How about I take a listen to it first, and if it seems satisfactory, especially knowing how much time you put into all this, perhaps we could work something out."

"That's up to you," Annie restated. "Stephen would have no problem with my changing a few words and putting it with another business. It would actually make a great restaurant song, I think. He said it was a shame to waste such a lovely tune on a car dealership."

"No!" Vivian replied a little too abruptly. "No, don't do that. Let's schedule an appointment and have a listen first. After all, I did sort of commission you first. That would only be the right thing to do."

Are we developing morals, Vivian? The right thing to do?

"I'm rather busy this week, having to catch up on my vacation time, but I do have a slot open this afternoon at 3:00 if you are available."

"I'll be there," Vivian said quickly. "Goodbye now."

That's it? No oozing about Kelly in Hawaii? No under-the-breath threats? Gee, Vivian, I must have really thrown you for a loop.

Annie was about to begin her series of phone contacts when Terri buzzed in again.

"Yes!" Annie answered in exasperation.

"The mouse is behind the copy machine!" she screamed. "Can you call someone to come get it?"

"Just a minute."

Annie got up and opened the door of her studio to find Terri on her desk squatting down, with her finger still on the intercom button.

"Where is it?" Annie asked plainly as she grabbed the still empty garbage can from beside Terri's desk.

Terri just stared in amazement and pointed to the copy machine. Annie peeked behind, but saw no mouse.

"Help me move this thing back from the wall," Annie asked Terri.

"No," she replied in fear. "I'm not going near it."

"Well, I can't move it myself," Annie said frustrated. "Either you're gonna have to help me now or Mr. Mouse has found a new home behind our copier."

"What if he runs out?" Terri wanted to know.

"That's the whole idea," Annie rolled her eyes. "And what if it's not a he, but a she?"

Terri's eyes grew big.

"A mother mouse?" she asked in horror. "Oh, my gosh! I'll help."

Terri climbed down from the desk, a major feat considering the clogs she was wearing. She got on one side of the copier while Annie prepared to move the other side. On the count of three, they pulled the machine from the wall. Immediately the mouse darted back toward Terri's desk. Terri screamed so loud that Annie's ear began to throb. However, Annie managed to drop the top part of the wastebasket over the mouse, thus trapping him underneath for the moment.

"Oh, my gosh! Oh, my gosh!" Terri began to chant. "Now what do we do? Call a man?"

Annie looked at her with slight aversion and shook her head in disbelief.

"What do we need a man for?" Annie wondered.

"You didn't kill it!" Terri exclaimed. "It's just trapped under there for now! It's still alive!"

Talk about your keen sense for the obvious.

"Terri, there's a garbage bag in this wastebasket. I'll simply pull it from the sides like this," Annie said as she demonstrated the process, "and you come lift the garbage can off. Then I will have little mousy trapped in the bag. See?"

"Oh, my gosh!" Terri yelled again. "But what if he runs out?"

Annie stared in unbelief.

"Pull the wastebasket off—now!" Annie said with a little more firmness.

Terri cautiously stepped toward the basket and slowly reached her hand to the garbage can. It was all Annie could do not to yell, "*Boo!*" but decided she might possibly get hit for doing so. Instead, she kept to the plan, entrapping the little mouse when Terri pulled up the wastebasket. Terri screamed the entire time that Annie captured the mouse and headed toward the door. Annie was glad to get outside to clear her ears.

"Did you kill it?" Terri asked her when she returned.

"No," Annie replied. "*That,* I couldn't bring myself to do. I let it go across the street next to the insurance office. Let's move the copier back to the wall."

As they each got their side to put the copier back in its place,

Annie noticed some fallen papers on the floor behind where the copier had been. She reached down to pick them up, planning to throw them in the garbage, but was startled by what she found.

"What is it, Annie?" Terri asked, having finally calmed down a bit.

"These are my songs," Annie said in disbelief. She held the papers out to Terri.

"So?" Terri wondered.

"Look," Annie said as she showed Terri the copies, "this one was too dark because I write them on that greenish manuscript paper. They had to make another copy and lighten it up."

"Who?" Terri asked. "Who makes copies of your music?"

"I have no idea," Annie said shaking her head.

"I'm really confused now," Terri said as they moved the copier. "I'm the only one who uses this copier, Annie. You don't ever make copies of stuff. You always ask me. Why would you say that someone is making copies of your music?"

"I don't know, Terri, but its time to find out."

When 3:00 rolled around, Annie was actually anticipating the meeting with Vivian McCall. She had the music cued up, had her blinds open in the office, and had forgotten all about her stolen music for the moment. Terri buzzed that Vivian had arrived, and Annie greeted her warmly at the door.

They exchanged very little small talk; just enough for the both of them to be considered polite, then Annie played the jingle. Naturally, Vivian was impressed. Annie knew she was probably more *overcome* than impressed, but she would settle for Vivian pretending to be impressed.

"Oh my," Vivian began, "that is exceptional. I mean it just makes McCall Ford sound so appealing and inviting. Stephen, and you *too,* of course, did a superb job with this. Oh, what to do."

"Like I said, Mrs. McCall, if you feel like you need to commit to this other agency, I understand. No hard feelings whatsoever."

"You are so *accommodating,* Annie," Vivian said trying to sound gracious. "That little tune just continues to jingle around in the head, doesn't it?"

"That's what makes a good commercial, *Mrs.* McCall," Annie said proudly.

"Well, dear, I hope you don't expect me to pay you more because it was co-written by Stephen Williams?"

"Not at all," Annie smiled. "After all, we did have a contract with a set price. I would never think of *breaching* a contract in any way, shape or form."

Good one, Annie!

"Yes, of course," Vivian smiled back. "You're such a good little thing, aren't you, the preacher's daughter and all?"

"I try," was all Annie would say.

Annie made sure she put the original contract in front of Vivian, noting that Vivian had signed in three separate places on the document promising her business. Apparently, Vivian was willing to swallow her pride for the privilege of having Stephen Williams' name on her commercial. She wrote Annie a check and left with a CD copy of the song to play for everyone she could think of. Annie grinned big—mission accomplished.

The rest of the month of June was hectic for Annie. She had only intended to take on two new accounts, but five of the businesses begged her so desperately that she gave in and agreed to have their commercials done by the end of August. She struggled beyond hope to pick five of her songs to send to Stephen for the tour. He would only choose one for her to perform, but deciding which ones were her top five was nearly impossible. She thought of calling Angie for advice, and then decided against it as she remembered her sister was now a country music fan.

When her songs were finally mailed to Stephen, she focused on learning the music for his new album. There was no way she could explain to anyone how she relished the fact that she had an early release of his album. Before she ever attempted to begin playing along with it, she had to listen to it over and over and over. She was star struck again. How could she help it? He was the most unbelievable musician she had ever heard. His new album was a step above anything he had ever put out before, and she was very proud of Alex's playing. His bass was a big contribution and complement to Stephen's style.

Annie had also spent time recording five of the commercials that had ripped off her songs, three radio and two television. She had called each of the companies to discover who had produced their commercials, but no one would ever give out any information. The people she needed to talk to were always out of the office or unavailable. She decided to make a personal visit to an old acquaintance who worked in Florence at a men's clothing shop, Billy Marcum. Maybe he could at least give her a hint.

"Annie Wright," Billy said smoothly as he greeted her in the store. "What brings you out of your little hole in Dockrey?"

"Nice to see you too, Billy," she teased as she gave him a small hug.

"I was wondering if we could possibly have lunch?" she asked.

"Wow," he said impressed. "This must be serious. Wait, did your father find out about the balcony?"

Annie rolled her eyes. Billy Marcum would never change.

"No," she said slowly. "I just need to talk with you about a possible favor."

"Let me guess, you need some good-looking man to escort you to an awards ceremony in California for jingle writer of the year?"

"Oh, you are so close," Annie teased back, when what she really wanted to say was, *Why would I be here if that were the case?*

Billy suggested Riccatoni's, but Annie did not want to mar the memory of that night with Stephen by doing lunch there with the balcony boy.

They opted for Famous Dave's, and after ordering, Annie revealed her plight, hoping frantically that Billy was the right choice for bearing her soul.

"Somebody is stealing your music?" he asked incredulously. "And my store is one of them?"

"Yes," she confirmed. "Do you have anything to do with the advertising?"

"No, not at all. That's way higher up than me. I just manage and order merchandise and stuff like that. They pay me well for it, but I don't make executive decisions like advertising."

"Is there any way you could find out who they used for this particular commercial? It would need to be done discreetly. Whoever is doing this is deliberately stealing my songs and then trying to cover the tracks. And understand, Billy, I don't care about competition. That's fine. What I want to know is how and why my music is being pilfered."

He nodded in understanding, then looked at her and smiled. "What do I get out of this?" he asked with one eyebrow lifted.

"I'm paying for your lunch, aren't I?"

"I could possibly lose my job playing Sam Spade for you. The stakes are a little higher than lunch, don't you think?"

"I'll give you Angie's phone number," she suggested, half jokingly, agreeing to anything just to find this information.

"Angie's in New Orleans," he shrugged off. "Any other offers?"

She thought for a moment and honestly could come up with nothing.

"I'll pay you," she suggested. "How much do you want?"

"Free tickets and backstage passes to Stephen Williams' Birmingham concert," he said quickly. "Since Alex plays for him, surely you have a few connections."

"You're a Stephen Williams fan?" she asked disbelievingly.

"Who isn't?"

"I'll see what I can do," she told him. That should be no problem. Stephen would be glad to help her get to the bottom of the song-stealing saga.

July 4 fell on a Sunday that summer. Jonathan Wright seldom cancelled church services, but he felt that a day with family was as much a priority as a day at church, so he allowed families to be together that Sunday evening. Angie drove up for the weekend so the festivities at the Wright household were full of celebration. Alex and Megan had talked of flying down but really wanted to spend their first official holiday as a married couple by themselves.

The Wright's managed a family ride on Saturday afternoon and a barbecue on Sunday. Andie was slightly troubled by morning sickness and didn't feel much like a game of badminton so Jonathan agreed to be Doug's partner in a grueling match with Annie and Angie. It got so silly that the points became moot. As the evening settled upon them, Doug and Andie took their exhausted brood home, while Jonathan and Barbara retired to their own room to recover from the day. Annie and Angie warmed up plates of ribs, then added potato salad, coleslaw, and baked beans to top off the leftover meal.

They sat on the couch in the great room, as it was too hot to enjoy the back porch in July. With the TV on to watch televised fireworks, they ate in silence as various performers sang in front of the capitol building in Washington D.C.

"Is Stephen singing?" Angie asked as she licked a huge clump of sauce from the side of her hand.

"Uh uh," Annie garbled with a mouthful of ribs. "He's in California tonight. Doing Leno tomorrow."

"Talked to him lately?" Angie continued as she took a spoonful of potato salad.

Annie shook her head as she tried to swallow before she spoke.

"He's been traveling around the country doing little bit interviews for various stations," she explained. "He e-mailed me his schedule before he left. That was about a week and a half ago."

"Does he not have a cell phone?" Angie probed.

Annie put down her fork and stared at Angie with wide eyes.

"Yes, he has a cell phone," she informed her sister with a bit of disdain, "but there is nothing to talk about at the moment. He's flying around the country and I'm writing jingles. Exciting lives we lead."

"Just curious," Angie smiled at her. "I wouldn't want you to lose touch with him."

"What about you?" Annie asked her. "Meet any nice men at seminary?"

"A lot," Angie answered back, "but they're either married or way too young for me. The truth is, though, most of them are unbelievably intimidated when they find out I'm a doctor. I've actually had a couple of these preacher boys make plays for me, but as soon as I start discussing my *education* with them, they run."

"Men," Annie grumbled. "By the way, your Billy Marcum is helping do a little investigating concerning the song-stealing situation."

"Really? How so?"

"The store he works for is one of the thieves," Annie told her. "He's going to see if he can find out the company they used."

"Watch out for Billy," Angie warned with a smile and raised eyebrows. "He can be very persuasive when it comes to repaying favors."

"We've already negotiated. He wants tickets to Stephen's Birmingham concert."

"That was easy," Angie laughed. "I should have been so lucky!"

"Any news about Padawin?" Annie asked her.

"Actually, yes," Angie said with excitement. "Michael Collins, the agricultural missionary there, has e-mailed me with some statistics. He says that between the two of us maybe we can convince the mission board that I'm needed there. He has finally gotten some of the tribal heads to agree to immunizations. They lost several people last month to measles. He explained about the shots and how they could prevent these diseases. He got straight "no's" until one of the chief's sons died. He said they were a bit more open now."

"How are talks going with the mission board?"

Angie heaved a sigh of disgust and shook her head.

"I don't think they like me very much," she griped. "Who would have thought that my biggest obstacle to the mission field would be getting appointed?"

"Just keep your cool and things will work out," Annie advised.

"Oh, you're one for doling out advice on keeping cool," Angie complained.

"See," Annie smiled, "I'm not even getting mad at you for saying that to me. I've changed, mellowed out a bit."

"Look!" Angie said pointing at the television. "The fireworks are starting!"

Annie gave her attention to the television just as the phone rang. She reached over to pick it up, wiping her hand on her shirt first to remove any excess sticky sauce.

"Hello?"

A mock British accent replied, "May I speak with Annie of Dockrey?" She recognized Stephen immediately and responded in like accent with, "I'm sorry, sir, she is indisposed at the moment sharing the viewing of fireworks with her wayward sister of Orleans."

Angie hit her and mouthed, *I'm not wayward.*

Stephen continued, "But I must speak with her immediately. It concerns specific music pieces upon which she desires to be played at the royal ball."

Annie got quiet for the moment. He wanted to discuss her music. This could be good or bad. What if he didn't like any of them? She got up from the couch and headed to her bedroom where she could be humiliated in private if necessary.

"Must be Stephen," Angie mumbled as Annie headed up the stairs.

Annie went into her room, closed her door, and plopped down onto her bed.

"So what's up?" Annie tried to sound light.

"Well, I'm really at quite a loss for words."

"Okay," Annie said hesitantly. "Just spit it out. I can pretty much take anything."

"For starters, how old are these songs?"

"They're all different ages," she tried to be pleasant. "Some are older than others."

"What do you do with your songs when you've finished them? Do you just file them away somewhere for future use? Do you sing them anywhere? Are there more where these came from?"

"Slow down, boy. Whoa, I say," Annie said calmly. "One question at a time, please. I just write them, that's all."

There was silence as Annie tried to anticipate the next question. She still was not sure where he was going with his comments.

"I've had a change of plans," he finally said.

Wonderful. I'm inept and you don't want me to go on tour with you.

"I had originally thought you would do *Autumn Sunset, I Knew it Was Love* and then another one of my songs. Then you would do one of yours, and we would back you up."

"You're not gonna make me sing *Autumn Sunset?*" she asked hopefully.

"Bite your tongue!" he scolded her. "You bet you're singing it. You're still doing *I Knew it was Love* too. But instead of adding a third one of mine, let's do two of yours. Annie, it was so hard to pick even one. They are all so good. I can't believe these songs have just been sitting on a shelf somewhere. That reminds me, I really want us to do that ragtime piece of yours too."

"My Howard Long commercial?" she laughed.

"Yes," he said seriously. "In fact, I think we'll end the first half of the concert with it. I want you to do the lead piano on that too. I flat out cannot play it. I don't have as many fingers as you do. I'll add some pretty strings or something."

"Now you're just trying to flatter me," she told him. "It's working."

"It's a horrible shame that you have never been exposed publicly. You are gonna take the world by storm, you know?"

"That's what you keep telling me."

"Well, believe it," he persisted. "After hearing these other songs, I've been fighting with myself over which two to actually do. Well, more like which three to eliminate. I love *Unlit Passion.* It has this sultry overtone to it that would blow every one away. It did me. Very vivid word descriptions used in that song, especially for a girl who had never been kissed."

"Who says I wrote it before I was kissed?" she teased.

"You're making *me* blush now," he confessed. "I didn't do *that* to you, at least not like you put it in that song!"

"A girl's first kiss can be quite impressionable."

She needed to stop. She was flirting with him now, and that was something she must not do. She did not need to send unclear signals to him when she had been very clear about her intentions.

"I'm just kidding," she released him. "It's none of your business when I wrote it."

She had written it shortly after he left. It probably was about him, but neither of them needed to believe that.

"Moving right along," he sighed. "I thought *Forever Free* was really excellent. No matter what I did, I could never anticipate anything in that song. It drove me crazy!"

"I did that on purpose," she laughed.

"How?"

"I wrote the melody first," she explained. "Whatever I felt like the next note should be, I wouldn't do it; I would put a different note there. When I finally finished the music, the words came easily. I mean, it had this whole sense of *freedom* about it."

"You're right about that," he agreed. "I really feel like that's a song my fans would enjoy. But then the other three are marvelous too. Look, do you have any preferences? Which two would you like to do?"

"I don't want that load on my brain," she was adamant. "You decide what is best and I'll just jump right on board with you."

"Okay," he sighed again, "but for punishment I'm going to make you wear four-inch heels."

"As long as you wear them with me, buddy."

Annie was back in the emotional dumps again. Angie was gone, and that familiar empty space had crept back in. Angie wasn't all that impressed with seminary and felt that she had more theological sense being raised in a minister's home than what she was getting there. She was also disappointed with the lack of enthusiasm the mission board was showing over her insistence on going to Padawin. Angie's visit had been a bit of a downer so the usual light and easy atmosphere that accompanied her presence was tainted somehow.

Annie was able to concentrate on the few remaining clients she had taken on. Moreover, she continued working on Stephen's concert songs. When things began to seem almost unbearably mundane, she reminded herself that in two months she would be on a world tour with Stephen Williams. It brought a smile to her face every time.

She spent a little more time with Andie also. This pregnancy was making Andie more sick than usual so Annie would pitch in to help with the children or dinner or the house. Andie was always so grateful as she would pick up her pale head enough to give a brief smile. Annie enjoyed the time with the kids too. She could imagine herself being a mother some day, but with all the uncertainty about her future, marriage and children were not even in the running. First, she had to finish the summer—then on to the tour.

As usual, when life seems about as routine as it can possibly get, a curve is inevitably thrown. This one came from Billy Marcum on a Thursday afternoon. Just when Annie had finished one of three final accounts, Terri buzzed her.

"It's a Mr. Marcum," Terri told her.

"Great!" Annie said enthusiastically. She crossed her fingers as she picked up the phone, and then remembered something Stephen had told her. "Those songs didn't magically appear in someone else's studio. Someone was handed your music because someone got into your office and your filing cabinet. So you need to take the word impossible out of this equation and start eliminating your suspects down to possibles."

"Hi, Billy," she said pleasantly. "I need you to do me a favor. Can you give me the number from where you're calling and let me call you right back."

"Sure," he obliged. "It's my cell. I'm driving to Dockrey right now as we speak."

He gave her his number and she wrote it down. She locked up her office and told Terri she had an appointment to keep as she headed out the door. Terri asked something that was totally unnecessary, and Annie promised to deal with it tomorrow. She got into her VW, cranked the car, turned off the CD with Stephen's new album playing, and dialed Billy's number before backing out onto the street."

"Hello? Annie?"

"Yes, Billy. It's me," she confirmed. "What have you learned?"

"It took a while, but I finally got enough info that I should be able to point you in a definite direction."

"Great," she said with relief. "Who is it?"

"Well, for starters, this guy is not even in Alabama. He lives in Chicago."

"You're kidding?" she shot back. "I was told a new company had been started here in north Alabama. I just assumed that's who everyone was using."

"Well, this guy has some kind of contact here who has been moving clients his way. Scott Adkins, the shop owner I work for, said a friend of his was talking about this guy in Chicago that was excellent and cheap. He could put a commercial together in no time, and do it for half the price of what anybody was offering around here."

"Who is his contact?" Annie wondered.

"*That,* I couldn't find out," he lamented. "However, I said that my sister in Hamilton was looking into some advertising. I asked if I could have the guy's name and number in Chicago for her to check with. He looked it up and wrote it all down."

"Wonderful!" Annie said in triumph as she threw her arm into the air. "You earned those tickets and backstage passes! But your sister doesn't live in Hamilton."

"Hey, as long as I was lying, I went the whole course. Felt kind of sneaky. The guy's name is Blake Henley, by the way. Here's his number."

Annie wrote it down on a piece of junk mail she had thrown onto the seat next to her. Progress was finally being made. Maybe this summer wouldn't turn out to be a total wash after all. She gave many thanks to Billy and could hardly stand the drive to the house where she would make her first call to Blake Henley.

In the privacy of her room, she dialed the number.

"Big Time Advertising," came the answer.

"Yes, I'm interesting in hiring Blake Henley to create a commercial for television," Annie tried to sound businesslike.

"Is this in the Chicago area?" the receptionist wanted to know.

"No ma'am," Annie replied. "In north Alabama."

"Would you hold a minute, please?"

Annie stayed on hold for nearly two minutes before the receptionist returned. Obviously, some eyebrows had been raised, if not a few red flags.

"May I have your name please?" she asked Annie.

Whew! She hadn't anticipated that. She half stole Stephen's phony name.

"Alice Andrews," she replied, perhaps a bit too shakily. She hoped she hadn't given herself away.

"And, Ms. Andrews, who recommended you to us?" the receptionist wanted to know.

Oh, man! I have no idea. What was Billy's boss's name? What was it? Something Adkins . . . something Adkins . . . Scott!

"Scott Adkins," she spit out. "He owns a clothing store in Florence."

"Thank you," the receptionist continued. "I'll put you on hold again."

Great. I've probably just blown the whole cover. He's gonna want a number, and if I give him any number I have, it will be traced back to me, and whoever is behind this will know something's going on.

"Ms. Andrews?" the receptionist asked. "If you will leave your number for Mr. Henley, he will call you back at a more convenient time."

Strike three and I'm out.

"I'd rather not do that," Annie said slowly, trying to find an excuse. "I don't have a permanent number yet. I'm just getting settled in. In fact, I'm at a phone booth right now." She winced at the ridiculous lie. "I was hoping mainly for some kind of a price from Mr. Henley. I'll call back later when I have some more concrete ideas in mind."

Hmmm, that didn't go well at all. I'm going to have to be more creative with this or perhaps just more direct.

ꟃ ꟃ

Annie checked her e-mail before she went to bed. Stephen, Angie, and Megan had all written her. She started with the least of her interests: Megan.

Annie!

Hope your 4th was super. Alex and I had a wonderful time.
We went to see the Macy's Fireworks Spectacular, and it lived up to its name. Afterward we went back to the apartment and had ice cream and cupcakes. Can't wait for you to join us! The other musicians are so wonderful. Their wives are super ladies too. You have caused quite a buzz among everyone here. They're all curious to meet this mystery lady that Stephen has invited to share the stage with him. I've told them all about how wonderful you are, and they are looking forward to meeting you. Give me a call sometime.

Every time I try to call you, you're busy. Slow down!!

Love, Your New Sis, Megan

It was a nice little note. Annie was glad that Megan and Alex were doing well. It was nice to know that he could actually live with somebody and bring happiness at the same time. Maybe one day things would change between them. Perhaps this tour would bring them closer together. Or not. It might drive the wedge even deeper.

Next, Angie or Stephen? Oh, why not read Angie's first. Her last few communications had all been on the negative side. Stephen was always upbeat and funny. She was not saving the *best* for last, just the more promising of a nicer note.

Annie,

Where have you been? I tried calling you all day on your cell. I didn't want your fruitcake secretary listening in on my conversation. I'm ready to throw it all in. The mission board told me today that it is highly unlikely that I can go on to Padawin when I finish seminary. They said there are many other places, however, in dire need of a doctor. Yes, I was impolite in my response to them. Michael Collins wrote me just this morning about the desperate need there. I don't know who the board is listening to?? Definitely not me, and sometimes I wonder if they're even listening to God. Enough of my blustering.

Call me, would you? I need to vent!!!!

Angie, the nice sister

Typical. Angie was going to close all the doors to the mission field if she didn't learn to control her mouth and emotions first. *They probably think she is a time bomb ready to explode at any moment. That would be a great testimony about American Christians.* However, the mission board did not see Angie's heart and determination to share the Gospel through medicine. If she could somehow communicate that passion to them, they would probably send her on now.

At last, Stephen's letter. She smiled before even opening it. He had a way of encouraging her no matter what. She was looking forward to laughing and talking with him again on the tour. She hoped there would be time for that.

Annie-Girl

(Megan told me that was your nickname for yourself . . . I rather like it!), I am worn to a tatter. The whirlwind press tour took it out of me. I am glad to be back home, alone in my own apartment. I try to be creative and unique with each interview, but after a while I just find myself using the same little jokes and lines. I bet you'll be good about things like that. The guys loved your songs, and I must admit, Unlit Passion really peaked their interest. Alex just smiled and told them all you were full of surprises. Hopefully, we should have our parts down pat when you get here. September 4 will be here before you know it. I'm sure you've probably got my simple melodies already memorized and worked out completely. Feel free to embellish in any way. Your arrangements you sent have blown me away. Where do you come up with this stuff? By the way, I have really been trying to play your ragtime piece. If I can get it down, how would you like to do a little dueling pianos on stage? Now, that would be fun! Just curious: have you washed her hair lately? (smile) I meant to bring a bottle of that stuff home with me, but I somehow managed to forget it. I'd better go . . . don't want to bore you stiff. Have a great day . . . or night . . . whenever you get around to reading this.

Yours, Stephen

It worked. Annie was still smiling as she turned off the computer. When she reached her room, she opened her closet and shoved the clothes aside. She reached in and unpinned the poster, bringing it out in all its glory back into her room. She pinned it across the room from her bed and sat at its foot to stare. Was it possible that she could actually miss someone so much having known him for so little? Yes. Definitely.

Chapter Fourteen

"What do you mean you're going to Chicago?" Jonathan asked his daughter in the middle of dinner.

"It's the only way I can find out exactly who is responsible for taking my music," Annie told him.

"You can't just pick up and go to Chicago on some kind of wild goose chase!" he insisted. "You don't even know if this company really exists. And, if this man is responsible for stealing one thing, there's no telling what other crime he may be willing to commit to cover his being caught."

"I think you're being a little over dramatic, Daddy," Annie bellowed back. Then she added, almost mouselike, "Besides, I've already bought a plane ticket."

"You've what?" her mother joined in. "Annie, you can't go by yourself!"

"For crying out loud!" Annie exclaimed. "I'm a 26-year-old who runs her own business, and I'm sitting here arguing with my parents about whether I can take a trip somewhere! All I'm doing is trying to get to the bottom of a big mess."

Jonathan leaned his head back and smoothed his thinning gray hair with his hand. He was trying to be wise and patient, but Annie was testing both of those virtues. He knew her mind was made up, and that generally meant there would be no changing it. If only she would listen to reason.

"Okay," he said in a sigh. "But you keep your phone on at all times. I want to know the address you're at, and I want a call when you get to this Henley guy's office. You call me again when you leave. Is that clear?"

Annie rolled her eyes. She felt as if she were 16 again and going to Tupelo with a few friends to catch a movie.

"Yes," she reluctantly agreed. "I will call you."

Annie did not like flying. She had only flown once before, and her father had accompanied her. It had been a national piano competition in Los Angeles. She came in second. One of the judges told her that it was her demeanor that had cost her the competition, not her talent. During a preliminary interview, she had donned a bit of an attitude that the judges found unpleasant. Over the years, there had been things to help sand that attitude out, but Annie still fought it regularly.

She had only brought a carry-on piece of luggage. Therefore, when the plane landed, she immediately found a cab and headed to her hotel for the night. She would awaken bright and early the next morning to search out Big Time Advertising and Blake Henley.

After settling into her room, she went downstairs to the restaurant and ordered a meal. She felt rather intimidated by the hustle and bustle of people in the city. Cars were constantly passing as well as people. Men were dressed in suits having business dinners; women were dressed professionally and discussing details over laptops. A few couples came in and lingered casually over their meals, but most of the patrons were all business. Annie felt completely out of place and found her appetite had waned significantly by the time her dinner arrived. She ate what she could then put the rest in a carryout container.

Back in her room, she turned on the television to cover up the intense silence, and then called her parents to let them know all was well so far. She pulled out a huge phone book from beneath the bedside table and looked up Big Time Advertising. There it was. She copied down the address and put the phone book back. She then sat silently on the bed, mindlessly watching the television. How strange it was to see unfamiliar faces on the news and listen to advertisements for places she had never heard of before. The bigness of the city became real to her, and then she thought about the bigness of the world as a whole. Since Chicago was Stephen's hometown, she assumed this would be a stop on the tour. Sometime this fall she would not be just a nobody sitting alone in a hotel room, she would be a featured artist sharing the stage with Stephen Williams. It was just a bit too overwhelming.

She fought the urge to call Stephen and opted for a nice, long, hot shower instead. When she finally turned in, she was so tired that she turned off the television, set her clock, and then drifted off to sleep immediately. She had fitful dreams all night, many of which included Stephen's mother reaching out to her with her gnarled hands.

"Here it is, lady," the cab driver said as he pulled up to a multi-story office building.

"Wow, that's a big place," she said slightly intimidated. "Is this whole thing Big Time Advertising?"

"I doubt it," the driver told her. "Most likely it's just one of many businesses in the building."

She paid the driver and watched him drive off. She checked the address in her hand with the number of the building. This was the place. Before going in, she called her father as promised, and then entered the lobby. Beside the elevator was a long listing of all the businesses in the complex. She carefully checked each floor until she spotted Big Time Advertising. It was on the 19th floor. Great. Annie was not fond of heights.

She stepped into the elevator with more people than she had imagined could actually fit in one. She looked at the capacity limit and began to count heads. She then made herself stop, wondering what she would actually do if there were more than allowed. Make somebody get off? Get off herself? Call the elevator police? She smiled at her insecurity.

"What floor, Miss?" asked a man near the front. He was looking right at her.

"Oh, 15th," she said. He immediately pressed the button. "Wait! No. It's the 19th. Sorry."

"You're not from here, are you?" asked a man standing next to her.

"No, I'm not," she smiled politely. "What gave it away?"

"Everything," he said bluntly.

The door opened and he got out.

Everything? What does that mean? My accent? My clothes? The fact that I couldn't remember what floor I needed to go to?

Annie breathed a sigh of relief when the elevator made it to the 19th floor. She exited and seriously considered taking the stairs when it came time to go back down. She straightened her clothes, tossed back her hair, and then began to bemoan the fact that she did not put her hair up. She would have looked much more professional.

She found Big Time Advertising immediately and told herself not to hesitate when she went in. She needed to act as though she knew what she was doing, remaining tough and insistent about finding out who was responsible for stealing her music. This would be one time when donning an attitude would be appropriate.

"May I help you?" asked the receptionist as soon as Annie walked through the glass door.

"Yes, ma'am," she replied confidently. "I need to see Blake Henley."

"Do you have an appointment?" the receptionist continued.

"No, I don't," Annie said, still trying to ooze with confidence.

Imagine being Vivian McCall. Handle this as she would.

"But I'm sure Mr. Henley will be glad to fit me in," she added with just a touch of insistence.

"May I have your name please?" the receptionist asked.

"He won't know my name," Annie told her bluntly. "But I guarantee you he will know my music. Tell him that, would you? And also, mention that I just flew in from Dockrey, Alabama."

The receptionist gave her an annoyed look.

"May I please have your name," the receptionist repeated.

"Annie Wright."

"Ms. Wright," she began.

"It's *Miss,*" Annie interrupted her. "I'm not married, and I don't have a problem with that."

"Very well, *Miss* Wright," the lady continued, "our offices are extremely busy. It is imperative that you make an appointment if you wish to speak with one of our associates."

"Miss . . ." Annie read the name on the desk plaque, "Miss Sella . . ."

"*Ms.*," the woman corrected her.

"I'm sorry, *Ms.* Sella, it is *imperative* that you allow me to speak with Blake Henley if you do not wish to have the pants sued off of your business. Tell him Annie Wright is here from Dockrey, Alabama, and would like to speak with him concerning commercials he has written using someone else's music."

"This is not proper procedure," Ms. Sella insisted.

"You're doggone right it's not!" Annie said a little more firmly. "And if you don't begin to make some kind of effort to contact Mr. Henley immediately, I'll become even a little more *improper.*"

"I don't know how business is conducted in Alabama, but here in Chicago we use a little more tact and etiquette."

"Is that so?" Annie began to fume. "Plagiarism, then, is acceptable as long as it is carried out with tact and etiquette? Wow, you're right; we don't handle things like that where I come from. When someone steals from someone else, we refer to that as a felony. We go to the courts, and then we have settlements where the one who was wronged is compensated handsomely for having her rights violated. So pardon me if I don't know how you *handle* things up here."

Annie turned to go, then quickly turned back to say, "Tell Mr. Henley a merciless lawyer from Alabama will be contacting him by the end of the day to begin proceedings. And trust me on this one—my lawyer knows exactly what he's doing."

"Miss Wright!" Ms. Sella called out. "If you will just be patient, I will take this matter up with Mr. Henley. However, it would have been more accommodating had you called for an appointment."

"Thank you," Annie smiled as she calmly sat down in the waiting area. "I eagerly await my meeting with Mr. Henley."

After a brief exit, Ms. Sella returned and informed Annie that Blake Henley would be with her in a moment. Annie smiled and nodded still trying to exude confidence. She hoped Mr. Henley would be as easy to intimidate as Ms. Sella, especially considering that Annie had no legal leg to stand on. Her unused files were not copyrighted, but no one knew that. She would have to make idle threats and hope that the fear of dragging the company's name through a lawsuit would be enough to elicit a name of the contact in Alabama.

Annie thumbed through some old magazines while waiting. She assumed Blake Henley was trying to get his facts together before bringing her in. Annie spied an old issue of *People* with a small picture of Stephen in the corner. She picked it up and opened the table of contents to find what the article might be about. Flipping to the page, she began to read:

Will Stephen Williams' (32) new love finally pin down the world's most eligible bachelor? Model Carrie McCarthy (27), best known as the new Freedom Faire Girl for Freedom Faire Makeup, was Stephen's date for this year's Grammy Awards. The couple arrived at the awards hand-in-hand and waved graciously to the crowds who were screaming their names. This is the third event that the duo has attended publicly together. Rumors have it that she may travel with him during his next tour. Don't bring out the tissues yet, girls. Stephen has courted many lovely ladies in his time, but has yet to make the trek down the aisle. Carrie may possibly be only another award for Mr. Williams to place on his shelf.

Annie cringed as she read the article. She actually felt a tinge of jealously. She thought of the few moments that she and Stephen had exchanged and began to feel embarrassed at the thought of his being interested in her. He was used to dating professional models; what would he want with an overly pretentious Southern girl? However, he had told her that he had not been with anyone for five years. Obviously, he had been with Carrie McCarthy at three public events. Who was he lying to, Annie or the public?

"Mr. Henley will see you now," Ms. Sella informed her.

"Thank you," Annie stumbled out as she remembered where she was. Stephen was an easy distraction for her these days. She tried to clear her head and keep in mind why she was here.

Just act like Vivian McCall. You'll get whatever you want if you can pull this off.

Annie walked through the door that Ms. Sella pointed out and was greeted by a man much younger than she had expected. Blake Henley could be no more than a couple of years older than she was. He was a thin man with round glasses, pale skin, and bright red hair with a goatee beard to match. He reached out his hand in greeting, but Annie refused to take it.

Vivian McCall would just stare blankly at him, assuming he was guilty and knew exactly what this meeting was about.

"Whether I shake your hand or not, Blake, depends on the outcome of this meeting, not the beginning," she told him firmly. She liked the way his first name could almost be spit out. When she said it, the sound was scathing and stinging.

"I feel there has been some sort of misunderstanding here, Ms. Wright," he began.

"Please don't call me *Ms.*," she said quickly. "If you want to keep this formal, Blake," she spit it out again, "then call me Miss Wright. But as far as I'm concerned, you might as well call me Annie, because you are way more familiar with me than you may be willing to admit."

"I'm afraid that you have an advantage over me in the fact that I am totally unaware of all that you are talking about," he said nervously.

"Oh, I doubt that," Annie persisted in the charade of pretending to be like Vivian McCall. "Exactly how much do I have to tell you in order for us to be on the same page here, Blake?"

"Apparently everything," he said innocently. "I have no idea what you're talking about."

"I write commercials from my own little business in Dockrey, Alabama. I could care less about *owning the market* there, Blake. I enjoy what I do, and it has been very lucrative for me. However, I have recently heard commercials on both radio and television that used *my* music, but they were not *my* commercials."

Annie pulled out a CD from her portfolio and walked over to a player in his office.

"May I?" she asked as she put the CD in.

"Certainly," he tried to sound calm and confident.

He loosened his tie and collar slightly as Annie programmed the CD. From the corner of her eye, she could tell he was very nervous despite his bravado.

She played the five commercials all the way through, then removed the CD and placed it back into her portfolio. She turned to Blake Henley and stared, waiting for a response.

"I don't know what you want me to say," he told her.

"Are those your commercials?" she asked point-blank.

"Possibly," he half admitted. "I do so many that I don't remember everything I've done."

"That's baloney," she said as she let her voice betray a touch of anger. "You remember every single thing you've ever written. Or perhaps, the reason it doesn't touch some deep recess of your memory is because maybe you didn't actually create it; you just took something created by someone else and doctored it up a bit."

"I don't like what you are insinuating, Ms. Wright," he began to defend.

"And I don't like being called *Ms.*!" she countered him quickly. "Did you or did you not create those five commercials, Blake? Have you been in contact with someone in Alabama and been turning out commercials for him or her? A simple *yes* or *no* is all that's needed at this point!"

"We write commercials for people all over the nation," he tried to explain rationally. "It is very possible that I wrote some commercials for someone in Alabama."

"That's not the answer I'm looking for, Blake," she spit out his name again. "Let me just clear all of this up for you. I have files that were obviously stolen and copied in some way."

She reached into her portfolio and pulled out her file of "Unused Songs" and threw it on his desk.

"Those five commercials all used melodies from this file," she went on, trying to rant and rave slightly. It was getting easier. "The thing about this file, Blake, is that I am no idiot. I copyright everything I stick in there."

She lied. She had to hope that she appeared just crazy enough to copyright even the single-lined musical phrases that were on some of the pages in that folder.

"You copyright things you don't even use?" he asked in unbelief.

"Call me crazy, Blake," she continued, "but you never know when someone might up and steal your stuff. It's always a possibility. These aren't registered copyrights. They're sealed in envelopes at the post office with an official postal seal and then sent to me. I have boxes under my bed, Blake, with envelopes, all sealed and dated, legal enough to stand up in any court of law."

She opened her file on his desk and pulled out a piece of manuscript music.

"See this?" she asked as she waved the music in front of his face. "This was number one on that CD, Muchos Music, I believe. I called it *Wonderland Theme.* It's in an envelope under my bed dated and sealed three years ago."

If it were possible, it appeared that Blake Henley's paleness just went a degree deeper.

"And this one," she said as she pulled out another piece of music, "was number two on that CD, Adkins Clothing. My melody was simply called *Untitled Seventeen.* Sometimes it's hard to give them all real names, Blake. But you know what? It's in an envelope under my bed, labeled *Untitled Seventeen,* and sealed. Legally and unmistakably sealed, and dated last year."

Blake was now starting to turn a few shades of red. He was not confessing yet, so Annie continued with what was now becoming a slight tirade. How much would it take to make this guy confess?

"And here's number three on that CD," she continued as she pulled out another piece of music on the green manuscript paper.

"I think I have seen quite enough, Annie Wright!" he finally blurted out. "I don't know exactly what you are accusing me of, but I have done nothing wrong here, and I believe it is time for you to leave this office."

Annie stared at him with a blazing look. She picked up her music and put it back into her file, then placed the file into her portfolio. The silence was deafening after all the raised voices. She straightened her clothes then looked him dead in the eyes.

"Fine, Blake," she rolled out his name again in contempt. "For the record, I could care less about the commercials. Whatever. What angers me is that someone, someone who knew me well, managed to get behind two locks that only I have keys to, and deliberately stole my music. Then they gave it to you, a man who is quite competent enough to write his own music, I *assume.* It was all done to get at me for some reason. Blake, I don't want to prosecute you nor your company. I really don't care. But what I do want is a name of whoever is doing this to me. If you refuse to give me *that* name, then I *will* take this to court. The result will be that your company will be humiliated by some down-home Southern girl from the boondocks of Alabama who will be awarded a huge sum of money because you used her copyrighted music for five commercials."

Annie swung around toward the door with her fingers crossed mentally in her mind. She hoped he would buy her bluff, but before she reached for the doorknob, she quickly turned back around to add the exclamation mark.

"My lawyer should contact you by tomorrow," she said firmly. "This is a big company. Perhaps the payoff you have to give me will ease the violation I've been dealt through all of this."

She went back for the door and made sure there was no hesitation in her step. She turned the knob and jerked it open.

"Stop!" Blake finally called out. "Just close the door and calm down, please."

Annie smoothly shut the door and turned back to face Blake Henley.

"I'm not exactly sure what has happened here," he said calmly, his face getting redder with each second that passed. "Yes, I am familiar with those commercials."

Annie walked toward the desk.

"I don't want to prosecute you, Mr. Henley," she said more gently now. "I just want this stopped."

Blake rubbed his hand down his beard as he tried to phrase his words carefully.

"I was told the music was written by this man's sister," he confessed. "I had no reason to doubt him. He wanted to use her music in a series of commercials for North Alabama. Fine. People do that occasionally. I was impressed. It's great music! So I did what I was paid to do. It was easy not having to come up with a tune."

"Who is the man?" Annie probed.

"Look, Miss Wright," he said nervously, "I was paid a large amount to never mention his name. I just assumed . . . well, I don't know what I assumed. It was money on the side, and it was a lot."

"Does it compare with the money your company will pay out in a lawsuit if I have to bring this to court? All I want is a name, Blake. I don't want anything more. But if I have to prosecute to get that name, that's what I'll do."

"For the record, it was a total of nine songs so far," he told her as he sat at his desk.

He pulled out a file and handed her the music he had received.

"Someone at least had the decency to put them in computerized script," she said as she looked over the notes. "These match note for note, you know?"

"I would never have done this in a million years," he said in defeat. "I wouldn't steal someone's music. I didn't even file my name with the copyright office; I did it under the sister's name."

"And what is that name?" Annie continued to demand. "Who is your contact in Alabama?"

"Do I have your word that you will not prosecute?" he asked her.

"Not only do you have my word on that," she promised, "but your name will never come up in any conversation I have with anybody after this."

"You can't promise that," he told her. "These people are crooks. You'll have to tell them where you got the information. Then I'll have to give the money back, the money that I've already spent."

"How much did they pay you to keep quiet?" Annie asked.

"$150,000," he said meekly.

Annie's eyes grew huge. Who would pay that kind of money to see her this mad?

She asked him slow and deliberate this time, "Who did this?"

"His name is Wade McCall," he said timidly.

Annie dropped into the extra chair and put her head into her hands. Unbelievable. Wade McCall, Vivian's son, Kelly's brother. So the enmity was returned.

"I take it you know him?" Blake asked her.

"Oh yeah," she moaned. "Very well."

Annie stood up and tried to pull her emotions back into control.

"I will do my best not to mention your name," she told him. "If it comes down to you having to return the money, I'll see what I can do."

"They aren't finished with me yet," he added. "I'm to meet with Mr. McCall and his mother next week about two more commercials, using the sister's music again."

"I'd suggest you cancel it," was all Annie could get out before she left the office.

Back in her hotel room, Annie called her father. He had been worried sick and was about to call the police in Chicago to go after her. She apologized for forgetting to call him right after leaving the office, but when she explained the situation he calmed down slightly. She then called Angie to tell her about the meeting. Angie could not believe that anyone from Dockrey could be so conniving.

"The thing that still gets at me," Annie lamented, "is that someone had to give them a key to get in."

"They could have picked the locks," Angie suggested.

"On the file cabinet, yes," Annie agreed, "but not the office door. It's metal and it's dead bolted. Someone had to have a key to get in."

"What about your fruit loop secretary?"

Annie blew her hair out of her face as she changed hands with her phone.

"I know everyone keeps putting her in the suspect list," Annie explained, "but I don't think Terri is capable of doing something like that and then be able to face me every day without somehow giving it away. She's not smart enough to be so devious."

"Okay, then who else would have access to your keys? Daddy? Moms? Me? Who else?" Angie began to interrogate.

"I don't know!" Annie yelled out. "I'm just gonna have to think on it for awhile."

"What are you going to do with this information?" Angie asked.

"I have no idea," Annie confessed. "I know who's responsible, but how do I go about putting a stop to it . . . or shoot . . . just confronting them about it? I never considered what I would do if I ever found out."

"Well, start considering," Angie told her. "I'll put my thinking cap on down here and see if I can concoct some type of plan. Meanwhile, stay out of trouble."

"What does that mean?" Annie asked a bit miffed.

"It means trouble follows you. Avoid it. I don't know that I'm all that comfortable with you crossing swords with the McCalls."

"That's what Daddy said."

"Then play smart, Annie. Don't jump into something without knowing where it's headed."

"I'll agree with everyone on this one," Annie admitted. "I'll be careful. Still, I just get mad all over when I think that Kelly McCall's name is on my songs registered somewhere in the copyright office."

"I'd get rather mad myself," Angie agreed, but then quickly warned, "but I wouldn't dare confront any McCall with anything until all my ducks were in a straight row."

"Warning heeded," Annie told her.

Annie ate lunch again at the hotel, but had nothing else to do. Her flight out was not until the following morning because she had not figured she would get her answers in one simple meeting. She sat back on the bed in the room and flipped through the channels. She considered calling Stephen, but decided against it. Perhaps he was having lunch with Carrie McCarthy somewhere. That thought did not bring a smile.

She pulled out the phone book, fat with only yellow pages, and began to look through it.

This is nothing but businesses and such. What do you do if you want to call someone's house?

She looked back under the table and spied another phone book with apparently only white pages.

Cool. A residential phone book too. If they did this in Dockrey, you'd only have two thin-line brochures.

She began glancing through the pages. She started with *Blake Henley.* Found him easily, the only one in Chicago. She looked up the name *Sella* and found several listings. She could not remember what

Ms. Sella's first name was.

Stephen's from Chicago. What was his Dad's name? Really weird. Let's see, Andrew? No, too normal. What was it?

She pictured them lying on the overlook and remembered asking him his mother's name: *Ellen.* Then she had asked his father's name. Something *drew.*

Annie turned to the Williams' section and began to glance through each name, hoping she would recognize the name if she saw it. Not in the A's, not in the B's. She kept going. Then it jumped off the page at her: Edrew Williams. She jotted down the address and grabbed her purse. This would be fun! She would drive by and see where Stephen grew up.

She hailed a cab and gave the driver the paper with the address.

"Yeah, I know where dat is," he told her. "Not da best section o' town. You know da people there?"

"Well, I'm a friend of the family," she stretched the truth.

He drove for about 20 minutes before finally pulling onto the street. He stopped in front of an old, dilapidated home and assured her this was the address. The house needed painting and one of the upstairs windows had a broken pane taped up with plastic and duct tape. She stepped out of the cab a bit uneasily, still not knowing why she was getting out. She imagined Ellen Williams sitting on the front steps with her gnarled hands waiting for Stephen to come home from school. She tried to picture Stephen's blue eyes and curly blond hair on a little boy, and the image was adorable.

"Are you gonna be okay, lady?" the driver asked through the window.

"I'm not sure," she said as she vacillated between staying and going. "Could you wait here for me?"

"How long you gonna be?"

"I honestly don't know," she told him.

"Look, I don't really want to leave you here, but time is money."

"How much could I give you to stay and wait? I'll pay you," she offered.

"Time is money," he repeated as he pointed to his meter.

"Okay, then," she smiled and shrugged, "start your meter. I'll be out when I'm out."

He smiled back and nodded. He realized she was clueless that he was paid by the mile and not the minute. Had she not been so beautiful and obviously naïve, he might have driven on. *Why am I always such a good Samaritan?* he thought to himself.

Annie could not believe she was actually going to attempt to talk to Stephen's father. This was ridiculous! What was she going to say? She forced herself up the steps and then knocked on the front door. She half hoped no one would be home, but her curiosity had gotten the best of her. She knocked again, a little harder. The description Stephen had given of his father was not flattering. She herself had to wonder what kind of man would totally reject his son.

"What do you want?" came a yell from the inside of the door.

"Mr. Williams? Edrew?" she called back.

"I know who I am!" said the voice. "Who are you and what do you want?"

"My name is Annie," she began to explain as she tried shouting through the closed door. "I'm a good friend of Stephen's. I'm in Chicago on a business trip and thought I would check in on you."

"You're a liar!" he called back. "I ain't talking to the press! You want to know something about Stephen, hunt him down yourself!"

"Mr. Williams," she continued, "I am not with the press. I write music for commercials. Stephen and I are colleagues. I just wanted to meet you."

"Why?"

"Because I want to know what kind of man would totally reject his son when his son is a wonderful person."

Edrew didn't yell back this time. She waited quietly until she heard the door begin to unlock. Slowly the door opened, and a thin face peeked between the crack.

"You're meddling, lady," he said to her.

"I know, sir," she replied. "Would you please let me meddle just a little bit more?"

"You don't know what you're into, miss. You need to just leave."

"My name is Annie," she said as she stuck her hand up to the crack in greeting.

He wouldn't open the door any more, and he would not extend his hand in return.

"I don't care who you are, Miss Annie," he said firmly. "I don't want to talk to you."

"Please," she began to plead. "I think I'm in love with your son."

Why on earth did she say that? She really was meddling, and she was desperate to talk to this man. Was she grasping at straws?

"You don't know if you love him or not?" he asked in puzzlement.

"It's hard to tell," she tried to explain. "It's not like Stephen is the boy next door, you know? I can't exactly decipher my feelings toward him. Sometimes I think we have a special connection, and then I'll turn around and think I'm just star-struck again."

"What does that have to do with me?" he wanted to know. He wasn't giving in easily.

"I'm not sure," she tried to come up with something. "Maybe if I can somehow connect with Stephen's past I can get beyond his being some superstar. He knows my family well, and to him I'm just this normal person. But I know nothing about him except his life right now, and I'm afraid that's not enough to build a relationship on."

Edrew stared at her for a bit longer. He was sizing her up completely. Annie still did not know why she was there, or why it was so important for her to talk to him. Her reasoning, however, surprised her. Maybe that was how she really did feel inside. As much as she found herself caring for Stephen on one hand, there was this other side that she could not get beyond. Stephen was not a real person. Maybe speaking with his father would bring him more into a normal light.

"I may be crazy," Edrew said as he opened the door fully, "but you are either one creative press agent or you're telling the truth."

Annie held up her hands to show she had nothing hidden with her.

"No recorders or note pads, sir," she promised. "I just want to talk to you about Stephen."

Edrew finally pulled the door all the way open and then motioned her him. Annie followed him through a small foyer into the living room. The house reeked with the smell of alcohol, and paint was peeling off the walls. A huge plasma TV covered the greater portion of one wall, and a portrait of Ellen and Sandy hung on another. Newspapers and beer bottles, along with empty frozen dinner trays littered the room, but a massive sound system in one corner stood in stark contrast to the trash.

Edrew shoved some papers aside on the couch to make room for Annie to sit, while he went to his plush recliner and dropped down.

"Not what you expected, huh?" he questioned her. "Bet you didn't think Stephen Williams came from a dump like this."

"I'm guessing it didn't always look like this," she said as she watched a roach scurry off one of the dinner trays.

"You're right," he admitted. "It was a beautiful place once. Guess I lost my motivation for fixing it up after Ellen died. You know about her, I presume."

"Yes, sir," Annie told him as she scanned the room for any more bugs. "She was killed in a crash along with your daughter."

"Told you all that, did he?" Edrew mused as he sat back in the recliner. "Did he tell you where they'd been?"

Annie nodded and said, "At one of his competitions."

"I guess you are telling the truth," he finally admitted. "As far as I know, Stephen's never told anyone that."

"Why do you hate him so? He wasn't driving the car. He had no control over whether Ellen went or not."

Edrew didn't look at her; he merely gazed at a spot on the carpet and nodded.

"He is your *son,*" she added.

Edrew looked up at her and halfway squinted as he barely nodded.

"Don't you feel like you owe him some sort of respect or support?" Annie wondered.

"He ain't my son," Edrew drew out slowly.

"That's very cold, Mr. Williams," Annie said flatly. "You may not want to claim him, but he's still your flesh and blood."

"No, he ain't," Edrew said again. "He ain't my son."

"You're unbelievable!" Annie rebuked. "He lost his mother at 15, and believe me, he has guilt about that. But you've done nothing but reject him since that day, and he still tries to buy your approval. Look at this house! Plasma television, expensive sound equipment, all just examples of a 15-year-old still trying to win the approval of his father. Is your heart so cold that you can't find any room in there to accept him just a little?"

"You ain't listening to me, lady," Edrew said again without any emotion. "He ain't my son. He ain't my flesh and blood. My name's on his birth certificate, but he ain't mine."

Annie tried to process what Edrew was saying. Was Stephen not really his son, or had he just disowned him?

"Are you saying that Stephen has another father somewhere? A blood father? Ellen was with another man when she conceived Stephen?"

"That's what I'm saying," he said with no emotion.

"Ellen had an affair?" she asked.

"No," Edrew pushed back the recliner, breathed a deep sigh, and began the long tale. "Ellen was a beautiful, talented, vibrant young lady. All she wanted was to play her music. She was a pianist and singer at a night club in Indianapolis."

"But she was handicapped," Annie blurted out.

"Not yet, she wasn't," Edrew went on. "She was—beautiful. I'd get off at the factory and go in just to hear her sing. Sometimes, I would walk her home if she stayed late at night. She was kind and full of life and laughter. One night I dropped by after work, and she wasn't there. The owner said she had to quit, that it was none of my business, and to go on home. That didn't sound right to me. I went to her apartment and heard crying inside. Not just crying, but wailing and mourning. I called to her and begged her to let me in. She trusted me. She let me in."

Edrew had slight tears forming as he recalled the story. She wondered if he had ever told anyone this before. This family was obviously very good at holding secrets.

"She was bruised and battered, but the thing that caught my attention most was her hands. They had been beaten, with a hammer I found out later. They were bloody and broken. She'd discovered she was pregnant. He was Jewish. Her family was Catholic. He was a musician, a conductor. He had promised her big things, but only gave her an unwanted child. He said he'd pay for the abortion, but Ellen wasn't that kind of girl. Out of desperation, she told her parents. Her father beat her, smashed her hands, and told her that was God's punishment for cavorting with an infidel."

"Stephen said it was a birth defect," Annie told him.

"Yes," he nodded. "I know. She didn't want him to know the truth. I took her to the hospital that night, but there was no hope. I told her I would marry her and take care of her for the rest of her life. She wouldn't do it unless I would promise never to tell the kid the truth—about his father or about her hands or about her family. I agreed. We moved to Chicago. Her family never even knew that she had died."

"Her parents are still alive?" she asked in amazement.

"As far as I know. Stephen's father is too."

Annie looked at him and felt pity for him for the first time.

"Why did you tell me this?" she asked.

"Because someone should know the truth," he said simply. "I

had intended to take it to the grave with me. But since you asked so adamantly, why not empty the Pandora's box and be rid of it?"

"You said his father is still alive. Where is he?"

"You mean *who* is he?" Edrew corrected her. "Does the name Benjamin Brenner ring any bells?"

"The conductor/composer Benjamin Brenner?" she asked stunned.

"Oh yeah," Edrew mulled over in his mind. "Good old Ben Brenner. Musician par excellence, but failure as a man."

"Benjamin Brenner is Stephen's real father?" she asked again as she dealt with the blow of this shocking revelation. "The movie composer and conductor?"

Edrew just nodded, almost expressing relief at having finally told his secret.

"If you married Ellen to take care of her, and you gave Stephen your name, why did you hate him so much? Why did you reject him like you did when you knew he would always think your were his father?" Annie asked beginning to feel a little irritation.

"I loved Ellen," he said sadly. "I figured becoming her savior would help her to love me back. She never did, but she loved Stephen. She always made that clear to me too. He was first in her life, and nobody would take a back seat to him. She showered him with enough encouragement and attention to last anybody a lifetime. I couldn't help it; I couldn't love the boy because he had all her love."

"He was just a child!" Annie tried to defend.

"It didn't hurt him none, did it?" Edrew said loudly and clearly annoyed. "Was I right or what? That boy had more attention showed to him that even when his only source of love was gone, he went on to do great things. He's rich! He's famous! He's a phenomenal success! Me? I worked in a factory for minimal wages in order to support him and his mother! Then he took her from me before she ever found any real love in her heart for me!"

"She died in an accident," Annie corrected him.

"Following him hours away just to hear him play that blamed piano!" Edrew shouted at her. "He didn't need me! He didn't ever need me!"

Annie stood up in disgust and turned to leave.

"Don't you think bad of me, lady!" he called out. "I did my best to protect her and live my life. He ain't my boy. He never was; he never will be."

"I'm sorry, Mr. Williams," Annie said scathingly, "but I feel like a bigger man *could* have done better. You could have accepted him. Do you ever think maybe that's what Ellen wanted to begin with? Had you actually been a loving father to Stephen, she may have found room in her heart to love you like you desired."

"Think what you want. I don't care," he seethed. "All I know is that the weight is on your shoulders now. Mighty heavy, ain't it?"

Annie wanted to agree, but she wanted to leave more. She left the rundown house and saw that the cab was still waiting. She hopped in quickly and asked the driver to return her to her hotel. Her mind rushed through all the information she had received that day. First, the deliberate deception of the McCalls was overwhelming enough. These people were trying to do something to hurt her, even stooping to illegal means in order to carry it out. Why? She did not care for any of them either, but to out and out destroy them was not in her makeup. Then Edrew's revelation concerning Stephen was a whole other matter. And now, what should she do with the information? Do you tell a 32-year-old man that the guy who raised and hated him is not his father? But instead, another man from an illicit relationship, who happens to be one of the most successful movie score composers in the world, is his father. This was too bizarre and too much for Annie to handle.

"Miss, we're here," the cab driver told her as Annie tried to control her sobs. "I'm really sorry about what happened in there."

Annie took out her money and paid him, but still sat in the cab.

"This has been a rough day for me," she tried to explain. "Too many surprises and too many let downs."

"I've had days like dat myself." He looked back over the seat at her. "You like sub sandwiches?"

Annie nodded as she blew her nose.

"Around da corner up there, over on da right, is da best sub shack in all of Chicago," he said with a smile. "Forget da fancy shmancy stuff in da hotel. You go get yourself a good sandwich tonight, pick up one of their big cookies for dessert, then kick back in your room and just relax. Me? I'd watch da Cubs play, but I'm guessing you ain't a Cubs fan."

She shook her head and smiled as she said, "Marlins."

"Well, to each their own," he laughed. "But you need to do something to settle down. Take my word for it. Cab driving can get quite stressful at times. Not every body is as polite as you."

"Well, thank you for that positive note," Annie told him as she reached for the handle. "It's nice to know that someone in this city will think of me as a nice person."

Chapter Fifteen

It was August 2, Monday morning, and Annie was still in a fog as to how to approach the McCall's concerning her music. She knew they were behind it, but the only evidence she had was the word of Blake Henley in Chicago, whom she was sure had probably already broken any ties with them out of sheer fear. She could not just sit down with them and say, "I know you stole my music; Blake told me so." They would laugh at her and call her a paranoid, precocious little dear. The very idea that she would accuse the McCalls of something so vile would totally appall them—at least they would make it appear so.

That was not what plagued Annie the most, however. The idea that someone managed to steal her keys and get into her office and files was the biggest concern. She went over her mental checklist yet again, probably for the 30th time. Everyday, she came into her office and placed her keys in her top drawer. She never left her office without her keys. When she left for lunch or home or for an errand, she took her keys with her because she had to drive. The only possible time she would not be in her office while her keys remained in the drawer would be to use the restroom. That would mean the only possible person who could have access to her keys would be Terri. Terri would have to somehow get into the drawer, make copies of the two keys, and get them back to the drawer, all before Annie returned to the office.

Terri can't even find the nose on her face without someone showing it to her. There's no way she could do something this devious and complicated without showing evidence of stress.

Annie turned back to her piano and stared at the music she was working on. She was down to one final commercial—Pizza Palace. She had a lovely little Italian tune going but was stuck as to where it should end up. She could go dramatic, fun, or outright frivolous. The first two lines were the basis of the song, but which attitude should mark the rest? She decided to just go ahead and write all three endings, then later she would pick which one sounded more like Pizza Palace.

She reached to her filing cabinet for another piece of the green music manuscript paper. It was empty.

Rats! I thought I told Terri to order some more.

She left the piano and cracked open her office door.

“Terri,” she called out. “Did you order the manuscript paper?”

“Sure did,” Terri said happily.

“Is it in?” Annie wondered.

“Not yet,” she said with a shake of her head. “It comes from Florida. With all the hurricanes down there this year, there’s a good chance things are running really slow.”

“Oh,” was all Annie said as she shut the door back.

She sat down again at the piano and stared back at the music. She wanted to write all three endings. Finally, she picked up the music and headed out the door to the copier.

“Watcha doin’?” Terri asked her as she passed by her desk.

“I need to copy this so I can write some different stuff for the endings.”

“Do you want me to do it?” Terri piped up.

“No. I think I can manage it.”

Annie stuck the paper on the glass inside the copy machine and closed the lid. She pressed the green button and waited for the copied page to appear.

“Oh, rats,” she moaned as the paper came out dark.

“What?” Terri asked as she came over.

“This green paper comes out dark in the copier,” Annie said as she held up the sheet.

“You have to lighten it,” Terri explained as she started to press buttons. “You have to press this one first, see the little picture there? Then you see this on the display.”

She showed the images to Annie, little icons of varying degrees of shading.

“For this green paper you simply press this button three times. One, two, and three,” Terri demonstrated carefully. “Now press the enter key here. You’re ready to copy.”

Terri pressed the green button and out came a perfect sheet. *Wow.* Annie was actually impressed.

“I need one more,” Annie told her. “Do I have to reset it again?”

“No,” Terri explained. “It gives you about 30 seconds before it sets itself back to normal. Just press *copy* again.”

Out came another perfect sheet.

"All right," Annie smiled. "I guess you know your stuff with office equipment."

"I've been doing this for three years now," Terri said bubbly. "Copying your green sheets is like second nature to me."

Annie went back to her office and shut the door. She started with the first ending, the dramatic one, and wrote down the notes on the original green sheet. When she was ready for the second ending, she put up one of the copied sheets and just stared again.

This looks strange. I guess I'm so used to the green that this black and white looks weird.

She began to write the notes, but was having trouble with her pencil on the copied lines. The lines were slick and embossed, and her pencil would not mark well over them.

I've never had this trouble before. Maybe I should try ink. No. Never write music in ink!

Annie tried several more times to write the notes on the paper, but it was becoming a bit of a mess. She gave up with the pencil and pulled out a fine-point felt tip marker.

Just this once.

Annie lounged on the couch in the great room at home with her half-gallon box of ice cream beside her. She flipped channels on the television hoping to find something to occupy her time. August was going to be a long month. She had finished writing the Pizza Palace jingle and would have it recorded tomorrow. That meant she would be finished with all accounts and would have no work to do for the rest of the month. She did not fly to New York until September 4. How on earth was she going to bide her time until then?

One of her stolen commercials popped up on the TV, and she scowled as she thought of Kelly McCall's name being on that piece of music. She imagined Kelly, peroxide head Vivian, and self-absorbed Wade McCall sitting around laughing at the fact that they had pulled a good one over on Annie Wright. They probably thought all of this was real cute. If only Annie had actually copyrighted the music. She could have legitimately sued all of them and had the last word. As it was now, even if she were able to confront them, there was nothing legal she could do.

"Good afternoon, sweetie," Barbara said as she came in the front door with two bags of groceries. "You're home early."

"I finished all I needed to do today," Annie explained with a yawn. "I thought I'd just come home and do nothing."

"It's nice to do nothing occasionally, isn't it?" he mother smiled as she took the bags to the kitchen.

Not really. I am bored to death.

"Angie called today," her mother shouted from the kitchen. "She asked for you to call her when you get a chance."

Annie got up to put the ice cream back into the freezer.

"Honey, why don't you put that into a bowl?" Barbara asked with a frown. "That's so nasty to just eat it out of the box."

"I didn't have the energy to dip it out," Annie mumbled. "Where's Dad?"

"He and the three marijuana children are painting the fellowship hall."

Annie chuckled. Those kids had messed with the wrong pastor by planting those weeds in the church flowerbed.

"He's had them working all summer," Annie commented to her mother.

"I know. I'm so afraid one of the parents is going to ask him what he thinks he's doing forcing their children to work."

"I'm sure Daddy would tell them."

"That's what scares me," Barbara said hesitantly.

Annie sighed in boredom and decided to call Angie. That would occupy her for a while. She told her mother and went upstairs to her room. When inside, she took a moment to enjoy Stephen's poster. Maybe she would call him too. She lay down on the bed and dialed Angie's cell number.

"Hello?"

"Hey, Angie, it's me," Annie smiled, glad to hear her sister's voice.

"Hey! Where have you been? Do you never take your phone with you?"

"I tend to leave it in the car when I'm at work. Just call the office next time."

"I can't stand to talk to that fruit loop secretary of yours," Angie moaned. "She always engages me in some lengthy conversation about health problems. Besides, we *do* have a family plan, you know, for our cell phones? Remember? We can talk forever on them."

Annie rolled her eyes and picked off a piece of lint from her jeans. "Yeah, yeah," she mumbled. "What's going on with you?"

"Would you believe I've had two dates this week?"

Now *that* perked Annie up. She rolled over in her bed wide-eyed.

"You're kidding? With whom?"

"Too very different guys," Angie explained. "One guy, Eddie, is this real free-spirited type of guy, complete with the long hair and all. He looks like a hippy. He wants to be a music minister."

"Oooo, a musician? That's a stretch for you, isn't it?"

"Yeah," Angie snickered, "but he's a lot of fun. We kind of went out to eat, dutch of course. We're both as poor as can be, actually had to take *my* junk of a car. Then we walked around Jackson Square for a while, went into Jack's Brewery."

"A brewery?" Annie said startled.

"It's like a mall," Angie told her. "You'd like it. I think it used to brew something, but now it has all these cute little shops. Anyway, it was just a nice evening. Eddie's funny, a little strange, but funny. We had a good time."

"Okay, how about guy number two?"

"Total opposite," Angie went on. "John, even his name sounds blah, doesn't it? He's one of these real preacher type dudes. He actually wears dress pants and a tie to class. When he asked me out, I thought, *Why not?* I've got nothing better to do. He picks me up in this really nice car, a Lexus no less. We go to this fancy place to eat. His conversation was a bit forced, but he kept right on talking. I got beyond the point of actually caring what he was saying and started to look for redeeming qualities about him. He dressed nice, had perfect teeth, and his hair was stiff from hair spray. Other than that, I was struggling to enjoy the night. Then, as though it made perfect sense to him, we drive out to Lake Ponchatrain. You would not believe what he expected!"

"He wanted to park?" Annie asked her in unbelief.

"Yes!" Angie exclaimed. "I thought I was gonna die! I told him he was crazy! I was so humiliated! Here I was thinking I had done this guy a favor by just spending an evening with him, and he wants to have a little groping session!"

"You could have run your fingers through his stiff hair," Annie teased.

"Yeah, but it probably would have broken in half. I could have just died," Angie said mortified.

"What did he say to you when you refused his advances?"

"Refused his advances? That's putting it mildly, let's just say."

"Gave him a little tongue lashing, did you?" Annie said smiling.

"I told him I ought to put his name up in the women's dorm with a mug shot and a warning. Well, basically that's what I said, in a nutshell. He then had the nerve to tell me it was *my* loss!"

"Oooo," Annie squirmed. "I can't imagine him as a preacher. Is he going into televangelism?"

"I don't even want to think about it," Angie groaned, "but I did learn one thing from all this. As a potential minister, there needs to be a higher standard of attitudes and morals. My own behavior, especially my mouth, tends to be on a lower yardstick than it probably should be. I feel really convicted about it. Andie told me to sit back and trust God, but I never do. I tell God what He *needs* to do, and then I set out to help Him in the process. Not the best testimony for someone wanting to be on the mission field, is it?"

Annie would not comment on that if wild dogs had been set loose on her. Annie, herself, tended to use the lower yardstick when it came to attitudes and mouth.

"Anyway," Angie finished, "I think I have a new lease on this whole man thing."

"Which would be?" Annie asked her.

"Celibacy," Angie stated firmly. "I know what I want in life—mission work. I know what I do not want in life—a man like John or Eddie."

"I thought you said Eddie was all right," Annie wondered.

"No," Angie corrected her. "I said he was fun and a little bit weird, but I don't want to spend the rest of my life with him. Yuck!"

"Now, now, Angie. You are too gorgeous to not end up with a man."

"Not gonna happen," Angie said with resolution. "I'm 28. If I haven't found him by now, I don't think it's gonna happen."

"Don't give up on those tribesmen yet," Annie joked. "You never know what you might find in Padawin."

"Trust me, after my week here, I don't care about ever dating again. I'm through. In fact, I think I'm swearing off men."

"What on earth does that mean?"

"I'm not gonna look at men, think about men, or desire them in any way other than as good friends, and maybe not even that much" Angie pledged.

"Oh," Annie grunted meekly. "I guess I must have done that years ago."

Angie laughed and said, "There's still hope for you, little sister! Don't give up on them yet!"

The conversation went on for another 25 minutes, but when it ended, Annie felt unsettled. She did not like Angie being down. It used to be that a talk with Angie always ended with lightness and a longing to see her again. Now, however, it was quite the opposite. Angie was moody and discontent most of the time, and this last leg of her education was proving to be more trying than all of her medical training put together.

Before Annie could even put the phone down, it began its little tune, *Toccata and Fugue.* She reached for the button.

"Hello?" she answered.

"Annie? Annie! Finally!"

It was Stephen. Annie smiled as she stared at the poster across the room from her bed.

"Yes, it's me," she laughed. "Have you been trying to get a hold of me too?"

"All day long," he said with exasperation. "Does your cell not list calls that you've missed?"

Annie winced. "Well, yes," she said tentatively, "but I don't usually look at them, nor do I call people back. I figure if it's important that they'll try me again. I get a lot of unwanted calls at times. People will get a hold of my cell number from someone else, and then call while I'm on the highway or whatever. I'd rather take business calls in the office."

"How about those of us who aren't business people, just friends who want to keep in touch?"

Annie smiled now. So he considered her a *friend.* She still struggled with his stardom, but *friend* sure had a nice sound.

"Friends keep on trying," she said plainly. "See, you're persistence paid off."

"I was beginning to wonder," he complained. "But now, let's talk for real. How are you coming on the music for the tour?"

"Got it down pat," she said confidently. "Also, I wanted to talk to you about *The Eve of My Life*. Love that song."

"Really?" he questioned. "That's my least favorite on the whole album. I thought it lacked something."

"It does. The arrangement is too plain," she said hoping he meant the whole friendship thing. "I made some adjustments, added a little bit around the edges. Well, basically kind of gave it a Native American feel."

Stephen was silent, which gave Annie cause to worry. Okay, she now believed she had stepped over the line. She should not have said anything.

"Or not," she added as she shut her eyes tight.

"I'm thinking," he told her. "That is an idea. It deals with a lot of nature kind of stuff, but it doesn't really have enough minor chords to sound Native American."

Annie hesitated, and then said, "It does now."

She wished she could see his expression. Was he smiling or frowning? Was he angry at her audacity or pleased with her doctoring up his song? This was the story of Annie's life—see a problem or flaw, face it, and fix it without thinking who she might hurt or dismay in the process. This was probably the biggest blight between her and Alex.

"Where did you put in minor chords?" he probed.

"Everywhere," she said very meekly. "I only left the V chords major. Everything else I swung into a minor."

"So basically, the song is not in E flat anymore? Is it C minor?" he asked, still not giving away whether he was pleased or insulted.

"No, just in E-flat minor," she said, now wishing she could accidentally drop her phone out the window and have it crushed to pieces. "The melody is still exactly the same, only the G's are now G-flats, and the C's are C-flats. But in the bridge it's all still the same—sort of a positive sway when you start there with all the major chords."

"Wow," Stephen said softly. "You've got to send me that. Can you just make an arrangement and write it out, or is that too much extra work for you right now?"

"I've already written it," she said, still lacking the comfort in what she had just revealed. "I haven't recorded it, but it is written out." She paused and then added, "All parts are written out."

"Please tell me it took you days and days to do this."

Annie sighed and squinted her eyes again as she rolled her head from side to side. She did not want to answer.

"Yeah," she managed to get out. It was a lie. It had only taken her about three hours to rewrite and arrange the entire song. "Does your woodwind guy play any kind of recorder or pan pipe?"

"If he doesn't, he will," Stephen assured her. "Hang with me here just a second. I'm going to the piano."

Annie waited as he went to his piano. He told her he was putting the phone down, but to not get off the line. He found his E-flat chord, then immediately dropped it into the minor key. He played through the first verse, changing the chords to minor, and then went on to the chorus.

When he finally stopped, he picked up the phone and said, "You do know that you're a musical genius, don't you?"

"No, that's not it," Annie stated. "I didn't write it; I don't know where your song came from. I was just simply able to take an objective look at it and see a different facet. When you wrote it, you had certain images and feelings about it. You arranged it that way. When I heard it, I was seeing something else. I do this a lot. For the record, it's called *having no life.*"

Stephen laughed at her description.

"You are full of baloney," he bellowed. "The truth is, that song had great potential. I felt like the lyrics were wonderful, but from the day I started putting it together, I knew it lacked something musically. But you found it, and not because you have no life," he laughed again, "but because you are a whiz kid!"

"I shouldn't have said anything," she began to back down. She was still mad at herself for telling him. Why can't she leave situations like this alone?

"Annie-girl," he said gently, "in my humble opinion, you just saved a song. My only regret is that it won't be on the album like that."

"Forget business for now," Annie said to change the subject. "Tell me something personal about your life that nobody else would know."

"Okay," he paused as he tried to redirect his thoughts. "I'm at my home in the Adirondacks," he began. "I asked the staff here if my fireplaces were log or gas, because I have never used them. I thought the descriptions you gave of your family around the fireplace in the winter sounded so warm and inviting. Leonard said the one in the den was wood burning. The one in the formal dining room is gas. The one in the

. . . gosh . . . what is that room anyway? The big, boring, fancy room? It's for wood; it's really huge—the fireplace, I mean. Well, the room is too. And then the two upstairs, the one in my studio and the other in my bedroom, are both gas."

"Sounds like your day was exciting," she said as she gave an obvious yawn.

"But that's not all," he interjected. "I got online and started looking at four-wheelers and motorcycles."

"You're kidding?" Angie snickered. "Did you buy one?"

"No way," he said quickly. "I wouldn't even know where to start! I did learn a few things, however. Hondas tend to be red, Kawasakis are green, and Yamahas are blue."

"You know that's only for dirt bikes?" Angie asked. "You can get street bikes in all kinds of colors."

"Yes, I figured that out; however, I am *not* in the market for a street bike. That could be fatal for someone like me. If I'm going out on the street, it's going to be in a limo with tinted windows and secure door locks."

"Do you own enough land to ride on?"

"Not yet," he gave details, "but I am looking into about 50 acres that connect to my property. I do want to know, though, how you make trails."

"Four-wheelers are pretty good at that," she explained. "They can be like tanks going through the woods. Sometime, though, you need a good chainsaw."

"Chainsaws are too loud for me," he complained. "Maybe I could hire someone to do it."

"Get Daddy up there," Annie suggested. "He's great at making trails, and *he's* not afraid of a chainsaw."

"I didn't say I was *afraid* of them," he clarified. "I just said they are too loud."

"Oh," she was smiling. "The noise doesn't bother Daddy either."

"I guess he is Superman then?"

"No, Daddy is far from perfect," Annie insisted.

"Actually, I think you're Dad is about as close to perfect as any man I've ever known."

That comment sunk to the bottom of Annie's stomach. It had been so hard for her to hold on to the information Edrew had given her. She knew, at this moment, that Stephen was bemoaning his miserable relationship with his father as he compared it to Jonathan. Part of her wanted to jump right out and tell him that Edrew was not his father—that instead it was Benjamin Brenner. Yet the smarter part told her to keep her mouth shut. She had prayed for wisdom concerning this knowledge and pleaded with God to never let it just slip out. She would only tell Stephen if it seemed absolutely necessary to tell him, however that might be portrayed.

The conversation continued. They both shared their mundane details of their boring lives and ended up finally discussing Annie's stolen music. Stephen suggested that she stop trying to discover facts on her own, but hire an investigator and a lawyer to give her some concrete suggestions. Annie reminded him that this was Dockrey. No PI's lived anywhere close to Dockrey, and if a strange man were to start investigating around, people would become edgy and concerned. As for a lawyer, what could she do? Her unused songs were not copyrighted. There was no place for a lawyer to even begin.

After hanging up, Annie went over to her piano and began to play out the piece *The Eve of My Life* using her minor arrangement. She smiled at what she heard. She still felt slightly guilty at just throwing it out to Stephen as she did, but her changes actually gave the whole song a mystical feel to really match the lyrics.

She reached into her portfolio and pulled out the music she had decided on for the Pizza Palace commercial. She scowled at the fact that she had to write the parts on the copied paper in ink. She wondered why the pencil didn't work; she had never had trouble with using pencils before.

Wait a minute. I would have remembered the pencil thing and chosen to just print out some paper from the computer, wouldn't I? I don't think I've used a copied piece of my manuscript paper in years. In fact, I know I haven't.

Annie tried to think back over the years concerning ever having copied anything from the copier using her green paper. Normally, she would just use a new sheet if she had anything to add or change because she hated going into the office with Terri. She would always get sidetracked into some obscure conversation and would then have to redirect her thoughts back to the project at hand. When she was working, she liked to continue working. If she ever needed a copy of music for someone else, she always used her computer program to transcribe the music. She never gave anyone a handwritten piece of music, copied *or* original.

Annie grabbed her purse and her keys, and as she was about to head out the door, she went back to get her cell phone. Apparently, people were always trying to reach her but she never seemed to have it with her at the time.

Inside her office, Annie began to remove every file with music that she had. There were literally hundreds of pages to look through. She would pick up a file and carefully flip through the pages, looking for a piece of white paper that would have been copied. There were plenty of white computer printed pages, but nothing that had come from the copier.

After going through a file, she would double-check, then place it back and start on another one. After an hour and a half, she had searched every file in her office, but had not found a single copied piece of music.

What have you been up to, Terri? You knew exactly how to set the copier when you copied that page today without even having to give it a thought. Plus, what was that copied music I found behind the copier. I didn't even glance over it. Who knows what it was? Maybe it was one of my unused songs? This is ridiculous! Terri is not capable of anything so devious, and she is especially not capable of hiding it all. Like today, copying that song, she didn't flinch or think twice about doing it. If she were guilty, she would be trying to cover her tracks; she wouldn't have offered help.

This whole mess plagued Annie's mind. Angie and Stephen had both insisted that Terri had to be involved. When Annie considered the circumstances, it only seemed feasible that Terri could get the keys. During a bathroom break, she could have gotten into Annie's desk and somehow copied the keys. But how? There would be no time for Terri to take them down to the hardware store and have copies made, then replace the keys. Unless, perhaps, she took a chance that Annie would not be going anywhere. She could have copied the keys, waited for another bathroom break, then replaced them in the drawer.

This is impossible. I'll just have to face Terri with the facts and see if she is willing to own up to any of it. How? I don't know, but tomorrow Terri gets a lesson on the price of deceit.

༄ ༄

Needless to say, Annie slept fitfully that night. Her father had warned that if Terri were involved, the first people she would go to after the revelation would be her accomplices. This might put Annie in danger of some sort. Annie still held to the conviction that this was not about the crime itself; it was personal. The McCalls were out to destroy her, not for money but for the sake of just doing it. Besides, what should she do? Continue to merely sit by and allow it to happen?

The next day Annie called Terri into her office shortly after getting to work. Terri offered to make her a cup of coffee and brought it in with her. She set the coffee on Annie's desk and sat expectantly in the chair.

"We've got a problem," Annie began. She thought that if she just laid out the facts, not showing any suspicion toward Terri, her behavior might give her away. "Do you know what this is?" she asked Terri as she dropped her unused songs file on the top of her desk with a nice, dramatic flair.

"Some kind of music?" Terri responded in innocence.

"Exactly," Annie went on. "This file contains bits and pieces of music that I have never actually completed or used for anything. It has things in it that I worked on but for which I couldn't find any use at the moment. Sometimes a melody would run through my head, and I would find it catchy, write it down, and then store it in here for later use."

"How cool," Terri smiled at her. "You think of everything. If I was half as organized as you, my life would probably be so much simpler."

Okay, she's still playing it naively. No obvious change of behavior or guilt.

"I've got a problem with this, though," Annie said as she stood up and began to pace in front of her window. "Someone has been copying these files. Then they either give them or sell them to someone else."

"Why?" was all Terri could ask.

"To use in commercials that are produced by someone else."

"Really? How do you know? I mean, has someone told you?"

"I've heard them," Annie said a little forcefully, still hoping perhaps to intimidate something out of Terri. "I've heard five commercials so far."

"Who's doing it?" Terri asked in unbelief. "Do you leave that file in here?"

"I don't know who's doing it," Annie told her, and then added, "and yes, the file stays in my office, locked in that file cabinet."

"My gosh, who has a key to that cabinet?" Terri wondered, and then suddenly her eyes grew wide. "For that matter, who has a key to your office? Annie! I thought no one had a key to your office but you!"

"That makes two of us," Annie said severely. "Someone has another key. They had to in order to get through the door and into my office. Now the file lock could have possibly been picked, but I've seen no evidence of tampering."

Terri stood up and began to inspect the door. She looked around all the edges, then closed the door and searched carefully at the connections.

"What are you doing?" Annie asked her slightly perturbed.

"Checking for evidence of someone breaking in," she explained. "Your door opens in, so no one could have removed the hinges."

Annie was actually impressed. She had never considered that possibility. Either Terri was completely innocent, or she was the best liar in the world. She still tended to pull toward the former simply because of Terri's background. She had been an abused wife from South Carolina. She had moved as far west as Alabama in hopes of hiding from her husband. She had an incredible resume', and everyone Annie had checked with assured her that Terri would be exemplary as a secretary. Each former employer or friend also mentioned how horrible the abuse had been and expressed his or her hopes that Terri could have new start. Annie's heart was definitely softened toward her, and she hired her without even considering anyone else. In truth, being Annie's secretary was not a hard job. Annie did all the hard work. All that was required of Terri was to type up letters, answer the phones, arrange meeting schedules, and write out the checks that Annie would sign. Each year Annie gave her a significant raise, and Terri was always extremely grateful. Terri gave Annie Christmas and birthday gifts every year and was always prompt and efficient. Her personality grated on Annie a bit because Terri was the epitome of flighty. Still, she worked hard, and that is what Annie had hired her for. It was probably a good thing overall. Had Annie hired a kindred spirit, she would have spent more time socializing than working.

"This door has definitely *not* been tampered with," Terri

announced. "There is nothing even remotely marred here."

"How would you know?" Annie asked her.

"Please," Terri said as though it should be obvious. "Max tore off so many of our doors that I stopped putting them back up inside the house."

"Max? Your husband?"

"The jerk," Terri spat out. "My only regret is that we are not divorced, but I don't want him to know where I am. Filing papers would probably mean he could find me."

"Maybe not," Annie told her. "Surely there are protection programs."

"I've done protection programs," she said sourly. "The last one cost me a broken arm. The only person who's going to protect *me* is me."

Terri really seemed sincere. Perhaps Annie should just tell her everything. However, Terri did not see the McCalls as anything but a group of great people. She did make a joke one time about how blonde Vivian's hair always was, but when she realized the statement had been derogatory, she quickly added that as successful as Mrs. McCall was, she could look anyway she wanted and just start a new trend. No, Annie should not play all of her cards yet.

"Will you keep your eyes open for me?" Annie asked her instead.

"Absolutely," Terri said enthusiastically, "but don't you think you should remove that file from your office? If someone has done it before, they're bound to do it again."

Now it was Annie's time to play her trump card. She had at the present copyrighted all of the music through the post office, and indeed, every piece she had created in the file was in an envelope beneath her bed *now.* Any more stealing and the thieves would indeed by in trouble.

"No," Annie answered about removing the file. "I think I'll just leave it here. All of that stuff is copyrighted anyway."

Terri looked at her with a slight jerk and asked, "Are you kidding me?"

"No, I copyright everything. The more they steal, the deeper they're getting themselves under the law."

"But I've never mailed any copyrights out on things like this," she gestured toward the file on the desk. "These are like bits and pieces of music," she said as she opened the file and thumbed through the pages. "Everything I send out for copyright is done on the computer, and it's always something completed."

Nervous, are we, Terri?

"There are other ways to copyright than just the national copyright office. All of my bits and pieces are stuffed in envelopes in a safe place after being sealed at the post office," she tried to sound matter of fact. She could not tell if Terri looked concerned or confused.

"You mean all these little scraps of music are legally copyrighted?"

"Sure. Like you said, I'm very organized."

"And that post office seal would stand up in a court of law?" Terri kept inching toward a conclusion.

Annie pulled out the top piece of music on the file and named the commercial it had been used for by the pirates.

"This music was used for Adkins' Clothing," she explained. "This music was sealed four years ago in an envelope at the post office. It is dated on the seal. If a judge were to open that envelope in court, having verified the seal, and he had a musician on hand peck out the melody on a keyboard, it would match the Adkins' add perfectly. It would prove that I own that song."

Terri was silent now and barely managed to slightly shake her head in disbelief.

"Somebody is in big trouble," Terri finally said. "I'd be willing to bet money they didn't know that."

"Yep," Annie said, deciding it was time to end the conversation on a nice, tense note. "Somebody was awfully smart to get a key to my office and probably my files, but someone never anticipated that I might have copyrighted seemingly useless pieces of music."

"You're right," were Terri's final words as she got up to leave the office for her own desk. She shut the door behind her.

You did really well during the first part, Terri, but I am afraid you failed the last, Annie thought. *I don't know what you've done, but I'm beginning to think that trouble is a-brewing in Dodge. And I didn't even have to badger you about knowing how to copy the green paper on the copier. Perhaps I can save that for later.*

After explaining the conversation with Terri to her parents, Annie thought she might get a nice pat on the back for being so perceptive. Instead, she got what her grandmother would have called a *good, old-fashioned tongue-lashing.*

"Annie! How many times have we told you *not* to take this thing into your own hands?" her father half yelled, half screamed. "You are playing with people who have no problem with breaking the law! Now you go and tell their biggest accomplice that as soon as you can figure out who they are, they're all going to court! What were you thinking?"

"I am *thinking,*" Annie emphasized, "that it's time for these people to know that I am not some ignoramus sitting back idealistically believing that all is right in my little world. They need to know that I know, and they need to back off!"

"What they need to do and what they might do are two totally different options here," her father went on to explain. "Yes, they *need* to own up to what they've done, they *need* to pay for their crimes, and they *need* to be exposed, but what you pulled today doesn't mean that *any* of that will happen! All it means is that *before,* they were stealing your music; *now* they need to keep you quiet. How do you weigh those odds, Annie?"

Annie stood up from the table in a huff. She took her plate to the kitchen, rinsed it, and put it into the dishwasher along with her fork. On her way back by the table, she grabbed her glass and headed up the stairs.

"Annie!" her father shouted. "You can't ignore AIDS!"

She spun around on the stepped and barked back, "I do not have AIDS! What type of comparison are you trying to make?"

"All I'm saying is that you have awakened something that is potentially deadly, but you don't seem to recognize that. However, your blindness does not remove the facts. It's like sin, Annie. Just because the results of sin don't jump on you immediately, doesn't mean there are no consequences. It just means that the time has not come yet."

Annie turned back to go on upstairs, but her father called her again.

"Annie, do you at least understand what I am saying in all of this?"

"Yes," she sighed loudly, "but this is Dockrey! Nothing as severe as what you are suggesting could ever happen here!"

Chapter Sixteen

Annie cradled her coffee mug on the back porch the following morning. The sky was extremely overcast, a cool breeze was blowing, and the air was thick with humidity. Any moment there was going to be a downpour, but the reprieve from the endless dry, sunny days was welcomed. She had slept fitfully that night, and the second cup of coffee was beginning to buzz through her body and zing her back to life. She could not bring herself to eat anything so the caffeine was working on her fast. Her senses were now keen to the weather, and the anticipation of rain enlivened her.

She had spent most of the night trying to weigh her conversation with Terri yesterday. On one hand, Terri seemed innocent and ignorant of the whole situation. Yet on the other hand, Terri's unusual response concerning the copyrights of the music worried her. In fact, it was almost a completely different Terri than she had come to know. Her Terri was an "A-Number-One" space cadet. It was even hard to carry on a meaningful conversation with her. However, yesterday a totally different Terri appeared at the mention of the copyrighted songs. It was almost odd to watch her expression change to one of deep thought and concentration. Also, Terri's abrupt exit with no bubbly goodbye was completely out of character. Annie was very glad now that she did not bring up the fact that she had never asked Terri to copy any music from the green manuscript paper. Annie did not want her to think she suspected her in any way.

"Annie," her father called to her as he cracked open the door, "telephone."

"You're kidding," she mumbled as she glanced down at her watch. "It's 7:30 in the morning."

"It's Stephen," he said with a smile.

"I'm coming," she groaned as she stood up and stretched.

She walked into the great room and picked up the remote phone as she dropped down onto the couch.

"Hello?"

"Annie, it's your favorite singer," he teased.

"Pavorotti?"

"Very funny."

"What would possess you to call me so early?" she grumbled as she tried to find a comfortable position on the couch.

"Bad night's sleep, I assume?"

"Yeah. I feel like a swamp thing," Annie tried to describe.

Stephen was silent before he responded. "I'm not sure what that is," he confessed, "but the mental image I'm forming isn't very attractive."

"Then you know roughly what it is."

"Are you excited about coming to New York? It's only one month away, well, a month and a couple of days."

"Right now, a tornado couldn't excite me," she confessed.

"Hmmm, this may not be the best time to have this discussion with you," he said forebodingly.

"Do you have bad news?" she asked with trepidation as she sat up on the couch.

"No, no, no," he said immediately. "It's just a *thinking* conversation. I want you to be ready and alert when I pose the possibility to you."

"Oh," she relaxed. "Spit it out then. I can handle thinking; I've done it all night long."

"How committed are you to coming back to Dockrey and writing commercials when this tour is over?"

"I don't know. It depends on whether the tour brings any better offers."

"What would you consider a *better* offer?" he asked pointedly.

Annie laughed slightly and said, "Just about anything!"

"Glad to see your sense of humor is still intact. I'm serious about this though. I know you can't imagine this right now, but when this tour is over, there will be company after company seeking your talent. Your biggest problem is going to be deciding whom to go with. I'm hoping you will take my advice when you're choosing."

"Aren't we getting ahead of ourselves? The tour hasn't even started. What if it doesn't go as you planned? What if after one week we realize this has been a big mistake and that I need to go."

"Annie," he growled. "I'm asking you to trust me on this. If you don't, you are going to have to deal with quite a shock adjusting to it.

After the night of September 11, your life will never be the same. This is why I'm trying to get you to think ahead. You need to decide right now if your jingle writing business is something you want to continue after the tour."

"Okay, let's just make this hypothetical," she began. She could hear his sigh through the phone. "Suppose it turns out like you say and I have offers to start some type of new musical career. No, I would not want to come back to Dockrey and start back up the old business. However, what if that isn't so?"

"Let's stick with hypothetical probabilities then," he told her. "There is a 99.9 percent chance that every record label from America to Australia to around the rest of the globe is going to make you an offer. You are saying that if that happens, you will not come back to Dockrey."

"That's a big 10–4, good buddy," she said sleepily as a yawn escaped.

"You need to evacuate your business," he said plainly.

"What? Are you crazy? I have a great office and facility!"

"Ninety-nine percent chance, Annie," he reiterated. "Think on those odds for a moment.

She did. Could it be possible that the odds were really that much in her favor?

"Annie," he tried to persuade her, "you need to pack everything up and store it somewhere at that big house of your parents. You need to give up the lease on the office and plan to do something new. Trust me, you will not want to come back there and have to close doors when things take off. You're going to want the freedom to make immediate choices with no strings to pull you back. An office full of expensive musical and recording equipment, not to mention a pretty steep lease, would all be extremely immense strings."

"But what if . . ."

"Ninety-nine percent chance!" he repeated.

"You can't know that!"

"Yes, I can!" he said in a raised voice. "I know what I'm talking about here! Okay, look, I'll make a deal with you. If, for some totally bizarre reason, nothing happens . . ."

"You mean if the .1 percent actually takes precedence?"

"Yes," he was getting exasperated. "If the .1 percent prevails, you can work with me personally. I will hire you as a full-time musician, and we will co-write the entire next album. You will play and sing with me, for way more than what you're making now, and you do not have to return to Dockrey until your heart really desires to go back there."

Annie leaned back on the couch. Shoot, she would rather do that anyway. Work with Stephen Williams? Write with him? Play music with him? Record with him? Be a hired musician for him? This was a win/win situation.

"Are you serious?" she wanted to know.

He moved the phone away and shouted in frustration. He then pulled it back and stated, "Yes, I am serious. Do I need to write this in *blood?*"

"I just never seriously considered the fact that my life would change like this. I can actually leave Dockrey for good and become a professional musician?"

"That's what I've been basically trying to say," he said patiently. "Do you understand? Are you listening *now?*"

"Yeah," was all she could muster up. She still could not share Stephen's enthusiasm.

"So let's try this again. Do you want to return to your commercial business when the tour is over?"

"That would be a big, fat, resounding *no,*" she confirmed.

"Then move out your stuff and cancel your lease," he said calmly. "And fire that little weirdo secretary of yours."

"Wow," she said slightly stunned. "I wondered how I would be filling the rest of August. This ought to do it."

ꟷ ꟷ

"You're giving up your lease?" Terri asked almost in horror. "I thought you were just taking a leave of absence!"

"I was," Annie told her, "but it looks like some other possibilities have opened up, and I would like to pursue them."

"Doing what?"

"There are several different options," Annie said trying to keep it vague. "Maybe playing as a musician, maybe writing. For now it just appears that I will be working with Stephen Williams."

"You and Alex both? That is so awesome, but what about the commercial business here in north Alabama? You pretty much have the market."

"Not any more," Annie said cheerfully. "Apparently someone

else has volunteered to take my place, and I am now free to move on to bigger things with no sense of guilt. Kind of a neat coincidence, wouldn't you say?"

There was that new and unusual look of perception on Terri's face again. What was going on with her?

"What am I supposed to do?" Terri asked her with an almost dismal expression.

"Get another job. I'll give you a good recommendation," Annie smiled as she picked up a packed box to carry out to her father's pickup.

"I don't want another job," Terri protested.

"But I do!" Annie yelled back as she headed out the front door.

Annie took her time moving, but she was totally finished by the end of the week. The man who owned the office building asked her if she was sure she didn't want him to hold it for her because it would be gone within the month. She assured him she would *not* be coming back to Dockrey to do anymore business. She was trying to get used to the fact that these were her last days in this pokey little town.

She spent a lot of her free time riding her motorcycle out on the trails. She and her dad rode often, and occasionally her mother would come along. They were good times and would be good memories to carry with her as her life took a new turn. No matter how far away she may be from *home,* she knew she would always carry the love and support of her parents with her.

The only unanswered question that continued to plague her was the stolen music issue. She tried her hardest to lay it aside and think about more positive things, but whenever she got still and quiet, it would always come screaming back. She knew that somehow the McCalls were involved, but were they in this alone? And why did they seem to think it was necessary to steal her music? They could have hired ample musicians, starting with Big Time Advertising, to do the writing. There was a personal vendetta involved here, and Annie wanted to know why.

Her father had told her that she was playing with something that had deadly potential. For a long time she assumed he meant her own life, but the more she thought about it, the more she realized that she had compromised herself in other ways. The first was with bitterness. She had never been fond of the McCalls, but this whole situation just ate at her until she found her thoughts consumed with revenge. The second aspect dealt with all the lying. In order to elicit information without giving herself away, she had stretched the truth—no, lied—on more than one occasion. She had excused it as just investigative work; any undercover cop would do the same type of pretending. Yet the inside guilt that kept gnawing away led her to believe that she was driven by the bitterness to the lying, compromising principles that she had always held to as important

After two weeks of stewing about the whole thing, she finally could take it no more. She was tired of the bitterness, tired of the lying, and tired of wondering who in this town, besides the McCalls, was out to get her. Without telling her father or mother, she took off one Thursday for McCall Ford, aiming to speak with Wade McCall about his dealings with Big Time Advertising. She tried to psyche herself out one more time, imagining how Vivian would handle the situation were the roles reversed.

Of course, the roles would never be reversed. I would never steal from anyone to promote my own . . . my own . . . I don't even know what this is about! That's what kills me! Why are they doing this? What is the point?

As Annie pulled into the Ford dealership, she saw that both Wade's and Vivian's cars were there, his Cadillac SUV and her Jaguar. She often wondered why Ford dealers would not drive Ford cars. Apparently, they did not mind *making* their money off of Ford, but just did not want to *spend* it there. She parked, took several deep breaths, thought about the Vivian persona, and then made her way inside the showroom.

An eager salesman immediately greeted her with an extended hand and said, "Good afternoon. I'm Dean. How can I help you?"

"I'm here to see Wade McCall," Annie told him.

His expression dropped slightly as he pointed her toward a desk with a lady sitting there looking completely bored. She thanked him and walked toward the lady.

"I need to see Wade McCall," Annie said forcefully.

"He's unavailable at the moment," the lady responded.

"That's unacceptable," Annie said soberly.

"Excuse me?" the lady spoke back.

"That is unacceptable," Annie repeated. "I am here to see Wade McCall. I intend to speak with him right now."

Annie began to head down a narrow hallway in search of door that she knew would bear his name. The lady jumped up and followed after Annie.

"Miss!" she yelled at Annie. "You can't see Mr. McCall right now. He is in a meeting. It would be very inappropriate for you to barge in on him like this."

"Do I actually look like that might bother me?" Annie asked her as she continued to walk.

Vivian McCall came out of her office to see what the commotion was about.

"Annie!" Vivian called out in shock. "What are you doing here?"

"Getting to the bottom of something," Annie said, finding the door with Wade's name written in gold. She knocked as loudly as she could.

"Wade McCall! This is Annie Wright! Open the door now!"

"Annie Wright! You are out of order!" Vivian insisted as tried to get between Annie and the door.

"Very well," Annie said sternly, "you and Wade and I can have this conversation right here in hallway." Annie put her hands around her mouth to amplify the yell, then she shouted, "I would like to talk to you about some very unethical advertising you have been involved with!"

"Hush your mouth," Vivian said with fire in her eyes.

Annie continued yelling, "Let's start with unauthorized breaking and entering and then end up with using someone else's copyrighted materials . . ."

"I said to hush! Try and show a little pretense at least of propriety!" Vivian insisted as she put her hand over Annie's mouth. "For mercy's sake, open the freaking door, Wade!"

Annie could hear scrambling inside the office, but the door was not opening. She grinned to herself as she thought of Vivian accusing her of having no propriety and then yelling at Wade to "open the freaking door."

Vivian juggled the knob incessantly and said with total irritation, "Did you not hear me, Wade McCall? Open the door, now!"

After a few more seconds, the door finally opened. There stood a very disheveled Wade at the door and an equally disheveled Terri in the background. Annie tried her best not to look surprised, hurt, or out of control in any way. She calmly stepped into the office, followed by

Vivian McCall, and stood with her hands on her hips. Vivian closed the door, and Wade tried to finish stuffing his shirt back inside his pants.

"Does anyone want to tell me the actual version of all that is going on, starting with the stealing of my music, or do you want to hear my version, which is what my lawyer will be spilling out all over the courtroom?"

All three of the accused looked extremely uncomfortable. If Annie got nothing out of this confrontation but their expressions at this moment, the whole fiasco would have been worth it.

"I suppose your silence means you want to hear my version?" she asked.

Terri fell back on the couch, and Wade leaned on the edge of his desk while looking at his mother for some clue as to how this should be handled. Annie looked at all three of them one at a time and eye-to-eye. Terri just shook her head and turned away. Wade continued staring at his mother, and Vivian kept gazing at the ceiling.

"All-righty then, I'll start the talking," Annie said with a victorious smile. "For starters, I am not leaving this one-horse town because of *your* conniving thievery. I know each of you would probably like to take credit for that, but the credit must go to Stephen Williams who has made me a very lucrative offer."

"You're kidding," Vivian said with bile. "What kind of offer?"

"None of your business really," Annie shot back at her, "but let's just say he wants to do more *collaborating.* I really owe that to *you,* Mrs. McCall. Had your account not been hanging over my head, he would have never offered the help and realized how much he liked working with me. Ironic, isn't it? You scored this whole little sting to bring me down, but in the end, you have set me up with the dream of a lifetime. I leave for New York City in two weeks—permanently."

"You're kidding?" Terri said amused. "I knew you were good."

"Shut up, Terri!" Wade yelled at her.

"Thank you, Terri," Annie said somewhat sincerely. "Other than being responsible for copying my keys and copying the music, I don't know how else you are connected with this. I will say this—you picked a bad bunch to fall in with in this town."

"You little snit!" Vivian said slowly and contemptuously. "You always thought you were better than anyone in this town, didn't you?"

"Not *anyone,*" Annie clarified. "Just your bunch. I never meant anything toward any of you, but you have always tried to drag me through the dirt. It was either rise above you or be destroyed by you! I'm sorry that I am not a quitter and didn't just lay down and die for you!"

And did it ever feel good for Annie to say that. For several years she had really believed that she had chosen to just lie down and wait for death. She realized now that she still had the fire to survive, and she had a future. She felt her confidence return with a passion, and she gladly directed it toward the three who had tried to destroy her. It was like being back at Clarksville College in Music Composition 301 with Dr. Stanley challenging her all over again. This time, however, she knew where she was headed and that no one in this room could change that fact.

"Let me say this," Annie said gravely, but calmly, "I really have no desire to take this to court. Fighting over the copyrights of these menial little songs has no appeal to me, other than to make you pay for what you've done and have your names plastered all over the Dockrey newspaper." She smiled. "The truth is, I just want the whole story from beginning to end. That's it. You tell me why you did it and you tell me how you did it, and I will walk out of here, call my lawyer, and tell him to drop the case."

Wade and Vivian stared at her in obvious hatred. Terri, however, appeared to find the whole thing amusing. She wasn't smiling, but Annie could see something in her eyes that twinkled.

"By the way," Annie added, "I'm sure your lovely wife, Wade, would love to hear my take on the relationship between you and Terri. Wouldn't your kids like that too?"

"Don't get dirty with this," Wade said in warning.

"Excuse me?" Annie said in disgust. "Dirty? Your idea of dirty does not include all the felonies you committed to pull this off?"

"My wife has nothing to with this, and there is no need to involve her now."

"I suppose she'll have to find out about it in court," Annie told him, "because it appears that no one is going to tell me about this straight."

"Do you mean that?" Wade asked her. "If we tell you the whole story, you won't prosecute us or make this public."

"All I want is the truth," Annie assured him. "I really don't want vengeance."

"She's lying," Vivian said hatefully. "You can't believe her. She doesn't know anything! She's bluffing to get information from us which she will take straight to her lawyer!"

"I doubt that," Terri said from the couch.

"Shut up!" Vivian snapped. "You stay out of this!"

"Why? My job for you is done. Annie knows, she's leaving, and there's nothing left in this for me," Terri said matter-of-factly and with a whole different demeanor than Annie had ever seen in her before. "Are you going to pay me now to keep my mouth shut?"

Terri did not have a Southern accent, and she could talk in complete sentences without using a colloquialism or perky exclamation.

"Wow, Terri," Annie said with surprise, "I might actually have liked you like this. You played one ditsy girl. How long have you been carrying out this whole thing?"

"You hired me September, three years ago. That was the start."

"Shut up, Terri!" Vivian shouted again. "That is enough from you!"

"Mother," Wade interrupted, obviously agitated by the whole conversation. "Let's get this over with and get on with our lives."

Vivian paced toward the window and ended up at Wade's seat behind his desk. Wade folded his arms after wiping the sweat from his forehead. Annie wondered if the sweat was from nervousness or the session he was having with Terri before she entered the office.

"We have your word on this?" Wade asked her again. "You won't take us to court or make any of this public?"

"I promise," Annie said with certainty. "I want nothing out of this except the truth."

Wade went over to the couch and sat on the opposite side of Terri. He placed his head in his hands as he weighed the consequences. Vivian swiveled her chair and opened the blinds to look out the large picture window. Terri actually smiled at Annie now. She raised her eyebrows a bit and almost snickered. Who was this girl that had worked for Annie these three years?

"Okay," Wade finally sighed. "I'll tell you."

"You're a fool," Vivian said with her usual bite. "I suppose we'll finally see how honorable the preacher's daughter really is, if she is capable to keep her word."

Wade began by telling how Kelly had always despised Annie. Any time Kelly tried to accomplish something, Annie always came back to claim the glory. When Kelly finally won the title of Miss America, she thought she had found compensation, but all she ever heard from anyone in Dockrey was that it was a good thing Annie Wright hated beauty pageants.

It galled both Kelly and Vivian that Annie set up shop in Dockrey and created a lucrative business that only highlighted her creative talents. Once again, Annie was the talk of the town. Everyone sang her little jingles and talked about the gold mine she had found. Even Kelly's talk show fame was worthless to Alabama seeing that she was thousands of miles and an ocean away. And as much as Dockrey loved football, it was not all that impressed with a second string player for a California team.

Vivian decided to do something to make Annie pay for her thoughtlessness and overshadowing of years past. When Wade came back from a convention, he told Vivian about a woman he had met, Terri. He wanted to bring her to Dockrey, but keep her reason for being there unknown to anyone. The very day he told Vivian his idea, Annie advertised for a secretary. Vivian immediately began to think that if someone worked inside her office, they were bound to discover something they could use to bring her down.

They talked with Terri and offered her a nicely furnished house with a significant monthly bonus if she would take the job as Annie's secretary and basically spy on her. They knew that it would take more than just an application to guarantee the position so they created the whole story of Terri being an abused wife and needing to hide from a horrible husband. They also created phony references and paid the informants well to tell of Terri's capability and blight.

Terri made clay impressions of Annie's keys during a trip to the bathroom one day. Wade knew a man who easily duplicated the keys. After two years of searching for something, Terri discovered the unused songs file.

"Let me just take it from here for a moment," Annie interrupted. "So you then contacted Big Time Advertising in Chicago. You were hooked up with a man named Blake Henley. You solicited a few business friends to use a different advertising company from mine and handed Mr. Henley copies of my music with Kelly's name on them. Am I hitting anywhere near home?"

"So that's why Henley said he wouldn't work for us anymore," Wade heaved a sigh. "He was slick, said they had too much business in his own area to keep up with us."

"Of course, Terri," Annie looked at her, "when I realized I was being plagiarized, I knew you were in on it." She was lying again. She was getting too good at this.

"So that whole little talk was to try and get me to confess?" Terri asked.

Annie smiled, nodded, and explained, "But I didn't know you were acting this whole thing out. I really thought you were loopy so I hoped that finally confronting you would maybe get you to spill the beans. The whole checking out the door thing really threw me off. I almost believed that you were innocent."

"What made you still think I was involved?" Terri wondered.

"I never asked you to copy any music off of manuscript paper."

"Really?" Terri asked as she thought back over the three years. "You never did?"

Annie shook her head and said, "I couldn't use my type of writing pencil on copied paper. I finally remembered that and never tried it again."

"You don't miss much," Terri confirmed.

"It was when I went through all of my files and found no copies whatsoever that I knew you were absolutely guilty."

"How?" Terri asked.

"When you knew exactly how to copy that piece I was doing for Pizza Palace."

"Oh yeah," Terri nodded in recognition. "Never crossed my mind."

"That was your only mistake," Annie congratulated her.

"Idiot," Vivian mumbled. "This whole thing is your fault."

"Oh, please, Vivian!" Annie exclaimed. "I knew about this long before. I knew everything except who was breaking into my office. Even before Terri's little blunder, I had already come to the conclusion that it had to be her; there was no other possible choice."

"Well, that's all there is," Vivian said with finality as she stood up behind the desk. "I suppose we should all be on our ways, assuming that you will actually keep your word."

"I will most definitely keep my word," Annie stated with conviction. "I would like to add just one little observation here."

Vivian dropped back down into the chair and sighed heavily.

"I think Kelly is a beautiful and talented lady. I think she always was," Annie said with sincerity as she realized for the first time that her hatred of them had been started and fueled by them alone. "I really hate the fact that her accomplishments, her incredibly great accomplishments, have all been tarnished by my apparent insensitivity. I am so happy that she has a family, twin girls. Now there's something I haven't done! And she has this great-looking husband, a nationally renowned man, something else I haven't managed to be able to produce either."

Terri laughed.

"So, please tell Kelly that I wish the best for her," Annie continued. "As for you, Terri, I wish I could have known the real you. Like I said, I think we might have gotten along great. However, the fact that you are having an affair with a man who has a beautiful wife and two beautiful kids really takes you down to a new low in my eyes. I doubt that matters, but that's how I feel."

"I understand," Terri told her. "Good luck, too, with Stephen Williams. Would you believe he's my favorite singer?"

"You're kidding?" Annie asked in unbelief. "I thought it was Travis Tritt."

"All part of the game," Terri smiled as she flipped the end of her hair and reverted back to the deep Southern accent.

Annie absorbed it all and then turned to Wade. "I don't know what to say to you," she confessed. "You had all any man could dream of, but you wanted more. I would say I hope that it's worth it, but what I really hope is that you come to your senses and decide to repair your life and do the right things."

"Annie Wright," Vivian mused as she stood up again and headed for the door. "Always so pure and so pristine. I suppose all is right in your eyes now. We've been humiliated once again, and you've come out on top."

Vivian walked out and slammed the door behind her.

"I don't think Mother will ever forgive you," Wade said sadly. "Personally, I'm grateful to you. I could have just lost everything these past few minutes, but instead, you offered me a second chance. Thanks."

Annie nodded again and sighed. She wasn't sure how to leave this situation. It was definitely time to go, but how?

"Why don't you walk out with me, Terri?" she finally asked.

"Sure," Terri said as she got up off the couch and followed Annie to the door. "Call me later?" she asked Wade.

"I don't know," he replied, refusing to look at her.

When they reached Annie's VW, Annie leaned against her door and looked at Terri. Terri only smiled and shrugged her shoulders.

"Why would you do something like this?" Annie asked her. "Why would you choose to be with a man who didn't want you permanently or at least want you enough to make you his wife?"

"I never did love him," Terri confessed. "He was a nice distraction for a while, and I'll have to confess loving this whole spy thing. My life is not like yours, Annie. I come from a completely different environment. I know you judge and condemn me, but so what? You have this whole God thing going on, but I don't even believe He exists. Because of that, I don't have the hang-ups you do about life."

"Boy, are in for a great surprise," Annie said as she turned to open her door.

"Surprise about what?" Terri asked.

"Eternity," she replied as she got into the car. "Have a nice life, Terri, but always remember what I'm telling you: God is for real and He plays for keeps. And at this point in time, you are *not* a keeper."

Annie shut her door, cranked her car, and left the Ford place. When she had finally made it three miles down the rode, she pulled into the hardware parking lot, parked away from anyone else, and broke down and cried. How could someone hate her so much? How could people be driven to live as these people did? Where was the sense of doing what was right? Yes, she had been legitimately violated, and during the whole process even lost some sense of her own priority of values, but these people thrived on the complete abandonment of principles, and it sickened her.

Dear God! Never let me get caught up in anything like this again. Teach me to be honest, to be loving, to be forgiving, but most of all to always encourage others when they succeed. I deserved this because I was vengeful. I would rather fail a million times now than succeed at someone else's expense. I need grace, Lord—grace from you and grace for others.

Angie was home for the last week of August between her seminary terms. She was tired and listless, much like Annie. Their first day together was spent watching television and eating ice cream. Had their father not made so much fun of them, it would probably have continued. Barbara suggested they go shopping, but even Annie did not have the energy for that. They settled for a ride and ended up at the overlook.

"That whole McCall thing was bazaar," Angie said as she lay on her back staring at the clouds.

"I know," Annie agreed, "and the thing that gets me is that I don't have this feeling of accomplishment through it all. I feel like I hurt them even more for finding out."

"They needed to be found out. People like that can buy their way out of anything. You confronted them with a lot of nasty stuff. Maybe they can change as a result."

"I hope so," Annie contemplated. "I would hate to think that all of that happened for no reason."

"God has a purpose for everything," Angie said almost cheerfully for the first time. "Maybe this wasn't for them, but for you. You really seem to be a little more levelheaded than before."

"Really?" Annie laughed. "So that's what I've become? What's happened to you then?"

"I think I'm just plain despondent," Angie moaned.

"Why?"

"A combination of things," Angie said as she brushed a few gnats away from her sweaty face. "I really hate seminary. I am tired of school. I'm tired of studying. I'm tired of feeling like I don't own my life and like I haven't owned it for ten years. I keep hitting all these blanks when I mention Padawin to the board. They always say they're looking into it, but they never have any answers when I call them back. Meanwhile, I keep getting all these e-mails from Michael saying that he is desperate for help. The best thing they could do is send him a doctor."

"Michael?"

"The missionary there now, the agriculture guy."

"I remember," Annie nodded. "Is he in contact with the mission board?"

"Regularly. Between the two of us, they probably have very little time to think of anything else."

"Maybe that's the problem," Annie suggested. "Maybe you guys are trying too hard to do the work of God. Maybe its time to stop tackling this head on and just relax and pray."

"This from the queen of tackling it head on," Angie said sarcastically.

"Not anymore," Annie said resolutely. "I have turned over a new leaf. I am going to sit back and let God do whatever He wants. I'm just gonna follow where He leads."

Angie clapped her hands and laughed. "That'll be the day," she continued to laugh. "There is no way you can do anything without confrontation and opinionation!"

"What the heck is 'opinionation' ?" Annie asked as she slapped Angie's thigh. "There's no such word."

"There ought to be," Angie insisted. "It describes your conversation perfectly."

Andie had definitely decided to stop teaching and stay at home with her children. Annie and Angie both found it hard to believe, but they admired her courage. Barbara had never worked as long as children were at home, and it had been wonderful to know she was always there. Annie doubted she could do the same. She really wasn't the motherly type. She liked kids and wouldn't mind having a couple of her own one day, but to be home with them 24 hours a day was probably not a reality. Angie thought it was great and hoped that she could do the same in Padawin. Then she began to grumble about the fact that it was unlikely she would ever get married, much less have children, but that she could still dream.

Annie did begin to pack for the tour with Angie and Andie by her side. The idea of Annie on a world tour, singing her songs, and playing with a world-famous musician was exciting. They knew Annie's talent was exceptional, and Angie swore that she had always known it was only a matter of time before Annie would be discovered. Annie, however, did not share their confidence. She knew that it took more than talent to be successful in this business. There had to be a charisma and star quality that emerged with it. She knew she had talent, but she did not know if anything else was there.

Stephen seemed to think so, but how could he know? She still found herself plagued with the idea that perhaps he thought of her as this innocent girl he could conquer. By offering her the world, knowing it would not happen, he could still win her over to be seduced by his charms, his fame, and his incredible good looks. He had promised he would ask nothing more of her than to participate musically, but maybe all that was part of his plan. Maybe when she had the wind knocked out of her sails, his plan was to be patient and be there to pick up the pieces.

This is absurd! Stephen is not like that. He is a good man with a good heart. If he really wanted to seduce me, he could have found easier ways to attempt it. Inviting me to share his stage isn't exactly subtle or wise. He's been nothing but a gentlemen over the summer. I have no reasons to doubt him, or do I?

ꕥ ꕥ

"We are stupid, you know?" Angie commented as she wiped the sweat dripping down her face with a small towel. "Why are we in the hot tub during the last week of August?"

"For old time's sake," Annie reminded her. "Think of the calories we are sweating off doing this."

"We are way beyond calories now, sister," Angie complained. "We are starting to dip into the reserves."

"Maybe the thermal pools will be like this in Padawin."

"Maybe," Angie thought.

Minutes of silence went by. The girls knew time was running out for them. This would be a passing of an era in their lives, never to be regained. Both wanted to savor it, perhaps even hold on to it, but each had a path to take, paths ordained before they were even created, and each had to follow her own.

"Promise me you'll have fun on this trip," Angie broke through the silence.

"What does that mean? Why would you tell me that?"

"That is not a difficult statement to understand, Annie," Angie growled. "Don't try to analyze it to death. This is the chance of a lifetime, the thing that will change your life forever. Enjoy the places you visit. Enjoy the crowds screaming out your name and asking for autographs. Enjoy being with Stephen and a bunch of professional musicians. Pretend that this will be the best three months of your life and give it all you've got. I know you; you will try to imagine it being everything else but that. Don't, okay? Just don't."

"Is that a doctor's order?" Annie teased.

"No, but getting out of this sweat pool is," Angie moaned for the last time as she popped up from the tub and immediately got out. "Remind me never to do this again in August."

"What if you're in the Southern Hemisphere and August is cold?" Annie replied with her typical smart aleck flair.

"I'm going to Padawin, not New Zealand," Angie reminded her.

Chapter Seventeen

"May I get you something, Miss?" the flight attendant asked Annie after being in the jet for an hour.

Yeah, how about a Valium? she thought to herself. "No thank you," she answered instead.

Annie really did hate flying. This was the biggest thing she was dreading about the next three months. Why did Stephen have to have a plane? Couldn't he use a tour bus like normal musicians? Annie's present flight was only from Memphis to New York City, and her stomach was in knots. There had been a lot of turbulence, and with every bump of the plane came a deeper level of stress. It was supposed to take just under three hours for her to arrive. She glanced at her watch and frowned at the idea of still having to travel close to another two hours. She wanted to promise God that if He got her off this plane safely she would never fly again, but she knew it would be a worthless promise. Instead, she tried to imagine *happy* thoughts.

If only Peter Pan were here to apply the pixie dust. Then I could fly away all by myself. Now I know why they serve alcohol on these flights.

She reached into her portfolio for a crossword book. Maybe she could kill some time working through a puzzle or two, or ten. She pushed out the lead on her mechanical pencil and opened her book. Stuck in the middle was an envelope with her name scribbled across the front. Angie's handwriting was unmistakable. Annie smiled as she removed the envelope and opened the note.

Dear Annie,

I hope this goes as planned . . . you finding this note sometime after leaving for New York. I asked Moms to place it strategically in one of your bags before leaving on your flight so it's highly possible that you're already in Europe or something. You know Moms (grin).

I just wanted to let you know how proud I am of you and how excited I am about your possibilities. I know that you have had some hard times in life because of your . . . well . . . how should I put it? Your opinionated stubborn-headedness? I guess that pretty much works, huh? I am still in awe of how you handled the McCalls and your fruit loop of a secretary. To just forgive them all and let it go took a bigger person than me. I want you to know, however, that I learned something from you—I learned that we don't always have to go with our instincts. I tend to follow my gut, and you have always done so too. But I am beginning to realize that our "guts" are probably more full of the flesh than the Holy Spirit. Don't get me wrong, I know that God made us like He did, you know—opinionated and stubborn-headed—for a reason, but I don't think He did it for us to blow all barrels at once, regularly, whenever we feel like it.

So I am really going to take your advice and just relax about this whole mission field thing. However, I still believe that God has called me to Padawin, and if they won't send me there now, I will work somewhere stateside until they "see the light." I will not get sidetracked and be sitting somewhere in Africa when an appointment to the island comes up.

Now I want to encourage you again to just plain have a good time. And remember, we Southern girls know how to have a good time! (No, I am not referring to Billy Marcum!) We know that real fun is the result of good relationships and meaningful friendships. While you're in the middle of all that glamour and glitz, take the time to bury yourself in the Word of God and to get to know those on this tour. Life is about relationship; God is about relationship. Daddy has pounded that concept into us for years now. Don't ever get sidetracked from that! It must be easy to do, just look at Stephen. Here is a man with total and complete success, but he is lonely and empty because he has done it by himself. Give him a little break by being a real friend to him. He thinks he's helping you, but maybe God intended this whole trip as a way to bring him out of his hermit hole by dropping you into his life.

And so, we turn another page, don't we? I'll be checking my e-mail daily for updates; however, knowing you, there is no such thing as a

"daily" update. I will take whatever I can get. I'll keep you posted on things down in the south, and will look forward to the New Orleans concert. I love you more than anyone—know that. You are my dearest sister and my most cherished friend. (Don't tell Andie, although I think she's probably already figured it out!) I wish you the best of everything and will pray for you daily. Take care and remember I'm only a phone call away, if you actually remembered to take your phone! Love that family plan . . .

All My Love, Angie

PS–Feel free to dedicate a song to me during the New Orleans concert!

Angie. Tears were burning Annie's eyes as she clutched the letter close to her heart. What a treasure in a sister. Every one should be so lucky. How was she going to exist without her, and how was she going to make it when Angie actually left the country? If this were God's plan, He would give Annie the grace she needed to make it fine.

The landing was bumpy, too bumpy for Annie's comfort. Her face must have turned pale because the attendant asked if she needed a drink of something before exiting the plane. Annie shook her head, picked up her portfolio, and entered the line in the aisle to make her exit. Her stomach, already twisted and turned from the flight, now took a few more leaps as she realized she really was in New York City. She took a few deep breaths and tried to calm herself down. Had she made a big mistake?

Once in the gate area, she looked around for a familiar face. She knew Stephen could not meet her; his being in a public airport would be impossible. She glanced around until she saw a man in a uniform holding a sign that said *Annie W.*

That would be me.

She walked up to him and asked, "Are you looking for Annie Wright?"

"Yes, Miss," he said seriously with a slight British accent. "May I assume that I have found her?"

"I'm Stephen Williams' friend," she nodded.

"Very good," he smiled. "May I take your things?"

"It's just a portfolio. I can carry it."

"Follow me, then," he said as he turned. "Did you mark your luggage with the bright pink tape, Miss Wright?"

"Yes, sir, wrapped it all around it," Annie replied, then added, "and you can just call me Annie."

"Would you like for me to lose my job?" he asked her gravely.

"No, sir," she said quickly.

"Then I need to refer to you as *Miss Wright.*"

Annie continued following closely behind as she commented, "Well, at least you called me *Miss* and not *Ms.*"

"Yes," he smiled back at her. "Mr. Williams gave specific instructions that you were to be *Miss Wright.*"

Annie tried to keep up with his fast pace, but she was finding it slightly difficult. She wondered if everyone in New York was in a hurry. He wound through the airport hallways until they reached the doors to the outside. He led her to a blue limo surrounded by many girls and a few guys who were being held back by security guards.

"Mr. Williams is not traveling today," the driver told the crowd as he opened the back door for Annie.

"Is he not in the car?" yelled one girl who tried to look in.

"No ma'am," the driver told the girl as he practically pushed Annie inside the vehicle.

"Let me see! Let me see!" she screamed as she tried to keep the door open. A security officer immediately pulled her back and allowed the driver to close the door. He briskly walked to the other side and got into the driver's seat.

"Who is she?" the crowd started to yell.

Annie was taken back by the group, but was more worried about her luggage.

"Will we be getting my bags?" she asked the driver.

"No, miss," he said as he pulled away from crowd slowly. "Someone is there now at baggage claim picking up your things. There are four pieces? Correct?"

"Yes, sir," she affirmed. Now she understood why the bright pink tape was to be wrapped around her luggage.

The drive through New York City was unnerving for Annie. She was thankful that the limo itself was smooth, but she had to give the driver great credit for weaving in and out of traffic without making her throw up. Her stomach was beginning to settle slightly, but now her head was swooning. The crowd at the airport was a bit much for her. Stephen had said to do anything in public was impossible, but she had somewhat doubted him.

"How did that group of people know this was Stephen's limo?" she asked the driver, wondering if it were actually possible to talk and drive in New York at the same time.

"They camp out everywhere and follow his every move," he told her. "There will be a group at his apartment building when we arrive. Do you see the scooter behind us?"

She turned around to look. Sure enough, a man was riding a scooter and matching their every turn.

"Who is he?" she asked.

"Ever heard of the paparazzi?"

"You're kidding?" she said in amazement.

"There are people in this city who know every move Mr. Williams makes. You are going to throw them all into quite a tizzy."

"Why?"

"Because they have no idea who you are or why you are here," he explained. "Your picture will be pasted on some website within the hour, and there will be chat lines opening up all over the place trying to find out what you're doing here. Some of the ideas will be less than noble."

Annie nodded in understanding as she blushed slightly. She knew what that comment meant. She turned around to watch the man on the scooter again. He was feverishly trying to stay with the limo. She had never considered any rumors concerning her and Stephen. This began to make her stomach flip-flop again. She leaned back in the seat and tried to calm her nerves.

"It will be okay," the driver told her as he looked at her in his mirror. "Mr. Williams will take care of you. There will be four security men at the entrance to his apartment building when you arrive. I will open the door for you, and two bodyguards will immediately escort you inside the foyer. The officers will keep the crowd back. They will take you up to his place right away. Do you have any sunglasses?"

"No, I can never keep up with them."

"With your dark brown eyes the sun probably doesn't bother you as much as others," the driver smiled.

"I guess not," she agreed.

"If you'll look inside that small compartment beneath the television, you'll find several pair. I suggest you put them on."

Annie complied. There were four identical pairs of extremely dark glasses. She took one out and tried them on for size.

"Why am I wearing sunglasses?" she asked him.

"Like I said, you're pictures will be all over the website today. It generally helps if you don't reveal too much at a time."

Annie nodded again, not sure what all this meant. Before arriving, she had been rather nervous about seeing Stephen again, but now she was looking forward to it. He would be the one familiar sight in all this strangeness, and it gave her a slight sense of comfort to know he was waiting at the other end.

Sure enough, the limo slowly moved through a huge crowd gathered at the front of the building. The driver explained again what was to happen. Annie took a few deep breaths as she watched him move around to her door. The security team was insisting that the people move back. Two large, muscular, intimidating men came up to her door as the driver unlocked it with a remote button. He opened the door and smiled at her warmly.

"You'll be fine," he assured her.

"Miss Wright," said one of the two large men as he offered her a hand.

Annie took it but could barely see anything with the dark glasses on. He immediately pulled her to her feet and put one strong arm around her waist. The other man flanked her open side, and they moved quickly toward the door. She heard the clicking and winding of cameras as she passed, and people were shouting out wanting to know who she was. The men pushed and shoved people aside and were at the door in no time. A doorman pressed a buzzer, and the three swiftly moved into the foyer.

"That went well," said one of the men. "Welcome to New York City, Miss Wright," he said with a smile.

"Yes, thank you," she said shakily. "That was quite the adventure for me."

He remained sober as he pressed the elevator button. The men stepped onto the elevator with her as she watched the people still taking pictures of her through the glass windows of the foyer. When the doors finally closed, she breathed a huge sigh of relief.

"That really wasn't very much fun," she said unsteadily.

"You'll get used to it," the talkative man told her. "My name's Guy. This is Bull."

"Nice to meet you Guy and Bull," she smiled.

"You'll be seeing a lot of us," Guy told her. "Mr. Williams has hired us as extra hands while you're in town."

"Are you like—bouncers or something?" she wondered.

"We are your human barriers for the next eight days," he explained. "You won't go anywhere in this city without us. Ideally, you should just pretend that we are invisible."

"That's a bit hard, don't you think?" Annie said with a slight chuckle. "I mean, it's like having Rocky I and II by my side."

"Invisible Rockies, Miss Wright," Guy laughed. "We'll have to tell Sylvester about this one."

Bull just nodded, never smiling.

When the elevator stopped and the doors opened, Bull entered the hallway first while Guy held Annie's arm to keep her from walking out. Bull glanced quickly back and forth down the corridor.

"Clear," he said flatly looking back to Guy and Annie. Annie wondered if he were capable of showing emotion.

Guy motioned his arm for Annie to exit the elevator, and the two men led her down the hallway to a white door, the only door on the floor. Bull buzzed the room and waited patiently for a reply.

"Yes," came a voice from the intercom.

"Bull and Guy here with Miss Wright," Bull said with no emotion.

The buzzer sounded again, and Bull opened the door.

"Mission accomplished," Guy said with a smile as he moved Annie inside the door. "We'll be stationed right here if you need us."

"Thanks," Annie said, really unsure of what proper etiquette was in dealing with personal security men. "Can I get you guys anything? A Coke, a crossword book, a good novel?"

Guy laughed at her again and shook his head saying, "No, Miss Wright. We are well taken care of," and he shut the door.

"Annie," came Stephen's warm voice behind her.

She spun around immediately, and there he was about eight feet away. She smiled in relief to see his familiar face and felt like she would start to cry all over again just from the reprieve of all she had experienced. He held out his arms, and she walked over to him and embraced him. He held her tightly, and she smiled as she heard him breathe in the scent of her hair.

"I washed it this morning," she confessed, as she pulled back from him to see him eye to eye. "Not for you personally, but I suppose it doesn't really matter why."

"I'm so glad you didn't cut you hair," he said with a big smile. "In fact, it looks even longer than when I left in June."

"Why would I cut my hair?" she asked puzzled. "I've never cut my hair, except to trim up the ends."

"You mentioned one time about being fed up with it and that you might ought to get it cut," he explained.

Annie shook her head and said, "I doubt that will ever happen. I'm rather attached to my hair."

"So am I," he laughed. "Come in and let me show you my place."

"Wait!" Annie called out. "I left my portfolio in the limo!"

"It's okay. It's my limo. It would be like leaving it in your VW."

He went to the intercom beside the door and buzzed it once.

"Bull," came the answer.

"Miss Wright left her bag in the limo," Stephen told him. "Would one of you retrieve it, please?"

"Right away," came the response.

Stephen led her down a small hallway to a massive living room. It was stylishly furnished and looked like something you would see in a magazine layout. Along the wall facing the street was nothing but glass. The remaining walls contained framed posters and shelves with various artistic figures strategically placed about.

"Sterile, isn't it?" he said almost sadly.

"No," she said quickly, "it's beautiful."

"No, it's not. Your home was beautiful. This place is practically barren. Every few years I'll have someone come in and totally redo it, but it's always more of the same."

"Well, for the record, I'm impressed," Annie told him.

He showed her the massive dining room and then the kitchen with its cozy breakfast nook. He took her into his private screening room with a wall-sized plasma television and comfortable seating.

"This will be your room," he said with a smile as he opened another door.

Annie walked in and was dazzled. The walls were a beautiful textured blue, identical in color to her VW. On them were scenes of barns and country houses, and the curtains over the massive picture window looked as thought they came out of *Southern Living* itself. The bedspread was a beautiful double wedding band quilt with blue satin sheets turned back. In the center of the bed was a Teddy Bear playing a grand piano.

"Is it a coincidence? This whole room?" she asked him.

He shook his head and said, "No, and it was great fun planning it all summer."

In one corner of the room was a Roland keyboard. Annie walked over and ran her hand along the top of it.

"Brand new?" she asked.

"Yes," he smiled. "My gift to you for agreeing to all this. When you find your own place, it goes with you."

"Isn't it going on the tour?"

"No, this is a console. The one on the tour is portable," he told her.

He stared at her quietly for a moment and then shook his head as he smiled. "I can't believe you're actually here."

"Me either," she grinned as she walked into her personal bathroom. "This is a pretty blue. Oh, my gosh! The soap dispenser is a motorcycle!"

"I thought that was pretty cool," he said as he joined her. "I got it off the Internet."

"Would you believe I've never bought anything off the Internet?"

"Yes," he said firmly. "I don't believe you care too much for the computer."

She rolled her eyes. She was bad about checking e-mail and even worse about responding.

"It is great for transcribing music," she admitted. "I would be lost without it in that sense. Other than that though. . . ."

"Come on," he said pulling her out. "There's more to see."

He showed her his own bedroom. Yes, she would admit to it being *sterile.* His in-home studio, however, was very impressive. She looked over all the equipment and gave him a thumbs-up. He smiled proudly, though she couldn't imagine why her opinion should matter. Everything was state of the art, and he knew it.

ꕥ ꕥ

Stephen and Annie spent the afternoon catching up. As they sat in his stately living room, he told her of the places they would visit on the tour. He was animated in his descriptions, and she was glad to see him excited about something in his life. Why shouldn't he be? This was what he lived for.

"Are you hungry?" he asked her as he began to rub his tummy.

"Not really," she confessed. "This has not been a good day for my stomach."

"We need to leave for the practice hall in about an hour," he told her. "We'd better get something to eat now."

"What do you have?"

"Nothing," he said plainly. "We'll order something in. What do you feel like?"

"I don't feel like eating anything," she reiterated. "You pick something, just make sure its kind of light."

"How about a good deli sandwich?" he suggested. "We can have a side of potato salad each."

"Sounds like a plan," she smiled as she leaned back against the couch to relax. "While you're ordering, could I e-mail my family?"

Stephen put his hand up to his heart in shock.

"You want to use the *computer?* Absolutely!" he exclaimed. "Right this way!"

He took her to a desk in a small room off the kitchen and showed her how to get online. He then left her to communicate on her own.

Dear Family,

Just wanted you all to know that I made it to New York in one piece. I have definitely decided that I hate flying and must confess that the prospect of flying all over the world on this tour has got me a bit antsy. Angie, could you send me a prescription of something, perhaps Valium or Demerol? Just kidding, Moms! I will handle this just fine.

Stephen has been a perfect gentlemen, but the array of fans bombarding my limo was rather unsettling. Would you believe I have two bodyguard guys assigned to me personally this week?

Their names are Guy and Bull. Toto, I definitely do not think I am in Alabama anymore! We are going to get a sandwich for supper. We're not making them; he's ordering them. Can you imagine? I mean I'm not stupid, I know you can get sandwiches at a restaurant, but what's the point of ordering them in when you can just make them yourself? After eating, we'll be going to some practice hall where I will play with the band for the first time. Am I nervous? Like a cat in a cage full of Rotweilers! Alex and Megan will be there. They had a meeting with the bank all afternoon to work out the closing for their apartment. I am looking forward to seeing them as a married couple. I hope Alex has cut his hair. I guess maybe he is trying to fit in with his sisters more. (smile) I don't know when I will write again, but I wanted everyone to know that all is well and my flight did not crash.

From New York City, Annie

Annie ate what she could, which wasn't much, and then went to her room to freshen up for the practice. She knew her music well. That was not what was making her so nervous. It was everything else connected with the rehearsal. She would be meeting the rest of the band. She would have to deal with hateful glares from Alex. She would have to sing *Autumn Sunset* and *I Knew it was Love* for Stephen's professional musicians. It would all be new to her, and it was a bit much to add to her already unfamiliar day. At least tomorrow would be Sunday and she could take the day off.

Stephen notified *someone* that he and Annie would be ready to leave in ten minutes, so Annie went to her room to grab her portfolio that *someone* had delivered to the apartment that afternoon. *Someone* called after several minutes to notify Stephen that everything was in place and the limo had been pulled to the front of the building.

"Are you ready?" he asked her as he stuck on a hat and sunglasses.

"I'm not sure," she replied tentatively. "Should I put the sunglasses back on that I wore today?"

"It would probably be best," Stephen agreed. "Of course, no one has any idea who you are so they are going to be snapping pictures like crazy. The glasses will help to hide you for the most part."

"Will it be like this always?" she wondered. "Will we ever be able to go anywhere without this entourage?"

"No," Stephen said bluntly. "Are you ready?"

Annie heaved a deep sigh and closed her eyes to brace for the exit. Stephen took her hand, causing her to jump and open her eyes rapidly.

"I told you life would be different," he smiled at her. "Just wait until after the concert on Saturday. Right now people are only curious about whom you might be. When they hear you, even *this* will change another degree."

Annie squeezed his hand and indicated she was ready. Bull and Guy were waiting at the door, along with a third man.

Rocky III, Annie smiled to herself.

The five of them entered the elevator and left the 7th story for the 1st. Annie had not even realized what floor Stephen's apartment was on. Seven was a bit too high. She would definitely close the blinds so she would not have to look out. However, the more she thought, the ceilings in his apartment seemed 20-feet tall. Seven stories in this building were not like seven stories in a normal building. Sweat began to bead up on her forehead. The ding of the elevator brought her back to the present problem—the crowd. There they were, lining the building, the sidewalk, and the street.

"Are they always out here?" she asked Stephen as they stepped off the elevator.

"Not like this," he told her. "There's always a big group, but you've got them curious. They know my practice schedule so they wait for me to go and return each evening."

Annie merely nodded as Bull and Guy flanked each side of her. Rocky III stood next to Stephen and nodded to the doorman who pressed the buzzer releasing the bolts in the door. As soon as it opened, the sounds of the crowd screaming were deafening. Bull and Guy literally pulled Annie along as they pushed people away.

"Who is she, Stephen?"

"Does Carrie McCarthy know about her?"

"Are you married, Stephen?"

"Stephen, I love you! I love you!"

"Just talk to me, Stephen! I'm your biggest fan! Please give me your autograph!"

"Stephen, pose with the brunette for us!"

Another security man stood ready to open the door as soon as Annie was next to him. Bull threw a man to the ground that tried to jump inside the car when the door opened. Guy helped Annie inside the car, and Stephen was right behind her. He stopped, however, and turned to the crowd and waved.

"I'll see you all Saturday night!" Stephen yelled to them, at which they went wild.

Stephen sat next to Annie, and Rocky III closed the door. The driver looked in the rearview mirror and asked, "All set, Mr. Williams?"

"Take off, Buddy," Stephen replied.

Immediately the limo began to wade through the crowds, almost as if it were parting water. Annie sat back and leaned her head against the seat after removing her glasses and placing them back inside the compartment.

"That went well," Stephen said as he patted her knee.

"Did it?" she really wanted to know. "Bull had to throw a guy down because he tried to get inside of here."

"He'll be arrested for that too," Stephen let her know.

"Is it a far drive?"

"Depends on traffic. Saturday night in the city? Probably."

Stephen picked up a remote from the side of the back seat and pressed a button. Suddenly Annie heard her own voice singing *Unlit Passion.*

"Oh, my gosh!" she said in surprise. "Why are you playing that in here?"

"I happen to be a huge fan," he winked. "I especially like this song. I'm still choosing to believe you wrote it about me."

Annie had, but she would never tell him so.

"Couldn't you play something else? What about the television? I'd like to see the news in New York."

"You're kidding, right?" he asked her.

She shook her head. He pressed one button that turned off the music, then another to turn on the television. Annie smiled in triumph. This was the one thing that had gone right today.

Thirty minutes later they arrived at the practice hall.

"Why are we practicing here?" she asked Stephen as she retrieved a pair of sunglasses, feeling ridiculous about it because the city was now dark. "Your house would do fine."

"If it were just the musicians, no problem," he explained. "But we have a sound crew, a lighting crew, and a video crew. They have to practice too. They are pretty much ready except for the little curves you might possibly throw them."

"What curves?" she asked defensively.

"Who knows," he smiled as he put his glasses back on. "I told them you were one unpredictable lady—moody too."

"You did not!"

He pulled down his glasses to the bridge of his nose and just grinned.

"There they are," he said.

"Who?"

"Security."

"Where did they come from?" she asked. "It's the same guys!"

"Of course. They were in a car right behind us. They will travel everywhere we do for the next week."

The same pandemonium that had happened at the apartment building was happening now at the practice hall. People were screaming and pushing to get a word with Stephen. Many questions were yelled out, asking about Annie's identity. Stephen pushed right behind Annie, and then stopped again, just before he went inside the door, to wave and make a comment. When the door closed, the silence was heavenly.

Stephen took Annie into a large hall complete with lights, screens, and massive speakers. In the center of the room was the sound control center. Stephen waved to the man behind the board.

"Steverino!" called the man.

"Bobby Bravo!" Stephen called back. "I have someone you need to meet."

Stephen led Annie to the sound center and shook hands with Bobby.

"This," Bobby said extending his hand, "has got to be *the* Annie Wright."

"That she is," Stephen said proudly.

"Hi," Annie said trying to sound confident but feeling as though she were failing miserably. "Nice to meet you."

"Let's get you sound checked before everyone shows up," Bobby said as he sat back at the controls. "Thanks for bringing her in early."

"Early?" Annie said as she looked at her watch. "It's 7:30 at night!"

"We practice from 8:00 until 10:30, just like the concerts will be. It gets our clocks on the same time as the tour," Stephen explained.

"So we'll be finished 9:30 *my* time?" Annie asked already feeling exhausted from her day and so looking forward to dropping into the comfortable bed awaiting her back at Stephen's apartment.

"Yes," Stephen nodded. "Sorry. A musician on tour keeps strange hours. You'll adjust. But for now, we need you up on stage. Go find your Roland."

Annie walked with awareness toward the colossal stage, taking in everything she could see or hear. As she walked up the steps to the stage, she realized for the first time how high a stage was. She found the Roland immediately; it was in symmetry to Stephen's Korg. He had placed her almost next to him. Was that on purpose?

"Okay, Annie," came Bobby's voice. He was talking into a small mic on the board. "I need you to say something in your mic so I can get an idea of your speaking volume."

Annie wanted to say, *What should I say?* but she knew that would be unprofessional. How many times had she seen people do that? She would always tell them to quote a Scripture or say a poem.

"One thing I ask of the Lord, this is what I seek," she began, "that I may dwell in the house of the Lord all the days of my life, to gaze upon the beauty of the Lord and to seek Him in His temple."

"So she's a Christian," Bobby stated.

Stephen only nodded.

"Okay, that was perfect, Annie," Bobby said back into the little microphone. "Now let's get a singing volume. Would you please sing *Amazing Grace* like you mean it?"

"A cappella?" she asked.

"Please," Bobby confirmed.

"Like I mean it?" she asked again.

Stephen leaned down into the mic and clarified by saying, "Put a little bit of soul into it."

Okay, let's jump right into it, she thought nervously.

She began. Bobby played with the knobs on her mic section until he had them tweaked perfectly.

"Thanks, Annie," he said to stop her. He then turned to Stephen and said softly, "What a voice!"

"I know. How do you think I felt when she started singing *Autumn Sunset?* Wait until you hear her tonight."

"Next, Annie, I need you to pound something out on your piano," Bobby told her.

Feeling mischievous, Annie told him, "I don't *pound* the piano."

"My bad," he said quickly.

"I tickle the ivories," she shot back quickly, "or in this case, just tickle the plastic."

Bobby laughed and winked at Stephen, then leaned back into the mic and said, "How about playing a little of that Ragtime number your wrote."

Bobby turned to Stephen and said, "This girl is gorgeous. If she can play half as good as she sings. . . ."

At that moment, Annie began the Ragtime piece. Bobby literally stopped and stared. "She's unreal!" he said in amazement. "She's about as good as you."

"She's better," Stephen told him.

"You're kidding? You'd admit that?"

"You're hearing her," Stephen offered as evidence. "I can't do that. I come close, but I can't do it."

"But I thought the two of you were dueling on this song."

Stephen just smiled and said, "We are; she wins."

"In concert?"

"What do you think? I can't top that, and *that* is exactly what she needs to be heard playing. *That* is Annie Wright's biggest talent."

"You must have a strong self-concept, my man," Bobby said shaking his head as he turned back and began to adjust the knobs and buttons. Annie was right; she didn't pound the piano at all. Her fingers danced so fast across the keyboard that he found himself turning up many of the gains on the adjustments.

"That's it, Annie," Bobby told her. "The camera guys will be here in a second to get your lighting and angles set. Just relax for now, or . . ." he smiled big, "you could sing *Unlit Passion* for me."

Annie shook her head and stood away from the piano. This was so surreal to her that she almost believed it was a dream. She found herself fighting an overwhelming sensation again in the pit of her stomach as she watched Stephen step across the room and join her on stage.

"Sing with me for a moment," he asked gently. "Let's do your *Autumn Sunset.*"

Annie shook her head and her eyes pleaded *no.*

"Okay," he said with a smile. "Loved that verse, by the way. Where is it found?"

"Psalm 27," she replied. "Read the whole Psalm; you'll love it even more."

The lighting and camera crews came in and set permanent spots, varied in colors, where Annie would stand when behind the piano, in front of the piano, and at the front of the stage. The cameramen explained to her that when a red light was showing on the top of the camera, it meant that particular camera was filming at that time. Occasionally, it's nice to look directly into the camera so that the audience feels as though you are singing to them personally. Annie nodded, but was beginning to think she would be lucky to actually stand on stage without her knees buckling beneath her.

The first musician to arrive was Chip, the woodwinds player. Stephen introduced him to Annie immediately.

"I love what you did with *Eve of My Life,*" Chip said excitedly. He was definitely what Annie often referred to as a cool musician. "When Stephen told me to try for that Native American sound, my first choice was a tin-penny flute 'cause I had one on hand."

Annie frowned, and he immediately followed up with, "Exactly! Did not work at all. So I went to the music shop to try out some recorders. I went soprano first, still didn't have the sound. Tried the alto recorder? Sweet."

Annie thought for a moment and then nodded, "I bet that *is* perfect."

Chip continued admiring her arrangements as she studied his beret, obviously worn to cover his thinning hair. She wondered if he was actually bald or not. His eyes looked tiny from behind the John Lennon glasses with thick lenses. His shirt simply said, *I'm in the Band.*

Sam, the drummer came in next. He joined the trio at her piano and was introduced.

"You know that you are a drummer's nightmare, don't you?" he said with a laugh.

A Southern accent! Great! Another one from the South, Annie thought.

"And how am I a nightmare?" she asked Sam.

"I am assuming all your little percussion parts are done on a machine and programmed in?" he wondered.

"You gotta love Roland," she smiled over at Stephen. "They

make it easy to do."

"Next time," Sam continued, "try and remember that you may have ten fingers, but I only have two hands and two feet! That little percussion lick in *Unlit Passion . . .*"

Annie interrupted him, "Between the bridge and the last chorus?"

"Yes," he said agitated. "It's humanly impossible, but Stephen insisted it be done. Kurt has to run over and do triplets on the big tom while I'm doing all that cymbal work."

"We could program it in?" she suggested.

"Bite your tongue!" he exclaimed. "No drum programming as long as I'm playing the tour! If you can program it, I'll find a way to make it happen live and in person."

Annie thought Sam was charming. His shaved head and dark goatee, along with a well-worn tank top seemed to define him perfectly. Slightly rebel, very talented, and eager to do it right.

She kept scanning the area hoping to see Megan and Alex. She had seen neither since the wedding and was hoping to spend a couple of minutes visiting before rehearsal started. No luck. The next musician was Jason, Stephen's guitarist. He had been with Stephen for many years, and she recognized him immediately when he came on stage. He was tall, long stringy blond hair, and a slight limp. She knew from articles that he had been a twin and was born with a severe defect concerning his right leg. Several surgeries had improved it somewhat, but he would always struggle with it.

"Hi," Jason said walking over. "I'm Jason and you're awesome."

"No, I'm Annie," she said shyly. This was almost as inspiring as meeting Stephen.

"Sense of humor, nice," he smiled. "Unlike your brother, I suppose?"

"He has a sense of humor," Annie told him, "he just uses it sparingly."

"Very," Jason nodded. "I'm looking forward to hearing you tonight. This ought to be fun. We've never played with a girl before."

"I hope I don't embarrass ya'll," she confessed. "My nerves are pretty shot right now."

"Oh, you'll embarrass Stephen," he added quickly. "That piano duel? You know you'll be covering his tail on that. He has yet to play it right."

She looked over at Stephen and he simply shrugged.

Megan and Alex finally made it in, right at the last moment. Megan ran across the stage and threw her arms around Annie.

"I can't believe you're here! I can't believe you're here!" she shouted into Annie's ear.

"Isn't this unreal?" Annie asked her as she pulled back. "Us in New York?"

"You're gonna *love* New York!" Megan told her. "You can do anything here."

"How's married life?"

"So great!" she said in exaggeration. "And with Alex being a musician, it's like we have all this time in the world. It's been kind of like being on summer break from school, only you have money—and a husband! It's awesome! You have to come over some day. I wish you could have stayed with us, but Stephen has the whole security thing down where he lives. He seems to think you're gonna require bodyguards at all times. He feels very promising about you."

"I know," Annie said nervously. "I hope I don't disappoint him."

"Are you kidding?" Megan asked in incredulity. "Your gonna knock 'em dead."

"Let's get started," Stephen said into his mic from his Korg. "This rehearsal will run long tonight, but you all know that. We need to get Annie acclimated in, and we need to do a little staging. I'm having some food brought in for the break. Megan, could you let us know when it's delivered?"

Megan gave a thumb-up and then winked and waved at Alex. Alex had refused to even acknowledge Annie's being there. Some things will never change.

The first half of the rehearsal went smoothly. Annie knew every song perfectly, and Stephen did not have to stop once to change a thing. They did have to work with her concerning her introduction during the 4th song. She just gave a slight wave, but Stephen explained that she needed to make a *statement* with her wave. All the other musicians did some kind riff on their instruments, but Stephen didn't want that for Annie. He insisted she come to the front of her keyboard and give a full bow with a double-handed wave over her head. After about five tries, she managed to do it right.

The most fun part of the first half of rehearsal was the ending song, the piano duel with Annie's ragtime piece. It began by Stephen humbly talking about his masterful piano-ship, at which Annie had to break in by clearing her throat. After several of her interruptions, he would ask if she needed to say something, to which she would respond that she was rather masterful herself. What followed was a bantering of piano playing of her composition, in which she overwhelmingly won at the end. To finish the song, Stephen would grab a fire extinguisher from the side of the stage and act as though he needed to put out the *fire* she had caused on her keys from playing so hard. The band thought it was great and admitted that having Annie would add a whole new dimension to the tour this year. During break, the guys in the band and the crew congratulated her on a stellar performance and reiterated the love the audience would show.

The second half of the rehearsal put Annie in the spotlight. The hall went dark as each musician found his place with small penlights. Annie began by playing the intro to *Autumn Sunset.* As soon as she started singing, the spotlight opened up on her. The band joined in when she started the first chorus, and Stephen began to harmonize with her. That was simple. What came next was a lot of staging.

After about 20 minutes of working on *Autumn Sunset,* Alex became exasperated. "Couldn't we just finish the rest of the practice and then let you two figure out this little dance routine on your own?" he yelled out.

Stephen turned to him and said sharply, "No. This little *routine,* as you put it, is more than just an added bonus, or have you not been paying attention? I am directing from the stage here. Every movement that I make is a cue to you as a backup musician to do something. Do I need to review all those cues again?"

Alex glared at Annie and mumbled out, "No. I'll try to pay closer attention."

Annie's heart sank, but apparently Stephen was unfazed by the outburst. She did not dare look at Alex now. She knew he probably hated her more than ever.

When *Autumn Sunset* was perfect, they began *I Knew It Was Love.* The staging was not near as complicated, so they sailed through it fairly quickly. Following that, Stephen introduced Annie's own compositions: *Forever Free* and *Unlit Passion.* Stephen let her stay behind the Roland for these so she could be free to express herself on the piano as well as through singing. They ended the concert practice with several more of Stephen's songs, including Annie's arrangement of *Eve of My Life.*

"That *Forever Free* is one weird song," Chip told her as he packed up his instruments, "but I love my sax solo in *Unlit Passion.*"

"I love *Unlit Passion* period," Kurt, the brass player told her. "I really like *Forever Free* too. You've got me doing some funky things with the trombone on that."

"We're all doing funky on that," Chip grinned. "See you Monday, Annie. You were great."

As the band and the crew left, one by one, Annie glanced at her watch. It was 12:30 her time. They really had spent a lot of time rehearsing *Autumn Sunset.* She set her watch up to 1:30 so she could begin to adjust to Eastern Time.

"We'll see you Monday," Megan told her with a hug as she passed by to leave. "If you need anything, give me a call. Maybe we can do shopping this week."

"Sounds like fun," Annie told her as she tried to keep her eyes open. "We'll make some plans."

Annie sat in a folding metal chair and tried to stay alert as Stephen covered a few last details with Bobby. He finally finished and came over to leave. He put out his hands and pulled her up to him. She found herself slightly off balance, and he caught her in his arms.

"Wo," he said softly as he kept her balanced. "You look exhausted."

"That's nothing," she smiled up at him, "you should see how I feel."

"Let's get you home and tucked in. You can sleep as late as you want in the morning."

He put his arm around her, and she walked to the exit with her head on his shoulder. Bull, Guy and Rocky III were waiting.

"You're kidding?" Annie asked in utter fatigue. "People will be out there at two in the morning?"

"Afraid so," Stephen said as he handed her the sunglasses.

"Forget it," she told him as she pushed them away. "Too much effort to put them on."

Bull and Guy flanked Annie's sides again, and Rocky III and Stephen gathered behind her. The door opened and the shouting began. Annie just closed her eyes as she let the two rocks guide her to the car.

Once inside, she moved immediately to the seat that faced the back and she lay down. Stephen got in and Rocky III closed the door.

"You will get used to this," Stephen told her as reached over to pull back the hair that had fallen into her face. "At least, you'd better."

"Wake me up when we get home," she groaned. "Or not. Let Bull and Guy just carry me in."

Stephen smiled as he watched her quickly drift off to sleep. He could not believe that he had discovered such a jewel. As he stared at her face, he swore she was the most beautiful woman he had ever seen. He thought of practicing with her on *Autumn Sunset,* face-to-face, hand in hand. He had only dreamed of finding someone like her, but here she was, sleeping in his limo, looking like an angel sent from Heaven. He had three months to win her heart, and he prayed with all that was in him that God would grant him this one thing—to live with her *happily ever after.*

Chapter Eighteen

"She is not coming to our home!" Alex said emphatically as he stomped down the hallway from the bedroom to the kitchen.

"She's your sister, Alex," Megan offered hopefully. "What will everyone think if you totally shun her this week in New York?"

"She will not come into this apartment," he firmly stated as he poured a cup of coffee from the programmed coffee maker. "Not this week, not ever."

"Alex, she is innocent of all this."

"Annie is never innocent of anything," he said through gritted teeth.

"You have got to stop blaming her for things."

Alex spun around and glared at her harshly. "You don't know what my life was like all those years. You don't know the humiliation and degradation and misery that I put up with for her sake."

"I don't know fully," Megan said softly as she put her arms around him and held him tightly. "But Alex, she doesn't know either. If she did know, she would tremble and weep. I know Annie. I know her well."

"Megan, we've been through this. What you know and what I know stays between us," he pleaded as he sat down his cup and stroked her hair.

"But you are bearing the burden of something you should have put behind you long ago," she said as she looked up into his light green eyes. "You really should see a counselor."

"I don't need one," he said for the hundredth time. "I've got you." He pulled her back to him and whispered, "You are all the healing I need."

When Annie found the strength to open her eyes, the room was a swirling mass of blue. She closed her eyes again to refocus, and then opened them slowly. It took a moment for her to remember where she was, but the events of the previous day finally came back fully. She was at Stephen's, in a huge blue bedroom, and was so tired she doubted she could pull herself from the bed.

She leaned over to the bedside table and lifted her watch. It was 11:30! She hadn't slept that late since probably high school or college, with the exception of the time she had the flu. She had missed church. Her father would be highly disappointed. However, where would she have gone, and how would she have gone? If the crowds yesterday were indicative of what she might face today, Bull and Guy would have to escort her and flank her side each step of the way. She understood why Stephen had given up trying.

She pulled herself from the bed and realized she was still wearing her clothes from yesterday; she hadn't even bothered to pull them off before climbing into bed. She walked over to the large window and pulled the blinds. New York City! Unbelievable. She glanced down to the building's entrance, and there was the crowd as large as ever. She needed coffee and breakfast before trying to take any more of this in, and she most definitely needed to get away from the high window.

She left her room and entered a hallway, and then tried to remember which way to the kitchen. However, she heard her father's voice strong and clear coming from one direction of the apartment.

I must be feeling really guilty about missing church. I'm actually hearing Daddy preach.

She followed the voice, and it was unmistakably getting stronger. She came to a door that was slightly cracked and then peeked through. There was her father on the huge plasma screen, preaching his heart out to an audience of one. Annie opened the door and walked on in. Stephen did not even notice her. He was sitting near the front of the room on a couch with his Bible open and notebook and pen in hand.

"Am I interrupting?" she finally asked.

Stephen turned abruptly and dropped his notebook in the process. He quickly reached for the remote and paused her father in mid sentence with a horribly funny expression.

"Good morning!" Stephen said brightly. "I'm having church. Want to join me, although you heard this last Sunday already."

"How did you get a video of my dad?"

"DVD," he corrected her. "That's what the new camera at the church records."

"Our church has a camera?"

"You didn't notice?" he asked puzzled. "I've been getting your father's messages on DVD and CD for almost three months now."

"Wow. All right," Annie said sleepily. "Is that coffee beside you?"

"Sure is," he smiled. "There's a pot on in the kitchen."

Annie turned to leave, the turned back around slowly to ask, "And where is the kitchen?"

"Take a left and then a right."

Annie walked down the hallway to the left, and then turned right as she got to the end. There it was, the kitchen. She poured herself a cup, added cream and sugar, and then began to rummage through the cabinets for something to eat. They were totally bare! They contained dishes and pots, but nothing more. She went to refrigerator and found the same thing. There were only Diet Cokes in the fridge along with a few juices, nothing more. With her cup in hand, she headed back down the hall to the television room.

"Stephen, you have no food!" she informed him.

"I know."

"What did you eat for breakfast?"

"I don't eat breakfast," he said sheepishly with a guilty grin.

"You ate it at my house," she reminded him.

"Someone prepared it there," he explained. "I don't make anything here. I can order you some breakfast," he said getting up." "There are ten restaurants within a five-block radius here. Seven of them serve breakfast. What are you in the mood for?"

Annie just stared, half in her sleepy stupor and half in total unbelief.

"I'd rather just go to the grocery store," she managed to get out. "I have no intention of ordering out every meal while I'm here."

"You can't," he said quickly.

"Can't what? Order out or go the grocery?"

"Grocery," he stated. "What happened yesterday with the crowds will be par for the course the rest of the week. If you want to make a list, I can have someone shop for you and bring the food back."

Annie found a chair next to a sidewall and eased herself down.

"I can't even go to the grocery store?" she said incredulously.

"I suppose I should have at least gotten a loaf of bread and a chunk of cheese for you," he confessed as he got up and came over to her. He kneeled down in front of her and put his hand on her knee.

"I haven't been a very good host, I guess," he apologized.

"You're right," Annie smiled. "Order me breakfast, and I will make a grocery list. I don't have to drink Diet Cokes do I?"

"Drink whatever you like," he said getting up and offering her his hand. "What would you like for breakfast? Eggs, bacon? I don't believe you will find any *cheese toast* on the menus up here."

"No eggs or stuff, too heavy. Doesn't New York have great bagels?"

"Aha!" he exclaimed. "Yes, it does! I know exactly where to order now. Do you want cream cheese or lox with that?"

Annie grimaced and shook her head.

"Yuck," she frowned. "Just some butter and jelly would be fine."

"Yuck," he responded back. "You will ruin the bagel."

"If I remember correctly," she chided, "I'm the one eating it, not you."

Sunday passed rather slowly, even considering the fact that Annie had gotten up so late. She did manage to get several bags of groceries, and she loved cooking on all of the high-tech kitchen equipment in Stephen's apartment. He told her a maid would clean the kitchen the following morning, but she insisted that the two of them finish it that night.

"It was ingrained in me," she tried to explain. "You never leave a kitchen dirty when you go to bed."

Annie taught Stephen how to play Liverpool Rummy, and they played several rounds that afternoon. In the evening, they listened to another of Jonathan's sermons, and then Stephen forced her to play video games in his screening room. Annie had never cared much for games like this, but with her competitive spirit in full force, she found herself screaming at her defeat. By 9:00 she was exhausted.

"You really don't need to go to bed yet," Stephen warned her. "It would be best if you would go ahead and try to adjust to the tour's schedule."

"Exactly what is the tour's schedule," she yawned.

"Each night a concert begins at 8:00," he started explaining. "We wind it up somewhere between 10:30 and 11:00. The other musicians pack up their instruments, their mikes, and all their chords. The crew breaks everything down as quickly as possible. We go out and do the whole autograph, publicity thing. Sometimes that can take up to two hours or so. After that, we head back to either a hotel or the jet. "

"I'm must have been crazy to think I could handle this," Annie sighed.

"But you do get to sleep late every day," he smiled.

"I don't think my biorhythms were cut out for this."

"You'll be surprised how quickly you will adjust," he told her.

"Well, I'm not adjusted yet, and everything in my body is screaming for me to go to bed. Tell me, how do I handle that?"

"Follow me," he said energetically as he pulled her up from her seat.

He led her down the hallway to his studio. He began to turn on various pieces of equipment. He handed her a mic, took one for himself, and then started the music for *Autumn Sunset.*

"What on earth are we doing?" she whined.

"We're practicing our two songs," he said cheerily. "If you're like me, a little music always energizes me."

"We're going to sing at 9:00 at night?"

"It will be later than that when we sing this on the tour," he informed her. "I believe you just missed your cue. Let me start it again. Just stand back here somewhere and pretend you are behind your piano for now."

"I can't believe I am doing this," she mumbled to herself. "I said I needed to get a life; I've obviously got one now."

ᘛ ᘚ

Monday and Tuesday's rehearsals went fabulous. Annie had finally begun to relax, and the musicians took great pleasure in teasing her. She could not have ever imagined being able to fit in with such a group of professionals, but they admired her greatly and felt honored to have her on board. Alex refused to speak with her, but Megan spent as much time during rehearsal breaks as possible to talk.

On Wednesday, a rehearsal free day, Annie and Megan, flanked with security, managed to take a riding tour of New York City. Annie was able to see all the sights, but only from a distance. They ate at a quaint little restaurant, but it required a major security setup in order to do so. Annie in reality was relieved when she finally returned to Stephen's apartment and no longer had to look over her shoulder for someone trying to press in on her. At one point, a man grabbed her long hair and began to yank her toward him. Bull took control immediately. For the rest of the day, Annie's head ached.

༄ ༄

"You look miserable," Stephen told her as they lounged in the screening room watching an old movie channel.

"I have a headache," she griped. "My body is tired, my voice is hoarse, and I think I pulled a muscle in my arm when I tried to jerk away from that guy today."

"Why didn't you tell me?" he asked her. "Can I get you some Ibuprofen?"

"You have medicine?" she asked in wonder. "Where? Not in your kitchen."

"In my medicine cabinet."

"Yes," she almost pleaded as she rubbed her temples. "Any Valium in there? Nyquil? Benadryl? Something to knock me out?"

"Oh, I think you'll manage to sleep fine tonight," he consoled her. "How about something to drink with it? A Sprite?"

Annie nodded. She hoped that by Saturday night she would be on this new schedule and feel up to the challenge. As for now, she was downright miserable. She should probably call her parents or Angie or someone, but she didn't have the energy to pick up the phone. It was only 8:30, concert-starting time, and she felt like a ton of bricks was sitting on the top of her head. She was so thankful there was no rehearsal tonight.

"Here we go," Stephen said as he brought in her Sprite and capsules. He sat next to her and handed her the pills first. She popped one into her mouth, took a drink, and then threw her head back trying to get it down. She always had trouble with pills. When it finally went down her throat, she repeated the process. She took a few more swallows of Sprite and then leaned back on the couch.

"Want to play cards?" Stephen asked her.

She shook her head no.

"Video game?" he tried again.

"No," she sighed. "I am just . . . I don't know exactly."

"Homesick?" he offered.

Annie looked up at him and wrinkled her eyebrows.

"Maybe?" she thought. "I could be. I just know that I am really out of sorts. I am tired and misplaced."

"I haven't been the best host, have I?" he asked sadly.

"No, that's not it," she quickly assured him. "You've been wonderful, well, once we got the food situation sorted out."

"I feel a little selfish," he confessed.

"Why?" she asked as she sat up now. "What do you think you've done?"

"I'm in Heaven," he admitted to her. "You are here with me. I'm not alone. You bring so much life and energy, even when you're tired. Just sitting here with you watching silly old movies is like a breath of fresh air. Leaving with you every night for rehearsal is wonderful. I almost wish we had practice tonight because I love the whole process of hearing you complain when we get into the limo. Then when we come back here together, I love walking you to your room and telling you *goodnight.* And then I know, I'm not alone; you're just down the hall."

Annie smiled at him. As usual, she had only thought about herself during this transition. She had not really considered the fact that Stephen's loneliness was at bay briefly during this week at his apartment. She remembered what Angie had told her—maybe God had more in store than just Annie promoting her music. Perhaps Stephen needed this as much as she.

"Okay," she moaned as she stood up. "Let's play some cards. You need to get a Scrabble game too."

"And take the place of my video games?" he said in mock horror. "I can beat you at video games. I'm afraid you would have the advantage over me when it comes down to words."

"Was that a compliment or a criticism?" she asked as they left the room.

"Compliment about the words, criticism about the video games," he clarified.

She turned him around and pointed him back to the screening room.

"Don't ever challenge me again," she said smugly as she pushed him back into the room. "Turn on the stupid game and see who wins tonight."

After Thursday night's rehearsal, everyone felt great about the program. It was close to 11:00, and the usual last minute discussions about problem areas did not follow. Everyone felt confident and comfortable with the run through. They talked and decided that a Friday rehearsal would be overkill.

"How about an alternate suggestion?" Annie asked.

"Like what?" Chip replied as he packed up his sax.

"Something fun," Annie grinned. "Like everybody coming over to Stephen's. We could have a covered dish supper, and then we could play a game or something afterward. The kids could watch a movie in the screening room or play video games, and we could just spend the evening relaxing. I'll cook the main dish, just have the wives bring whatever moves them."

"If it involves food," Jason smiled, "we'll be there."

"Wow, people actually at my apartment?" Stephen said as a smile began to grow across his face. "I never thought of that."

"What time?" Sam asked. "And we'll bring dessert. Sharon makes this great chocolate éclair cake."

"Annie?" Stephen asked turning to her. "What time?"

"Well, since no one had any plans to begin with, let's say 6:00."

The plans were made and everyone left in a great mood, everyone except for Alex.

"We won't be there," Megan told Annie sadly before they left. "Alex just won't do it."

Annie nodded in understanding, though she really did not understand. How could he so detest her that he wouldn't even show up for a dinner at Stephen's? What on earth had she done? Was she really beneath his forgiveness?

The Friday covered dish dinner was a great success. It gave Annie a chance to get to know the musicians and their families in a more intimate way. She worked with the ladies in the kitchen and found each one charming in their own ways.

Chip's wife, Tracy, was full of life and energy. She tended to laugh loudly, talk loudly, and reprimand loudly when her kids got rambunctious, all three boys. Sam's wife, Sharon, was rather quiet, but had a wonderfully dry sense of humor. She had this knack for saying something so off the wall that everyone else would hold their stomachs from laughter, while she managed to stay calm and collected. Jason's wife, Diane, a little older than the rest, carried her maturity well. She was definitely motherly and very sweet in her demeanor. In fact, Annie had already decided that if there ever came a time that she needed to spill her guts, Diane would be her first choice. They had two older children, 13 and 14, who were well behaved and great with conversation. Kurt's wife, Krista, was as full of mischief as he was, and their six-year-old son kept everyone hopping from the moment he walked in the apartment.

As Annie surveyed the group as a whole, she felt so much more comfortable. In this setting, they were more like family than business partners. She made sure she spent time with each one, including the children, to begin building bridges of relationships that would be vital to her for the next three months. The absence of Alex and Megan was extremely noticeable to her, but no one else seemed bothered.

When it came game time, Annie pulled out a computerized disc from her room called *Catch Phrase.* Jason's teenagers even stayed in to play the game. By the end of the evening, the other four kids came in just to watch. It became hilarious as the guys began to lose considerably to the ladies. Their competitiveness began to drive them so much that they resorted to body contortions trying to win. Annie found herself genuinely laughing and having a good time for the first time in a week. This was the medicine she needed for homesickness—a new family of sorts.

"That was unbelievable," Stephen said to Annie as they closed the front door behind the last guest. "I have lived here for six years and never done anything like that. I've had a couple of socials, with like record executives and such, but it wasn't fun. It was strictly milling around and business. Rather boring to be honest."

"Well, I thought it was great!" Annie said, very pleased with its success. "I needed to feel like I was a part of this group."

"I hope you feel that way, then, because you were the life of the party tonight."

"No, I wasn't," she protested.

"Yes, you were," he insisted as they sat on the black leather sectional in his living room. "You were in your element. I guess socializing and Southern hospitality run in your veins."

"Some of it is just being raised in a minister's family," she told him as she pulled her feet up on the couch. "We always had people over, every week. Daddy felt it was important to get to know everyone personally. We would eat, play games, sit around a bonfire, sing—anything to get to know others better."

"I am certainly thankful he trained you well," he said as he took up one of her feet and began to massage it. "Maybe one day we can do this at my home upstate. You even have beautiful feet. How did you manage that?"

"I would complain that you might possibly be trying to be fresh," she said as she laid back and let him continue, "but that feels too good."

"You think so?"

"Uh huh," she sighed with a smile.

"Stick your other one up here too," he told her. She obliged.

He continued to massage both feet as he watched her close her eyes in delight. He had never seen anyone more beautiful in his life. How did he handle moments like this, moments when he wanted to come out and declare his feelings for her, but knew he had promised her he wouldn't? He sighed deeply as he told himself to be content with just holding her feet in his hands.

"Tired?" she asked him.

"No. Why? Are you?"

"Not really," she said, eyes still closed, still smiling. "You just sighed deeply."

"Ah," he said with understanding. "Just content. A good sigh, not a frustrating one."

"Why didn't you ever get married?" she asked him out of the blue.

He was taken back by the sudden change in subject, but collected his thoughts and answered, "I never fell in love."

"What about Carrie McCarthy?" she asked with one eye open.

Stephen gave a small laugh. "Carrie is what you might call a decoy," he explained. "If a successful man shows up without an escort in public too many times, they begin to start rumors. My best defense is to stop them before they start."

"Rumors like what?" she asked, eyes closed again.

He wouldn't answer, but just stared at her. When she finally opened her eyes to find out why the pause, she was taken back by his expression.

"What?" she asked him. "What's the deal?"

"You really don't know?"

"No," she said as she pulled her feet away and sat up again.

"I've been accused many times over the years of being gay," he said somewhat embarrassed.

"It's not true, is it?"

"No," he said definitively. "But if I go too long without a public appearance with a woman, somebody starts the rumor again. To be honest, the rumors don't bother me; people are free to think whatever they want. It's when men begin to assume it's true that I have the problem."

"Oh, my," Annie said troubled by the thought. "I'd heard rumors but never believed them."

"Thank you," he smiled. "I have to be careful how I handle it. I always deny the rumors, begin being seen with someone, and eventually things subside. But there are many gay people in this business. I rub shoulders with them a lot. It's hard to look at a man and say, 'I'm not interested in you that way,' and then just go on about my business."

"Is this some kind of arrangement you have with Carrie, then? She knows what you're doing?"

"Yes," he confessed with another deep sigh. "She's so busy right now with her career that it serves us both comfortably. However, with you in the picture, there will be a lot more rumors."

"What do you mean?"

"We've been seen together so much, people will begin to put two and two together and pin us as an item."

"Really?" Annie said more amused than upset. "So people will think we're dating or something?"

He nodded.

"Like I've replaced Carrie McCarthy?" she asked in unbelief.

"Some will," he told her. "Some won't believe anything until it comes out of my mouth. You'll notice I never answer any questions yelled out as we go from building to car or vice versa."

"Cool," she said with a big smile. "So I'm like Stephen Williams' girlfriend for the week! You should get me a ring or something and let the rumors really start!"

"You have no idea," he laughed. "They would then have us secretly married with pictures of a mourning Carrie on the side."

"You're a very nice guy, Stephen," she said as she reached out for his hand. "And you're a perfect gentlemen. My dad would have never agreed to letting me stay alone with a man in his apartment for a whole week had he not trusted you."

Stephen nodded, acknowledging the compliment of trust from her father.

"What about you?" he asked. "Do you trust me?"

"Shouldn't I?"

"We had this little agreement about you going on tour," he reminded her. "We would only focus on you getting exposed musically. I was to initiate nothing else."

She pulled back her hand and nodded. She remembered the agreement well.

"Just curious," he began, "was there ever any attraction toward me? Or was it all on my part?"

"Cry Baby Bridge," she said softly. "There was definitely attraction there."

"No other time?"

"Stephen, where are you going with this?"

"Apparently up the wrong tree," he said awkwardly. "I didn't mean to get into all this. I shouldn't have brought it up."

"No, it's okay. We should probably discuss it and get it all behind us. It will help us to not be unsure of each other during the tour."

"But see," he said with almost a look of agony, "I don't want to put it behind us. You are the most beautiful, talented, and intriguing woman I have ever met." His blue eyes almost pleaded with her as he explained. "When I'm with you, I want to stay with you," he said softly. "Right now, I feel like I have somehow discovered Paradise, but am not allowed to get off the boat. I just can only watch you from the deck and take in your beauty, but I can never have it for my own. I watch you sing, I watch you laugh, I have even watched you sleep in the limo, and you take my breath away. But I promised you I would not act on these feelings so I stay on the boat, continuing to take in every detail about you, hoping and praying that dreams can still come true."

"Wow," she said as she stood up. "That was . . . wow."

"Annie, I didn't mean to get into this," he said exasperated as he stood up to apologize.

Annie walked over to the large window and peered down to all the people still waiting outside the building for another glimpse of Stephen.

"Can they not see us?" she asked him.

"Reflective windows," he told her as he looked down on the crowd also.

They stared in silence at the many views offered by the window.

"I've never been in love either," she told him honestly. "I don't know if I've ever wanted to be before. . . ." she paused in mid-sentence.

"Before what?" he asked her.

"Before you," she confessed. "I have to tell you, when you touch me, hold me, sometimes just even speak my name, I feel like I'm going to fall apart inside."

"Really?" he smiled.

"Yes," she admitted, "but then I get so scared because I don't think I could ever get over losing you. And I feel so out of control when I feel like this with you. I can't think straight; I can't make sense of any of it. This is why we have to put it all on hold."

"Why?" he asked confused.

"Because I can't *even* process all of *this,*" she gestured to the city, the street, the crowd, and the apartment. "Right now, I can't go to a grocery store. I have Rocky I and II by my side whenever I leave this building. Tomorrow night I sing for New York City, and I'm scared to death. Then I look at you, and I am almost willing to give it all up."

"For me?" he asked amazed.

She nodded.

He couldn't bear it. Was she confessing her love for him, or was she telling him to stay away? They stared at each other in complete silence. He wished he could read her mind to know what he should do next. All he wanted right now was to pull her close and tell her she could have everything, but he knew that her small life was already being turned upside down. He did not want to lose her.

"What do you want me to do, Annie?" he asked as he kept his distance.

"Kiss me again—or leave me alone," she sighed. "Hold me—or keep your distance. I don't know."

She turned toward the window and folded her arms around herself. Stephen ached for her. He softly came up behind her and wrapped his arms around hers.

"I'll just hold you for a minute," he said gently. "This is all. You trust me, your father trusts me, and I never want to lose that trust. If you need me to keep my distance until you can think through all that is happening, I will be an arm's length away. Do you understand?"

She laid her head back on his shoulder and nodded. This felt so good and so right to her. Why did she doubt him? He had done nothing to ever indicate that he was not an upright, honest, and trustworthy man. If only he was *not* Stephen Williams, this was *not* New York City, and she was *not* in an opening concert with him tomorrow, then things would be so much easier. Right now, the thoughts she was thinking were not right thoughts. She was thankful that Stephen was a gentleman.

"Now," he said as he turned her around to face him, "you'd better go to your room, and I'll go to mine. We'll sleep on all of this, and when we wake up in the morning, we'll have a good laugh over coffee and cheese toast, and we'll finish packing for the tour."

She took a deep breath and nodded. "See you in the morning," she smiled. He melted inside but managed to wave goodnight. He watched as she went down the hall to her room and shut the door. *I am so in love, it hurts. I need to write a song.*

Chapter Nineteen

Annie awoke the next morning with her stomach in knots again. The opening concert was tonight, and regardless of the encouragement she had received from all involved, she was a complete bundle of nerves. At least she had managed to sleep until 9:30. Stephen was right. She was slowly adjusting to the schedule. The American tour would not be near as disconcerting as the jet leg to follow the trip to Asia and Europe. Stephen warned her that you just learn to sleep when you can over there.

She got out of bed and pulled on her scrubs, then whispered a little prayer for Angie. These pajamas always made her think of her sister, and right now she wished she were here with her. Angie had always been Annie's biggest fan, and when she needed to hear an encouraging word, generally Angie had one for her.

She glanced out the huge window from her room. The height was still dizzying, but she was even beginning to adjust to that. In one week, she had gone from small-town Southern girl to big-city dweller. She smiled at the thought. She was far from big-city in her heart. In fact, she wondered if a life like this would ever become second nature to her.

Annie left her room and headed toward the kitchen to scrounge up some breakfast. Tonight after the concert, they boarded Stephen's jet and headed for Cincinnati. Because of that, food supplies were waning in the house. As she entered the kitchen, she noticed Stephen sitting at his computer clicking away with the mouse.

"Morning," she said sleepily as she gently tousled his hair on her way by.

"Hey, look at this!" he said rather loudly.

She turned back to see what was on the computer screen.

"My, gosh!" she exclaimed. "That's me! What am I doing?"

"Trying to hide," he laughed. "Aren't you glad you had those dark glasses on now?"

"What does it say underneath?"

"It talks about the new mystery woman in my life," he told her.

"You've been spotted here for a whole week at my apartment, and you accompany me to every rehearsal. They think we're an item. They have no clue you're going to be on stage tonight."

"Is that good?" she wondered.

"That's great!" he said as he spun around. "You are going to blow this city away! This is one of many unofficial sites on the web. Your face is plastered all over all of them. People have already assumed you'll be going on the tour with me, but not as a musician. That idea hasn't even come up."

"You actually check your websites?" she asked surprised.

"All the time. Sometimes it is hilarious to see the things they come up with. You just wait, tomorrow you will be the buzz of the Internet, Annie-girl."

"Did you eat anything?" she asked him as she went toward the refrigerator.

"You've been with me a whole week, and you still haven't realized that I don't make food for myself?"

"I'm beginning to think you're a bit spoiled," she said with pointed finger. "We're out of cheese. Do you want some sugar toast?"

"If you're making it, I'm eating it."

"What it I were to get sick or something?" she asked him. "Would you make me breakfast?"

"It would depend."

"On what?"

"On whether we were married or not," he said with his head cocked to the side.

"Okay, we're not married, and I'm sick," she said rolling her eyes. "Would you make me breakfast?"

"No," he said matter-of-factly as he spun back around in his chair to face the computer again.

Annie frowned. He *was* spoiled.

"Okay," she tried again. "We are married, and I'm sick. Would you make me breakfast?"

He spun back around in his chair smiling, and said, "If we're married, I'll make you anything you want."

Annie blushed a bit, but Stephen immediately spun back around and continued his search on the web. She made sugar toast and got her coffee. As unfamiliar as all this was, she had to admit she was liking it—a lot.

ꕥ ꕥ

At 1:00, Stephen, Annie, the band, and their families along with the tour crew, were transported to the 9/11 site of the World Trade Center Bombing. Stephen had postponed starting his tour until September 11 so that he could kick it off in honor of the victims.

As they sat in the limo awaiting the final clearance by security, Stephen asked Annie, "How do you like Bull and Guy? I should have checked with you concerning them long ago."

"They're fine," she said as she stared nervously at the crowd that had gathered around the area. "Why?"

"Then you're okay with them continuing as your personal security for the tour too?"

She looked back at him and nodded, saying, "It won't get easier when we go to different cities?"

"No," he said with a slight grimace. "In fact, it will get progressively worse. People will be awaiting your arrival in each city, everyone wanting to get a glimpse of the strange, new lady who's touring with me."

Rocky III knocked on the window and held up two fingers.

"Two minutes," Stephen interpreted. "Got your glasses?"

She reached into the compartment and pulled a pair out.

"I'll go out first with Jeff," he began to explain, "and then you follow me with Guy and Bull."

"Who's Jeff?"

"My security," he said with a funny look. "You didn't know his name?"

"You mean Rocky III?" she smiled. "I don't recall an introduction."

"You're really not supposed to fraternize with them anyway," he told her. "They're supposed to be invisible. You just know they're there when they need to be." He smiled and shook his head as he repeated, "Rocky III."

"Look," he continued, "when we actually get up to the memorial area, you come and stand by me. I'll say a few words, and then we'll have silent prayer. Stand by me during that time. Guy and Bull will be scanning the crowds well. Security is all over this place. When it's time to go, Guy and Bull will escort you back. Got it?"

"Does it matter?" she mumbled sleepily as Rocky III, a.k.a. Jeff, came back to the window and knocked to let him know all was ready.

The door opened and Stephen stepped out to a screaming crowd. Rocky III led him quickly up a walk toward a microphone. Annie was right behind him with Guy and Bull on either side. The band and crew were already at the memorial area. Stephen stepped up to the mic and motioned Annie to join him. The crowd went even wilder.

Stephen bent down and spoke into her ear, "That last scream was for you."

Annie felt herself blush a bit.

Stephen bent down again and told her, "Give them a wave and see what happens."

She held her hand up to her shoulder and gently waved it, at which the crowd's screaming grew deafening. She was a bit taken back by it all. They had no idea who she was, yet here they were screaming at her as though she were a celebrity too.

Stephen held up his hands and began to calm the crowd down. Slowly the noise subsided, and Stephen began to speak.

"September 11, 2001, was a day we'll never forget," he began. "I was not here in the city that day. I was on a jet headed toward Denver for a concert that night. I was awakened by a friend who told me that New York City had just been attacked. I sat up in unbelief. Why? Tonight, I will kick off my tour with a tribute to those who were the victims of this vicious plot. Every song, every word, every note is dedicated to those people, to their families, and to the residents of this, the greatest city in the world."

The crowd went berserk. Annie just stared in unbelief at the emotions that were being expressed at that moment. Stephen let them continue for nearly two minutes before he put up his hands to silence them again.

"Now," he went on, "I would like for us to offer up a moment of silent prayer. We need prayer, not just for those who experienced a great loss that day, but also for our city itself, for our nation, and for our world. Let us pray."

Everyone silently bowed his or her head. Annie could not bring herself to pray. She stared at the crowd from behind her dark glasses. Stephen had managed to have full control of such a large group, and it was intimidating to her. Just last night, she had almost confessed her love for him, thinking that maybe she could learn to know him as a normal person. But this experience put it all back into perspective. Stephen

Williams was a man who was out her league.

"Amen," Stephen half-whispered into the mic. "God bless New York City, and God bless America."

The crowd went wild again. Stephen waved and smiled at the crowd as Rocky III came up and took his arm. Immediately, Annie was flanked again by Guy and Bull who pulled her back down the ramp toward the limo. The crowd was polite—loud, but polite. They continued to yell and scream, but no one was pushing in on them as always happened at Stephen's apartment or the practice hall.

Once inside the limo, Annie removed her glasses and stuck them back inside the compartment. Stephen placed his up on his head and then gently slapped her knee.

"This crowd is going to fall in love with you tonight," he said with excitement.

"This crowd loves you already," she corrected. "You had total command over them. How did you do that?"

He waved his arms around mysteriously and said, "Magic."

Annie nervously finished gathering the last of her luggage and let Guy and Bull know that she was finished. They each grabbed armfuls and took them out the front door of the apartment. She got her garment bag from the closet that contained her two outfits to wear for the concert and hung it on the hanger by the front door. Stephen was right behind with his.

"How you feeling?" he asked her with a concerned look.

She slowly spoke, "Very, very nervous."

He put his arm around her and gave her a little squeeze.

"That's actually good," he said as he hung up his bag. "Nervous adrenaline really does increase your performance. It's a God-given blessing."

"I don't feel very blessed by it right now," she moaned. "I feel more nauseous than blessed."

"Just wait until the ragtime duel," he smiled. "They'll be yelling for more when the intermission hits."

Annie double-checked to ensure she had packed everything. As far as she knew, all was in her luggage that was now in route to Stephen's jet. She would not see this apartment again until the tour was over. Stephen had told her that the next time she was here, they would be meeting with executives to determine which label would have the privilege of recording the first Annie Wright album. That thought did not bring comfort to her at the moment. It just made the butterflies grow in size.

"Time to go, Annie!" Stephen yelled from the living room. "Your Rockies are waiting!"

She smiled at his humor. She hoped he could somehow soothe her nerves on the ride to the concert hall.

As the elevator doors opened, the crowd began to scream. They had not even left Stephen's apartment building yet, and the frenzy had already moved up several notches. Guy and Bull both held Annie's arms tighter than ever before as they went up to the glass door leading to the outside.

"No hesitation, tonight," Guy told her. "We walk fast and straight toward the limo. Understand?"

She nodded.

"By the way," he said with a smile, "thanks for keeping us on. You're the nicest celebrity we've ever worked with. Here we go. Ready?"

Did it matter?

The door buzzed and the crowd immediately began to push in on them. There were several more security men there so they shoved the crowd back while Guy and Bull practically drug Annie to the car. People were screaming things at her, but she was so frazzled by the frenzy that she could not make out anything. Once in the car, Stephen followed right behind. He did not stop this time to wave or say anything. Rocky III hit his hand twice on the roof, and the driver slowly parted the crowd again.

The arrival at Carnegie Hall was even worse. People were thick lining the street and the sidewalk. At least yellow police tape had been stretched along the route they would be walking through. Security and police were stationed everywhere, but as the limo pulled up to the drop-off, the crowd began to push in on the tape. Immediately all the security kicked in, forcing and threatening the crowd back. Stephen inched toward the limo door and waited for Rocky III, Bull, and Guy to appear. He gave Annie a thumbs-up and waited for the door to open.

As Rocky III pulled Stephen out, the crowd went fanatical. Annie was hoisted out immediately, and Guy and Bull quickly moved her to the entrance. The crowd was kept away behind the tape by security so this was actually the least physical resistance Annie had seen. Once inside, Annie sighed and shook back her head in relief.

Guy told her, "Tonight, I will be on the left side of the stage, and Bull will be on the right. We'll be watching your every move and constantly scanning the audience for problems. If someone happens to jump on the stage with you, don't panic. We will be there immediately to remove him. Okay?"

"Okay," she nodded. "Sure you don't want to just stand beside me at the keyboard?" she teased.

"And take away from your big night? Not on your life! We're to remain invisible, remember?"

Stephen came to her and took her hand. "Let me show you something," he smiled. "Follow me."

He led her to the hall where the concert would be that evening. It was breathtaking.

"Welcome to Isaac Stern Auditorium. This is the largest hall at Carnegie, but it will actually be the smallest group we play to on the entire tour," Stephen explained.

"It's awesome," Annie whispered as she looked around the auditorium. "I never realized there were so many tiers in here."

"It has five levels. The seating is wonderful, not to mention the acoustics. It seats around 2,800."

"Twenty-eight hundred is a lot," she said with a sideway glance.

"No, 28,000 is a lot," he corrected her.

There went the butterflies again, apparently African butterflies, massive and all aflutter. Annie tried to breathe deeply and relax, but nothing was calming anything at this point. Carnegie Hall, what a place to start.

"Mr. Williams," came a voice from the back, "we are about to let the crowd in."

"Thank you," Stephen called back to the man. "Shall I show you to your dressing room?"

He offered his arm and Annie took it. There was a slight sense of comfort in knowing that at least she would be with Stephen through all of this. He led her to a small room with her name on the door.

"I'll see you just before show time," he smiled. "And remember, the blue outfit is for the first half, the orange for the second."

"Blue, orange, blue, orange," she repeated. "That may be the only thing I get right tonight."

He laughed and left her to herself.

Annie walked inside the room and found several bouquets of flowers. She saw the blue carnations first and knew they were from Angie. She smiled as she reached for the tag. Angie knew Annie's favorite flowers were blue carnations.

Annie,

Go for it! You'll do great!

Love, Angie

Several of the arrangements were from various businesses in the area. They weren't even personal, just complimentary arrangements for whoever used the dressing room. A dozen white roses were on the table in front of the mirror. She picked up the card to see if these were also complimentary.

Annie,

Tonight you will light the hearts of many.
I am honored to have you on this tour with me.
No matter what happens in the end,
I will treasure the friendship you have allowed me to share with you.

Break a Leg!

Yours, Stephen

She felt a warm appreciation inside. He had gone overboard to make her feel welcomed and a part. She really felt like she could trust him and was finding herself drawn to him more and more. He was offering her the world in a way that only he could do, and she hoped she could live up to his expectations.

"Now, blue," she mumbled as she reached for her garment bag. "Or was it orange?"

Guy knocked on Annie's door and told her it was "five minutes 'till show time." She opened the door and was greeted by a warm smile.

"You look absolutely beautiful," he said as he motioned for her to turn around.

She turned around slowly as he whistled.

"Stephen has great taste," he nodded as he took her arm to lead her to the backstage area. "In clothes *and* women."

Annie felt her face grow warm again. As they approached the wings of the stage, everyone was there waiting. Stephen immediately came over and took her hand.

"You look unbelievable," he said to her softly.

"So do you," she smiled.

He was also in blue, but not a deep one like hers. His blue matched his eyes perfectly. He gazed at her briefly, causing the Africans in her stomach to grow even larger, and then he led her to the rest of the group.

"Let's have a prayer, and then we're on," he told them.

Everyone joined hands and Stephen led in prayer. Annie tried to relax, but she could hear the crowd murmuring in the background.

I must be crazy to be doing this! What was I thinking? I can't breathe! Inhale, exhale, be normal, be relaxed. This is what you've dreamed of all your life. Get a grip, and go out there and do what you know you can do.

"Amen," Stephen concluded. "Let's get ready."

Everyone took their places and prepared to enter the stage. Stephen grabbed Annie's hand and gave it a squeeze.

"You better stop looking like a cat with her tail in the fan," he told her. "You're about to change music history, Annie-girl."

"No pressure," she laughed nervously.

"When you get started, it will become second nature to you," he assured her. "Nerves are good, *remember?* Adrenaline."

"I don't like adrenaline, *remember?*" she said tersely.

He laughed and shook his head in amusement. "Yes," he said still laughing. "One of the many things I love about you."

The lights dimmed and the crowd went wild. Annie and Stephen placed their earpieces in and prepared to go onstage. There was screaming, whistling, clapping, and pure excitement generating in the whole room. Guy led Annie to her Roland with a small penlight, as the others also went to their places.

"I've got my eye on you the whole time," Guy assured her before he left.

She felt her keyboard to get her bearings. She placed her fingers in the starting position and waited for Sam to start the click-off with his sticks. The crowd was still screaming, anticipating the opening song.

Suddenly, Annie heard Bobby's voice say, "We're ready to roll guys."

Sam began the click-off," One-two-three-four-five-six-seven-eight!"

The lights flashed on as the first notes were played. The audience screamed even louder. Annie refused to look up. She concentrated on her keyboard and made sure every note was played in perfect time. She was next to Stephen but slightly at an angle so, when he began to sing, she was able to watch him. She could not believe she was actually doing what she was doing. She had seen him in concert so many times that it was almost déjà vu, yet she was no more than 10 feet away.

As the concert played on, Annie began to relax and enjoy it. Stephen looked over and winked at her several times. She had tried to see the audience, but the lighting made it impossible. However, she could feel and hear the energy. She could not see Bull nor Guy either, but she knew they were right where they had told her.

When it came time for introductions, Stephen went through each member of the band, allowing each to play a brief impressive lick after calling their names. Annie was saved for last. When Stephen finally got to her, she was not to play, just do the thing with her hands as she stepped to the side of her piano.

"And last, but definitely not least . . . ," he yelled. The crowd began to scream louder than ever. "Playing incredible keyboards," he went on, more yelling, "and adding her vocal stylings to my songs this tour . . ." The crowd seemed out of control to Annie. "Miss—Annie—Wright!" he finished.

Annie did her hand thing and stepped to the side of her Roland. She was able to see the crowd at last as various spots scanned over the audience. She was floored. People were standing and shouting, and then they began to chant her name. She simply did what she was supposed to do and went back to her keyboard to finish the introduction song. The crowd would not quiet down.

The concert continued. When it came time for the ragtime duel, Stephen pulled his microphone off the stand as planned and walked out to the center of the stage.

"Now as most of you know," he spoke to the audience, "I am a little bit famous for being a pretty good pianist."

The crowd went crazy again, but Stephen held up his arm just as he did when quieting the crowd at the 9/11 site. They quieted down.

"But I believe I might possibly have met my match."

They laughed this time.

Annie replied, as practiced, "Possibly?"

The crowd screamed again, and Stephen quieted them.

"That's what I said," he said turning back toward her. "I might *possibly* have met my match."

The crowd laughed and clapped.

"Now, Annie here is quite the composer," he continued as the crowd yelled again. "She's worked up this little piece that we'd like to do for you next."

There it went. The crowd was practically out of control. Stephen held up his hand and waited for the room to get quiet before continuing.

"Now, I have to confess, this piece is what I would put into the *hard* category," he explained.

"Really?" Annie responded in disdain. "You think it's hard?"

The crowd laughed and cheered again. They were loving the exchange. It was a total departure from anything Stephen had ever done before.

"Well, in a relative sort of way," he replied back.

"I think it's easy," Annie sort of seethed out in a challenge.

There went the crowd again. They began to chant, "Annie! Annie! Annie!"

Stephen quieted them one last time.

"Well, what I *think,*" he said pretending to be slightly agitated, "is that you need to put your money where your mouth is."

More yelling, screaming and chanting ensued.

"How 'bout I just put my money where my fingers are," she countered.

The crowd blared as Stephen said aloud, "Deal!" and went back to his piano replacing his mic.

Sam counted off and the ragtime piece began. Stephen began by playing several lines, to which Annie would respond by playing them slightly more involved. Stephen would go on with something new, and again Annie would follow him by showing him up. In the middle of the song, Stephen was supposed to have grabbed a fire extinguisher, but they changed it so that one of the stagehands ran on with one and pretended he needed to put out her keyboard because it was so hot from being played. Stephen yelled for him to get off, all staged of course, setting the audience screaming again. As the song neared the end, Stephen gave up, pulled up a chair, and sat down, while Annie played an incredible finale.

When the song ended, the lights fell immediately, and the crowd roared with applause. Annie waited patiently for Guy to show up with his penlight to lead her from the stage. He was there almost immediately. He took her arm and gently led her to the wings where dim lights were a welcome sight.

"That was awesome!" Chip yelled as he patted her on the back.

"They may have to change the name of this tour," Jason said to Stephen. "I think you not only were outplayed, you were definitely outscreamed."

Annie basked in the moment, but was quickly brought down by the scowling look Alex gave her as he left the area. Her smile faded, but there was little time to think on it anymore.

Stephen took her hand and led her back toward her dressing room.

"What did I tell you?" he asked as they walked quickly.

"I still have to sing *Autumn Sunset,*" she reminded him.

"Just wait," he said as he opened her door for her, "you haven't seen anything yet. When you start that song, they will be stunned. They haven't heard you sing. Get dressed quickly. See you in the wings."

Annie walked in her room and was startled to see Megan there.

"Ah!" Annie screamed slightly.

"Wasn't that amazing?" Megan said as she squeezed the breath out of Annie. "I think everyone in that hall has fallen in love with you! I knew it would be like this!"

"Not everyone out there loves me," Annie rained. "Alex wasn't the least bit pleased."

Megan sighed and said, "Don't let Alex pull you down in this. This is your moment, your chance of a lifetime. He'll just have to get over it."

The intermission went by quickly. Annie, now dressed in her orange, not a favorite color of hers, stood in the wings next to Guy. He patted her back as they prepared to go onstage.

"Give it all you've got," Stephen told her. "Belt out these songs. Exaggerate your movements when you get the mic and go center stage. When I get out there with you, pretend that I am the man of your dreams and we are actually living through this at that very moment."

Annie laughed. *Pretend?*

The lights dimmed and the crowd yelled again. Guy led Annie out with the penlight, placed her at the piano, and walked on. She listened for the go signal in her earpieces. She was *it* for this one; she started the whole thing off.

"Let's do it," Bobby said into her earpieces. "Go get 'em, Annie."

She smiled. She placed her fingers on the keyboard, took a deep breath, then exhaled. Softly she began the prelude for *Autumn Sunset.* Immediately the crowd screamed in recognition. She heard Bobby slightly turn up the keyboard in her earpieces. She was thankful.

Early November

Immediately the crowd began to hush.

Gaze out my window

Slowly an orange spot and a red spot began to emerge on Annie.

Watching the leaves barely hanging on

The crowd gave a few whistles, but most remained quiet. Annie was nervous. Were they mad? Was she intruding on Stephen's song?

Pour me some coffee
Pick up a novel
Ready to spend another evening alone

"Sing it Annie!" someone yelled near the front.

Never thought it would be this way
I simply played it safe
And somehow I never gave my heart away.

She let the keyboard fade, then listened for Sam to click off three beats before the entire band joined in, with Stephen singing background.

So while I'm waiting for someone to love me

The screaming started again. Annie had to concentrate to hear the music.

Someone who knows me through and through
I'll watch the Autumn Sunset
From my single room apartment
And hope and pray that dreams can still come true

She heard Bobby slightly raise the sound level again.

And long to hear the words, "I love you"

When the chorus ended on the deceptive cadence, the crowd roared louder. Annie now removed her microphone and came to center stage. From this angle, she could see the crowd jump to its feet.

Cool early morning, stretching and yawning

They quieted slightly to hear her voice better. She could now hear shushing around the room.

No reason to get up, but no reason to stay.
Hear children playing, watch couples swaying
Down in the courtyard as they face the day

Now the audience was completely still. Annie continued to fight her nerves; were they upset?

Never thought it would be this way
Just focused on other things
And somehow I let my time slip away.

As the next chorus began, Stephen was beside her on stage.

So while I'm waiting for someone to love me
Someone who knows me through and through

The crowd was the most out of control she had yet heard. Bobby turned up the volume another notch. Annie hoped her ears would not burst.

I'll watch the Autumn Sunset
From my single room apartment
And hope and pray that dreams can still come true

They looked at each and sang the last line of the chorus.

And long to hear the words, "I love you."

Stephen winked at her and gave her a warm smile. They separated on the stage and Stephen echoed her phrases on the bridge.

Nobody warned me (nobody warned me) Nobody said (nobody said)
There's more to living (there's more to living)
Than just success (than just success)

Nobody moved me (nobody moved me) Nobody dared (nobody dared)
Nobody showed me (nobody showed me) Nobody cared (nobody cared)
Slowly they began to back toward each other.

Nobody told me about the sunrise
Nobody told me, nobody tried.

They were now back to back. Each, including the band, gave a silent count of seven, and then Annie and Stephen came in together, in a new key.

So while I'm waiting for someone to love me
Someone who knows me through and through

The crowd was frenzied. Annie could barely hear. She took Stephen's hand on stage, and just continued to sing, belting it out as Stephen had told her.

I'll watch the Autumn Sunset
From my single room apartment
And hope and pray that dreams can still come true
And long to hear the words, "I love you."

The room quieted again as Stephen and Annie faced each other and moved in closely. She could feel his breath and the warmth radiating from his body as he stared into her eyes. As they sang the final phrase, he leaned his forehead to touch hers.

I long to hear the words, "I love you."

ꟃ

When the music was totally faded, the audience was screaming again. The applause went on and on and on. Stephen bowed and continued to acknowledge Annie with his arm. She would bow and mouth out "thank you's," but the audience would not stop. After two minutes, they began to chant her name again. This continued. Finally, Stephen put up his arm to quiet them down.

When they were back in a range where he could speak over them, he yelled into the mic, "There's more where that came from!"

The crowd started again, "Annie! Annie! Annie!"

Stephen motioned for her to return to her piano. They walked back and the crowd settled slightly. Sam counted off *I Knew it Was Love,* and the whole thing started over again.

By the time they had finished with *Forever Freedom* and *Unlit Passion,* Guy and Bull had had to remove three guys from climbing onstage. The energy that Annie felt hearing the roars for her own songs was beyond description. She knew the time was nearing 10:30, and that the concert was almost over. She could not believe that she was ready to go another two hours. Stephen had been right again; adrenaline definitely had its upside.

When the final note was played, the band members, along with Stephen and Annie in the middle, gathered in a line at the front of the stage. They bowed in sync several times then waved as they walked off the stage. The crowd, however, began to chant Annie's name again. Stephen took her hand and led her back to center stage. People began to throw flowers, shirts, programs, anything they could find to show their appreciation. Stephen picked up a bouquet and gave it to her. They screamed again. He took her hand and led her from the stage, with both of them waving until they left.

"So, what do you think, now, Annie-girl?" Stephen said with a big grin.

"This is not real," she said shaking her head. "This is not happening."

"Oh, yes it is," he assured. "And realize this—this is only the beginning. By Cincinnati tomorrow night, everyone will know who you are and be anticipating the moment you sing."

Annie bit her lip and closed her eyes. It was too much to process. Is this what they meant by *overnight sensation?* How on earth could this be happening to her?

After changing back into comfortable jeans and a red silk button-down shirt, she handed her garment bag to one of the crew and stood with Stephen and the three Rockies as they prepared to leave the building. Stephen handed her a sharpie.

"We'll take several minutes to sign autographs and talk," he told her. "Sign anything they ask: shirts, programs, books, even skin. Don't hesitate. Give as many as you possibly can."

"Skin?" she questioned.

"Just do it fast," he said pointedly. "They will talk to you 100 miles an hour. Smile, say your thanks, and don't tell them anything you don't want them to know. Don't tell them where you're from, don't tell them how old you are, and don't tell them where you went to school. Just be gracious and move on to someone else. Bull and Guy will make sure no one gets a hand on you. Security is thick out there right now. If for some reason somebody senses danger, you will be moved to the limo or back to the building immediately."

"What do you mean by danger?" she asked cautiously.

"Whatever," he shrugged back. "You have fans now. You learn

to anticipate anything."

Bull and Jeff stood next to the door, while Guy stood by Stephen and Annie.

"We're ready," Stephen told them.

"Let's face the music," Guy said with a smile. Annie liked him more and more.

The door opened, and the crowd began to go wild. When Stephen and Annie stepped out, they began to chant her name again. Immediately people began to hand things to her to sign from behind the yellow police tape. She signed as quickly as possible and smiled to herself as she thought of all the times over the years she had actually practiced this. People were yelling questions and comments to her, most of which should couldn't make out clearly because of all the noise.

"You're awesome!" she managed to hear.

"Thank you very much," she said back.

"Annie, do you have an album?"

"Not yet," she would smile and say, signing something else.

"Are you and Stephen married?"

"He'd better practice more if he wants to marry me," she teased. The group nearest her laughed.

"Where are you from?"

"Not here, that's for sure," she said in her Southern accent, handing a paper back to someone.

This went on for several minutes. Annie found that talking with the people was very easy. They expressed their admiration for her, and she found it undemanding to reply back in kindness. Soon Guy was at her side telling the crowd she had to go. They complained greatly, but Annie smiled warmly and told them all how much she appreciated their support. She left with Guy as people continued to beg for another autograph. She waved and smiled until she got inside limo. Stephen followed directly behind her. The door closed and Jeff smacked the top very loudly two times.

"Well," Stephen said with a huge grin, "I am rather pumped up and ready for Cincinnati. How about you?"

"I don't even know what to say," she confessed.

"I know what *I* should say," he said mischievously.

"What?"

"I told you so," he said as he reached up to touch her face. "New York City has just fallen in love with you, Annie Wright. Are you ready for more?"

Annie could not hide the smile that spread across her face. She wanted to be modest, to act humbly, but it was impossible. Stephen had been right about it all. Her life had just changed in a matter of two and half hours, and she could not imagine what the end of this tour would hold for her.

"I guess I owe you a big thanks," she told him.

"Not at all," he insisted. "That is the most fun I have ever had in my life. I was sharing the stage with someone. It was great! Our give and take was invigorating! Do you know what its like to suddenly have the life pumped back into you?"

"Really? It means that much to you?" she asked confused.

"Annie, this is old hat to me. Every year it's the same old thing, but not tonight. Tonight I felt alive again! And, trust me, it wasn't my music that did this."

Annie took his hand and looked into his bright blue eyes.

"I do trust you, now," she confessed with the same smile spread across her face. "Thank you for knowing what was best for me."

Chapter Twenty

Stephen's jet was truly beyond description. Annie could not imagine anything more plush and luxurious. However, all the fanciness could not hide the fact that she was back in a plane thousands of feet above the ground. She took no comfort in everyone else's security. She did not like heights, and she did not like planes. An even greater task was that she was somehow supposed to go to bed and attempt to sleep while the thing was still in the air.

Her bedroom was small and scantily equipped. It was twelve by twelve with a full-sized bed, which she hoped was bolted to the floor, a rack for hanging clothes, and a medium-sized bureau containing four drawers. A full-length mirror was on one of the walls, and a lamp was attached to the wall behind the bed. Stephen told her to go ahead and unpack, and then she could return to the seating area and buckle in for the take-off if it made her feel better.

Why certainly! I would much rather be safely strapped to a seat if we're plunging at a rate of 500 miles per hour to the ground from an altitude of 2,000 feet.

After the jet was in the air, Annie went back to her room hoping that somehow she would be so exhausted that she would forget where she was and drift off to sleep immediately. Impossible. They were only in the air for an hour, but Annie felt every bump, turn and joggle of the trip. During the landing, she believed she was having an all out panic attack. Was it actually possible that the rest of the band and crew had just gone to bed and fallen asleep?

She glanced at her watch. It was 4:20 in the morning, still Eastern Time. If she could actually be asleep by 4:30, she could sleep until 12:30 and still get eight hours. She rolled over in the bed and closed her eyes. The last time she checked the clock, it was 5:15. Somewhere shortly after that, sleep found her, but it was fitful and sporadic. She believed that subconsciously her psyche knew she was still in a plane and would not let real rest come to her. They would not actually be in a hotel until the next Saturday night so she had better learn how to deal with her psyche and her subconscious.

ꕥ ꕥ

The concert in Cincinnati was as huge a success as New York City, only with four times the people. Annie was still apprehensive at the beginning of the concert, but by her introduction on the fourth song, the crowd already loved her. The *Autumn Sunset* duet with Stephen was extraordinary. The audience did exactly as in New York—stood to their feet and cheered for several minutes. There were a few that had obviously heard about Annie from the web sites and brought along posters and banners with Annie's name.

She enjoyed signing autographs again, posing for pictures, and talking with the people after the concert. She remembered Stephen's advice not to give out any information whatsoever. As far as she knew, no one had yet realized that this was Annie Wright, preacher's daughter from Dockrey, Alabama.

Normally Stephen did not do concerts on Sunday nights, but because of a programming problem with tickets being sold at a later date, a date when he would have been in China, he agreed to start off the tour by allowing the second night to be on Sunday in Cincinnati, transferring all tickets to the new time.

They boarded the jet and took another brief flight to North Carolina for the Monday night concert. When people actually heard Annie speak in a Southern accent at the introduction of the piano duel, the crowd went crazy even more. During the autograph section, her fans pleaded to know where she was from. She would just smile and tease, "Let's just say I'm from the Promised Land and leave it at that."

Tuesday night they performed in Atlanta. Anticipating the excitement of the crowd over Annie's obvious Southern heritage, Stephen played that up considerably during his introduction of her during the fourth song. It was a smart move. The crowd was totally behind her and frenzied by the time she actually started *Autumn Sunset* after the intermission. However, this crowd responded more to her *Unlit Passion.*

With no concert on Wednesday, they flew to Boston during the day. Annie found that she preferred flying in the daytime to the black of night. Stephen made sure the band and crew listened to the DVD of Jonathan's mid-week service from the week before, and the two chefs cooked up a marvelously gourmet meal for everyone to enjoy. Annie had to confess that being cooked for, morning, noon and night, had its perks. However, she finally convinced the chefs, after four days, that she did *not* eat eggs, pancakes, or any type of greasy meat for breakfast. All she wanted was some kind of bread with something stuck on it: cheese, butter, sugar or jelly, and a cup or two of coffee.

As September 28 approached, a Tuesday, the concert in New Orleans was at hand. The jet was approaching the runway at 2:20 in the afternoon. After Annie's incessant complaining, the pilots begin to file flight plans in the daytime whenever possible. She was finally able to sleep at least six to seven hours a night. Occasionally, she would even make it eight or nine hours, but she was adjusting well to the tour. She was even beginning to wonder how she ever managed to get up at 6:45 every morning, and if she would ever go back to that schedule again when her life returned to normal. Or would her life ever return to normal?

As soon as they landed, Stephen had Annie call Angie to say that a limo would pick her up from the seminary and take her to the Hyatt downtown. When everyone had packed, the cars began a convoy to the hotel. At the hotel, a massive crowd had already arrived, and the police had put up security tape to keep the crowds back. As each band member and his family, then crewmembers, exited the limos, the crowd would yell and wave. But when Stephen and Annie stepped out of the last one, the crowd went berserk. Stephen and Annie waved as Guy, Bull, and Rocky III led them quickly to the foyer, then to the see-through elevators. As they hurriedly went up to the top floor, a little too quickly for Annie's stomach, the crowd downstairs continued to gawk and wave.

When the elevator door opened, standing directly across was Angie. Annie screamed in delight and ran to hug her immediately.

"I don't suppose I'll be seeing much of you tonight," Stephen said forlornly to Annie as he grabbed a quick hug from Angie.

"Oh, I don't know," Angie answered instead. "If you're a real good boy, we might let you take us *out* to dinner."

Annie laughed, as did Stephen.

"What?" Angie wondered at their response.

"We won't even try to eat *out* some place here," Stephen told her. "That crowd down there will be all over New Orleans this evening. You'll need to order in."

"Oh," Angie said softly in comprehension. "Well, then, see you when its concert time."

"Wait," Stephen halted her, "do you want to sit backstage or front and center?"

"Wow, I don't know. If I sit in the front, can I still come backstage during the intermission?"

"Absolutely," Stephen assured her. "In fact, we'll stick you with Jeff for the whole night. As soon as the concert begins, he'll seat you, and then get you back for intermission and the end of the concert."

"Who's Jeff?" Angie asked.

"Rocky III," Annie cleared up.

During their afternoon together, the girls lay around in their suite and tried to catch up. They both had so much to say that it was nearly impossible for either to finish a thought. At 6:00, Annie said they needed to order some supper so they could be ready to leave for the Super Dome by 7:30. A hotel attendant delivered their trays, complete with silver platters and coverings by 6:30.

"This is awesome," Angie said in unbelief as she pulled the top from her Jambalaya. "It's like we're in a movie!"

"You have no idea," Annie tried to explain as she doused a small tad of hot sauce on her skewered shrimp. "Even though nobody knows who I am, it's almost like I'm already a celebrity. By the time I get to another city, pictures and autographs and facts are already on these websites and people have these printed pictures of me to sign at the end of a concert."

"Is it scary? Or do you like it?" Angie asked excitedly.

"It's awesome!" Annie confessed. "They don't even know who I am or where I'm from. There's no album for them to buy, no T-shirts for them to nab, although one guy did have a T-shirt he had printed out from the Internet somehow. I definitely signed it."

"Wow, Annie on a T-shirt," Angie said in awe. "So what happens after the tour?"

"Oh, gosh, I don't even know," Annie rolled her eyes. "All these people have been contacting Stephen's agent about trying to get me on board, but Stephen told him to tell everyone to wait until the first of the year. He says I need to get through the tour, think on all my options during the holidays, and then we will make a decision about what I really want to do."

"*We* will make a decision," Angie grinned slightly.

"Yes, *we,*" Annie confirmed. "I am trusting Stephen to help me make the best deal and the best contacts. I mean, I could get lost in the middle of all this."

"Or you could get lost in those blue eyes of his," Angie teased.

"We're not going there again," Annie said soberly. "Stephen and I have agreed to keep anything like that on hold until the tour is over."

"Why?" Angie asked incredulously. "I mean, really, why?"

"Because everything is so *tumultuous* and fast-paced right now."

"You could say it is *passionate,* maybe."

"You are a totally hopeless romantic," Annie said scornfully. "Stop trying to hook me up with someone and start digging for yourself."

"I told you," Angie reminded her, "I have sworn off men and sworn myself to celibacy."

"Yuck," Annie scowled. "Like—forever?"

"Forever!" Angie confirmed.

༺ ༻

The trip to the concert included Angie joining Stephen and Annie in their limo. There was a little confusion in the crowd as to which girl was Annie. Both sisters had long, dark hair and full lips. It didn't take long however for the majority to pick out the correct one.

"Annie, I love you!"

"Sign this, Annie! You're beautiful!"

"Are you and Stephen married yet?"

"When are you doing an album?"

"Where are you from?"

Once inside the dressing room, Annie dressed quickly while Angie read the notes from all the flower arrangements.

"Do you know any of these people?" Angie asked her as she read another note.

"Only that one," she said pointing to the dozen white roses in front of her mirror.

"How do you know? We haven't even read it yet."

"I get them every night," Annie smiled.

"Oooo, a secret admirer?" Angie teased her. "May I read it?"

Annie nodded as she pulled the sides of her hair back and clipped them behind her head. Angie removed the note from the bouquet and then the card from the tiny envelope. She read:

Annie-girl,

Have fun beating me again tonight!

Yours, Stephen.

"He does this every performance?" Angie asked with wide eyes.

"So far," Annie said while adding a little more powder to her face.

"Does *everyone* get flowers from Stephen?" Angie wondered.

"I don't know," Annie replied with slight sarcasm. "I don't go into anyone else's dressing room."

"Hmmm," Angie mulled.

"Yeah, yeah, yeah," Annie mumbled as she pointed Angie toward the door. "Put your mind somewhere else for a change. Let's get with the rest of the group, and then Rocky III will take you to your seat."

"Does he know you call him that?"

"I don't know," Annie confessed as they walked down the hallway. "I've never actually spoken with him; he's supposed to be invisible."

Stephen asked Angie to lead in prayer, and then had Jeff escort her to her seat. To her surprise, Megan was sitting next to her. They quickly exchanged warm greetings then hushed as the lights went down. When the concert began, Angie was totally baffled by the performance she saw. She knew Annie was above average, but as the ragtime duel came to its end, Angie could not even speak. This was inconceivable. Annie was a full-fledged performer who could work the crowd every bit as much as Stephen Williams himself.

"I cannot believe what I just heard and saw," Angie told Annie back in the dressing room.

"Wasn't it fun?" Annie said smiling. "The crowd loves it when we do that."

"You don't get it," Angie said trying to explain. "That wasn't some little half-hyped performance you guys just gave. That was like, top of the line, cream of the crop, doesn't get any better than this kind of performance."

"Couldn't you think of any more clichés to add in there,

Angie?"

"My clichés don't even begin to describe what happened tonight," Angie said dumbfounded. "You guys were *totally* awesome."

"Totally awesome," Annie smiled. "Congratulations, you just found another cliché."

Angie continued to try and explain how impressed she was as Annie put on the orange outfit.

"Orange?" Angie questioned.

"Yeah, funky color, isn't it?" Annie frowned. "Stephen wears it too, though, so I don't look like the only Halloween moon on stage. We've got to go."

Annie rushed Angie to the wings where Rocky III escorted her and Megan back to their seats. When the lights went down and Annie began to sing, Angie was more astonished than before.

This is my sister! My Annie! This is unbelievable! She does Stephen's song even better than he does it. Why would he let her do that? She is literally showing him up all over the stage, and he just smiles at her like—like a man—like a man in love.

Whoa! Did Annie know? She sure didn't seem to. She bantered with Stephen like a big brother, but never gave evidence of anything else. She did say that they *possibly* felt something, but it was all on hold. For Annie, perhaps, but it was written all over Stephen's face. He was hopelessly in love with her sister.

When Annie sang *Unlit Passion,* the only thought in Angie's mind was, *Where the heck did that come from? She wrote that? For crying out loud, about whom? Annie-girl, you are holding a lot of secrets from your big sister. I certainly hope you didn't plan on doing any sleeping tonight in that big hotel room. Nope! You will be doing a lot of explaining instead.*

After autographs and such, they made it back to the Hyatt around 2:00. Annie showered and changed into her scrubs while Angie flipped through channels. Shortly after Annie joined Angie on the couch, a knock came from the door. Annie looked at Angie with a look of question.

"I have no idea," Angie responded. "You want me to get it?"

"Okay," Annie yawned.

Angie went to the door and peeked through the eyehole.

"You're not gonna believe this," Angie said turning back toward Annie. "It's Stephen, and he's got one of those carts with the silver trays and stuff on it."

"Food?" Annie smiled. "Let him in!"

"But he gets to see you every day," she protested. "I only have tonight and tomorrow with you."

"Just see what the food is," Annie said with excitement. "I'm really kind of hungry,"

"At 2:30 in the morning?"

Angie opened the door and slightly glared at Stephen.

"I have to confess," he started, "that the idea of you two in here carrying on conversations all night long has gotten the best of me."

"And . . ." Angie said sternly.

"And I thought that perhaps I might bribe you just to let me join you for 30 minutes?"

"It's 2:30 in the morning!" Angie exclaimed.

"Well, yes, I know that," he said hesitantly. "But just 30 minutes with the both of you is all I'm asking."

"What's he got?" Annie half yelled as she left the couch to join them at the door.

"Whatever it is, I'm sure we can order it up ourselves," Angie insisted.

"No, no, no," Stephen quickly corrected her. "I had these specially ordered prior to leaving the hotel this evening. They would take much too long to bake at this late time of night."

"What are they?" Annie asked excitedly as she rubbed her hands together.

"You sure are easy tonight," Angie mumbled at her.

Stephen laughed and said, "Your sister is *never* easy."

"Come on, Stephen," Annie pleaded. "Show us what it is."

Stephen smiled mischievously as he carefully lifted the silver cover from the platter. Annie gasped. Before her was an entire plate of brownies, chocked full of pecans, with a gallon of milk and three champagne flutes.

"Okay, you win," Angie gave up as she let the door fall all the way open. "How did you know that brownies were our weakness?"

"With pecans, no less," Annie added as she grabbed one and began to dig in.

"Ladies, ladies," Stephen said as he pushed the cart into the room, "I will never reveal my sources."

"Well, one thing we know for sure," Angie piped, "it wasn't Alex!"

"You're right about that," Stephen affirmed. "In fact, I don't believe Alex has actually spoken a word to me since the tour began."

"I guess then that you've got the *Annie curse* too," Angie said with a mouth full of brownie.

"Exactly what *is* the 'Annie curse'?" Stephen asked them both.

Annie just shrugged, but Angie answered, "We have no idea. Pour me some milk, please. I am *assuming* that you are acting as our servant in all of this?"

"Absolutely," Stephen said as he opened the jug and poured out three champagne glasses full. "Can I get anyone anything else?"

"This is heavenly," Annie sighed as she took another bite. "However, as long as you're offering, how about one of those foot massages?"

Stephen came over next to her immediately and pulled one of her feet into his lap where he began to knead it methodically. Angie tried not to show any emotion, but she was flabbergasted again. The exchange was purely platonic, but Angie had never seen her sister with a man in any way at all before. The ease with which Annie and Stephen touched each other and spoke totally baffled Angie.

"Get him to do yours next," Annie told her. "He's very good at this."

"I'll pass," Angie said trying not to show her shock.

"So what were you two talking about before I came in?" Stephen grinned. "Feel free to pick right back up and act as though I'm not even here."

"So what shade of makeup did you decide to use?" Annie jumped in quickly. "I found that whole idea of switching brands invigorating."

She winked at Stephen who nodded his defeat at getting to hear anything personal during his brief 30 minutes.

When he finally left, Annie and Angie dropped into the king size bed in the sleeping area.

"That was a bit surreal, was it not?" Angie asked. "Stephen Williams serving us brownies and milk?"

"Not," Annie replied plainly. "He's a very personable guy. I've actually had fun getting to know him on the tour."

"Is he more *normal* to you now, as opposed to his superstardom that you struggled with back at home?"

Annie leaned up on one elbow as she looked to her sister and considered the question.

"Actually, I think he is," Annie said with a smile. "He's become sort of like a mentor to me. I still respect who he is greatly, but he has shown me so much and exposed me to so much in this business that I feel now like he is my right arm."

"Interesting analogy," Angie nodded. "What happens after the tour?"

"I go home and chill. I spend the holidays in Dockrey with my wonderful family and that includes my *exceptionally* wonderful sister." Angie smiled. "Then," Annie continued, "I head back to New York in January to meet with Stephen and make some plans. He keeps telling me that *I* need to know what *I* want before *I* make any decisions. He seems to think there will be so many different directions that I can go, and that I will need to chart it all out. He says I need to be the one making offers, not just taking what people will give me. Apparently, I will write my own ticket."

"And what about Stephen when all of this is through?" Angie tried to ask without sounding as though she were prying.

"He'll be helping me through it all," Annie said simply. "Now, enough about me! Tell me more about you. What's something new and exciting going on in your life?"

Annie, the queen of changing the subject. Okay, you don't want to talk about Stephen. You will, one day, and you will spill it all out, sister.

"Remember Eddie?" Angie asked, deciding to just move on.

"No. Who is he?"

"The musician guy I went out with?" Angie reminded her.

"Oh, the weird one with the long hair," Annie remembered.

"Well, he wasn't *that* weird, just a little different."

"Are you dating him again?" Annie asked curiously, now sitting up fully in the bed.

"No," Angie waved it off. "He's teaching me how to play the guitar."

"Get out of here!" Annie exclaimed. "You've decided to take up something musical? Why?"

"I've always been around music," Angie sighed. "My family adored it, and it sort of *is* the universal language, you know? The more I imagined myself on a desert island with no source of music, except for maybe a tribal drum here or there, I began to get very depressed about it."

"Wow, I never imagined you picking up an instrument."

"I'm not the best, but Eddie says I'm doing really well. By the time I go to Padawin, he says I should have a nice 'command' of the instrument."

"I wish I could hear you play," Annie smiled. "Maybe you could be on my album?"

Angie laughed and rolled back down on the bed.

"Yes, I'll be the featured guitarist on *Unlit Passion,*" she giggled. "Speaking of which, who on earth is that song about?"

"I'm a songwriter," Annie said plainly. "I can write about anything."

"Not like that, you can't. You're holding out on something with me."

"Think what you like," Annie said as she lay down too. "Stephen swears it's about him."

"Is it?"

Annie slapped her sister playfully and rolled her eyes. "Its not about *anyone,*" she emphasized. "I just have a vivid imagination."

"Very vivid," Angie murmured as the two began to drift out of conversation and into sleep.

༺ ༻

The next morning, the girls got up late, ate late, and talked until late in the afternoon. Angie had wanted to show Annie the seminary, taking her to her dorm room and introducing her to a few friends, but after checking with security, they were advised against it. The crowd was larger than ever, and most of them were carrying signs with Annie's name or picture on them.

"Do you think this will ever settle down?" Angie asked Annie as they prepared for dinner in Stephen's suite. "I mean, will you be able to go home in Dockrey and just do whatever?"

"Oh yeah," Annie said with certainty. "No one in Dockrey gives a flying fig about what I'm doing."

"Except maybe Vivian McCall," Angie said with a devious smile.

"Probably," Annie agreed. "I'm sure she's donned black and is officially in mourning until the tour is over."

"When do you leave for overseas?" Angie asked her as she removed a fallen eyelash from Annie's cheek.

"Sometime after the Saturday night concert on October 17."

"Aren't you excited?" Angie asked animated.

"About going around the world? Sure. About flying there? No."

"You don't like *flying?* In a jet like *that* one?" Angie asked with a stunned look.

"Hey, look," Annie said while opening the door to exit the room, "isn't the old saying 'the bigger they are, the harder they fall'?"

They knocked on Stephen's door and waited for him to answer. He greeted them with a gracious smile and invited them into the room. To their surprise, Alex and Megan were there. It was apparently a surprise to them also.

"Great," Stephen said with a clap of his hands, "now that the whole family is here, we can sit down and begin dinner. Alex, Megan, you can sit over there. Annie and Angie, how about here?" he told them all as he gestured to their designated seats.

Alex was extremely offended, but had apparently come to the conclusion that it would be better not to counter Stephen again. He pulled Megan's chair out to let her sit, and then he sat next to her. Stephen pulled out the chairs for both Annie and Angie and then sat down, insisting they hold hands as he asked the blessing. Annie wanted to peek at Alex desperately, but feared he may be glaring back at her. She hoped he did not think this was her doing.

"I asked for several dishes of Cajun food," Stephen said as he removed the lids from the trays on the carts. "Here they are. Help yourselves."

Silently everyone filled their plates and then sat back around the table. There was no conversation. None. No smiles. In fact, there was barely any eating. Stephen stood the silence for a while, but then finally broke in.

"How strange," he began. "This is a family that I remember sharing much love and laughter. Those eight days I spent in Alabama were some of the best in my life. And the truth is, it was because of this family. Now, here I sit with three blood members and one lovely addition by marriage."

Megan smiled at him.

"Yet, I am confused. Why is it, Alex, that whenever you are present with your family, it is like a wet blanket on a warm and inviting fire?"

Alex said nothing, but he did put down his fork and stared at his plate. Megan reached over and took his hand. Stephen continued to stare at him, hoping that he would offer some kind of reply. He would not.

"Have you nothing to say, Alex?" Stephen asked him again.

Alex put his napkin on the table and scooted his chair back. He looked up at Stephen and said, "I am eating at this table because you are my boss. Had you been anyone else, I would have rudely left this room immediately when I realized what you had done. Right now, I am merely trying to be polite, to hold my tongue, and to oblige whatever it is you're trying to do. You made this tour miserable for me by bringing her on to begin with. I will play for her, and I will play for you. But nothing in my contract demands that I do anything more. Let's go, Megan."

Megan stood at once and began to follow him.

"You don't have to go too, Megan," Angie told her. "I'd really like to spend some time with you before you have to leave for Miami.

"I know," Megan smiled warmly, "but I need to go. Good to see you, Angie."

They left. Stephen turned to the sisters and raised his eyebrows in question. Annie, however, was livid.

"What were you trying to do?" she asked in anger. "That was embarrassing and humiliating for everyone involved, with the exception of maybe you."

"I wasn't embarrassed," Angie insisted. "I think he's a little twit."

"Shut up!" Annie yelled back at her. "I have tried for years to atone for whatever it is that I did to Alex, and all to no avail! I have learned that the best point of action is no action at all."

"That's a very passive approach for someone with such an aggressive nature, don't you think?" Stephen asked her. "Demand it from him!"

"You don't get it!" she said as she threw her linen on the table and stood up. "I have tried everything! I have yelled, I have cried, I have pleaded, and I have even threatened, but all he does is literally tell me he hates me and to get out of his life!"

"He didn't have a problem auditioning for me," Stephen reminded her. "You were responsible for that. Why did he follow something you had initiated?"

"I have no idea," Annie bellowed, "but to this day, he has yet to thank me for lining this up! Why? What in heaven's name have I done to him?"

Annie went toward the door and turned to say, "I don't have much of an appetite any more. Knock yourselves out."

She then opened and slammed the door as she went back to her room.

"Interesting family," Stephen said as he went back to his dinner.

"Why *did* you set this up?" Angie asked him.

"I supposed that if I could actually get them into the same room in a somewhat social, civil setting, that maybe something miraculous would happen."

"Apparently you don't understand the meaning of miraculous," Angie told him as she decided to go ahead and continue her own meal. "Making Annie an overnight success was *miraculous*. Getting Alex to forgive Annie is *impossible*."

"Oh," he nodded as he chewed his food. "I think that may be a little clearer now than before."

ꟷ

"What is the deal with Alex?" Annie asked Angie again as they prepared to go to bed. "I mean, there has to be something more to all of this than just a little twinge of jealousy. Know what I mean?"

"Who knows?" Angie said between brushes of her teeth.

"At this point, it would seem like he would have forgotten whatever it was. Maybe he *has* gotten past it, but is just too embarrassed to let it go."

Angie looked at her with a scowl.

"You're right," Annie said defeated. "That's reaching. I just get so frustrated with him that I don't know what to do."

Angie spit in the sink then looked up at Annie with toothpaste-covered lips and said, "You know what gets me more than anything? The way that Megan just follows him around and lets him throw these little pity parties."

"Tell me about it," Angie rolled her eyes. "Megan and I got really close this past year. I mean, I almost hate to admit it, but we were like best friends."

"I'm jealous," Angie said with a grin as she started to rinse out her mouth.

"Not *that* good of best friends," Annie assured her, "but we got close. She would talk to me about Alex and how much she loved him and couldn't wait to marry him. Meanwhile, he continues to treat me like the scum of the earth. She can't be oblivious to it, but she certainly won't do anything about it or talk about it. I guess she just shrugs it off as some kind of *normal* sibling thing."

"Normal!" Angie practically screamed. "Augh! There is *nothing* normal about this."

Once in bed, they continued chatting about this and that, their futures, their plans, and their dreams. Slowly they drifted off, without either being really aware of when it happened. Those were Annie's favorite kind of sleeps—no pressure to go to sleep and no pressure to get up.

They said their goodbyes at the hotel the next day, just shortly after lunch. When Annie returned to her room in the jet, she almost felt a sense of comfort in its familiarity. She smiled as she realized this was yet another enormous change in her life. She threw her bag on the bed and then fell into it herself. It had a familiar texture and a familiar smell. Perhaps the trip overseas would not be so bad after all.

A knock on her door elicited a moan, as she got up from her comfort to answer it.

"Hey," said Stephen cheerfully when she opened the door. "Got any plans?"

"Yes," she said direfully. "I'm going to lie in my bed all afternoon and do nothing until I have to leave for the concert."

"Ooo that does *not* sound like fun. How about I suggest an alternative?"

"Like what?" she asked cautiously.

"I'm not telling," he said with a finger to his lips. "Just follow me, and I will explain it when we get there."

Annie figured, *Why not?* She really did not want to lie in her room all day. And with the plane already in the air, she was definitely ready for a distraction. She followed him to the area of the plane where the dance floor was located. He led her to a keyboard at the edge of the room.

"Please tell me we are not practicing," she complained.

"No," he said quietly, patting the bench for her to join him. "Nothing like that."

"Then what?" she asked as she sat next to him at the piano.

He smiled, then sighed, and then shook his head.

"I can't believe I am actually shy with you about this," he confessed.

"Shy? With me?" she asked in unbelief. "What on earth for?"

He chuckled slightly then placed his hands on the keyboard.

"Just listen," he told her.

He began to play a very sultry sounding piece. Annie smiled immediately as she liked the melody and how it mingled with the unusual chord progression. She watched him play it and realized that she was hearing an original Stephen Williams song for the first time, before anyone else had heard it. She felt her face go flush at the honor. She wondered if there was any possible way for him to show her a deeper respect.

"That was incredible," she said in total honesty. "When did you write that?"

"I started it right before we left on the tour," he began. "You really like it?"

"I love it," she assured him. "What's it called?"

He smiled, and she almost thought she could see him blushing.

"What?" she really wanted to know.

"Well, I've always wanted to do a sequel to *Autumn Sunset,*" he explained. "The whole seasonal theme would be a great thing to try. I've attempted many times to come up with something that was winter, but they were all pitiful. I don't know why. Then the other night I began to play around with this, and before I went to bed, I had this whole little theme going. I'm calling it *Winter Passion.*"

"I like that," she said in awe. "It has that sound about it."

They sat quietly for a moment then Annie burst in with an idea.

"Oh, you know what would be great!" she nearly exploded. "What's that Christmas song that almost has a mournful feel? You know, uh, the Judy Garland one?"

"*Have Yourself a Merry Little Christmas?*"

"Yes," she said with a high-pitched squeal. "You could play that somewhere in there, the beginning, the end—somewhere—to connect the winter theme even more."

"Bingo!" he yelled as he slapped his knee. "I was hoping you would collaborate with me on this! That's why I brought you in here."

"No way," she said in horror. "I can't work with you on the *Autumn Sunset* sequel! That would be almost plagiaristic."

"Annie," he said in amazement, "do you not yet realize what you did with *Autumn Sunset?* You changed the whole mood of the song. When you do it, it's almost a different song. That's what I want with this one. I couldn't do it before because *Autumn Sunset* was never complete; now it is."

Annie stood up.

"Stephen, that's not true," she insisted. "I take every song and make it mine. That's just who I am. Your *Autumn Sunset* is beautiful. Mine is just a little different."

"Annie," he said as he got up and went over to her, "I am *not* complaining. I have waited all my life to find someone like you! Do you realize how incredible you are? Man, I tell you that all the time," he turned away. "I bet you're tired of hearing it."

"Stephen," she went over to him and touched his face, "I am honored beyond description at how you have treated me and included my interpretations and my music. I sometimes need to pinch myself to make sure it's all true. And the thing that is amazing me more than anything else is that I really consider you my friend now."

He looked up at her and reached for her hand.

"Do you really?" he asked.

"Yes," she admitted. "I don't know when or how, but somewhere in the middle of this whole tour thing, you became my confidant, my partner, my colleague, and my friend."

"Then, as a friend," he smiled, blue eyes twinkling, "would you please write *Winter Passion* with me? We deserve this. You and I. Let's start now, and then sometime before the tour ends, we can introduce it in the concert."

Here she was again. She remembered this feeling well. She was face to face with him, barely and inch from his body. She could feel his breath, she could smell his wonderful scent, and she could see the flecks of color in his eyes even in the dim light. His hand tightened around hers. Her knees went weak again.

"Will you? Please?" he asked her again.

She had already forgotten what he had asked so she just nodded. Whatever he wanted, she was ready to give.

"Yes!" he whispered in triumph as he pulled her hand up and gently kissed it.

Missed, she thought with a smile as her hand began to tingle.

"Shall we start right now?" he said anxiously. "I haven't even attempted to put any lyrics to it."

Annie closed her eyes to regain her composure and then nodded in agreement.

Winter Passion? I'm definitely in the mood to put some words to that right now.

Chapter Twenty-One

Miami, like every other city on the tour so far, had its own unique reaction to Annie. But also like every other city, it loved her. South Florida was very warm and humid, but the tropical atmosphere put everyone in high spirits. When the jet left for Detroit, another game of Catch Phrase ensued, for which Annie was extremely thankful. While she was involved in the game, she did not think so much about the long flight. Shortly after arriving in Detroit, it was time to pack into the limos and leave for the concert center.

No one bothered checking the weather. It was to be unseasonably cold that weekend in Michigan, and when Annie stepped out of jet for the ride to the concert, the bitter wind blew straight through her long-sleeved T. The waiting limo was warm and toasty, but it took her body several minutes to actually get heated up again. When at the auditorium, she went through the whole process again, only the backstage was nowhere near as warm as the limo had been.

She dressed through chattering teeth and prepared for the night's concert. While onstage, the lights helped to warm her some, but not significantly. After the piano duel, she raced to her dressing room, still cold and shivering, to change for the second half. By the end of the concert, Annie was miserable, and a sore throat was definitely in the making.

"Are you okay?" Stephen asked her as they prepared to face the crowd outside in now sub-freezing weather.

"I'm a little chilly."

"Why don't you head on to the limo? I'll explain to the crowd."

"I can't do that!" she insisted, teeth still chattering away. "They'll be very disappointed."

"Yes," he admitted, "but they'll also understand the need to get you back to warmth."

"At least give me five minutes."

Annie stayed out for 15 minutes in biting wind and was finally forced by Bull and Guy to head to the limo. Her lips were blue, her face was pale, and her teeth would not stop rattling. Stephen held her close and rubbed her arms as they started back for the jet.

"I shouldn't have let you go out," he regretted.

"As I saw it, you tried to stop me."

"Yeah, but I *didn't* stop you. That's the whole point."

"I'll be fine once I get warmed up," she told him as she leaned her head on his shoulder. "Maybe a cup of hot coffee will help."

"No coffee tonight. I'll have one of the chefs brew you some tea."

"Yuck," she complained. "Hot tea?"

"Don't try to buck me again," he warned her as he continued trying to warm her up. "How's your throat?"

"Sore," she confessed.

"Tea with honey, then."

When they arrived back at the jet, Stephen walked her to her room and then went to find a chef. Annie collapsed on the bed, kicked off her shoes, and snuggled beneath the covers. Her body was still shivering as she balled up to try and stay warm. A knock came on the door.

"Come in," she could barely yell out.

It was Diane, the guitarist Jason's wife.

"Hey," she said gently. "You weren't looking the best after the concert. Are you doing okay, now?"

Annie nodded slightly and said, "Just cold and tired."

"Can I get you anything?"

"Stephen's bringing me some hot tea."

"Good. That should help warm you up," Diane smiled. "Would you like another blanket?"

"No thanks. I'm sure I'll warm up soon."

"If you need anything later, look me up. I mean it, okay?" Diane waved as she closed the door.

After several more minutes, Stephen appeared with a travel mug full of hot tea and honey. He sat down beside her and helped her to sit up. She was still shivering.

"Why did let yourself get so cold?" he asked her as he handed her the mug.

"I didn't realize I was . . ." she stopped mid sentence to drink some tea. It soothed her throat a bit.

"You look so pale," Stephen told her as he reached up to touch her forehead. "Annie! I think you've got fever!"

"How can I have fever when I'm freezing like this?"

"I'll be right back."

Stephen left quickly and returned with a thermometer.

"You have everything on this plane," she smiled, still shivering, as he placed the thermometer in her mouth. When the device beeped, he removed it and his eyes grew wide with concern.

"Bad," she asked him.

"I would consider 102.5 pretty bad," he nodded. "I'll be right back."

This time he returned with Diane and Tracy, the woodwind player Chip's wife. They had a rather large first aid kit with them. Tracy immediately felt Annie's head and propped a pillow up behind her so she could continue to drink the tea without having to force herself to sit up.

"When did you start feeling bad?" Tracy asked her while Diane dug around in the bag.

"I don't know. Maybe at the auditorium—it was so cold in there."

Tracy smiled and said, "It wasn't that cold; you obviously already had fever by then."

"I wish we had known," Diane commented as she pulled out a bottle of Tylenol. "I'm guessing you had a pretty miserable night up there on stage."

"You wouldn't have known," Stephen said shaking his head. "You were quite the trooper. I didn't pick up on anything until after the concert was over."

"Take these," Diane nearly commanded as she held out two pills for Annie.

Annie scowled. The only thing worse than taking pills when she was not sick was taking pills when her throat was killing her. She knew there was a huge possibility that she would gag on them. She took them from Diane hesitantly and just stared at them in her hand.

"Problem?" Tracy asked her.

"She doesn't do well with pills," Stephen explained. "Is there any other option?"

"We've got a kid's liquid," Diane said looking into the kit. "I'm not sure how much to give her though."

"Let me see it," Tracy said with her hand held out.

Diane gave her the bottle and Tracy began to calculate in her head.

"How much do you weigh?" Tracy asked her.

All three looked down at her. Annie gulped. She was not in the habit of throwing her weight out for all to hear. She sort of stared back at them.

"You dose this out by weight," Tracy explained, waiting for an answer.

"Around 120 or 125," Annie finally told them. "It depends on whether its morning, night, after a ride, or after dinner."

"That's fine," Tracy assured her. "Hand me the little measuring cup."

Tracy measured out some of the medicine and gave it to Annie. She swallowed it down quickly, but it burned her throat. She gagged slightly anyway. Tracy took the cup and measured out another dose.

"More?" Annie asked, her throat still burning from the last swallow.

"This is it," Tracy assured her. "Swallow it down and chase it with the hot tea."

"You can't *chase* it with the tea," Annie complained. "It's *too* hot."

"I'll get her some water," Stephen said quickly as he got up to leave the room.

He returned about a minute later with a cup of water for her. She drank the medicine, gagged again, and then followed it with several swallows of water. Diane and Tracy stood up to go.

"Should we take turns watching her?" Diane asked Tracy.

"I'll be fine," Annie said firmly. "No one needs to stay with me. All I'm gonna do is sleep."

"We're flying tonight," Tracy reminded her. "You won't sleep well."

"I don't even think flying could keep me from slumber tonight," Annie told them as her head was swimming from the fever.

"We'll check in on you," Diane told her as she went toward the door. "I wish there were some way you could call us if you need us."

"I'll let you know," Stephen told them. "Thanks for helping."

"I'll be back with another blanket," Diane said as she followed Tracy out the door.

Stephen sat down next to her on the edge of the bed.

"Drink your tea," he said softly as he moved a long strand of hair from her face. "It will help warm you up."

"I'm so tired," she yawned, until the jet engines began to fire up. Her stomach turned over a few notches. She really hated flying.

Stephen smiled at her and shook his head. "You are one stubborn girl," he grinned. "I've had band and crew members before who hated flying, but all it took was a couple of weeks and it was over."

Annie drank another swallow and handed the mug back to Stephen. No more. She had downed all she could take. She pulled her pillow beneath her head and snuggled up under the cover again. Diane came back with a blanket and spread it out, doubled-up, over Annie. She still shivered, but she was so tired that she actually began to fall asleep right away, even as the jet began to take off.

Annie tossed and turned all night, but at least she did sleep. When she finally awoke the next day, her throat was killing her. She found it hard to even swallow at all. She rolled over to check the time—1:13. She had slept all night and then some. She was now sweating all over, but the shivering was gone.

Her door opened and Stephen peeked his head just inside.

"You're awake," he smiled.

As he came inside, he frowned and shook his head.

"You look horrible," he told her.

"That's nothing," she half-whispered. "You should see how I feel."

He smiled; she liked using that phrase. He came and sat down next to her and felt her forehead.

"Man, you are still so hot," he said with concern.

Annie grinned and said, "Thank you. I don't know that anyone has ever described me as *hot* before."

"Well, glad that sense of humor is still working. Let's take your temperature again. Put this in your mouth, and I'll get you something to eat and drink."

"I'm not hungry at all," she told him, "but I am dying of thirst. Got any Sprite?"

"I was thinking more along the lines of hot tea with lemon."

"Oh, please," she grimaced. "No more tea."

"It helps your throat," he explained. "You do realize that your throat is a major commodity now? You have a concert tomorrow night."

Annie rolled her eyes and stuck the thermometer under her tongue. How was she ever going to stand, much less *sing* tomorrow? She gave a thumb-up for the tea and lay back down.

ꕤ ꕤ

Her temperature was rising so Stephen began calling all over Denver to find a doctor willing to come visit the jet. Finally, a Dr. Michaels from one of the hospitals agreed to the *house call.* Stephen sent a limo for him and waited anxiously at the door for his arrival.

When he did come, Stephen was surprised at his age. The man couldn't be over 30.

"Dr. Michaels?" Stephen asked as he extended his hand.

"Yes, sir, Mr. Williams," he said with a smile. "Let's see this famous patient of yours."

"Annie? You know about Annie?"

"I've got tickets to the concert tomorrow night," the doctor grinned.

"Really?" Stephen asked in amazement. "For me or for Annie?"

"Originally, for you," Dr. Michaels confessed, "but after the news and websites, I have to confess, Annie is the big pull right now."

"Let's hope she makes it tomorrow night, then," Stephen told him. "And I'll tell you what, if you can get her there tomorrow, there's front row center tickets for you."

The doctor smiled and motioned for Stephen to lead the way. He was the most unassuming looking doctor Stephen had ever seen. His bushy blond hair looked as though it hadn't been combed in weeks, and he definitely had the forming of a three-day beard. He was tall and gangly and looked more like a college basketball player from the seventies than a doctor in the twenty-first century.

Stephen knocked on Annie's door and cracked it slightly.

"Doctor's here," he said softly as he stuck his head inside.

"Great," Annie whispered out. "I hope you got a miracle worker."

Stephen and Dr. Michaels walked inside the room.

"Good afternoon, Annie," the doctor said as he walked over and reached out his hand. "Wow, you *are* strikingly beautiful."

"This is nothing," Stephen smiled. "You ought to see her on a good day."

Annie was probably blushing, but she couldn't tell because her face was already flushed from the fever. The doctor felt of the glands in her throat, listened to her heart, looked into her throat and her ears, and asked a few questions.

"Without a culture, there's no definitive way to determine the real problem," he began. "But I'm willing to place my bets that it is tonsillitis or strep throat."

"Is tonsillitis bad?" Annie asked him.

"Well, it's by far one of the lesser problems with the throat," he smiled. "The best and quickest course of action would be an injection of penicillin. They would take care of either problem."

"A shot?" Annie said with a wince.

"That's better than trying to get you to swallow any more pills," Stephen said firmly.

Annie nodded then asked, "How long before I'll be better."

"The fever should begin to break sometime late tomorrow or even the next day," he explained. "The sore throat should be about the same. Actually having an injection will speed up the process as opposed to taking oral medication."

"Will she be able to sing tomorrow night?" Stephen asked.

The doctor smiled and looked over at Annie, "I sure hope so. I would hate to miss the hottest act in the world right now."

"Wow," Annie said with mischievous grin, "I've been called *hot* two days in a row now. I'm gonna start to get the bighead if you guys don't stop."

"However," Dr. Michaels said as he lifted a finger in warning, "I have some very strict instructions for you to follow if you are going to even attempt to be on stage tomorrow."

Annie and Stephen both nodded and then listened intently.

"First, you must drink, drink, drink," he started. "Keep as many liquids inside you as possible. Take some hot tea several times a day too; it will help soothe the throat. Rest most of all. Don't attempt to do anything, even shower. Tomorrow evening, before the concert, shower. Keep bundled up when you go outside, especially your head. The wind is cold out there this weekend. If you need to wrap your head in a sweater, do it. Keep the cold from irritating your throat."

"We can do that," Stephen immediately agreed.

"I would suggest she do as *little* singing as possible tomorrow," he said unhappily. "I know the concert schedule," he confessed sheepishly. "Maybe no background singing whatsoever. Save her for the lead after the intermission."

"You're going to the concert?" Annie asked in amazement.

"Wouldn't miss it for anything," he winked at her. "Now, if you're throat is not considerably better in the morning, give me another call. We'll do a second injection."

Annie winced again.

"Second?" she said rolling her eyes.

"Hopefully not," he assured her, "but we don't want to take any chances."

After the shot, Stephen led Dr. Michaels to the exit and promised him not only front row seats, but immediate backstage access to check on Annie at intermission and the end of the concert. He also handed him a check for $500.

"That's a bit steep for a house call, isn't it?" the doctor grinned.

"Not if you helped Annie," Stephen told him.

"She's absolutely gorgeous," the doctor said in almost a whisper. "Those big brown eyes and those lips! Where did she get those from?"

"The lips? Her father," Stephen answered.

"Is she really that talented, or is everyone just awed by her beauty?"

"You won't believe her talent. She's incredible."

"Where did you find her?" the doctor wondered.

"Writing commercial jingles in a small Alabama town."

After almost an hour, Stephen knocked softly on Annie's door and peeked his head in again.

"How are we doing?" he asked her.

"*We?*" she complained. "There is no *we* here. It's just *me,* and *I'm* miserable."

"How about I try to cheer you up?" he offered.

"Just try," she said almost as a dare.

"First, let's get you out of this room," he said as threw her the bottoms to her scrubs.

"I'm supposed to rest," she protested.

"Get dressed, and get your pillow. I'll be waiting outside the door for you."

He left, and Annie shrugged her shoulders in compliance. She got out of bed, pulled on her bottoms, took her pillow, and headed out the door.

"What are we doing?" she asked.

"Just follow me."

He led her to one of the television rooms and had her sprawl out on a couch. He then handed her two wrapped gifts.

"Presents?"

"Let's call it an early birthday," he smiled.

"Not too early."

"Really? When's your birthday?"

"October 19."

"I had no idea," he smiled. "Just kidding anyway; this is not early birthday. We'll celebrate properly then. Come on, open them up."

She opened the large one first. It was a huge fleece blanket, blue and soft.

"Nice," she said gratefully. "This is wonderful. Thank you."

"That's not all. Next one."

She first spread out the blanket and covered her legs and feet. Then she opened the smaller package. Her eyes grew wide in recognition.

"A Cary Grant DVD collection!" she exclaimed. "How did you know I loved Cary Grant? *North by Northwest! Bringing Up Baby* and *Charade!* How many more are there? *His Girl Friday! The Philadelphia Story!* Stephen, thank you! How did you know?"

"Oh, I have my ways," he said mysteriously. "The point, however, is that you need to rest. So curl up here on the couch with your nice, soft blankie, hand me the movie you want to start with, and you can begin your resting process now."

She looked through the movies, then handed him *Charade.*

"Does any body want to watch them with us?" she asked as he went to the massive screen to start the DVD player.

"Nobody's here but us and Chef Martel."

"Oh, at the hotel huh?"

"Yep. Chef Martel insisted on staying to cook for you."

"For *us,*" she corrected him.

"No, for *you,*" he said as he put the DVD in. "He couldn't bear thinking of you here all alone with no one to provide nourishment.

Speaking of which, how about some chicken soup?"

"I suppose that counts as a liquid."

"Indeed. Shall I order some? The chef will be *thrilled* to know he is helping."

Annie nodded as he handed her the remote and left the room. She snuggled down with her pillow and blanket and smiled as she pressed the button to begin the movie.

Heaven.

That evening, Annie's throat was still sore and her fever still high. She had watched two movies, but now felt like she could sleep for a while. Stephen took her back to her room, still pushing liquids down her.

"If I have to drink anything else, I swear I'll throw up," she threatened.

"I don't care," he countered. "Throw up all over me if you must, but the doctor reiterated to me before he left that you *must* have liquids."

Annie took the tea as tears began to well in her eyes. She sat on the edge of the bed and took several sips. As she did, tears began to trickle down her cheeks.

"What's wrong, Annie?" Stephen asked with concern as he sat down next to her. "Does it still hurt that bad?"

She shook her head. It hurt, but not as bad as before.

"Then what is it?"

She handed him the tea and lay back in her bed, pulling only her soft fleece blanket over her.

"I miss Moms," she said. "I miss Angie. Whenever I've been sick, they've always been there. This is so hard. I feel so horrible."

He reached out to touch her forehead. She was still warm.

"I'm trying," he said slightly defeated. "I'm trying to take care of you."

"I know," she said as another tear rolled down her cheek. "And you've been wonderful. I guess it's hard to be out of sorts in an unfamiliar place."

He nodded, but felt helpless to do anything. He had tried everything he could think of to make her comfortable. He wanted her to appreciate his efforts more than he could admit.

"Is there anything else I can do for you?" he asked for probably the 50th time.

She shook her head and closed her eyes to rest. He gently ran his hand along the back of her hair. It was tearing him up to see her so miserable. In truth, he did not care whether she could sing tomorrow night or not. He just wanted her well and happy again. He thought of the times he had been sick growing up. His mother had always sung to him. He smiled at the memory. It was worth a try.

So while I'm waiting for someone to love me
Someone who knows me through and through

It was working. He saw a small smile creep up on the corner of her mouth.

I'll watch the Autumn Sunset
From my single room apartment
And hope and pray that dreams can still come true
And long to hear the words, "I love you."

Before he could complete the entire song, he heard her breathing become deep and rhythmic; he knew she was asleep. He wished there was a chair in her room so he could sit and watch . . . just to be near her. Instead, he carefully got up and went to the door, gently opening it. He looked back at her and felt his heart ache. He never thought he could feel so deeply for anyone. She had inched her way into his heart, into his life, inside his head, and it was all he could do not to tell her his feelings. But he had promised her to keep his distance. He had to prove he could keep that promise. He had to prove to her that he was trustworthy. He had started the whole thing off on the worst foot possible, kissing her on the balcony at her house that morning. If only he had known that she had never been kissed! He could not imagine someone that beautiful, 26 years old, having never even dated before.

He closed the door and headed to the piano for a little reprieve from thoughts about Annie. As he began to play, he found himself starting with *Winter Passion,* but ending up with *Unlit Passion.*

Unreal. Even when I try to avoid thoughts about her, I wind up playing her music. She has buried herself inside my soul, and she doesn't even know it. God, please grant me wisdom and patience. And please, if possible, grant me Annie.

Annie slept through the entire night. When she finally did awaken, her throat had calmed only a little. She could tell she was still fevered, but the extreme chills and sweats were gone. She moseyed out of bed and decided to actually dress today. In fact, she wanted to shower, but she remembered the doctor's orders. Instead, she threw on a pair of sweats and made her way toward the kitchen.

"Onnie!" the chef exclaimed in his unusual accent as she walked in. "Goot mornin'! How are shoo feeling today?"

"A little better," she admitted.

"Woult shoo like zum chees toast?"

"Yes, I think I would," she said with a smile.

"And zum hot tea?"

"No, some coffee, please," she said as pitifully as she could muster.

"No, no, no," he said with a shaking finger. "Shoo can haf no coffee until shoo are bettoor. I make shoo zum tea instead, no?"

Annie rolled her eyes and nodded. She felt as though she were drowning in hot tea. At least the hot tea would go much better with cheese toast instead of trying to slosh it down on its own. She sat at the counter in the kitchen and drummed her fingers against the counter top.

"Vill shoo zing tonight?" Chef Martel asked as he started the water.

"I shall try to *zing* tonight," she teased him.

"Oh, my. Shoo are feelink bettoor. After breakfast, shoo will, how shoo say, haf a new lease on life!"

Annie ate and talked with the chef until her breakfast was finished. She then went to the television room to watch another Cary Grant movie. After about an hour, Stephen finally appeared, followed by Dr. Michaels.

"And how is my most famous patient today?" the doctor asked as he came to the couch and joined her, having shaved and possibly brushed his hair.

"I'm actually feeling better," she admitted with a grin.

"Wow," the doctor said in awe as he saw her genuinely smile for the first time. "You are feeling better. Let me see your throat."

She opened up and he stuck the depressor inside. She gagged slightly and saw Stephen chuckle a little bit.

"You never need to go on *Fear Factor,*" he said with a smirk.

"I can't even watch *Fear Factor,*" she said with a scowl. "That is stupidity personified."

"You're right," the doctor told her.

"Hey, I like that show," Stephen told them both. "I've always wanted to do a celebrity version of it."

They looked at him in unbelief.

"I've got a bit of a wild streak," he said with a smile.

"Yeah, call it whatever you like," Annie said sarcastically.

She's back, Stephen thought to himself.

Annie's fever was still low grade by the time they left the plane for the concert, but her throat was significantly better. They did agree with the doctor that she should not sing until the second half, but she felt confident she could make it through the latter songs fine.

"I'll have a little raspy Janis Joplin sound," she grinned once they were inside the limo. "I'll really give them something to talk about tonight."

"We'll see," was also Stephen would say. He was still concerned.

"Lighten up," she said cheerily. "I'm much better. I even managed to swallow a couple of Tylenol without gagging to death."

"You've been in bed for two days, though. I hope your energy can hold out."

She nodded at that as she drank some hot tea with lemon that the chef insisted she bring with her. She leaned her head back and closed her eyes to relax. She was a little chilled again seeing how cold it was in Denver. This was not the typical October weather she was used to in Alabama, and she was having a hard time adjusting her mindset. At home, they would not have even had an indoor fire yet, an outdoor one possibly. She smiled as she thought of home, sitting around the fireplace with the family, drinking coffee and laughing or arguing, maybe even playing cards.

"Penny for your thoughts," Stephen asked her, breaking up the pictures in her mind.

"Home," she said simply.

He nodded in understanding. Her home and her family were everything to her. He wondered if it would ever be possible for her to feel that way about him. Would there come a time in their lives that she would dream and long to be with him as much as she did her parents and her sisters? He hoped.

ꕤ ꕤ

Dr. Michaels checked her throat and her fever before the concert began. Her tonsils were still swollen, and her temperature was 99.9, but at least she was up and active and excited about the night, a complete turn around from yesterday. Jeff escorted him to his front row seat, and he prepared himself for an enjoyable evening. However, he was not prepared for the Annie he saw on stage.

After the piano duel, Jeff took him backstage immediately so that he could check on Annie again. He spied Stephen heading toward his dressing room.

"Mr. Williams!" he yelled as he ran to catch him.

"Ah, Dr. Michaels," Stephen smiled, slightly sweating from the physical event that the piano duel had evolved into over the past weeks. "And are you enjoying the concert?"

"I'm, for lack of a better description, blown away."

"That's a great description," Stephen told him. "That seems to be the opinion of everyone who hears her for the first time. And just think, you haven't even heard her sing yet!"

"So she wrote commercial jingles in Alabama?" he asked Stephen in unbelief.

"Yes! Can you believe it?"

"How did you find her?"

"Her brother is the bass player," Stephen explained. "I went home with him to be in his wedding. And there she was."

"You often find beauty with minimal talent, or talent with acceptable beauty, but how often do you find both and in such great degree?"

"You know what is so refreshing about this whole thing, though? She's clueless. She knows she's a great talent, but she doesn't even begin to flaunt it or demand anything. As far as her beauty is concerned, she is totally oblivious. Would you believe that we had a big struggle getting her to wear the red lipstick for the concert because she thinks her lips are . . . uh . . . unattractive?"

"No, I don't believe that," Dr. Michaels said shaking his head. "That was *not* my opinion of her lips at all."

"Mine either," Stephen grinned.

"Well, I need to check on the patient. Can't wait for part two."

"You only *thought* you were blown away by her playing," Stephen said as he began to back towards his room.

Dr. Michaels went the opposite direction to see Annie. He passed her brother, Alex, on the way. There was a slight resemblance, but not enough to make a real connection between the two. Annie's dark eyes stood in stark contrast to the extreme light green of Alex's. Dr. Michaels was going to comment to him, but Alex never made actual eye contact with him as he walked on by.

He found Annie's door and knocked gently.

"Just a minute," she yelled. "I'm almost dressed!"

Dr. Michaels winced. She did not need to be yelling like this with her throat as bad as it still looked. After about two more minutes, Annie opened the door all dressed in orange.

"Lovely color," he commented as she invited him in.

"Trust me, I didn't pick it," she half complained as she went to the mirror to brush through her hair.

"How's your throat feel?"

"A little sore still, but nothing like yesterday."

"Finish primping and let me take a look," he said soberly, but with a hint of teasing in his expression. He smiled as he saw her roll her eyes in the mirror.

"I'm not primping," she said firmly.

"You certainly have no need to," he added.

This time her look was more of a warning. She turned to face him with a questioning expression.

"You're very beautiful," he said bluntly. "In fact, you're *exceptionally* beautiful."

"I guess I should thank you, but I am not in the habit of hearing men compliment my looks. It doesn't happen."

"Well, it should. Perhaps you have been in the company of the wrong men. Now, let me take a look at your throat."

She sat on the edge of the table and opened her mouth dully to let him know she was ready.

"Don't get *too* excited about this," he said in response to her expression.

"I know I will gag again; I might as well get it over with," she complained.

She did gag, but Dr. Michaels was shaking his head.

"Your throat looks horrible. Are you being completely honest with me about how sore it is *not* feeling?"

She shrugged.

"What does that mean?" he asked nearly exasperated. "Does that," he shrugged in imitation, "mean *yes,* it really hurts bad, or *no,* it really doesn't?"

"How do you know with all this adrenaline going on?" she said throwing her hands up in the air. "I don't feel 100 percent, but I definitely feel like going out there in a few minutes and making the earth move!"

"Stop yelling," he said as he tried to quiet her down. "At least save your throat for the singing."

"I'm sorry," she said more gently. "My throat hurts a little, but it isn't killing me."

"Good enough," he said as he felt her forehead with his wrist. "Good heavens, Annie, I believe your fever has gone back up."

He reached into his bag and removed a bottle of Tylenol.

"Please don't make me do that before I go on stage."

"Yes," he insisted. "Yes, yes, yes, yes. When do you leave for . . . where are you going next?"

"Las Vegas."

"Ah," he nodded. "When?"

"In the morning."

"What time?"

"I don't know," she said starting to get a little impatient. "Probably around 11:00."

"I'll find out for sure, and I'll be over with another injection."

Annie's eyes grew wild and she shook her head.

"Yes, Annie," he said unquestionably. "Listen, this is your career you're dealing with. Do you want to finish out this tour?"

She nodded.

"Then I'll be over in the morning with another injection," he said seriously, but then slowly a smile began to grow upon his face, "and a picture for you to sign."

"I'll be glad to sign 20 pictures if you won't give me the *injection!*"

"Stop yelling," he said calmly. "Please."

She zipped her lips and glanced at her watch.

"Show time," she whispered.

"Lipstick," he reminded her.

He smiled as she rolled her eyes and went back to the mirror.

Annie waved as Jeff took Dr. Michaels back to his seat. Stephen came up to her and looked her over seriously.

"Are you okay? Are you sure you're ready for this?" he asked soberly.

She saluted and smiled, saving her voice for the performance.

"Good girl," he winked back. He then stared at her for a moment.

"What?" she asked. "What are you looking at?"

He came closer to her and took her hand.

"You look absolutely beautiful," he said softly so no one else would hear.

Annie rolled her eyes and shook her head.

"You do," he insisted.

"Why is it that in my 26 years on this planet no one has ever called me beautiful, with the exception of my adoring family, and now I hear it so often I'm really beginning to doubt its sincerity?"

"Don't ever doubt my sincerity," he said without a smile.

"I'm doing my best."

Dr. Michaels was not disappointed by the performance. When Annie began singing *Autumn Sunset,* he had anticipated it because he knew about it from the web comments, but he did not anticipate the voice behind it. His mouth literally fell open.

How could she just sit in a small Alabama town and write commercial jingles? I wish I had been the one to hear her first then I could have been her hero.

ꙮ ꙮ

The next morning, Dr. Michaels showed up as promised to give the injection. He also showed up with a picture printed off the web. Annie insisted on signing the picture first because she knew she would have no desire to after the shot. He completed his assignment, said his goodbyes, and then left the jet almost mournfully. He had met the most incredible woman in the world, but he knew that she had already fallen for Stephen Williams. He felt sure that Stephen would treat her well.

Chapter Twenty-Two

After the concert in Los Angeles, Annie signed autographs and pictures with an unusual excitement. At the end of the concert, several celebrities had been granted backstage passes, and she had the opportunity to meet movie and television stars she would never have dreamed of prior to this tour. To be complimented by those in show business gave her another boost she did not think possible. She was beginning to actually believe Stephen when he insisted that she could write her own ticket when this tour was through.

Back at her hotel while packing to leave, she called Angie one more time before leaving the mainland. This night they would fly to Hawaii for a concert in Honolulu tomorrow night, followed by a day off staying at a lovely Hawaiian hotel overlooking the ocean. The next day they would leave for Moscow.

"Hello?" came Angie's sleepy voice from the dorm bed.

"Hey! Angie, it's Annie!"

"Do you know what time it is?" Angie growled into the receiver.

"Here its 2:00," Annie said looking at her watch. "I don't know what time that makes it in New Orleans."

"Four in the morning."

"Good, I caught you before its too late. We leave for Hawaii tonight, then we'll head straight on to Moscow, followed by Hong Kong, then down to New Zealand and Australia."

"You could have e-mailed," Angie continued to complain.

"Stop being so grumpy," Annie said with irritation. "This may be the last time I can actually talk to you for six weeks."

"What? They don't have phones in Asia or Europe?"

"Okay, I give up! Yes, they have phones, but do you want to stop and ponder the time difference we'll have to deal with then?"

"I'm sorry, Annie. I am so tired I can hardly think straight. I took way too many hours trying to cram all this seminary in so I could rush off to a place where no one wants me to go."

"Did you get another door shut?" Annie asked cautiously.

"Try slammed," Angie moaned. "They pretty much said, in so many words, that I need to make some serious changes in my plans. I am not going to Padawin; they just can't see funding that at the moment when there are more dire needs elsewhere waiting for appointments."

"Oh, Angie, I'm so sorry. Don't give up, yet."

"Hello?" Angie said sarcastically. "Anybody listening out there?"

She tapped the phone several times in emphasis.

"If the board won't appoint me, I don't have a job!"

"Maybe there are other options," Annie suggested.

"Oh, let's see," Angie continued with the sarcasm, "I could just go on blind faith! Yes! I could go over there with no equipment, no medicine, and no facilities! There's a good idea!"

"Okay, okay. You're not up to a real talk right now; I shouldn't have wakened you."

"I'm sorry," she finally backed down. "I just feel so helpless. I know where I'm supposed to go, but the powers in charge don't agree. I'm trying to keep a stiff upper lip and all. It's hard."

"How are the guitar lessons going?"

"The one bright spot in my life at the moment," Angie said slightly more upbeat. "I'm actually doing really well. Eddie and I sang a duet in student chapel on Friday. We played our guitars and did a nice little version of *Blessed Assurance.* Everyone was impressed and said I should be on your first album."

"Hey, you're there. Unless, of course, you actually *are* in Padawin."

"We'll see. You gonna see Kelly McCall in Hawaii?" Angie asked.

Suddenly Annie's demeanor dropped to the basement. Kelly McCall? The idea had never even come to her mind. Would she actually have to see her while there? Was it possible that the biggest enemy she had ever known would overshadow her first trip to Paradise?

"Yuck," Annie spat out. "Why on earth would you think that?"

"Big talk show host over there," Angie reminded her. "And you and Stephen on this tour are big news. I'm guessing she'll be front and center when you get off the plane."

Annie's face contorted horribly. Her dream weekend had just become a nightmare. So much for Angie giving her an encouraging word.

ᘓ ᘐ

Back on the jet, Annie changed into her scrubs, although she thought seriously about burning them at the moment after Angie's unbearable suggestion. At this mid point in the tour, everyone was tired and pretty much burned out. A little vacation in Hawaii was the only reprieve before heading for the other side of the world where their hours would really be turned upside down.

Annie lay down in her bed and snuggled beneath her fleece blanket. Surely Stephen would not expect her to speak with, much less be interviewed by, Kelly McCall. No, he wouldn't do that to her. Nah. Not a chance. Uh-uh.

ᘓ ᘐ

Despite her foul mood when going to bed, Annie still actually managed to sleep through the flight and even the landing. She drug out of bed around 9:00 Pacific Time; she had no idea what time it was in Hawaii or even what time zone Hawaii was in, much less what Alabama time might be. It was still early here, however, as the sun was barely evident. Still, Annie was hungry and anxious for the glorious coffee she had finally been cleared to drink again. She swore she would never drink hot tea again at any time ever, even if she were dying of dehydration, strep throat, or any other dreadful disease!

"Mornin' Chef," she said drearily as she strode into the kitchen. "What can I scrounge up for breakfast?"

"Shoo are up too urly," he said clicking his tongue. "Annie could not sleep, I seepose?"

"Actually, I slept through the whole flight," she said groggily.

Chef Martel handed her a cup of coffee.

"Ah, this smells wonderful," she smiled as she closed her eyes and took in the aroma.

"Shoo are an addick," he said shaking his head.

"An *attic?*" she asked confused.

"An addick! An addick!" he told her again. "Shoo drink too mush of dis stuff, and it is no goot for shoo."

"An *addict?*"

"Yes! Yes!" he yelled at her. "That's what I say! Shoo are an addick!"

Annie stirred her coffee and then took a careful sip as it was piping hot. She sighed deeply and the chef shook his head in disdain.

Stephen entered, still sleepy himself.

"Good morning, everyone," he said with a very sluggish smile. "Coffee, please, Chef?"

Chef Martel turned around to pour Stephen a cup, all the while shaking his head in disdain. He nearly sloshed the coffee out as he put it in front of Stephen.

"Shoo are an addick too," he said forcefully.

"I'm an *attic?*" Stephen questioned him.

Annie began to laugh as Chef threw up his hands and began to blabber in whatever his native language was.

"What?" Stephen asked Annie.

"He thinks we're coffee 'addicts,' " Annie explained.

Stephen looked over to where Chef was working with flour and said loudly, "We are coffee addicts! And we're proud of it!"

"I woodn't poor that stuff in my automobile!" Chef insisted.

"I wouldn't either," Stephen laughed. "It would kill it!"

"Point made!" the chef exclaimed as he turned pompously and left for the back kitchen.

Annie and Stephen sat quietly as they finished their first cups. They yawned occasionally, but generally were still. Annie, however, was dying to ask a question, but she hated to start the day off with it.

"Will we see Kelly McCall?" she finally blurted out of nowhere.

"Fine, thank you," Stephen said with a start. "And how are you this morning?"

"We will, won't we?"

Stephen took another swallow and kept looking straight ahead as he answered, "High probability."

"Rats," she said under her breath. "Maybe I could get tonsillitis again."

"Don't even think about it," Stephen said sternly as he turned to her. "Look, you can't let Kelly McCall eat at you anymore. Whatever she might have been in your past, even your recent past, is no longer important. What you have done these past six weeks has dwarfed her in comparison."

"*That,* I don't really care about," Annie confessed. "It's the whole oozing and shmoozing that I have to put up with while around her. It makes me nauseous to even think about it."

"Then don't think about it," Stephen said with smile. "Stop borrowing trouble."

She leaned over and punched him hard in the arm.

"Ouch!" he yelled. "That hurt!"

"Then 'don't borrow trouble,' " she said emphatically as she stood up and left in a whirlwind.

Stephen rubbed his arm and stared at the door still swaying from her exit.

I've got to learn to keep my mouth shut when I haven't been asked.

Annie made a point to make sure she looked better than usual, yet still casual as though she had not *really* tried, before unloading the jet. When it was finally time to leave, everyone made their way to the door to prepare to unload. Stephen smiled at Annie when she appeared from her room carrying her overnight bag.

"What are you grinning about?" she asked him in a huff.

"Nothing, just happy," he said trying to suppress his smile.

"If you make one smart remark, I'll slug you again," she warned.

"I wouldn't dream of incurring your wrath."

He turned his face toward the front of the plane, attempting to hide his amusement at the whole situation. Annie had become a ragged jeans, sloppy sweatshirt, Marlins' hat and big, black glasses girl whenever she left the plane, yet today she was close to being decked out. Her jeans were not baggy, but sleek and tight, and her shirt was the silk button-down he remembered her wearing to the Italian restaurant in Florence. Her hair had obviously just been washed and blown dry because it was full, silky. and shiny. No hat and stylish, thin sunglasses with a light blue tint as opposed to the fat, dark ones topped off the outfit.

Annie slung her bag on her shoulder defiantly as if to dare Stephen to make a comment. He tried to ignore her, but the smell of her freshly washed hair was getting the best of him. He found himself slowly moving backward so he could get closer to the source. He tried to act nonchalant, but when he tripped over a small rug and fell backward toward her, she knew he was up to something. Everyone turned to see what the commotion was about.

"Chef must have spiked my coffee," he tried to joke.

"You okay, Stephen?" Dianne asked with concern.

"Fine," he said as he got up and brushed himself off. "I'm okay," he assured everyone.

One by one, they turned back toward the front and waited for the door to open. Annie just glared at him. She had a way of making him feel totally foolish at times; however, he had to confess that it was because he was usually being totally foolish over her.

"You want to tell me what you were doing?" she asked him privately from the side of her mouth.

He leaned in toward her and placed his mouth right next to her ear as he said, "I was trying to smell your hair."

She rolled her eyes and now found herself trying to suppress a smile.

"I don't care," he continued to speak into her ear, "why you washed your hair or even for whom you washed it. I am so captivated by it that I will take whatever I can get."

"If you don't move your mouth away from my ear, I'm going to hit you once more," she muttered again.

"Sorry," he said as he moved away. "It was heaven for a moment."

The door finally opened and the crew, band, and security prepared to leave down the portable stairs that had been driven up to the jet's opening. Slowly the families moved to the limos, and everyone else began to drive away, except for Stephen and Annie. When they finally appeared at the opening, the crowd began to yell. They both waved, and then Stephen motioned for Annie to go down first.

"Annie! Annie Wright!" yelled a Southern accent from somewhere close by. Annie looked up to scan the nearest members of the crowd.

"Annie! Over here!" came the voice from the right.

Annie looked to her right as she landed on the bottom step and spied Kelly McCall, beautifully blonde, perfect features, and impeccably tanned, waving ecstatically at her from behind the yellow police line. With Kelly was a cameraman recording the whole scene on tape.

"Annie! Come here!" Kelly yelled out again.

Annie halfway shook her head at the thought of Kelly actually being behind the tape and calling her to come over. She almost considered turning her head deliberately away and going straight for the limo, but her sense of ethics made her walk on over to Kelly. When she reached her, Kelly put out her arms and grabbed Annie in a tight hug.

"Oh, my gosh!" Kelly exclaimed. "Can you believe all this? These people have been chanting your name since the plane landed!"

"Really?" Annie asked in true amazement. "They haven't even heard me yet."

"I know! It doesn't matter," Kelly continued to yell over the crowd. "Can you believe that two girls from dinky Dockrey, Alabama, are standing here in Hawaii?"

"You actually admit you're from Dockrey?" Annie couldn't resist the mock. "I thought you were officially from Birmingham now."

Kelly laughed heartily as she took Annie's hand and leaned in to say, "I only say that to eat at my mother! If I said I was from Dockrey, the press would look up my family, and she would be sickeningly thrilled!"

Annie pulled back slightly to stare at her. Kelly did not want to please her mother in every thing she did? That was news.

"Look," Kelly continued to yell over the crowd, "we just wanted to film you coming in! We'll see you before the concert tonight! If you need anything, here are my numbers."

Kelly handed her a card with her work number in print, but her cell and home phone scribbled in personally.

"Thanks," Annie said, still trying to pull herself out of the stupor caused by Kelly McCall attempting to be cordial. "I'll put this by my phone in the hotel."

"Great!" Kelly said hugging her again. "I'll see you tonight! Can't wait to hear you again! If anyone ever deserved this, it's you! Bye now!"

Kelly waved and motioned for her cameraman to head through the crowd to somewhere else. Annie just stood totally bewildered. Was Kelly trying to play act here as though nothing had ever transpired between them? Annie was completely oblivious to the screaming crowd until Guy came up to her and took her arm. She looked at him and then nodded that she was ready to go. She waved to the crowd continuously as she walked toward the limo where Stephen was waiting.

"What was all that about?" Stephen asked her as the car began to drive away.

"I have no idea. She was actually being civil to me."

Stephen didn't say anymore. Here was a new mood he had never seen. Annie was taken back. He had to admire her for at least being gracious enough to respond to Kelly after all her family had done. In fact, it had been Kelly's name that was used to register the copyrights of Annie's music. Stephen wondered if he could have overlooked such a thing, and the more he thought on it, the more he doubted he could.

Later that evening, as the limo pulled up to the concert location, Stephen could not help but notice that Annie was antsy and nervous again. She had stayed to herself at the hotel all day and was not talking much in the limo.

"You look beautiful," he said sincerely.

"Thanks," she replied offering a small smile.

"Washed your hair again, didn't you?"

She nodded and explained, "I spent a lot of time out on the little porch watching the ocean. I was soaking with sweat by the time I went in."

"I didn't think women sweated; I thought they perspired."

"Depends," she sighed. "I was out and out sweating today."

The limo stopped and the pair prepared for their escort to the back door. Guy, Bull, and Jeff appeared at the car and made sure a clear path was available. As was usual, when things started moving, they happened fast. Bull opened the door and Guy was there to immediately help Annie from the car and push her toward the door. Although all she could hear was the screaming of the crowd, she knew both from instinct and habit that Stephen was right behind her. She waved cordially to both sides of the crowd and smiled sweetly as she got to the door. Once inside, she sighed deeply and removed her blue sunglasses. Standing right in front of her was Kelly McCall.

"Annie, hi!" she said as though she were an old friend. "Hello, Stephen. I'm Kelly McCall," she extended her hand. "I interviewed you once after the charity concert."

Stephen shook her hand and said he remembered her.

"I doubt that," Kelly laughed as she reached over to hug Annie. "But thank you anyway. Annie Wright! I still can't believe all this has happened so fast. If anybody in the world ever deserved this kind of break, it was you."

Stephen took great pleasure in watching Annie try to analyze the situation. He knew inside that she was seething with mistrust and bitterness, yet outside she had all appearances of being calm and in control. When Kelly linked her arm into Annie's as though they had been the best of buddies in year's past, he nearly laughed aloud at Annie's expression of total surprise.

"I'll show you to your room," Kelly told her as she moved her toward a hallway. She stopped abruptly and turned back to Stephen to ask, "You don't mind, do you, Stephen? I haven't seen Annie in years."

Stephen looked at Annie for an inkling of what he should do. Predictably, she merely rolled her eyes.

"That's fine," he smiled. "Just don't monopolize her. She's my lifeline on this tour."

Kelly smiled and waved as she turned back and continued heading Annie toward her dressing room.

"How on earth did you ever manage to do this?" Kelly asked her once inside the room.

Annie was still reeling from the companionship that Kelly was assuming had always been there. She was afraid to actually say anything, for fear of it being turned upside down on television, or even worse, being twisted for Vivian McCall.

"He was in Alex's wedding," Annie said simply, deciding to not reveal anything more than basic details. "We sang a duet."

"I know!" Kelly exclaimed with a laugh. "That killed my mother! She was depressed for weeks after she found out. So is that how he heard you sing, working on the duet?"

"Actually," Annie explained, still being very cautious in her answers, "he heard my piano playing in the Harold Long commercial."

"That guy is a nut," Kelly chuckled again. "I told Mother she should jump around like that in her commercials. She was highly offended."

Annie actually smiled because the thought of Vivian McCall acting like a fool on local television was a sight she would *love* to see.

"I haven't heard your commercial, though," Kelly continued. "Did you do something really fancy?"

"You'll hear it tonight before intermission," Annie told her as she went into a small, private room to change into her blue clothes. "It's a piano duel."

"Cool! He must have been really impressed! I've never heard anyone play like you. I can't wait for the concert. You should read all the reviews."

"Stephen actually told me not to," Annie said from behind the screen. "He says reviews are only one person's subjective opinion.

Sometimes they're great, sometimes they're horrible, but either way, it's only an opinion. He said to let the audiences be my judge."

"He's smart," Kelly admitted quickly. "You could knock yourself out trying to please everyone. However, I've read absolutely nothing negative about this tour. Even the cable news networks have talked about it. You're a star and you haven't even put out an album yet! So are you worn out from all the traveling?"

Kelly continued to talk as though they were simply catching up with each other. Annie finished dressing while Kelly went on and on, then exited her little room to add to her makeup.

"Ah! Annie!" Kelly said in delight as she came over to her. "You look absolutely beautiful!"

"Thank you, Kelly."

"But you always were. I bet you've broken your share of hearts over the years."

Annie was glad when Stephen knocked on her door. She welcomed him in.

"I guess you guys need a little quiet time before the show?" Kelly wondered.

Stephen nodded and said, "Helps us know where we're going."

"I understand," Kelly smiled as she went to the door. "I'll see you two after the show for a very brief, and I promise brief, interview. Take care!"

When she left, Annie breathed a huge sigh of relief.

"Well?" Stephen asked her.

"I have no idea," Annie said as she rolled her head back trying to relieve the tension.

"Here," Stephen said as he came up behind her and began to massage her neck.

"You're getting pretty good at this," Annie smiled as she continued to roll her neck.

He kept working his hands as he asked her, "Did things go okay in here? I wasn't sure if you needed rescuing or not."

Annie chuckled. "You can rescue me from anyone at anytime," she was beginning to relax. "I will confess to great relief when you knocked on the door."

"Were you getting grilled?"

"Not really," Annie said in confusion. "I don't know what I was getting. It was almost as if we had been great friends in the past, and she was just chatting away. It was weird."

He stopped rubbing her neck and turned her around to face him.

"Are you okay, though?" he asked. "Is this going to affect your performance tonight, get you off balance in any way?"

"Here I thought you were concerned about me," she said teasingly, "but all you care about is whether I make you look good tonight or not."

"Actually," he smiled, his blue eyes dancing as he took her hands, "I'm more concerned that you can still make me look *bad* during the piano duel."

Annie leaned in toward him and said, "I could do *that* with my eyes closed."

Stephen reached up and gently took a strand of her long hair and brought it up to his face. He breathed deeply and smiled with a deep sigh. Annie giggled and took her hair back.

After the concert, Kelly appeared backstage in a near frenzy, telling men where to set lights and the camera. When Annie and Stephen appeared, Kelly screamed.

"My, gosh!" she yelled as she ran up to Annie, hugging her once again. "You were absolutely awesome! I knew you were good, but that was an unbelievable performance."

"Thank you," Annie smiled tiredly. She was five hours behind Alabama time, three hours behind California time, and her body was feeling it desperately.

"Where do you need us?" Stephen asked as he took Annie's arm, knowing she was exhausted. He was too.

Kelly directed them to the area and began the interview. She kept it short as promised, for which Stephen and Annie were both thankful.

"Now," Kelly said privately to them after wrapping up the interview, "I know you plan to stay here through tomorrow before leaving for Asia. You are going to be pummeled by crowds at the hotel. Why don't you let me host a barbecue at my house all day tomorrow? I've got a pool that you can actually swim in—no photographers or fans around. I even have a beach. We've got some horses . . ."

"Any motorcycles or four-wheelers?" Stephen interrupted.

"No," Kelly said sternly. "I don't share the Wright family's obsession with off-road vehicles. However, we have a couple of jet skis. You guys are free to just relax out in the open."

Stephen looked to Annie for a hint. She looked so tired he knew he would get no answer tonight. Neither Stephen nor Annie had actually had any genuine relaxing time, away from crowds or photographers, since she had come to New York in early September. If she could survive Kelly McCall, this would probably be a great opportunity.

He leaned into her ear and gently whispered, "This would really be nice, Annie. You could actually sit back in a chair and lounge around, outside, with no one watching."

Annie, exhausted beyond caring, leaned her head on his shoulder and simply said. "Sure."

There was a lot of excitement among the crew and band as they loaded the limos to travel to Kelly's estate. Swimming and horseback riding had captured the imaginations of the children, and everyone was ready for a reprieve from the monotony of life on tour. However, now back to her senses after a night's rest, Annie wondered why she ever agreed to such a thing.

The estate was most definitely *stately.* The house had three stories, overlooked the ocean, and was covered in lush green lawns that stretched forever. It was truly beautiful. Annie wanted to feel a bit of contempt toward Kelly, but why?

She deserves to have a good life as much as anybody else. So what if she's hated me forever? Everybody should have the freedom of life, liberty, and the pursuit of happiness. And she's been wonderfully sweet and accommodating so far. If all she's trying to do right now is impress me and make me jealous, it will be worth it for a day away from the hectic life I've lived the past six weeks. I can swallow whatever Kelly dishes out today.

After the bitter cold of so much of the northern states, Annie enjoyed sitting out by the pool in a pair of white shorts and yellow tank top while watching children take turns on the four horses. The older kids rode some on their own, while the younger ones were walked with workers riding with them. Several of the crew members were enjoying the jet skis, while one man was actually surfing. The wives alternated between swimming in the pool and lounging on the deck with Annie.

Kelly appeared with her identical twin daughters, two-year-olds who were anxious to get into the pool. They were copies of Kelly herself with bright blonde hair, blue eyes, and perfect little smiles. After putting on their swimmies and a bit of sunscreen, Kelly let them attack the pool. They had no fear whatsoever. Kelly motioned for one of her staff to keep an eye on them while she visited with the guests.

"Your girls are beautiful," Annie said sincerely as Kelly pulled up a lounge chair.

"Thank you," Kelly said proudly. "They are one of the biggest joys in my life."

"Is your husband here?"

"I wish," Kelly replied with a longing smile. "That's the biggest thing right now with what we do. He's playing in Jacksonville today. I'm here with my job *and* the girls. Being separated can be really tough."

Annie nodded. She could imagine.

"So what about you?" Kelly asked her. "Any marriage plans in your future?"

"Oh, wow, not at the moment. I have to find a man first," she laughed.

"Really?" Kelly said in surprise. "What about Stephen? Is there not a little *chemistry* there between the two of you?"

Maybe this was what the whole nice *thing* was about. Kelly was going to drill Annie about she and Stephen for information, then spill it out to the world; she would be the breaking reporter.

"No, there's nothing there," Annie said flatly.

"Well, he's missing it, then," Kelly shifted in her seat to look at Annie. "Maybe he really is gay."

"He's *not* gay."

"I never thought he was either," Kelly grinned. "At least I hoped. He has a thing going with Carrie McCarthy, doesn't he?"

"You'll have to ask him about that," Annie said hoping to divert the questioning. "How do you like Hawaii?"

"Honestly, it has its ups and downs," Kelly admitted. "I love the tropical weather, just not year round. The native people are wonderfully sweet. It's a nice place, but I miss home a lot."

"I can understand."

"I'd like to get back to the mainland one day. I really hate doing what I do right now with my girls growing up. I want to be with them, but it is such a crucial time in my career. It's almost like I have to choose between my family and fame. I really hate that."

"Andie felt that way too," Annie told her. "She's due with her fourth child in January. She stopped teaching this year to stay at home."

"Really?" Kelly smiled. "How wonderful. I'm so torn. My job is something that I have worked to attain my entire life, but suddenly the girls and Johnny have taken my focus elsewhere. You should have seen my mother when I tried to explain that to her. She nearly exploded!"

"I bet," Annie said imagining Kelly telling Vivian she just wanted to be a wife and mom.

"Oh, you have no idea," Kelly sighed. "My mother has always projected her ideals of what I should be. Frankly, it has always been a huge struggle. And now, it's almost impossible. It's like she still wants to control my life after all these years."

"What do you mean?" Annie asked, suddenly interested in the possibility that all was not well between Vivian and Kelly.

"All my life she has demanded that I *do this* or *do that,*" Kelly said as she leaned back in the lounge. "I was always pushed to be better and step higher. I could never just relax and enjoy life. In high school, *you* were the biggest obstacle in my life where she was concerned. If I made a 98, you made a 100. Not good enough! It went on and on."

"I studied a lot," Annie said halfway in defense.

"No, you were just smart," Kelly said with a chuckle. "I killed myself trying to make straight A's. In our junior year chemistry class, I finally gave up! I couldn't get an *A* in that class if my life depended on it!"

"That was hard," Annie admitted.

"You aced it!"

"I studied hard," Annie admitted.

"I did too, but I just couldn't get it."

"You should have called me," Annie smiled. "We could have studied together."

"My mother would have shot me," Kelly laughed. "You would not believe how it galls her that you are on tour with Stephen Williams right now. She made some comment last time she called about how you even pick the better men to be seen with."

"What?"

"Oh yeah," Kelly went on. "My marriage to Johnny is like the biggest joke to her. Why on earth would I marry a nobody when I had all these famous, successful men to choose from?"

"He's a football player!"

"Second string," Kelly reminded her. "The chances of his ever playing real football are minimal, but that's not why I married him. I love him, Annie, with all my heart. I sang the national anthem at a game he was playing at in Seattle once. He arranged a meeting. He was so wonderful. I can't tell you what it was like to meet someone who really liked me for who I was. He changed my life! After a year of on and off meetings, he just proposed and said we needed to spend our lives together. When I'm with him, life is good."

"And what about when you're not with him?" Annie wondered.

"It's like this," she motioned around her. "I have the girls, I have our home, and I have my job. I kind of exist. Then mother will call every week or two and tell me to leave him and get on with my life."

"You're kidding? Why?"

"He's holding me back, Annie," she said in mock disdain. "I was *Miss America!* I am way above all of *this!*"

"All of what?" Annie asked her. "To me it looks like you've got it made. A great husband, incredible home, two healthy, beautiful daughters, a fun job, I assume. What more does she think you need?"

Kelly shook her head and shrugged her shoulders.

"Who knows?" Kelly admitted.

They sat quietly as they watched the children ride the horses. Annie wondered if Kelly had any idea about the music fraud her mother and brother had pulled the past year. *This* Kelly was not the Kelly McCall she remembered from years past. Perhaps it really was Vivian's insane controlling that had driven the wedge from the beginning. Was it possible that Kelly was actually a normal, healthy, happy person doing her best to live with an insanely jealous mother?

"I need to ask you something," Annie finally got the courage to say.

"Sure," Kelly smiled as she turned back to look at her.

"Are you familiar with the little scam your mom and brother pulled on me this past year?"

Kelly had a confused look, and then cautiously said, "What are you talking about?"

Annie explained the story from the beginning. When she got to the part about Kelly's name being on the music that was stolen, Kelly became furious.

"I can't believe it!" she yelled in anger. "I *cannot* believe it!"

"You didn't know?" Annie realized.

"Are you kidding? I am humiliated! You must have hated me when you saw me at the airport yesterday, and last night," she closed her eyes in complete embarrassment, "and today."

"I just assumed, Kelly . . ."

"Unbelievable," Kelly mourned as she dropped her head. "Do you know why I took this job in Hawaii?"

Annie shook her head.

"To be as far away from Vivian McCall as I can. She is more like a cancer in my life than a mother. I feel like such a fool! Here I thought that for once in my life I could be with someone from my past and not have her hateful shadow hanging over me, but its looming there larger than ever."

Kelly stood up to leave, but Annie jumped up quickly.

"Kelly, don't," Annie assured her as she took her arm. "I never knew any of this. I assume that everyone's life is like my life. My mother is wonderful. I can't imagine how you have lived with this all these years."

"I never wanted to be your enemy," Kelly confessed, "but I had no choice. My mother daily painted you to be my biggest obstacle to everything she wanted me to be. I used to admire you from afar. You were so funny, and you and your sister Angie together used to crack me up. I was so jealous of how wonderful life was for you two. When Dad left us, I was only 11. Mother wouldn't allow us to have any relationship with him whatsoever. She would cry and go into hysterics if we ever went to visit him. She said we were choosing him over her, and we were all she had. Yet every week I would see you and your father laughing or talking, and I envied that relationship."

Annie sighed as she felt the remorse of years lost. "Imagine how much different our lives might have been had we been able to rise above all of that," Annie said.

"I swore I would never manipulate my children like my mother did," Kelly said firmly. "I want them to be free to be whatever they want to be."

They walked out toward the stables and talked a while longer. This time Annie let down her defenses and talked to Kelly as though she genuinely were an old friend. She told Kelly about her family, her struggles with Alex, and even her unsure feelings about Stephen. She asked some advice about her future in show business and promised Kelly she would come back and do an entire hour on her talk show.

By the time the day was over and all began to load up in the limos, Annie believed she had found a great friend. They hugged with tears as they said goodbye, and Kelly, with her two little girls by her side, waved long after the limo left.

"I take it you had a good re-acquaintance," Stephen asked with his sunburned nose shining.

Annie nodded, still stifling some of the tears.

"Very good," she told him. "It was very enlightening."

"Are you still sore at me for telling you how *charming* she was?"

Annie laughed. She remembered when he had said that during his week in Alabama. She had seethed at the thought.

"You're a good person, Annie," he said. "It's so hard in this business to learn to trust people. When you do find someone you really believe you can trust, you pull him or her on your team by hiring them to do something for you, anything. I hope you never lose the ability to give people a second chance when you've done this as long as I have."

"Sometimes that scares me," she confessed. "It's almost like you have no one, Stephen. I . . . I don't know if I could live that way."

"I started out with no one, Annie. Big difference. I had to pretty much claw my way through this whole process on my own. You've got a lot of people behind you already. And when things get tough, or even unbearable, you've got a family to turn to. You'll be fine."

His words were not all that consoling to her because his sadness seemed to prevail the comfort. She thought of his father and all the deceit that had gone into Stephen's life, and still he did not know. Should she tell him? Would it be positive knowledge or would it destroy him even more? Was 32 too old to start over with such information? She studied his face as he stared out the window. He was so handsome, and he had treated her so kindly on this trip. How could she ever repay him for all he had done? Maybe this secret could somehow figure in to that.

"Hey," she said as she reached over and took his hand, "you're a pretty good guy yourself."

"Tell me that after the time changes on the other side of the world," he smiled at her.

"If I can handle your jet, I can handle the time change."

"Don't be so sure. Jet lag can be a real misery, especially when you are trying to appear fresh and excited every night."

"Oh, don't be such a doomsday prophet," she said with a slight punch to his arm. "It's going to be fun."

"And I'm going to hold you to that," he said with a little doubt sounding through his voice.

"You make me sound like a moody old bat!"

"You are," he said with raised eyebrows, "but I like your moods. I'm going to miss them horribly when this is over."

"Look!" Annie exclaimed breathlessly as they turned the corner. "Look at the sunset over the ocean. Stephen, is that not beautiful?"

He peered out the window and nodded.

"You know what that's called?" he asked her.

"What?"

"It's an *autumn sunset.*"

He looked back at her and saw the orange glow in her eyes. She was smiling in acknowledgement. He reached up and moved a strand of hair from her face.

"And it's the most beautiful sunset I've ever seen," he said softly.

"You're not looking at the sunset," she said with a warm smile growing.

"Yes, I am," he whispered as he continued to stare into her eyes, "and it's never been more beautiful."

Annie leaned toward him, still smiling, and she gently ran her hand down his face. She was ready to break the rules she had set before the tour ever began.

"I think we're crossing your lines," he could barely say as her hand sent shivers through his body.

"I think we are too," she agreed. "Should we stop?"

He closed his eyes and tried to think clearly. She had set the limits; she was free to break them, but he could not. He could not take advantage of her at any time. He reached up and took her hand and placed it on his heart.

"Do you feel that?" he asked her.

She nodded as she felt his heart pulse against the back of her hand.

"That's what you do to me," he said gently. "Any time you are certain about what you want, my heart will still be right here. I'll be ready at a moment's notice to take the next step."

She smiled and nodded as she leaned back and regained her

composure. She was so thankful that he was a man of honor, at least where she was concerned. He continued to hold her hand on the ride back, gently stroking it with his thumb.

When they arrived at the hotel, security moved them through the crowds, but Stephen still held her hand. Up the elevator, down the hallway, all the way to her door he stayed with her. When they stopped for her to go inside, they just gazed at each other. Neither knew what to say or what to do next.

"I should go . . . now," he told her.

"I know."

"Tomorrow will be a long flight."

"I know."

"Are you dreading it?" he asked her.

"Not with you there," she admitted.

"You're killing me, Annie Wright. You know that, don't you?" he whispered as he leaned in to breathe the scent of her hair one more time.

"The feeling is mutual," she told him as she put her arms around his waist and pulled him closer to her. "I don't know what to do, Stephen."

He wrapped his arms around her and rocked her slightly back and forth.

"We'll know in time," he promised her. "Until then, however," he pulled back and looked down into her eyes, "we'll just be happy to be together."

"Very happy," she smiled at him.

"Good night."

"You too."

He left her door and went down the hallway to his own room. Neither of them saw the look of disgust on Alex's face when he rounded the corner with the ice bucket.

Chapter Twenty-Three

Annie found the schedule on the other side of the world to rate from grueling to nearly unbearable. The U.S. tour had been slightly difficult, but after a couple of weeks, she was able to adjust to the schedule. From Moscow on, however, there was never a real time to catch up. Although the concert time was less, not doing five to six shows a week, but more like three or four, the hours were impossible to negotiate. Annie seldom knew if she was coming or going whenever she entered a limo, and she found she could sleep absolutely anytime she closed her eyes, bed or no bed.

She loved the different cultures and the different foods. She loved meeting the diverse people from so many backgrounds and races. Stephen quickly met her request for a personal interpreter at each location to help her communicate personally with the fans. Her only struggle was having to say goodbye to the translators after a couple of days of intense togetherness. She would grieve over leaving them, and then move on to meet someone new, only to have to go through another separation again.

Even though a lot of time was spent on the jet, Stephen and Annie managed to keep their distance for the most part. When they were together, it was usually spent honing down *Winter Passion* to perfection. They were not ready to present it in a performance until Greece, and even then, they only used their keyboards, with Alex on bass and Chip on saxophone.

Annie had always been fascinated by Greek culture and architecture, so Stephen hired a limo to drive them around for a day. She did manage a stroll at the Parthenon, but that was it. Everything else had to be seen from the inside of the car. The limo had a sunroof, so Annie was able to stand through the top on several occasions to get a clearer view of the sight as well as a photograph. Whenever her head would pop up, fans would scream and begin to snap pictures from all over. As usual, she would wave graciously and smile to all. Stephen was proud of how she handled herself with the crowds.

The premier of *Winter Passion* sent the audience into a four-minute cheer. Stephen's usual quieting techniques did not faze them. He finally set down his mic and waited for the cheering to stop, which actually sent the crowd to a louder level. By the time they reached Rome, thanks to the Internet, people had posters that read *Winter Passion Tour* splattered all throughout the seating. The habit became that as soon as *Autumn Sunset* was finished, people began to scream for *Winter Passion.* Stephen finally cut *I Knew It Was Love* permanently from the lineup, much to Annie's chagrin. The segueing from *Autumn Sunset* into *Winter Passion* actually sent crowds to a new intensity not found on the tour before.

As the week before Thanksgiving approached, bringing the final three concerts of the entire tour, Annie's homesickness took on a whole new height. They still had to play Paris, Berlin, and London, three places she was looking forward to seeing, but the thoughts of being with her family once again overwhelmed her at times. She knew the fireplace would be blazing, the electric blankets would be welcoming, and the conversation and laughter would be warm and familiar. She felt her heart would literally melt if she didn't change her thinking immediately. Sometimes she could; other times she just cried. She had thoroughly enjoyed this tour, but she was so ready to go home.

The flight into Paris took place at night. Therefore, as the jet approached it's landing, the landmarks of Paris were breathtakingly visible. To actually see the Eiffel Tower from the air would be counted as one of Annie's most incredible moments in life. Even though it was late at night, a huge crowd awaited them to leave the jet for the convoy to the hotel. Annie was tired, but she waved and smiled to everyone as they shouted their admiration even though they had never heard her sing.

Once in her room, she opened the blinds covering the French doors to the balcony and just stared in awe at her perfect view of the tower. It was hard to imagine that she was here. It was hard to believe that she would sing here tomorrow night. It was even hard to comprehend all that had happened to her these past three months. Yet the more opportunities were offered to her, the less she knew what to do. She definitely wanted to do something, but to narrow it down to something specific seemed impossible. She breathed small prayers of wisdom, but found herself too tired to do much of anything else.

"Hello?" Annie answered her phone the following morning.

"Hello, Annie-girl," came Stephen's cheery voice. "Sleep well?"

"Yep."

"Wanna see Paris?" he asked her.

"Are you kidding? I'd love to! I've been staring out the balcony doors all morning pinching myself because I am actually viewing the Eiffel Tower. I can't go out, though. I was hoping to have coffee and a croissant out there."

"The crowd?" he figured.

"Yes," she sighed. "It was a little disappointing. I hope that someday I can come back to some of these places incognito."

"You can," he assured her. "When no one knows you're coming, you'd be surprised at what you can get away with."

"When do we leave?" she asked excitedly.

"Fifteen minutes?"

"I'll be waiting."

ಐ ಣ

The tour of the city was wonderful! They could be snuck inside a couple of the halls, but most of the monuments and landmarks had to be viewed from the limo. At lunchtime, however, Stephen had prepared a wonderful surprise. He prearranged a special table in an exclusive corner of one of the ever-famous sidewalk cafes'. It wasn't on the sidewalk, but up on a balcony where strict restrictions and security were in tact. Stephen ordered for her, anxious for her to try some genuine French cuisine, and they enjoyed a semblance of freedom and privacy for the hour they were there. The crowd was down on the street, but they could not see Stephen and Annie.

"You should be rewarded for this," Annie told him as she sipped the most wonderful coffee she had ever tasted.

"That could be arranged," he said with a grin.

"Oh yeah? What do you have in mind?"

"We'll talk about it tonight," he said mysteriously.

"Okay," she said not prying any deeper. He obviously had something planned. "I still can't believe I'm here. I feel like I'm living some surreal existence right now."

"All in all, how would you rate your tour experience?" he asked as he leaned back in his chair and crossed his arms.

"All in all? I'd begin by saying that it's most wonderfully unforgettable, but at the same time it has been demanding and hard. In some ways it has been the quickest three months of my life, then on the other, the longest."

Stephen threw his head back and laughed heartily.

"What?" she asked, surprised at his response.

"You!" he exclaimed still laughing. "Everything about you is a paradox! You are full of extremes with no room for mediocrity. How did I ever live without you?"

"I think you did all right for yourself," she teased him, smiling at her apparent contradictions of description. "Isn't Paris supposed to be the city of romance?"

"I believe so. Why? You looking for some French man to fill the bill?"

"Hardly," she said after another sip. "The communication barrier would be too difficult to break."

"Ah, but isn't love the universal language?"

"No, I think that would be music."

"What about music of love?"

She thought for a moment and nodded in agreement.

After finishing the afternoon tour of Paris, they went back to the hotel. Because there was plenty of time before dinner and getting ready for the concert, Annie suggested they sign a few autographs and talk with the crowd a little before going back to their rooms. Stephen spent most of that time watching Annie work through the people. She tried hard to understand their broken English and gracefully smiled for photographs while accepting gifts of flowers and candy.

He walked her back to her room and tried to find the courage to ask her for dinner. He did not want to push her for anything, but he had plans for the evening that included her, and he wanted to somehow move in that direction without overstepping her boundaries.

"Uh, before you go in," he began, "I was wondering if we might have dinner together before leaving for the concert?"

"Where?" she asked as she slid the card through the ID slot.

"In my room or yours, whichever you prefer."

She turned back to look at him and replied, "Yours, I guess. I don't usually care for anything heavy before a concert. You sound like you're talking about a *real* dinner here."

"Nothing heavy," he assured her. "Just good food and pleasant conversation."

"Sure," she agreed. "When?"

"Is 5:30 okay?"

Annie chuckled as she nodded and said, "Why not? My schedule is so confused right now that I am just running on automatic. 5:30, 10:30, whatever."

"Great," he smiled nervously. "See you then."

As 5:30 rolled around, Annie dressed casually and left for Stephen's suite. She knocked on his door and heard him yell, "Just a minute." One of the crewmembers passed her on his way back to his room, and she politely acknowledged him. When the door finally opened, she walked in unsuspectingly.

"Good heavens," she exclaimed breathlessly. The room was lit entirely by candles and was filled with dozens of red and white roses.

"What is this?" she asked turning to him. He looked wonderful. His hair was perfect, and he was wearing pressed jeans and a sweater to match his eyes. His smile, however, was beaming.

"How could I resist having a romantic dinner with you in Paris? I couldn't help it," he confessed as he held his arms out in vulnerability. "I've kept my end of the bargain on this tour as much as possible, but I hoped you could give me this one moment of weakness."

He took her hand and led her next to the opened balcony doors where the tower was in clear view and a table sat just inside, out of view from the crowd. He held out her chair and allowed her to sit, and then he went to the other side of the small glass table and took his seat. A tray with silver covers and a bottle in an ice bucket were on a cart next to the tables. He took the bottle and began to open it.

"That's not champagne, is it?" she asked nervously.

He smiled at her and said, "No. Sparkling white grape juice. It's actually delicious."

"Oh," she said slightly embarrassed.

He poured her a glass, and then followed by filling his own. He lifted his glass and motioned for her to do the same.

"To a great night," he smiled again.

They clinked their glasses together and took a drink.

"Mmmm," she said surprised. "This *is* good."

"Let's pray," he suggested as he reached over and took her hand.

The meal was wonderful, and yes, romantic. French music played from the stereo, and Annie was coming to the conclusion that she loved French food. The conversation was easy and relaxed. Being with Stephen had become comfortable and warm for her, almost familiar and natural. They didn't discuss the tour, just dreams and hopes for the future. Stephen asked most of the questions, and Annie answered them all eagerly. She managed to throw in a few questions now and then, but Stephen wanted to give her an opportunity to talk about what she wanted as a result of all that had transpired.

"Now, before you go," he said as he got up and took her hand, "we must share one dance on the balcony."

She took his hand and stood, but protested, "People will be watching."

"I know," he confessed as he reached over and turned up the music, "but this is Paris. We deserve a dance on the balcony as the sun sets behind the Eiffel Tower. Don't you agree?"

She simply smiled and walked with him to the balcony. He put one arm around her waist and pulled her close. She wrapped her free arm over his shoulder and began to sway with the music. They crowd in the street shouted, but the music was loud enough for them to ignore most of the noise. Stephen led her back and forth, around and around. He even dipped her once at which she laughed and insisted she would probably fall from the balcony if he tried that again.

"Just creating a memory," he smiled as he pulled her back to him.

"This is wonderful," she admitted, "but I've never really cared for dancing, you know?"

"Are you caring for it now?" he asked as the evening began to grow dark.

"I'm beginning to think that doing just about anything with you is wonderful."

He pulled back and looked down at her.

"Truthfully?" he asked.

"Scout's honor," she smiled as she held up three fingers.

"But you're not a scout," he said with a raised eyebrow.

"I know," she grinned mischievously.

He twirled her a few more times causing the crowd to squeal down below. She found herself laughing in pure delight at the whole scene. She was dancing with Stephen Williams on a balcony in Paris with the sun dipping now completely down behind the Eiffel Tower. As he pulled her close, she closed her eyes to let all her senses remember this moment. She knew the sights, but she wanted to remember the sounds, the smells, and the feel of his soft sweater against her arm. She laid her cheek against his chest and gently rubbed her face across the material.

"You're beautiful, Annie Wright," he whispered in her ear as he bent down to breathe in the scent of her hair again.

She turned her head to look up at him and said, "So are you, Mr. Williams. Inside and out."

"Are we back to formalities again?" he asked her. "Mr. Williams?"

"I am simply showing you honor for all you have done for me," she confessed. "You have been wonderful. I don't know what I ever did to deserve all of this or to deserve—well, you."

"Annie," he said as he took her hands and led her back into his room, "tonight, after the concert, I want us to meet and talk about things. Okay?"

"What things?" she wondered.

"Not now," he said slightly frustrated. "We have a concert hanging over us. But tonight, when the concert's over, I have a small interview about a charity thing I'm doing here in February. Come on back to the hotel and relax a bit, and then I'll be at your room as soon as I get back. Okay?"

"Sure," she said wondering what that talk would concern.

In her dressing room after intermission, Annie quickly changed into the orange outfit, breathing a sigh of relief that she only had to wear this color two more times after tonight. She had never asked Stephen about who chose this bizarre orange, or why, but she would bring that up to him tonight during their "talk." She left her room and went to the wings where everyone was gathering.

"You forgot to take your hair down," Stephen reminded her as she approached him.

"Oh yeah," she remembered as she reached back to unpin it. She shook it loose. "Should I go back and brush it out?"

"No," he said softly as he reached up to smooth it out. "You look beautiful. Do you know how hard it is for me to concentrate when you start singing out there? You totally mesmerize me."

"Good," she said as she placed the clip from her hair on a table. "I like that sense of control," she teased him.

"You are most certainly in control," he assured her. "Ready?"

"Ready!"

They found their places on the stage and waited for the "all clear" in their earpieces. As Annie began to play *Autumn Sunset,* the crowd quieted. Most knew that this was now her solo, and they eagerly anticipated the voice that was now the focus of the tour.

When Annie came from behind the piano to sing to the audience on the second verse, Bull and Guy had to remove several from the stage immediately. She continued singing, and then Stephen joined her for the chorus. She looked at him and saw total admiration in his expression. Her heart stopped and her stomach swirled again. It was dreamlike to be on stage with him singing this song and singing it face-to-face.

ꕤ

They moved to their perspective sides as they sang the bridge:

Nobody told me, nobody said
There's more to living than just success.
Nobody moved me, nobody dared.
Nobody told me, nobody shared.

They then came together, back to back, and finished the bridge.

Nobody told me about the sunrise.
Nobody told me, nobody tried.

When they turned face to face and took hands, the crowd screamed, but Annie saw complete adoration in Stephen's eyes. As they sang with all their might, belting out the last chorus, Annie felt Stephen's hand tighten around hers. He pulled her closer, but as she sang to him this night, all that had transpired between them came flooding through her mind. There was the balcony at home, Cry Baby Bridge, the deck behind the church, the moments at his apartment, his caring for her during her miserable illness, the writing of *Winter Passion,* and the evening dancing on his balcony to French music in front of the Eiffel Tower.

So while I'm waiting for someone to love me
Someone who knows me through and through
I'll watch the Autumn Sunset from my single room apartment

And hope and pray that dreams can still come true

As the song began to fade, Annie found herself drawing closer to Stephen than usual. She stood face to face with him, one hand cradling the mic, the other holding tightly to his hand.

And long to hear the words, "I love you."

I long to hear the words, "I love you."

When the last note cut off, she was barely and inch from him. For the first time in her life, she was glad to be 5'10', short enough to look *up* at him, but tall enough to see directly into his eyes. Despite the frenzy of the crowd, in her mind she was alone with him. She suddenly leaned up into him and kissed him. The crowd went fanatical. Annie didn't care. This was not about them. She realized that she had indeed fallen in love with him, and she was ready to let him know.

Stephen pulled back and stared at her in amazement. She simply smiled and mouthed the words "I love you" to him. He pulled her back to him in an embrace. The crowd cheered again. They thought this was just a part of the show, but the rest of the band and the crew knew it was not. Suddenly, the band themselves began to applaud with the audience, everyone but Alex.

As soon as the concert was over and the bowing at the front of the stage had ended, Stephen took Annie's hand and rushed her to his dressing room. He closed the door quickly behind them and stared at her in unbelief.

"Annie," he asked desperately, "did I cross a line again?"

"No," she said emphatically as she stepped up to him.

"I didn't mean to kiss you on stage," he said as he began to pace. "I don't know what happened! We were just there, and suddenly, the next thing I know, I'm kissing you, in front of everybody!"

"You didn't kiss me!"

"Hello!" he yelled. "I did too! Just upped and did it before I knew what was happening!"

"Stephen," Annie said calmly as she took his hand, "I kissed you."

"What?"

"*I* kissed you out there," she explained. "I realized during that song that—that I really care about you—that I, well, didn't you see what

I said?"

"Yeah," he said bewildered. "I thought you were just . . . I don't know, maybe trying to get me through that awkward moment," he paused. "I didn't kiss you first?"

"Not tonight," she smiled.

Stephen sat back on a table and ran his fingers through his hair. He then looked at Annie, still slightly confused.

"You kissed me?" he asked her again.

"Finally," she said with a sigh.

"Wow," he said as he took both of her hands and pulled her closer to him. "I don't know what to say, Annie. I have dreamed of this from the moment I first saw you."

"And I've dreamed of it for eleven years," she said as she leaned in and kissed him again.

"Do you trust me?" he asked her as he gently pulled her face back so that he could look into her eyes.

"With all my heart."

"Do you love me?"

She smiled and rolled her eyes as she said, "With all my heart there too."

He pulled her close and embraced her again. She could feel his body begin to shake. She leaned back and saw that tears were streaming down his face.

"Stephen?" she asked with concern.

"I was so afraid to dream this could ever happen," he confessed. "When did you know?"

She shrugged and tried to explain, "I'm not sure. I just knew that tonight, when we were singing, that I truly loved you. I don't want to ever be apart from you, Stephen. I'd give up all of what's happened to me just to be with you."

"Annie, you don't have to give up anything to be with me," he said gently as he kissed her again and again.

A knock sounded on the door.

"Mr. Williams!" came a yell. "They're ready for your interview!"

"Be right there!" he called back. He turned to Annie and instructed, "Go back to the hotel. As soon as I'm finished, I'll be there, and we can talk about all of this. I want to make some plans for us, immediately. Okay?"

"Okay," she whispered as she kissed him yet again. She could hardly pull herself away, but the second loud knock brought them back to reality.

When Annie returned to the hotel, she practically danced to her room. Her light mood was immediately spoiled by the brooding looks both Alex and Megan were wearing as they waited by her door.

"What are ya'll doing here?" she asked them puzzled.

"We need to talk," Alex said soberly.

"I've got plans," Annie told him, not wanting anything to interfere with her talk with Stephen when he returned.

"That's what I'm afraid of," he said, still austere.

"Look, whatever it is that you have decided to *actually* talk to me about, it can wait for some other moment. Your timing is lousy," she told him as she slid her card in.

"Annie, you really need to hear him out," Megan interrupted. "This is about Stephen."

"What about him?" Annie asked as she opened the door.

"May we come in?" Alex asked.

Annie rolled her eyes and sighed, "Sure. Why not?"

They followed her in and waited for her full attention.

"Okay, what's going on?" Annie asked feeling completely annoyed with them.

"You're not the first girl that Stephen's done this to on a tour," Alex nearly blurted out.

"What? What are you talking about?" Annie asked him.

"The band members had warned Alex that this might happen," Megan said.

"Megan," Alex said sternly, "let me tell this. She's my sister."

"What is going on?" Annie demanded to know.

"The band said that every tour Stephen picks some naïve, young girl to go with him. She always serves some unimportant purpose . . ."

" . . . like a photographer or a journalist or something," Megan interrupted again.

"They didn't think it was like that with you because you were actually part of the band and the act," Alex went on. "But these past couple of weeks, they've expressed concern about Stephen's actions toward you."

"You are way out of line with this," Annie said trying to control her temper. "It is not like that with me and Stephen. You don't know what's going on."

"Actually, everyone seems to know what's going on except you," Alex told her. "The guys said that normally by this time on the tour, the girl has already moved in with him, but you were obviously a harder challenge."

"You are lying," Annie said forcefully. "I am telling you it is *not* like that with us."

"And I am telling you that you have been used and been made a huge fool of because of all of this!" Alex began to shout. "Look! At first, I was like . . . whatever! She deserves whatever she gets! But the longer I watched it happen, regardless of what I may feel toward you, I couldn't just sit by and watch you be totally degraded like this!"

"This isn't true," Annie tried to explain to him.

"Then you're a bigger fool than I thought," he spat out. "Everyone's guess is that tonight he makes his big move. He comes waltzing in here, as though you're the first real love in his life, and he has you hooked for the next few weeks. That's his way. You'll stay with him just long enough for him to be satisfied, usually about three or four weeks, and then its over. He starts planning for the tour and looking for the next conquest."

Annie could feel herself begin to shake inside. This could not be true.

"Stephen hasn't been with anyone in five years!" she yelled. "You're either making this all up, or somebody's lying to you!"

"All right! Everybody's lying to me then!" he yelled back. "I guess I was a total idiot to actually try and protect you! Knock yourself out, Annie!"

He turned to go.

"Alex!" Megan called to him. "Annie! You've got to believe him!"

"This is not true!" Annie yelled out. "Alex, what makes you think that all this is on the up and up?"

"Because the guys in the band are good, decent guys," he said gently, the first time he had spoken to Annie with concern in years. "They like you and they admire you. They are literally sick over the fact that *you* were the one this year. They didn't realize it until it was too late. One of them even mentioned to him to please back off of you, and

Stephen said he would fire him if he said another word."

Annie fell down on the couch in total mortification. Could this possibly be true? Stephen had been wonderful to her. He had treated with respect and honor. Had he done all of this just to woo her into some kind of tawdry affair, only to dump her off when it was all over? He wasn't like that. She could not imagine him doing that with anyone, but especially not her.

"So, what do I do?" she mainly asked herself.

"Leave," Alex told her.

"Are you kidding?" she said incredulously. "There's only two nights left of the tour!"

"Then don't leave," he said bitingly. "Give him another week to try and seduce you even more. Maybe you can make the whole stage even hotter than it was tonight."

Nobody moved, nobody talked. Annie tried to weigh the evidence, but all she could see was the fact that Alex had reached out to her for the first time in many years because even *he* could not stand to see her used like this. Yet this was not like Stephen. However, if this had been his plan all along, from the balcony at her home to the balcony in Paris, he had played his cards well. He had told her earlier she could repay him tonight. Even before the kiss at the concert, he had intended to meet with her and *talk* about something. Had this been his plan?

"I'm sorry, Annie," Megan said with burning tears. "I really thought he loved you. I was so shocked."

Annie walked over to the desk and pulled out a phone book.

"What are you doing?" Alex asked.

"Making reservations for a flight home," she said wearily and defeated. Then she looked up at both of them and said, "I guess I was a complete fool to think that he could really love someone like me, some nobody from nowhere."

"Annie," Megan started, but Annie cut her off immediately.

"I don't want to hear any more," she said curtly.

"I'll make the reservation," Alex offered. "You just pack and get out of here as soon as you can. You don't need to be here to listen to his excuses when he returns."

Annie sat on the plane in the first class section and prepared for a long, miserable flight to New York. Her body and mind were totally numb. She had sobbed in the limo all the way to the airport, but now she just could not feel anything. She had gone from the highest height possible, declaring her love for Stephen, to the lowest low imaginable, realizing he had been seducing her for six months. How sick he must be to go to such lengths just to mar an innocent girl, and she fell for it completely. She tried to take comfort in the fact that Alex genuinely did care for her enough to stop the whole thing. She knew he probably had to battle with facing her after all these years of enmity. She admired him for his fortitude. Perhaps, after all this was over, they could begin to repair the things that had torn them apart for so long.

Stephen knocked on Annie's door for five minutes, but there had been no answer. He went back to his room and tried calling. No answer again. He called the front desk to make sure she had arrived. Perhaps there had been some problem with the car, or maybe she stayed to sign more autographs.

"She checked out," the desk clerk told him.

"What do you mean 'checked out'?" he asked in unbelief.

"She checked out over 30 minutes ago."

"To do what?" he said, still confused.

"I'm not sure, sir. She had her bag with her."

Stephen hung up the phone and tried to imagine what was going on. When he had last seen her, she had promised to meet with him and talk about their future. Now she's gone! Checked out? Taken her overnight bag? He loved her! How could he find her? Maybe he scared her away. No, she had confessed her love to him too. In fact, she initiated everything tonight. He had planned on doing it anyway after the concert, but she had beaten him to the punch. Where was she now?

He called the jet. Perhaps she felt the need to go back there. They had seen no sign of her. He called Bull and Guy, but neither of them knew she had left. They did tell him that Alex and Megan had been waiting at her door when she returned from the concert. Suddenly, Stephen put it all together and began to realize that something very sinister had taken place. The pit of his stomach began to gnaw away, and he feared that somehow Alex had done something awful to her.

Stephen banged on Alex's door and yelled incessantly for him to open it. When Megan finally did, she gave Stephen the most horrible look imaginable.

"I'd like to know where Annie is!" he said out of control.

"Oh, I bet you would," Megan said with a sneer.

Alex quickly came up behind her and said, "Megan, let me handle this."

"Handle what?" Stephen yelled out. "What have you done? Where is Annie?"

"She's gone!" Megan screamed.

"Megan, go to the other room," Alex demanded. "I will handle this."

"Where—is—Annie?" Stephen said as he towered over Alex.

"The musicians told us all about your little tricks," Megan continued.

"Megan!" Alex yelled at her this time. "I am handling this!"

"What tricks?" Stephen asked in confusion.

"The way you seduce girls to come on these tours and then finally end up with them in your bed!" Megan yelled out again.

Stephen's face turned pale and his jaw dropped.

"Admit it," Megan said in tears. "You brought Annie on this whole trip for one reason alone."

"I said to leave, Megan," Alex said firmly. "Do not say another word in here. Go!"

"What are you talking about?" Stephen asked as things began to suddenly make sense. "What musicians, Megan?" He realized that he would only get truthful answers from Megan, and that Alex had pulled something horribly deceitful out of the bag.

"Megan, do not say a word to this man," Alex commanded her. "Leave the room!"

"I will not," Megan replied innocently. "Your band says you do this every trip, get some girl and then woo her away."

"Megan, shut up!" Alex began to yell.

"Who told you this, Megan?" Stephen asked her.

"All of them," she said in sobs.

"Shut up, Megan!" Alex said again. "I am handling this! Leave this room now!"

"No!" Stephen yelled at her as she turned to go. "I want to hear this from Megan, not you, you conniving, worthless, snake!"

Stephen really wanted to use expletives, but he would not allow the burning deceit and hate that was buried inside of Alex poison his own life.

"Alex is just trying to help!" Megan defended.

"I told you to leave," Alex emphasized again.

"Then tell him what they told you," she pleaded.

"Yes, Alex, tell me what *they* told you," Stephen said through gritted teeth.

Alex's jaw was grinding. He stared at Stephen, then back at Megan. He could not bring himself to open his mouth. The one thing he hated most in the world was confrontation, yet here he was in the biggest confrontation of his life. All he did was seethe with anger.

"The guys in the band said you always bring some girl to seduce, and that this time it was Annie," Megan finally spoke up.

Stephen shook his head in disbelief.

"Megan," Alex said as he tried to control his rage, "if you say one more word to him, we are through. You can pack your bags and leave with Annie on the next plane out."

"What?" she asked in total surprise. "I'm just trying to clear things up while you just stand there with your mouth glued shut!"

"There is nothing to clear up," Stephen said to her.

Within five minutes, all four musicians and their wives were in Alex's room denying the story.

"Stephen has never done that," Jason said quickly. "In fact, it is a rule on his trips that no one fools around like that, not even the crew."

"They would be fired immediately and sent home," Dianne added.

"And as for girls, he's never brought anyone," Chip added. "Never."

"We were thrilled that he brought Annie along," Tracy jumped in. "I actually thought they were falling in love."

"We were," Stephen said shaking as he looked to Megan.

"Then what happened?" Megan asked in complete frustration. "Why did you tell Alex that . . ."

"No one told Alex anything," Sam finally concluded. "Looks like you finally found a way to get back at that sister you hated so much," he said in repulsion as he kicked the floor in anger.

Megan's face changed to horror as she suddenly realized what had transpired. She began to shake her head in unbelief.

"No," she began to whisper. "Alex? Tell me you didn't do this. Please."

Alex said nothing and did nothing. He just stood still.

"For the record," Stephen said barely controlled, "you will be fired when this tour is over."

"For the record," Alex finally managed to speak, "I could care less. I got what I wanted out of all of this—a chance to put that wicked, wicked woman in her place. And as for you," he turned to Megan, "get out of my room and out of my life."

Stephen packed his bag and went back to the jet for the night. He could not bear to be in the room where he had managed to finally sweep Annie off her feet. He dropped his bag inside his bedroom door and just stood there. He did not know what to do next. The thing that hurt him most of all was that Annie had believed Alex. She had admitted to finally loving and trusting Stephen, but all it took was one blow from her brother to bring the walls of love and trust crashing down.

He walked to her room and slowly opened her door. All her things, except what she had taken in her overnight bag, were still there. He walked in and glanced around. He could still smell the scent of her hair. He slowly laid down on her bed and felt the tears stinging his eyes for release. He then reached inside his pocket and pulled out a small white box. He opened it and saw the prisms of the diamond ring begin to spin together as the tears started to fall.

"I love you, Annie Wright," he cried, "and you still don't know it."

Chapter Twenty-Four

Annie got very little sleep on the flight to New York. From there, she switched flights to Huntsville with an estimated arrival time at 2:37 in the afternoon. She had tried to put the whole Stephen thing out of her mind, but it was impossible. The more she wished she had never met him, had just stayed in Dockrey writing commercials, had never seen the world or sang for an auditorium full of screaming fans, had never signed an autograph or posed for a picture with someone she had never met, the more she realized she would never be the same. Even if she did go back to the same old life, she was not the same Annie.

She had tasted something that she did not want to lose. The one thing, however, that continued to crush her heart was that it was not the fame and the recognition and the music that had affected her the most; it was Stephen. She had so fallen in love with him that every fiber of her being ached to be with him, to hear him say it was all a misunderstanding, to be held in his arms once again.

Stop it, Annie! How much of a fool do you need to become before you can wipe this little fantasy out of your mind? It's over. In fact, it never even started. The very thing you feared the most came true: Stephen used you.

Annie had not felt so totally destroyed inside since she was 13. Her father had a cousin named Toby; all the kids called him Uncle Toby. He was a bit silly, which often endeared him to children, but he was an irresponsible wanderer. Annie remembered overhearing a conversation between her parents when he had *wandered* to their home for several weeks. Her father kept saying he was harmless, just a bit off in the head somewhere. They just needed to show him some genuine kindness and let him move on. Barbara, however, was wary of him. She did not like him in her house and was not comfortable with him around her children.

Annie remembered the night her parents had gone to church for an adult Sunday School fellowship one Friday evening. Andie and Angie had gone to the football game with Doug, and Alex was sick in his bed. Annie stayed home because she had a project due on Monday and wanted to make sure it was perfect. She stayed up in her room all afternoon and evening to work, even bringing her sandwich up so she could work and eat at the same time. She made a feudal community and had taken great pride in crafting every detail to perfection.

Uncle Toby came into the room to check on her project. He asked her about various aspects, and even though Annie thought he was *totally weird,* she never feared him. After talking about the project, he came over next to her and began to touch her in uncomfortable ways. Annie's parents had talked with all their children about the possibility of situations like this arising. She instantly told him to stop and to leave her room. He then began to flatter her, telling her how much more beautiful she was than any of her sisters, or anyone he had ever known. He said that he loved her and that they should have a "special" relationship.

Annie stood up and told him to leave or she would tell her parents. He then began to threaten her. Annie's parents had taught her well. She knew this was the pattern that child molesters often took in order to scare their victims. He threatened to hurt, not her, but her parents and her sisters, if she told. He came toward her again, more forcefully this time, but she simply reared back her right leg and kicked him as hard as she could in the groin. He fell to the floor, writhing and screaming in pain. She remembered telling him that she would gladly keep her mouth shut if he left her room immediately and left their house the next morning. He did.

Annie remembered the feeling of being violated, even though nothing ever happened. She had thought about telling her parents, or maybe even just Angie, but the humiliation of it made her keep it inside. She thought of the few times guys had expressed an interest in her, and how it always made her feel the same way she had felt with Uncle Toby. That was why she would never date, but Stephen had been different.

When Stephen had kissed her on the balcony, she remembered using the word "violate," but that was not how she truly felt. In fact, she liked it very much. Yet she had so equated any relationship with a man to that night with Toby that when she did finally regain her senses, "violate" was the first word that came out. In retrospect, she now believed that her mind knew exactly what was going on, but that she was so caught up in Stephen Williams that she had convinced herself that he really cared for her.

"Miss Wright," came the attendant's voice. "You need to prepare for landing. Please fold up your tray."

Annie nodded and folded her tray. Apparently, she had missed the announcement. Everyone else was already set up for the landing. She sighed deeply trying to calm her nerves. She hated landings more than anything else. In her mind, they were equated with a controlled crash.

Once down, Annie unbuckled and grabbed her only bag. She wondered if she would ever get her things from the tour. Stephen had probably already dished them in the garbage, disappointed that his scheme did not work with her. One thing she was glad of in all this—she never got to the actual point of seduction. She wondered if she could have taken it well. She would have been so floored and crushed that she would probably have fallen apart right there in front of him.

"Miss Wright," the attendant spoke to her again, "I saw your concert in Baltimore. You were awesome."

"Thank you," Annie said graciously with a smile. There was no need to alienate anyone simply because her life had just blown to pieces.

"Would you sign this?" the attendant asked handing her a piece of paper.

"Sure," Annie smiled as she took the paper and signed.

"Thank you, Miss Wright," the attendant said as she excitedly took the paper. "Enjoy your vacation."

When Annie walked out of the plane, she scanned the terminal for her father. She had pleaded for him to come alone to get her. She saw him. His face had a grave expression, and he was already walking toward her. She ran to meet him and dropped her bag five feet back when she grabbed him in a strong embrace. The tears began to pour out uncontrollably as she held him tighter and tighter.

"Let's get your luggage and go," he said gently.

"That's all I brought," she said pointing to her overnight bag.

Jonathan grabbed the bag and then put his arm around his little girl, escorting her to his pickup in the parking lot. He said nothing until they had left the airport.

"Do you want to tell me what happened?" he asked her. Annie had said nothing yet, not even over the phone, about why she had left the tour.

"No," was all she could say.

"No? No what? No, not right now? No, not until we pass Decatur? No, not until we get home?"

"No, never," she clarified.

Jonathan shook his head as he maneuvered through the lanes.

"Annie, we've got to talk about this," he told her.

"I don't want to talk about it," she mourned. "I don't want to think about it."

"Is that possible?" Jonathan asked her. "Do you really believe you can just put this whole thing out of your mind and pretend it never happened?"

"No," she said weakly as she gazed out the window while crossing the Tennessee River, "but that's my plan anyway."

"Annie, I really thought that your stubborn, opinionated ways had begun to settle. But here you are, right back into them again."

"Daddy!" she screamed at him offended. "You don't even know what happened! You don't know the humiliation I've been put through!"

"Actually, at this point, I probably know a heck of a lot more than you."

"How can you say that? Who have you talked to?"

"Just about everybody, but Alex. He won't speak to me at all. I've talked with Megan, and I've talked with Stephen."

"Stephen?" she asked in unbelief. "Why on earth would you talk to him?"

"Because I have talked with him at least once a week, often more, for the past six months."

"What?" She couldn't believe that. "Why?"

"He asked me to mentor him, to disciple him," Jonathan explained. "I would give him books to read and study and passages to meditate on. I sent him sermons each week, until the overseas tour. We would talk regularly about his spiritual walk, and I would encourage him in his process of growth."

"Well, then," she moped sarcastically, "it looks like he pulled one over on you too."

"Let me ask you a simple question, Annie," her father said as he passed the last red light in Decatur. "Up until that last night when Alex told you all this stuff about Stephen, who were you more likely to trust or believe?"

"What do you mean?"

"Before Alex's big bomb, would you have been more likely to

trust Stephen or Alex?"

Annie thought. It was really a no-brainer. Of course she would have trusted Stephen.

"That is not the point," she tried to defend.

"Oh, but Annie, that is exactly the point," Jonathan insisted. "You have these ideas in your head about things. You think you are clever and well protected in your thinking, but you are so easy to read. You have always been an open book. Stephen knew you didn't trust him from the moment he kissed you on the balcony at our house to the night he walked you to your room in Hawaii."

"You knew about those?" she asked in disbelief.

"I know absolutely everything," he told her. "I know way more than you do, in fact. I also know that the night you walked out on Stephen, he had planned to propose. He never planned for the whole night to get caught up in passion on stage. All he wanted to do was to get you thinking in a more romantic way so that he could pop the question that night after the concert. In fact, he had told me he wanted to keep the physical aspect of the relationship at bay until you were married. He wanted to honor your purity for all these years. But when you kissed him, he couldn't help himself. He was so relieved that you finally returned his love, he was ready to drag you to a minister that night."

Annie sat quietly, stunned at the sudden revelation.

"But Megan and Alex . . ." she began.

"No!" her father said firmly. "Megan knew nothing. She simply took Alex's word in the whole scheme. He laid it out to her as deceptively as he could, and she believed everything he said."

Annie laid her head back in disgust. Alex had used her one weakness with him, her desire for him to actually treat her like a sister and care about her, to destroy her.

"He and Megan have split, by the way," he informed her.

"Unbelievable," she cried. "This thing just goes from bad to worse."

"What I am trying to understand, Annie, is why you gave up on Stephen so fast. Why didn't you defend him?"

"I tried to, Daddy," she said in desperation, "but every time I did, they started countering me with these conversations they had with the band. These are great guys! They're not slothful, good-for-nothing, ne'er-do-wells! They're all family men, and they're all Christians."

"You just couldn't believe that Stephen could really love you, could you?"

Annie turned her head back to the window. No, she could not. She had tried to convince herself that it was all true and that her highest hopes were really happening. However, she could not believe that Stephen, the man of her dreams, had really fallen for her.

"Alex knew that, you know," he told her as he took her hand. "You're an open book, Annie. I'm sorry that it all turned out like this."

"What a mess I've made, huh?" she said dryly. "I don't even know what to do or where to go from here, Daddy."

Jonathan remained quiet as he stared pensively down the road. "Do you want some advice?" he finally asked her.

"I guess," she said despondently. "What can it hurt? What do you think I should do?"

Jonathan sighed. He had already thought through this and knew Annie would fight anything that meant she must initiate the first step. "You need to start with a phone call to Stephen."

She groaned and rolled her eyes as she said, "No way! I can't even think about talking to him."

"Annie, you did him wrong. You left him, first of all, high and dry with two concerts left, as a leading act in his stage show. That was totally irresponsible and ungodly of you."

"But I thought . . ."

"It doesn't matter what you *thought,*" Jonathan said sternly. "That was wrong! There were a lot of disappointed people in Berlin, and he still has to go to London. That was terrible. Annie, he let you *become* the show. He tailored the entire thing so that his fans would fall in love with you and your music."

Annie nodded. He was right. That had been wrong and irresponsible.

"Then second, you owe Stephen a personal apology," he continued. "The least you could have done was face him with the truth after all you had been through. He had the musicians and their wives come into the room to confirm to Megan that Alex had created all of this for one reason—to destroy you. They were furious! They believed the two of you had fallen in love, and they had been flying high on that thought all evening. The girls were planning your wedding!"

"Daddy, Alex told me to leave! He made me believe it was the honorable thing to do!"

"Once again, Annie, where was your head? You just lost it all giving into your fears! That's always been your problem, you know? You could change the world if you wanted to, but you are so scared that the Vivian and Kelly McCalls are going to sabotage everything you do that you hide yourself in little corners and never rear your head until the winds are calmed or passed! Annie, you've got to grow up! And you will start by calling Stephen when we get home."

Annie shook her head. He was right and she knew it, but she would *not* talk with Stephen. She had lost him through all of this, and she could not bring herself to even apologize.

"You will call him, Annie," Jonathan said more firm.

"I can't, Daddy."

Suddenly Jonathan slammed on his brakes and pulled over to the side of the road. He pointed his finger into her face and said, "Do you think I'm trying to ruin your life too? Do you think I would do something as dastardly as Alex to destroy and humiliate you?"

"No, Daddy," she said weakly and trembling.

"Stephen Williams is the first thing in your 27 years, other than your music, that has ever brought you to life! He has given you meaning and purpose and a future and a hope, and I will not allow your stubbornness to drive him away from you!"

"I can't talk to him!" she began to cry. "How can I try to make up to him what I did after all he's done for me?"

"That's exactly why you will talk to him," he persisted. "If he never wants to speak to you again, that's your fault. Not totally, Alex wove this whole thing very well. Unfortunately, you were a victim too. Whatever he has against you, I'd say you're even now. But that still does not release you from owning up to your part of the problem with Stephen. You *will* call him when we get home."

"I can't," she continued to cry.

"Then get out of my truck," he said bitterly.

"What?" she asked bewildered.

"I let Alex get away with irresponsibility and wrong attitudes," he said harshly. "I'm not doing it anymore. If you have no plans to stand up here and do the right thing, you might as well leave now because you're not coming to my house with that attitude."

Annie stared straight ahead. Her eyes were so clouded she could not make out anything clearly. There was no way she could talk to Stephen.

"That's not fair," she said hurt beyond imagination.

"No, it certainly isn't," he agreed, "but it looks to me like someone in this whole mess has got to start cleaning up. And as I see it, you're the one to blame."

"Me?" she sobbed. "I was the victim!"

"No, Stephen was the victim," her father emphasized. "You told him that you loved him and trusted him. Do you remember that? After the concert? He remembers it clearly."

"I remember."

"Then you need to tell him that you either lied or that your vision was clouded beyond recognition by the bitterness of your brother."

Annie closed her eyes and put her face down in her hands. Her only reprieve on the flights back home was the fact that she would never have to face Stephen again. Now she had no choice.

"I'll call him," she said resolutely.

When they pulled into Dockrey, Annie did not feel warm and welcomed as she had expected. She felt hard and cold and lonely. As they passed by her old office on Main Street, she wondered what her life would be like if she had never met Stephen and never closed up shop to follow him around the world.

When they reached the Wright house, she was floored to see a twelve-foot fence in place and reporters and photographers scattered everywhere. As soon as the pickup pulled up to the gate, they began to flood the car, snapping pictures and begging questions.

"What's going on?" Annie asked in a near panic. "What's with the fence?"

Her father didn't answer. He merely waited until two armed guards motioned to another guard to activate the gate. The third man pressed a button on a remote, and the gate rolled open to allow him to pass.

"Three weeks after the tour started, people began appearing here," Jonathan explained. "Some were fans, others were press. When one actually broke into the house, Stephen offered to put in a security system and install the gate."

"Why didn't he tell me?" she asked. "Why didn't *you* tell me? Why didn't anyone tell me?" she thought of Angie.

"Because we all tried to protect you. We wanted this tour to be the dream of a lifetime. You could face the realities when you got back."

"Can you ride?" she wondered. He knew she meant the motorcycles.

"No," he said sadly.

As Annie saw it, she owed apologies to just about everybody now.

ꕤ ꕤ

Annie could not eat supper. Her schedule was still off from being in Europe, and her emotions had been drug through so much, she didn't know how she really felt. Her mother had been way more comforting than her dad. She had held Annie while they both cried more than once during the afternoon and evening.

"Annie, life is not over for you," Barbara promised her. "I know that right now it seems like the end of so much, but it's really the beginning. You have a following. We had to change our number because we literally got phone call after phone call of people wanting to sign you up with some kind of outlandish deal. Lucky for us we have that cellular family plan!"

Annie looked up at her in amazement.

Barbara continued, "People were talking about literally million-dollar contracts! We don't even know what to tell them. Your life is changing, and it is for the better. But right now, even though you may feel like Job, you will get through this. And God will bless you richly on the other side."

"Moms," Annie said sadly, as she attempted to halt a few more tears, "I don't even care any more. I don't want any of it."

"What do you want, sweetie?"

Annie leaned her head against her mother's shoulder and let the tears flow on.

"All I want is Stephen," she cried softly. "That's all I want."

"Then perhaps you should tell him so."

ꕤ ꕤ

That night Annie's parents left her alone with her phone in front of the blazing fire. Annie tried to calculate what time it would be in London, but she was still totally confused. The whole time zone thing never made sense to her. To her it was like Daylight Saving's Time. Why not leave it all alone and just realize that twelve midnight in Australia means its time for school?

She dialed Stephen's cell number and tried not to think about what to say. She hoped it would just come to her when he answered.

"Hello?"

"Hey," she said feebly. "This is Annie."

There was total silence. She winced and closed her eyes. Just hearing his voice made her long to be with him even more.

"I don't even know what to say, Stephen," she tried to begin. "I love you."

There was still silence.

"I'm sorry," she said quickly. "I shouldn't say that to you. I'm so sorry. You deserve better than this, better than me. I should go."

She simply pressed the end button on her phone.

How could I tell him that I loved him? After all I've put him through, I had no right to say that! He must really think I am a total fool!

The phone rang. She glanced at the display; it was Stephen. She couldn't answer it. She stared at the fire and watched the flames dance. She had even dreamed of his being with her here one day to sit by this very fire, warm and cozy, snuggled together on the couch. The phone continued to ring as tears started streaming down her cheeks again. How many tears could one person cry in 24 hours? She turned off the phone and went to her room. Maybe if she could sleep she would wake up and find the whole thing had been an awful dream.

The next morning, Annie did not awaken at 6:45. Her clock said 1:33. It was daylight so that meant she had slept past both breakfast and lunch. She pulled herself from her bed and dressed in a pair of warm sweats. The weather was extremely chilly, and she longed for a cup of hot coffee to sip in front of a roaring fire.

When she went downstairs, her father and mother were sitting on the couch waiting for her.

"I don't think you've actually lived up to your end of the bargain," her father began.

"Jonathan, give her a break," Barbara said forcefully. "Would you take her feelings into consideration with all this too?"

"I am taking her feelings into consideration!" he called out. "The sooner she gets this settled, the sooner she'll feel like she's part of the human race again."

He turned his speech back toward Annie.

"Stephen said he called you all night, but you turned off your phone."

Annie sighed in despair. There was no hiding anything from her father, especially with Stephen at the other end pushing the whole thing.

"I called him," she said in argument. "He wouldn't talk to me."

"You didn't give him a chance!" he yelled out.

"I'm sorry," Annie began to scream. "I tried to do the right thing! I apologized, but he said nothing! There was stone silence, and that silence said plenty!"

"Once again, Annie, running ahead of the game," her father began to scold. "He was totally shocked to hear your voice!"

"Honey," Barbara said in a much calmer demeanor than Jonathan, "please call him back, and let him collect his thoughts this time."

Annie nodded as she entered the kitchen. Yes, there was still coffee in the pot. She did not care how old it was. It was hot and it was coffee. That was good enough. She fixed her a cup and found the courage to leave the kitchen to face her parents. Her father had already left the room. Barbara just watched her sympathetically.

"Call him, Annie," Barbara softly pleaded. "He's still very much in love with you."

"How can he be?" she asked her.

"What you did didn't change his feelings," Barbara tried to explain. "If it had, then he never really loved you. Annie, he needs you as much as you think you need him, maybe even more. Stephen and your father have gotten very close. Stephen has sought your father's advice every step of the way with this whole relationship. When you talked with him last night, he was so stunned. He had believed that you were still taking Alex's side. When you told him you still loved him, he didn't know what to do. He was prepared to beg the point and plead with you to give it another try. He didn't expect your simple declaration. To be frank, that's not like you. Not at all."

Barbara got up to leave, but handed Annie the cell phone she had left down there from last night.

"Turn it on and keep it on," Barbara smiled. "Don't be afraid, Annie. God has not given us a spirit of fear, but of peace, of love and a sound mind."

Annie took the phone and turned it on. Twenty-seven missed calls. He was persistent, wasn't he? She drank another bit of coffee and went over to the fireplace and sat on the hearth. She gently laid another log on the top and then stared at the fire for a long while. How had life managed to get so complicated when six months ago it had been completely boring?

Her phone rang. She checked the display. Stephen.

"Hey" she said carefully, still wondering what they could say to each other that would ever remove the wall between them.

"Please don't hang up," he said quickly. "Just give me a chance to say it all."

Annie immediately tried to explain, "I'm sorry. I was so nervous and tired and gosh, scattered last night. I shouldn't have called to begin with."

"No," he jumped in, "I'm so glad you did. I was going crazy wondering if you would ever speak to me again."

"Me speak to you? How can you even think about talking to me after I ran out like that?"

"Oh, Annie," he said in desperation, "I don't blame you for that. Alex really pulled a number on us all. He's treated Megan horribly."

"None of this was her fault," Annie tried to reason. "Why did he leave her?"

"She was so mad at me that she revealed the whole thing in disgust. Apparently, Alex's plan was to get me alone and continue the web of deception by coming up with some excuse that would paint you as a really bad person who took off on me for no reason. Then I would be mad at you, you would be crushed, and he would look like the hero to both of us."

"I don't know what to say," Annie sighed as she thought of all the trouble she had brought into Stephen's life by insisting he audition Alex from the beginning. "I should have never gotten him the audition to begin with."

"Bite your tongue!" Stephen said adamantly. "Don't you ever think that! Annie, you need to understand something: I love you with all that I am. I don't ever want to imagine my life without you again. Don't think that anything has changed here."

"But it has changed. I said I loved you and I trusted you, then I turned right around, within an hour, and proved that both of those were lies."

"Do you not love me?" he asked quickly.

Annie was silent. Of course she loved him. She would give her life to be with him.

"Do you not love me, Annie?" he asked her again.

"Yes, I love you," she confessed, "but I didn't act like it in Paris."

"Yes, you did. All day long you acted like it. When the concert was over you acted like it. When Alex sabotaged you, you even acted like it then. You were hurt because you thought I had betrayed you. What else could you have done?"

"I could have stayed and asked you for myself."

"Why did you leave?" he asked her. "Why didn't you face me?"

Annie thought for a moment and told him, "Because Alex said I should go."

There was silence again.

"Did you defend me to him?" Stephen asked her.

"Yes. Up until he said the musicians were the ones who had warned him."

"As I see it, you were bamboozled. He even had it planned to suggest your leaving."

"He offered to call the airport and make the reservation," Annie admitted as she felt her anger rise. "I let him, still amazed that he was caring about me. And all the while, he was playing every trump card he had ever stored up at that very moment in time."

Annie and Stephen were both silent as the depth of Alex's bitterness sunk in. How could a brother be so intent on hating his sister so much? What would drive someone to that?

"You're not gonna hang up on me, are you?" Stephen asked as he broke the silence.

"No," Annie said as a small smile began to grow.

"How can I tell you how much I love you and how much I need you in my life?"

"You just did."

"No," he said softly, "that's not adequate."

"If you can ever forgive me for leaving like I did and putting you in the horrible position of the last two concerts that would be, well, more than I could ever ask."

"That was hard, Annie. Those crowds were unbelievably disappointed. I said there had been a terrible family catastrophe and that you had to leave for the States immediately. We edited a previous performance and put you on the screen instead. They weren't thrilled, but at least they got a small taste of what they came to see."

Annie hung her head. What she did was unforgivable.

"Annie, I do forgive you," he said quickly. "Please know that I do."

"How can you?"

"Because you were pulled into that trap like a fish with bait. You were." There was more silence. "Come see me," he finally suggested.

"When?"

"As soon as I get back. We should be in New York on Friday after Thanksgiving. We'll actually spend the holiday over the Atlantic Ocean."

Annie smiled sadly. She had hoped to spend that holiday with him.

"I'll be heading up to my house in the Adirondacks on Sunday. Come up there with me."

"Let me talk to Daddy," she said cautiously. "He let me come to your apartment alone because of all the security needs and the people present on your floor. I don't know about your house."

"Mabel and Leonard are there year round. They live there with me. They have their own place over the garage."

"I'll talk to him," she said again, "but I feel like I really need to be with my family for the holidays. I need a little grounding with them right now."

"Do you think you will ever see me as that place of grounding?" he asked with melancholy in his voice.

Annie smiled because she knew the expression that accompanied that tone of voice.

"No," she said teasing him, "you will never be my ground. You are my height, Stephen. You are the place I fly to when everything is said and done."

"I love you, Annie Wright."

"I love you too. I promise I do."

Thanksgiving dinner was both festive and sad. The family was grateful to be together, but with Alex's shenanigans still weighing heavily in each one's mind, along with the realization that Megan would no longer be a part of their family, the holiday was, for the most part, shattered. They tried not to talk about it, but it was hard to talk around it all day. Annie finally sat them down and laid the whole story out. Doug was ready to find Alex and teach him a lesson about family propriety.

Andie managed to get Annie off alone at some point.

"You are going to see Stephen when the holidays are through?" she asked Annie.

"I think so. Daddy even thinks so."

"If you have Daddy in Stephen's corner, then you can take that as a clear sign from God that he's a good man."

Annie chuckled. Who would have thought a father would fight so hard for a man for his daughter?

Later that night, Annie and Angie enjoyed some time in the hot tub. The weather had turned bitter cold, and the tub was more than relaxing.

"I love Thanksgiving," Angie said as she lifted a foot from the water.

"I do too," Annie agreed. "There's no pressure at Thanksgiving. No gifts to get or parties to deal with, just family and great food."

They both sighed, half in contentment, but half in frustration of all that had transpired.

"Do you think you could cook your own turkey?"

"Probably," Annie thought. "I never have, though. Come to think of it, Moms has never let any of us do the turkey."

"I was thinking the same thing today. Maybe she feels that if we never learn how, we'll have to keep coming back here for hers."

"I wouldn't put it past her," Annie laughed.

They sat and relaxed. The stress was slowly evaporating.

"So do you plan on marrying him?" Angie asked playfully.

"He has to ask first," Annie told her.

"What if he does? I mean, with Daddy pulling so hard for him, he's probably afraid not to."

Annie smiled, but her heart really ached to see Stephen again. She thought about him every waking moment and many of the sleeping ones. For the first time in her life, there was someone else she longed to be with more than her family, and as homesick as she had been on the tour, it was doubled now, only for Stephen.

"I bet you won't miss me near as much now when I go to Padawin," Angie teased.

"Oh, are you going?"

"I still have faith and hope," she said like a trooper. "Michael Collins insists he needs me there so I just keep praying for God to work some kind of miracle and get all the obstacles out of the way. We actually e-mail in the Padawin language," she added. "It has been fun to sort of *speak* the language with him. I still struggle with the sentence structure," she laughed. "They're going to think I'm the stupidest doctor they've ever seen!"

"Well, I don't. I could have really used you on the trip when I had tonsillitis. That was miserable."

"I can't believe you actually went on and did the concert."

"Me either when I think about it," Annie confessed. "It was hard not to, though. When you realize those people are packing out huge arenas just to hear your music, you somehow find a way."

That night Annie unpacked her overnight bag for the first time. She pulled out her scrubs, her jeans and sweater, and at the bottom was the blue fleece blanket Stephen had given her. She removed it tenderly and brought it up to smell it. Although it didn't smell like Stephen, it had its own unique scent that reminded her of everything about the tour, everything that was good. She glanced at her clock and wondered if she could possibly reach Stephen over the Atlantic. She dialed, but only got a recording of his voice mail. His phone was unavailable at the moment.

"Hey, Stephen, it's Annie," she spoke to the recorder. "I just wanted to say that I hope your Thanksgiving was as miserable as mine. All I did was think about you the entire day. Even when I was with Angie in the hot tub, I just thought about you. You've somehow managed to capture my complete and undivided attention, and there isn't a flipping thing I can do about it."

She paused, and then added, "I miss you—and I love you."

As the jet landed, Stephen pulled out his phone to check for messages. Three. He scrolled through the numbers to see who had called. He smiled when he realized Annie had left a voice mail. He pressed the buttons and put the receiver up to his ear.

"Hey, Stephen, it's Annie," he heard her say. "I just wanted to say that I hope your Thanksgiving was as miserable as mine. All I did was think about you the entire day. Even when I was with Angie in the hot tub, I just thought about you. You've somehow managed to capture my complete and undivided attention, and there isn't a flipping thing I can do about it."

She paused, and then added, "I miss you . . . and I love you."

He ended the call and glanced at the time—3:30 in the morning was not a good time to call anyone. He clipped the phone back to his belt and continued to the waiting limo. His old familiar driver saw him to his seat and shut the door.

When the car started, the driver asked, "How was the tour, sir?"

"Life changing," Stephen replied.

"For the better, I hope."

"Me too."

Back in his apartment, Stephen immediately went to his computer. He did not check e-mail or news, but instead went to one of the websites where he knew pictures of Annie had been posted. He scrolled through until he found the perfect one. He printed it out, turned off the computer, and fell straight into bed with her picture beside him. How did he ever find any reason to exist before her?

Chapter Twenty-Five

As wonderful as Thanksgiving was, Annie had still not adjusted back to Central Time. Her body was tired and out of order, her emotions had been tugged beyond anything she had ever known, and her frustrations toward Alex had reached an all time high. How could he have so deceptively tried to ruin her life? After Sunday dinner, she excused herself and went up to her room to sleep. And sleep she did, all afternoon.

Angie and her parents sat around the fireplace for a long time, just talking and relaxing, as the sky grew grayer with impending rain. In Angie's opinion, days like these invited gloom, but the gentle crackling of the fire and total freedom from responsibility at the moment brought complete contentment instead. Barbara had become so content, in fact, that she decided to hit the bedroom for her own nap, leaving Angie and her father alone.

"What are you reading?" Jonathan asked Angie who was sprawled on the floor in front of the hearth with her head laid back on an overstuffed pillow.

"Pure garbage," she said looking up at him with a smile. "It's one of those gossip magazines at the front of the grocery stores. It had Stephen's picture on the front. I couldn't resist."

"What does it say about him?"

"That he's gay and the whole stint with Annie was a cover-up."

Jonathan grimaced. "Does it say anything about Annie?" Jonathan wondered.

"Yeah," Angie mumbled, "but you don't want to know."

"I do now," he said as he glared down at her. "What does it say?"

"Well, the gist of it is that if someone as hot as Annie can't turn him around, performing with her like that for three months, there's no hope for him."

"I wonder if Annie is really ready to face this high-profile lifestyle. It's a stark contrast to how she was raised."

"I think she's tough enough to handle it," Angie said honestly.

"And besides, Stephen will probably be with her through the whole thing. After all the baloney they've written and said about him over the years, he can help her to keep her feet on the ground."

"I'm banking on that."

"How come you trust him so much?" Angie asked as she sat up and put down the magazine. "I can't believe you're actually sending her up there, all alone, to his house, for two weeks at Christmas. What about all the 'appearances' you preached to us all these years?"

"First of all, they're not 'all alone,' " he began. "He has a couple that actually lives in the house there, an older couple; they will serve well as chaperones. Also, I trust Annie. I trust Stephen too. Now you, I would never send off like that!"

"What? What have I ever done to cause you not to trust me? For Pete's sake, I'm going to the mission field!"

Jonathan gave her a funny look and said, "What have you ever done? Where I do I start?"

"What?" she asked him again.

"You have always had a bit of a wild streak. Dancing, sneaking out of the house, Billy Marcum, the balcony . . ." he began listing.

"The balcony!" she exclaimed. "What do you know about the balcony?"

"More than you'd like me to know."

Angie actually blushed slightly. Her father knew about the Billy Marcum fiasco?

"Annie snuck out too," Angie began to defend.

"Yes, I know. That night you guys went toilet papering the yards was very disappointing."

"Everybody did it, Daddy."

"But we had just had the talk about the fact that it was illegal in Dockrey. Because of *that, we* weren't going to do it."

Angie smiled slightly embarrassed.

"As for the dancing, all of us did it, you know?" she defended again. "And what about Alex and Megan's little dance for their friends before the wedding? You didn't complain about that."

"They're adults; what could I have done? Prohibited it? You all went anyway, and I understand you, the future missionary, cut quite the rug," he said with raised eyebrows.

"Dancing's in the Bible, Daddy."

"Dancing for the glory of God," he reminded her. "All the rest usually led to something horrific, such as cutting off prophets' heads and the like."

"I wasn't all *that* wild in high school."

He laughed softly and told her, "Yes, you were. I made it my business to know what you kids were in to, and what I didn't know, everyone else made it their business to know what the preacher's kids were up to! And they readily told me. Very little passed me by."

"Why didn't you ever say anything?"

"You were 15, 16, 17, you needed to make some choices and deal with the results. As long as you didn't go too close to the edge, I had to let you make some mistakes."

"I still can't believe you didn't *talk* about it to me," she groaned.

"I did a lot of talking, mainly in prayer," he said gently. "I had done my part in raising you. God would have to guide you at that point. I stepped in now and then, but figured He could probably convict you much better than me. It worked, didn't it?"

Angie lay back down. Her dad was a wise man, but she did not realize how wise until now. If he knew half the stuff she had done in high school, yet he had only prayed, apparently he had done the right thing.

"I still can't believe you're letting Annie leave us at Christmas," she mumbled again. "That's not wise; that's *mean.*"

"It's not 'mean' to Annie. Besides, I have an ulterior motive."

"You?" Angie said in surprise. "Daddy has an *ulterior motive?*"

"Yes, Daddy has," he said without excitement. "Alex needs to come home. He needs to be here with the family for the holidays, and he won't come if Annie's here."

"Good riddance!" Angie exclaimed. "Nobody wants him here! We'd much rather have Annie here."

"Exactly. That's why he needs to be here. Listen, Angie, we have got to pull together as a family and try to bring some kind of healing back to Alex."

"To Alex?" Angie began to get animated now. "What kind of healing does he need? What about Annie? What about what he did to her?"

"He's born the brunt of that. He lost Megan and he lost his job."

"And so, that's it?"

"Angie, do you have any idea why he despises Annie so much?"

"No idea," she admitted.

"That's why he needs to be here," Jonathan tried to explain. "Whatever it was that happened, it destroyed him inside where she is concerned. I think it's time we made him face it and confess it. He needs healing, and this family needs healing."

"Good luck."

"You know I don't believe in luck," he said with a quick glance toward her.

Annie wanted to motorcycle ride with her father so badly, but there was no chance. Once the press found out she was back home, they camped out along the fence everywhere. Even a trip to church had become impossible. On Wednesday evening, she sat in front of the fireplace and read while her parents went to prayer meeting. Her father called Stephen that night to apologize to him for being so harsh about his not attending church. He then handed the phone to Annie. She took it upstairs to her room.

"What do you want for Christmas?" he asked her.

"Goodness, Stephen," she said tiredly, "I don't even know what I want for breakfast anymore, much less Christmas."

"You don't want cheese toast?"

"I have no appetite whatsoever."

"So you're more on the 120-pound side these days?" he teased.

"You think you're being cute, but I weighed 114 last night."

"Annie," he said softly with concern. "Why?"

"I just can't eat much at all, Stephen," she said plainly. "I try, but nothing tastes right, I guess."

"Are you taking vitamins?"

"No, never have done that."

"Get a multivitamin then. Take it everyday," he nearly commanded.

"Aye-aye, sir. So, what do *you* want for Christmas?" she wondered.

"You."

She smiled and paused to ponder that comment.

"Done," she replied. "I'll be there the week before Christmas and right through the New Year. How did you manage that with Daddy?"

"It wasn't easy," he confessed. "I had to make some big promises to see it happen."

"Like what?"

"For starters," he began, "Mabel or Lenoard must be at the house any time we are there together. Second, I must see to it that you do not get too cold and wet in the snow and end up with tonsillitis again. And third, I cannot sleep with you unless we are married."

"He did *not* say *that!*" she said quickly and embarrassed.

"He did too, and rather emphatically, I must tell you. Apparently, he is concerned about *your* morals or something."

"Right," she smiled glad that he could not see her blush. "As for the tonsillitis, I don't care to go through that again. I'll keep myself warm, don't worry."

The next weeks drug by in Annie's opinion. Everyday was spent locked in the house, sitting near the fire either watching TV or reading a book. She remembered that it was this type of weather that had turned her into a bookworm. She could not stand any kind of cold climate. She even hated basketball practice during the fall and winter. The rest of the team would practice in shorts and tank tops, but Annie would wear her sweats the whole time. When home, she never went out. Her father had never let them watch television just to pass the time so she ended up sprawled out before the hearth with a good book, or even a bad book, to endure the winter.

Angie's seminary term was over on Wednesday, December 15, so that gave the sisters a chance to spend some time together before Annie left for New York. Angie had even devised a plan to get Annie to the mall. Angie went to the hardware store, picked up an appliance box, and put it in the back of her father's covered pickup. When she got back home, she and her father loaded the box onto a dolly borrowed from the church and acted as though it were miserably heavy. They rolled the box to the front door and on inside the house. It stayed there until Saturday morning, when Angie and Jonathan rolled the box back out on the dolly again, lifted it into the back of the truck, and Angie left. At the gate, she told the guards they had to return the appliance because of a huge nick discovered on the side. They waved her through.

When Angie got out on the road, she dialed Annie who was hiding inside the box. Annie climbed out, climbed through the windows on the camper shell and the truck, and took her seat beside Angie in the cab.

"This is great!" Annie said, excited for the first time in days.

At the mall, the girls shopped and shopped. They got most of what they needed knowing that it was unlikely that Annie could get by with this again. A few people did recognize her, and she graciously signed autographs and pleaded that they tell no one she was here. Every one understood and promised to keep it quiet.

Annie searched everywhere trying to find something she could give to Stephen. What do you get a man who has everything? She had heard that cliché many times, even used it a few times herself, but this was the first time that it literally applied to someone.

"So what are his hobbies?" Angie tried to help.

"Music," Annie said flatly.

"Come on! There has to be something he does while sitting around his apartment all those lonely days."

"He likes video games," Annie offered.

"Well, there's a starting place," Angie said with hope.

They thought quietly for a moment, then Angie said, "No, way too impersonal. What else does he like to do?"

"I think that's it."

"You could get him a sweater or something."

Annie rolled her eyes.

"Okay, you're right," Angie sighed. "No sweater."

"He wants to get a four-wheeler," Annie said half-enthusiastically.

"Can't get it on the plane," Angie reminded her.

Annie nodded. What had she personally observed him doing at his home? Playing video games, playing cards with her, sitting at the computer, watching some TV, but it was usually one of her father's sermons. Wait—his faith. That was something that he held onto strongly.

"How about something to do with his walk with the Lord?" Annie suggested.

"Oh, yeah! Great idea!" Angie said with a big grin. "What is something that could be symbolic of his faith, something he could have to remind him of his trust in God and then you at the same time?"

"A Bible?" Annie suggested.

"No, no," Angie was still thinking. "What about jewelry?"

"He doesn't wear any."

"Why?"

"Gee," Annie thought. "I don't know."

"Maybe its time he started," she said with a playful smile.

The family had an unofficial going away party for Annie on Monday, December 20. She was to leave the next day for Stephen's. Everyone wanted to exchange their gifts with her then, but she insisted she would take them all with her, and they would wait and open hers on Christmas morning also. Annie wanted them to be connected on Christmas in some way, and she felt like this might accomplish that.

Angie and Jonathan took her to the airport the following morning. They had a good time on the trip over, with Jonathan treating them to a buffet breakfast out. Annie still struggled with her appetite. She wasn't sure if it was stress or still the jet lag, but she hoped that it would return within the next couple of hours before seeing Stephen again.

They sat in the waiting area for an extra thirty minutes since the plane was late. When it came time to board, both Angie and Jonathan felt the need to talk with Annie alone. Angie pulled her aside first.

"Look, we'll take care of Alex down here," Angie told her. "We're gonna get to the bottom of this, and things are gonna work out on our end. You work on Stephen at your end."

"What am I supposed to work on?" Annie asked her confused.

"Please, girl," Angie rolled *her* eyes this time. "Do I need to explain the facts of life to you again?"

"No, thank you," Annie said hastily. "I don't want to go through that conversation again! I'll do my best, but I can't force anything. If the chemistry is still there, then maybe things will push forward. If not, however . . ."

"There you go," Angie exclaimed as she tossed her hands into the air. "You have to analyze everything, don't you? Give romance a chance, sweetie!"

"This from a girl sworn to celibacy?"

"I haven't sworn to it," Angie corrected her. "Just considered it's probably my best option right now."

They hugged and parted, knowing they would be together again in two weeks. Then Jonathan took her aside.

"Give this a chance, Annie," Jonathan told her. "I know you; you already have fears and doubts about whether it can really work out."

"What makes you think that?"

"I know *you,*" he repeated. "You've probably already figured a way of escape from this if it doesn't work out perfectly. Don't do that. And for the record, you've always done the *reasonable* thing, at least *reasonable* from *your* perspective."

"What on earth does that mean?" she asked totally puzzled.

"It means exactly what I said," he did not clear up the confusion. "At some point during this visit, you may feel compelled to be unconventional, to do something that your family wouldn't necessarily think is, well, conventional. You do what your heart tells you."

"I have no idea what you're talking about, Daddy."

"That's fine; I just wanted you to know that some decisions you make don't necessarily need to include always thinking about what your family might like the most."

Annie was still befuddled, but she nodded and said, "I'll keep that in mind, Daddy. Anything else?"

He reached over and pulled her into a long hug.

"Merry Christmas and happy New Year," he said cheerily. "This will be my first Christmas without you."

"I know," she said a bit drearily.

"But it will be your first with Stephen."

"I know that too," she said as a small smile crept across her face.

ꟸ ꟹ

The flight to New York was a rough one. In fact, it was the absolute worst flight Annie had yet experienced. She could not touch a bite of food on the plane, and truth be known, she was very tempted to try one of the little bottles of alcohol just to calm her nerves. She tried doing some crosswords, but nothing took her mind off the jolts and drops of the flight.

There were several in first class that recognized her and asked her about this trip. She explained she was going to New York for a brief visit to make some decisions about her future. It was true from a certain point of view.

"Miss Wright," the steward said to her. "Security is asking for you to leave the plane first."

"Really?" she was surprised. "Okay."

She grabbed her portfolio and her coat and started toward the door. Many of the passengers bid her a warm farewell. She had not spoken with them all, but she knew they must have realized who she was, and she was thankful that they had respected her privacy. The steward led her to the door and through the collapsing hallway to the terminal. She was not prepared for the sight that welcomed her.

There were many security guards in the area, and people began to scream when Annie appeared. Security immediately started to control the crowd. Annie wondered how they could know she was flying in. She began to search the area for Stephen's driver. She could not remember his name; it started with a "B." Bill, Bob, Buzz, Bull? No Bull had been her security. She tried to look graceful and not as scared as she really was as she scanned the crowd for the familiar face. Instead of the driver, however, she saw someone else.

Stephen stood in the center of the waiting area with a bouquet of white roses. When Annie finally made eye contact with him, he smiled at her and held out his arms, shrugged his shoulders, and gave a sheepish grin at the silly thing he had done. She shook her head, wondering how he had managed this, and began to walk toward him. How wonderful that he would choose to be the one to greet her, even though it had to have been nearly impossible to pull this off.

When she reached him, she merely fell into a long, warm embrace. He was wearing the same sweater as in Paris, the blue one that matched his eyes, and Annie buried her face into it, remembering its softness. Cashmere. The crowd screamed even more, and although her eyes were closed, she could still see the flashing of cameras and hear the clicks and winds as photographers and fans shot away. She felt herself blush slightly as Stephen's face leaned into her hair, and he took a deep breath.

"Thank you," she whispered into his ear as she lifted up her head.

"My pleasure," he replied, still with his face buried in her hair. "Are you ready to try and make it out of here?"

"Is this safe?" she asked him.

"Probably not," he told her, "but I'm counting on the people being nice to us seeing that it's the holidays."

They broke apart and Stephen handed her the bouquet. The crowd sighed in understanding. He took her hand and began the walk away from the terminal, waving to the crowd with his free hand. Security surrounded them immediately. Annie waved slightly with the roses, but was more concerned at the moment with simply making it out of the airport and to the car that she knew would be waiting. She tried to smile and acknowledge the onlookers as much as possible, but Stephen and security were walking much faster than she was used to.

"Put on your coat," Stephen told her as they approached the doors.

She complied, handing him the roses and retrieving her coat from an officer who had taken it and her portfolio shortly after their walk began. When the doors opened, another crowd was waiting outside around the blue limo. They screamed as Annie and Stephen approached, but the only thing Annie noticed was the biting cold air and the pouring rain. She wondered if the low pressure had followed her right on up to New York.

Once inside she shivered slightly and rubbed her arms to warm up. Stephen followed her inside and smiled at her being so cold from a 20-second walk to the car from the building.

"Sit back and relax," he told her. "It's about 5 ½ hours to Saranac. You'll be plenty warm in a jiffy."

"Will it still be light when we get there?" she asked, hoping she could be able to see the house when they arrived.

"I doubt it, but it's Christmas. Things will be lit up well."

"So you do a lot of decorating?"

"Mabel and Leonard do."

"Oh," she said nodding, beginning to feel slightly awkward at seeing him again.

"Do you do a lot of decorating?" he asked.

"Embarrassingly so," she confessed. "We just seem to get bigger and bigger each year."

"I'd like to have seen it."

"I'm sure there will be plenty of videos to watch; there always are."

They sat silently for a little while as the car turned and swayed through the city. Annie remembered the familiar sights, but New York still did not feel anywhere close to home. Everything was beautifully decorated. It made Dockrey's dinky decorations almost seem like a joke.

"Are you hungry?" he asked her. "You look really thin, Annie."

"No, thank you," she said politely. "I've been struggling to get back on track after Europe. In a couple of hours I could probably eat."

They rode on in silence again until the car turned onto I-87.

"Now," Stephen spoke, ready for a real conversation, "we'll be on the interstate for a couple of hours. We need to talk about all this stuff here, now, and get it all out before we get home. I don't want to bring any of this negative thinking into the house."

Annie just nodded without looking at him. She knew exactly what he was talking about. The unspoken tension between them was strong.

"First, I want you to know that I completely understand what you did," he began.

"It was inexcusable," Annie said quickly.

"No, it wasn't," he said gently. "Annie, I don't blame you for what happened."

"I could have at least stayed for the last two concerts," she said with her face still looking toward the road. "Then I would have faced you with what I had heard, you would have immediately cleared it all up with the musicians' testimonies, and none of *this* would have ever happened."

"But that's not how it played out," he said frustrated that she would not look at him. "What happened, happened, and you need to know that's it okay, and that I understand, and that Alex planned everything in such a way as to manipulate you into the worst possible situation."

Annie closed her eyes and leaned back against the seat. The heat was beginning to get to her now. She removed her coat, and Stephen took it from her, laying it across the facing seat.

Finally, looking at him, she asked, "How can you forgive me so easily?"

He smiled and shook his head in disbelief, "Don't you know?"

"No! I was horrible! I don't deserve anything from you except disdain and . . . and a whipping!"

He laughed and rubbed his face in amusement and frustration.

"Oh, Annie," he continued to chuckle, "you were set up. Besides, I'll leave all the whippings to your dad."

She turned back to face the road, but Stephen scooted over next to her.

"Look at me," he said.

She turned slowly to face him.

"I never got the chance to tell you something in Paris," he told her. "I was waiting. You need to know that I love you too. I truly and wholeheartedly love you. When I found out that you had left, I wasn't mad or even upset at you. I was hurt for you. When Megan spilled out the truth, I could have beaten the snot out of Alex! I literally had to hold myself back. I was hurt, Annie, not because of you, but for you. I could only imagine how you must have felt when he pulled all of that on you!"

"But I had just told you, not even an hour earlier, that I loved and trusted you," she said shakily. "What does that say about my love and trust?"

"Okay," he sighed as he took her hand and patted it. "It doesn't really say anything about you and me. What it says is that you had longed for some kind of relationship with your brother for so long that when he finally appeared to reach out to you, you grabbed it with all you could. I don't think you *wanted* to believe him. Megan told me that you even accused him of lying, but when he began to unravel his carefully crafted defense, you were speechless. You thought he cared. You thought all those years of being hurt, ignored, and despised had faded in a single moment. You had 24 years of history with him; you had six months with me. I want you to stop beating yourself up about this. It's over. And when we leave this car tonight, I never, ever want to talk about it again. Understood?"

She nodded lightly and leaned over on his shoulder. He bent his head down above hers and could smell the scent of her hair.

"I don't want to try to live life without you, Annie," he said softly. "You have been the first person in 17 years that I have loved. I'm so afraid to lose you. Please don't ever think you could do *anything* to change my commitment to you." He paused, then continued with a simple, "I *need* you, Annie."

Tears began to burn her eyes as she realized the depth of his care for her. She had imagined that this trip would either make or break their relationship, and being the pragmatist that she was, she leaned strongly toward the *break.* She squeezed his hand tightly, trying to communicate in touch what she could not say in words at the moment. He responded in like and gently kissed the top of her head. He then started singing softly to her:

So while I'm waiting for someone to love me
Someone who knows me through and through
I'll watch the Autumn Sunset

She smiled as a tear trickled down her cheek.

From my single room apartment
And hope and pray that dreams can still come true
And long to hear the words, "I love you."

She pulled her head up to look at him.

"I do love you," she said sincerely, "and I do trust you."

Somewhere down the road, the car stopped at a deli, and Annie and Stephen went inside. They managed a corner booth where they could sit unnoticed and ordered some sandwiches and French fries. Two people did recognize them, and they gave autographs before leaving. Annie was freezing again, however, by the time they made it back into the limo. The rain was still pouring, and the weather was getting colder and colder.

"I thought when it got this cold, it was suppose to snow or ice or something," she complained through chattering teeth. "I hope Leonard knows how to build a fire."

"It will probably turn to snow tonight," he said rubbing her arms to warm her up. "And yes, Leonard builds a wonderful fire."

Darkness did set in before they arrived at his house outside of Saranac Lake. The rain only added to the low visibility. Annie knew they were at a gate house, and to her surprise, there were actually people standing in the freezing rain outside of the wall that surrounded Stephen's estate. Two security guards left the small house and went to man the gate as the car pulled through to ensure no one passed by and made it onto the grounds.

When they drove through the opening, Annie gasped at the sight of his house. It was a glorious two-story mansion, lit up by floodlights with wreaths on every window, and two on each of the double front doors. Matching fir trees lined the driveway, all decorated with blue lights that seem to twinkle as they drove past. Each wreath wore a satin blue bow, and the lights on the lower porch area gave a bright welcome home.

"It's beautiful," Annie breathed as she continued to gaze at the house. "It's big."

"And it has always been lonely," he sighed, "until now."

"I don't know," she said as she shook her head. "It may still be lonely. I'll probably get lost in there and never found again."

"No way," he assured her. "I'll just check all the fireplaces. You're bound to be at one of them."

A man, whom Annie assumed to be Leonard, met them at the front with a large umbrella. He was very tall and thin, probably in his sixties, but had a pleasant face and a charming accent.

"This way, Lady Annie," he said as he helped her from the car. "Have a nice trip, sir?"

"Yes, Leonard," Stephen replied.

Annie could smell smoke in the air. She hoped that meant that a fire was roaring somewhere inside. Leonard walked slowly with Annie and Stephen until they reached the massive porch. He then removed the umbrella, closed it up, and shook it out.

"Mabel's brewed ye up some fresh tea inside," he told them as he opened the door. "It ought to warm ye nicely."

Annie stuck out her hand in greeting and said, "Nice to meet you, Mr. Leonard."

"And ye too, Lady Annie," he replied with a gentle handshake. "I've heard an awful lot about ye these past sev'ral days. Let's get ye out of this weather." He motioned her inside.

Annie walked through one of the double doors into a huge foyer. Garland and bows were draped across the walls. Stephen took her coat and handed it to Leonard who immediately hung it in a small closet. He then took Stephen's coat. Stephen took Annie's hand and led her into a colossal room with the biggest fireplace she had ever seen. The logs were at least three feet long, and the height of the fireplace itself was close to six feet. She immediately walked to it and began to warm herself.

"Was this place made for giants?" she asked Stephen as he joined her.

"It is a large fireplace, isn't it?" he laughed. "I've never used it except for big parties and such. I thought tonight though would be a good time to kick it in again."

"Can I just sleep here?" she asked with a grin. "I love camping. We used to pull the cushions off all the chairs and couches in the house on cold nights, and then we'd lay them in front of the fireplace and sleep there."

"Oh, I don't think that will be necessary," he told her. "Your sleeping quarters should be amply warm and toasty."

Mabel came into the room with a tray containing a teapot, two cups and saucers, and small carafes of cream and sugar.

"Oh, Mabel, wonderful," Stephen said as she approached.

"Would ye like to take it here or in the den?" she asked him, speaking in the same charming accent as her husband.

"Mabel, I'm Annie," Annie said quickly, waving her hand slightly at her shoulder since Mabel's hands were too full for a handshake greeting.

"Yes, love," she said with a pleasant smile. "'Tis lovely to finally meet you. Mr. Stephen has talked of nothin' else."

"We'll take it in the den, Mabel," he said as he took Annie's hand and led her down a small hallway toward the rear of the house. Mabel followed. Stephen opened a set of double doors that were aglow from the fire in yet another fireplace. It was wonderfully warm in there, and Annie's chill immediately began to fade.

Annie sat on a white leather sectional couch near the fireplace as Mable placed the tray on a coffee table and began to pour the tea.

"Will there be anythin' else for ye, sir?" Mabel asked Stephen.

"Do you need anything to eat, Annie?" he asked her.

"No thank you," she said to Mabel, "And thank you so much for the tea."

"My pleasure, love," Mabel said pleasantly as she left the room and closed the doors.

"I know you don't care for tea," Stephen said as he put cream and sugar into her cup and passed it to her, "but it's decaf, and it's better for you than coffee, and you need to be warmed up from the inside out."

"I think I can manage it," she said with a smile as she took the cup and stared around the room. It was decorated with a rustic flair. Along the walls were black and white photographs of various western places she recognized: Colorado, Arizona, Montana, and Wyoming. A large plasma television hung on the wall opposite the couch, and doors stood on each side of the fireplace that she assumed led to the outside. On another wall was a large entertainment center with many shelves containing what looked like a large collection of antique books.

"Nice place," she said as she took a sip of her tea. "I could get used to this."

"I hope so," he said as he sat back on the couch with his own cup.

"I do have a question, though," she said looking back at him. "You have Christmas decorations all over this house, inside and out, but nothing in here? Is this your bah-humbug room?"

He laughed again and shook his head saying, "You're very observant. Actually, I wanted *us* to do this one together."

"Really?" she said wide-eyed.

"Yes," he nodded. "I haven't decorated a tree since Mom and Sandy died. I never wanted to. All the decorations here were for the visitors and the passing fans, not for me. This room I would never decorate anyway. It *was* my bah-humbug room. However, this year, you and I will go cut a tree. We'll make a list of what we want on it, and then Leonard will go to town for us and bring all the paraphernalia back."

Annie smiled warmly at him and leaned back next to him on the couch, cradling her cup for warmth. She just stared at him for the longest time. Was it actually possible that she was here at Stephen Williams' house, drinking tea with him in front of a blazing fireplace, talking of decorating a tree with him for Christmas, and knowing that for the past six hours he had declared his love for her over and over?

"Pinch me," she asked playfully. "This can't be real."

"I will not *pinch* you," he said firmly.

"Then I must be dreaming," she said closing her eyes. "Don't let me wake up."

"I feel the same way," he confessed. "Do you know how many Christmases I have spent alone, with no one at all?"

She shook her head. She could not imagine any holiday alone.

"I know that to you this seems surreal because of the grandeur and the stark contrast to your cozy home and family environment," he told her.

"That's a nice way to put it," she snickered, "cozy."

"Annie, that wasn't a cut. I love your home, and I love the people that fill it and make it a home. This place has been large, cold and empty for as long as I have owned it, but the light of the fire on your face has brought more warmth and joy here in the past few minutes than it has ever seen before. So if I seem overwhelmed or if anyone needs to be pinched, that would be me."

Annie reached over and pinched him through his sweater.

"Ouch," he squeaked. "Are you always so literal?"

"You don't know that about me yet?" she teased. "Always."

"I'm imagining a fun holiday," he smiled as he rubbed where she had pinched.

"I do have one simple request."

"Anything."

"If it snows, can we build a snowman? I never have. We get a few inches now and then in Dockrey, but nothing substantial. And I have *never* had a white Christmas."

"I'll see if I can order one up," he winked, knowing that many Christmases in New York were white.

"Well, then everything will be perfect," she sighed as she turned to face the fireplace.

"Really?" he wondered. "Even without your family?"

"At first, I wondered how I would fare," she confessed, "but each minute here I'm beginning to feel more and more at home."

Stephen did not reply aloud, but he looked up toward Heaven and mouthed a heartfelt "thank you" as he whispered a prayer in genuine gratitude.

Chapter Twenty-Six

Annie was generally a heavy sleeper; it took a lot to rouse her, with the exception of trying to sleep on a flying jet. When she awoke the next morning at Stephen's, she had slept so soundly that she could not remember where she was. The soft down mattress pad along with the down comforter literally enveloped her body like a gentle hug. She rolled over slowly and caught sight of the gas fireplace softly burning and tried to jog her memory.

Stephen's. I'm at Stephen's.

She smiled, stretched, and then gradually emerged from the covers. There was a bite in the air so she scampered toward the fireplace as she grabbed the bottoms of her scrubs. In front of the hearth was a plush brown sofa with recliners built into either end. Her father had always wanted a couch like this. Maybe one day she could afford to actually buy him one. She pulled on her bottoms, and then fell back into the center of the couch. This was Stephen's personal bedroom. He had insisted she take it because of the fireplace. She felt like a queen.

Annie stuck out her feet toward the fire and let the warmth penetrate her socks. She glanced around the room, which was larger than the great room at her home in Dockrey. Stephen certainly did like books, which reminded her of her parents' bedroom at home, but his were either antiques or beautifully bound sets. She wondered if he actually read much or if his interior designer had a thing for literature.

Deciding that it was probably too chilly and too informal to wear her scrubs downstairs, she changed into jeans and a red and blue sweater. However, she refused to put on any shoes. Stephen had insisted she make herself at home, and at home she never wore shoes unless there was a valid reason. Her socks would do just fine. As she dressed, she peeked out the window and gasped in delight; the rain had indeed turned to snow, and the entire land was covered in white.

She opened the bedroom door and walked into the hallway. A delicious aroma hit her nose immediately and she wondered what on earth it could be.

Definitely not bacon, she smiled to herself.

The hallway and stairs were hardwood, and they had apparently been waxed recently. Her sock feet slipped slightly on the floor, and she thought of sliding down the hallway at her grandparents' house growing up. She and her siblings would have contests to see who could slide the farthest in one run. She never won because she had a fear of crashing or falling. For old times' sake, Annie took a little run and slid toward the upstairs railing. She nearly slipped to the floor during her stop, but managed to regain control. She immediately looked around to make sure no one had seen her. She was alone and laughed slightly at her silly feat.

Heading down the stairs, the aroma became even stronger. It was something baking for sure, but she still could not decide what. She came down into the massive room with the giant fireplace, now smoldering in coals, and took another run and slide. No problem. She wove around the downstairs, following the smell and the sounds of clanking dishes, until she discovered the kitchen. Mabel was working away.

"Good morning, Miss Mabel," she said cheerfully as she entered.

"Mornin' to you, love," the woman replied. She was short and stocky, pretty much the opposite of Leonard, but that pleasant look and same brogue connected the two unmistakably. "Did you sleep well?"

"Like a princess," Annie smiled at her.

"My, you are a beautiful lady, even so early in the mornin'," Mabel said shaking her head. "No wonder Mr. Stephen's so smitten' with ye."

"After a night in that room, who wouldn't look great in the morning?"

"I'm supposin' ye want som' coffee, do ye?"

"You read my mind," Annie said as she sat at the bar on a high stool with a padded seat and back.

Mabel poured her a huge mug of coffee and sat it down before her, sliding a tray with cream and sugar down the bar to her.

"What smells so good?" Annie asked her.

"Ah, yeer nose got the best of ye, this mornin', I see," Mabel said with an inviting grin. "Irish pastries I call them. Made just this mornin' with fresh apples bought at the market yest'rday."

"Oh, anything with *pastry* on the end of it has got to be heavenly!"

"Imagine that?" Mabel laughed. "Such a skinny girl likin' the idea of pastry! Stay 'round here long enough, and you won't be havin' that figure no more!"

Annie laughed with her and replied, "I could use some fattening up right now!"

"Yer not kiddin' about that, now, are ye?"

The timer buzzed and Mabel hurriedly grabbed two potholders and reached into the oven. She pulled out what were the most sublime looking baked pastries Annie had ever seen. They were large triangles with flaky crusts, and apples and sauce oozed from every seam. Mabel placed down the tray and quickly retrieved a saucepot from the stove. She then liberally spooned a whitish, sugary glaze over the top of each pastry.

"Miss Mabel," Annie whispered in awe, "I believe you are a true artist in the kitchen."

"But ye haven't tasted 'em yet," Mabel smiled. "It don't matter if they look good if they taste like rocks in yeer mouth. How many ye want?"

"How many?" Annie asked wide-eyed. "They're huge! If I can finish one, I deserve a trophy!"

"Well don't be expectin' any trophies then in this house," Mabel laughed at her as she dished a pastry onto a plate. "Mr. Stephen can down three in one sittin'!"

"Three?" Annie exclaimed. "I would put that into the *sinful* category."

"Oh my," Mabel said cautiously, "then ye need not be eatin' 'round me much. As ye can see, I indulge that sinful category right often now!"

Annie carefully cut a corner of the pastry with her fork and placed the first morsel into her mouth. *Heavenly!* The flaky crust melted as she chewed, and the mixture of the apples and the glaze was beyond anything she had ever tasted before.

"Oh, Miss Mabel," Annie gushed as she continued to chew, "you should open a restaurant and sell these."

"Tried," Mabel said slightly sad as she began to wipe up her work area with a cloth. "Leonard and I came over to the States with the hopes of openin' a little pub and restaurant. Spent all we had on a dream, but it didn't go well with us here. Mr. Stephen's hirin' us was a big blessin'."

"I can't imagine a restaurant failing if you made these things for breakfast!"

"We couldn't either, but it wasn't to happen," Mabel told her.

"However, livin' and workin' here and getting' paid what the boss pays us, we could'a never made that well on our own."

Annie smiled as she took another bite. She knew Mabel was probably right. They lived in this huge mansion most of the year by themselves, and if what Stephen paid his other employees compared to their pay, they probably did do very well.

Alex and Jonathan said very little from the airport to the house. Jonathan tried to keep the conversation down to pure small talk, but Alex was horrible at small talk. They stopped for gas and a cup of coffee, but the lag in conversation made the trip seem longer than ever. Jonathan wondered how his relationship with his one son had become so stressed. He had only countered him once in his life, and that was when he suggested Alex might want to do something more than just play guitar in a band. When Alex insisted that was his life goal, Jonathan backed off. He never wanted to be accused of killing his children's dreams.

When they arrived at the house, Alex was floored to see the fence, the gate, the security, and the crowd.

"What is this?" he asked his father in total bewilderment.

"Annie," was all Jonathan answered.

Jonathan rolled down the window in his pickup and yelled to the crowd, "I told you she's gone! She's with Stephen in New York! Why don't you all go home for the holidays?"

"When will she be back?" someone yelled.

"Are she and Stephen seeing each other?" screamed out another.

"We just want to talk to her," came a pleading fan.

Jonathan rolled up his window and shook his head as the gate opened to let him pass. Would their lives ever be the same here?

Barbara greeted Alex with a warm hug, but Angie stayed a cool distance away. She had no intention of suggesting she was even remotely happy at his being here and Annie's being in New York for Christmas. She had felt like mourning ever since Annie had left yesterday. She wondered if Annie was as miserable as she was, or if Stephen had actually managed to become the number one person in her life.

"What are we doing?" Annie asked Stephen as they trudged through the snow into the woods at the back of his house.

"You'll see," was all he would tell her.

She followed, struggling to make the trek as easily as him because walking in the thick snow was troublesome for her. He was carrying an axe; obviously he was going to cut something. Was he going to split wood? Chop down a tree? Murder her?

For crying out loud, Annie-girl! You have a vivid imagination. You've watched too many horror films with Angie over the years.

"I want to make a snowman," she reminded him as they continued tromping in the snow.

"Later. We have more pressing things at the moment. First, we work, and then we play."

Annie smiled. What was he up to? Stephen finally stopped and pointed toward a beautiful blue spruce.

"That's our tree," he said proudly.

"It is?" Annie replied, admiring its perfect symmetry. "It's a beauty."

"Stand back," Stephen ordered as he lifted the axe and brought it down cutting into the bottom of the trunk.

After several minutes, the tree fell. Stephen looked at her and smiled, breathing heavily from the exertion.

"Congratulations," she said weakly. "You just killed a tree."

Stephen began to rear back and laugh loudly as he shook his head in wonder. He actually slapped his knee in near jubilation.

"What is so funny?" she asked him, wishing she could laugh like that too.

"You!" he managed to say. "I've had Leonard show me for an entire week how to chop down a tree just so I could impress you with my *manliness,* and you weren't the least bit impressed, were you?"

"You could have done that with a chainsaw in probably 1/20th of the time," Annie explained. "You're gonna have to take a chainsaw to it anyway in order to even out that bottom. It'll never stay in a tree stand looking like that."

Stephen laughed and leaned against the handle of the axe.

"I better stick with the piano, in other words," he said still out of breath.

Annie kicked the bottom of the axe so that it went out from under him, but he caught himself before hitting the ground. He gave her a look of revenge, and she realized she had probably better begin running. She took off back toward the house, but it was no use. Running in the snow was impossible for her, and Stephen caught up to her in no time. He tackled her around the waist and tugged her to the ground gently. He pinned her hands and arms down and sat on her tummy as he tried to decide what to do with his catch.

"Gee, how do I get even?" he wondered.

"I would tell you what my sisters used to do with me in this position, but I'm afraid you might try it."

"That was awfully ugly of you, kicking out my axe after I worked so hard to impress you. I should make you carry the tree back all by yourself. So tell me what your sisters would do when they had you pinned."

"Not on your life," she said firmly.

"I would tickle you," he said thoughtfully, "but I don't imagine you would feel a thing through this parka."

"My hair is getting wet and cold, you know? You promised Daddy you wouldn't let me get sick."

He smiled down at her and felt his whole body go warm. Annie Wright was here with him in New York, at his house, for Christmas. The cold had turned her nose and cheeks a bright pink, and her dark brown eyes were teasing him even though she was helpless to move. Then there were her lips. They were wet with gloss to prevent chapping, and they were the most inviting he had ever seen. He had never in his life known anyone more beautiful.

"I bet your sisters never did this," he smiled as he leaned down to kiss her.

Annie met his lips with a warm response. He settled in and loosened his grip, expecting more of the same, but as soon as Annie felt him let up, she flipped him over and jumped up.

"You're right," she said triumphantly. "My sisters would have never relaxed until my torture was over."

He began laughing again as his head lay in the cold, wet snow.

"Pull me up," he said as he stuck out his hand. "Let's get our tree and drag it back to the house."

She hesitated then put out her hand to take his. She pulled it back quickly and asked, "You're not going to pull me back down, are you?"

"I wouldn't dream of it," he said emphatically.

Annie helped him to his feet, and they went back for the tree.

Andie and Doug walked through the front door of the Wright

home with bags of gifts in every arm. They had been shopping without the kids, having left them with Doug's mother.

"Alex!" Andie exclaimed warmly as she went to the couch to greet her brother. "It's so nice to see you."

Alex stood and let her hug him, but as usual, he was distant and the expression was awkward. Doug did not even attempt a greeting.

"Moms," Doug called to Barbara who was in the kitchen with Jonathan, "we forgot to buy tape. Do you have any so we can go ahead and get these wrapped up?"

"Sure, honey," she called back sweetly, "in the utility room. Look inside one of the clear boxes."

Doug looked over to Angie in the recliner and shrugged his shoulders saying, "There's got to be 30 clear boxes in there. Do you have any idea which one holds tape?"

"I'll find it," Angie said as she got up.

Doug took the bags and brought them to the floor in front of the fireplace, along with a large package of wrapping paper. He dropped the items on the floor and began to stoke the fire with the poker. He added a log and then turned back to Andie who had flopped herself onto the couch.

"Ready to start?" he asked her.

Andie simply moaned as she rubbed her now large belly.

"I wrap ugly presents, honey," he reminded her.

"My back hurts," she complained. "Let's take it to the table."

"No, that's okay," Angie said coming in with two rolls of tape. "I'll help you, Doug. Maybe it'll put me in the holiday spirit."

Angie plopped on the floor and began to help Doug sort the items. The array was enormous. Angie tried to organize everything, but there was just too much.

"You have too many kids," Angie mumbled as she decided to just start wrapping and stop categorizing.

"*Now* you tell me," Andie grinned as she tried to find a more comfortable position.

"I vote you stop at four," Angie said with silly glare. "If not, you'll have to start wrapping in August to get it all done."

A knock on the door got everyone's attention.

"I'll get it!" Barbara yelled as she left the kitchen.

She went to the front door, wiping her hands on her apron on the way. She opened the door and exclaimed in glee, "Megan!"

Everyone, except Alex, looked up to the door in delight.

"Megan!" Angie yelled as she stood up and hopped across the mass of toys now cluttering the floor in front of the hearth. She grabbed Megan and hugged her tightly.

Andie stood up and hobbled over to greet her. "Hey, sweetie," Andie said gently as she carefully hugged her. "It is so good to see you."

"You too," Megan smiled at her. "You're getting so big. Is it a boy or a girl?"

"No idea," Andie said as she patted her tummy. "At this point, who cares?"

"Come on in and sit down," Barbara said with a gentle smile. "I'll get you some spiked cider."

Angie's eyebrows went up as she exclaimed, "*Spiked* cider, Moms!"

"*Spiced!*" Barbara corrected quickly. "*Spiced* cider! *Spiced* cider!"

"No thank you," Megan said politely. "I needed to return this shirt to Annie. I had borrowed it while on the tour. Is she here?"

She held out Annie's red silk button-down blouse.

"In New York with Stephen," Angie told her.

"Really?" Megan said with a smile. "How wonderful!"

"Come on in and have some 'spiked' cider," Angie suggested again with a teasing look toward Barbara. Barbara shook her head in embarrassment.

"No, really, I should go," Megan insisted.

Alex stood up and began to head toward to the stairs. "It's okay. I'll leave," he said harshly as he began up the stairs.

"I don't think so," Jonathan said as he came out of the kitchen, himself also wearing an apron. "I think we're all adults here and that we can stay in this room together and act civilly."

"It's okay, Pastor Jon," Megan said quickly. "I really am going."

"Stay a while, Megan," he said more commanding than requesting. "Sit down, Alex."

"I'd rather not," Alex said still facing the stairs.

"Oh, I'm sure," Jonathan continued, "but there are some things I'd like to get to the bottom of. Seeing that Megan's here, this might be a great opportunity to learn more about what happened that fateful night."

"Please, don't do this," Megan nearly pleaded. "You don't understand."

"You're right about that," Angie popped up. "I don't understand any of it. I especially don't understand what happened between the two of you that night!"

"Leave it alone. *Please,* Angie," Megan said hopelessly.

"Come here, honey," Jonathan said tenderly as he walked over to Megan and put his arms around her. "Sit down and talk to us."

"No," she said as she pulled away from him. "I betrayed Alex. I can't stay."

"Betrayed?" Doug nearly yelled as he stood up. "How did you betray him? What about what he did to Annie? Was that not a betrayal? What about Stephen?"

"Stay out of this," Alex said barely controlled as he spun around to face Doug. "This has nothing to do with you!"

"Megan is a part of this family, now," Doug said with a sting in his eyes, "and so am I. And what you did was inexcusable."

"None of you know what you are talking about," Megan burst out, nearly in tears. "There's so much more to it than just that night! Please, leave him alone. It's not his fault."

"You're as crazy as he is!" Angie screamed as she threw up her hands. "Why do you insist on taking up for him even when he has cast you off like old rags? He's treated you like the scum of the earth, totally dishing his vows of marriage, and you stand here defending him still! What is going on?"

Megan stared at Alex who gazed at her with a hateful glare. He shook his head slightly, as if to warn her to keep her mouth shut.

"Alex?" she said weakly. "Why? Why not tell them?"

"Keep your mouth shut," he warned her. "You betrayed me once; don't do it again."

"But, Alex . . ." she tried to protest.

"What is going on here?" Jonathan began to demand. "Megan, sit down! Alex, sit down! Angie, calm down!"

"I can't do this, Pastor Jon," Megan began to cry. "I can't do this to him. If the truth is going to come out, he's going to have to say it. I promised him I would never tell."

"And he promised you 'until death do us part'!" Angie said in a loud reminder.

"Shut up!" Alex yelled at Angie.

"You shut up!" Doug yelled at Alex.

"This is not your family!" Alex retorted.

"Oh, yes it is," Andie defended as she stood next to Doug and took his hand.

"I'm not telling anybody anything," Alex said defiantly. "I don't throw my problems around on other people like you all seem so eager to do."

"Really?" Jonathan said in surprise. "You mean you don't *tell* your problems to others. You put them on us, all right. For years we have borne the brunt of whatever your problems are. We have dealt with your sarcasm, your distance, and your bitterness. And now, the love of your life, your wife, has also had to bear your problems. As I see it, you have projected your problems on every one in this room and some who are not even present. So, as I said, sit down. We are getting to the bottom of this now."

"I'm not saying a word," Alex said resolutely as he sat on the couch and folded his arms in defiance.

"I guess it's up to you, then," Angie said to Megan as Megan took a seat opposite Alex on the couch.

"I won't say anything," Megan said wearily as she glanced at Alex.

"Why?" Angie began to scream again. "What does he have over you? He's ditched you as though your marriage was some minor inconvenience in his life! You stuck with him for six years waiting for the day when he would finally commit himself to you, and he throws you away before your six-month anniversary!"

"Sit down and be quiet, Angie," Jonathan commanded her. She did.

"She does bring up a good point, Megan," Jonathan said gently. "You have nothing more to lose with this; we have a lot to lose. He has torn our family apart, literally. We had to choose between his or Annie's being here for Christmas. What more can he do to you, Megan?"

Alex glared at her even harder, and her demeanor continued to sink. Her eyes were already swollen and leaking with tears, but she only shook her head. She was not going to say anything. Barbara sat next to her and gently held her with one arm. Megan laid her head on Barbara's shoulder and cried.

"I believe this has taken an ugly turn," Barbara told everyone.

"Jonathan, let it alone."

"No," he replied sternly. "This family is being ripped at the seams, and there is a reason. Apparently the only two people who know that reason are sitting in this room and are refusing to talk."

"Be a man, Alex," Doug said scathingly. "How can you watch her squirm like this and do nothing."

Alex just stared at the floor, arms crossed, expression blank.

"For crying out loud, Megan!" Angie yelled again. "You've got nothing more to lose!"

Megan sat up and looked at Angie and said, "Yes, I do. I still carry the hope that if he wants to abandon me, I can't change it, but perhaps he won't have the heart to abandon his child too."

Everyone, including Alex, was taken back by her revelation.

"You're pregnant?" Andie asked in astonishment.

Megan nodded slightly as she looked to see Alex's reaction. He simply stared at her, still with a blank expression.

"Oh, my gosh!" Angie screamed in anger. "Do you even care?" she asked Alex.

Alex only stared. No one could make out what he was thinking.

"Good question," Doug shot out.

"Megan," Jonathan asked, "when did you know?"

"I suspected it for the last month, but didn't know for sure until this morning. I just saw the doctor."

"How far along?" Barbara asked her.

"Three months," Megan said feebly.

"Were you gonna tell me?" Alex finally spoke.

She shrugged. "I don't know. Eventually, I guess. But I didn't know how you would respond. I couldn't bear hearing you tell me you didn't care."

Alex ran his fingers through his long, dark hair and then placed his head in his hands as he sighed deeply. No one said anything. Everyone, except Alex, traded glances. Who would have thought the moment could get any more awkward than it already was?

Finally Megan had the courage to speak, but only Alex understood when she said, "What if it had been your son? Would you want to know? Would you want to help?"

He nodded slightly, but kept his head down.

"Tell them, Alex," she begged gently. "I know they love you. I know they'll understand."

Jonathan sat down next to his son and draped his strong arm across Alex's shoulder.

"Whatever it is, son, we'll understand and we'll deal with it," Jonathan told him. "You have got to let this go, for your own sake, for Annie's, for your family, and if for no other reason, for your wife and your child."

Alex sighed again and lifted his head. He slowly stood up and put his hands in his pockets. He paced slightly before the hearth, still refusing to look at anyone.

"This whole mess," he said almost choking, "can be summed up with one word." He stopped, still struggling with actually telling them the truth.

"What is it, Son?" Jonathan asked.

"Tell them, Alex," Megan pleaded softly. "They'll understand."

Alex looked at Megan with an expression of total defeat as he said, "Toby."

Barbara was the first to respond as her head jerked up. "Oh my God," she whispered in a slow panic. "No."

Alex nodded in humiliation.

"He messed with you too?" Andie suddenly understood.

"What do you mean 'messed with you too'?" Jonathan asked in a controlled anger.

"He molested me several times," Andie explained. "He tried to threaten me, and it worked for a little bit. I finally had enough and told him I would shoot him if he ever touched me again."

"Why didn't you tell us?" Barbara asked in tears.

"He threatened to kill all of you if I did," Andie said. "I told him if he stopped, I would keep my mouth shut."

"He tried with me," Angie confessed. "I wouldn't let him near me. I always thought he was a pervert."

"He tried with Annie too," Alex told them.

Everyone looked back at him.

"He was home alone with just me and Annie," Alex began, his words choppy and emotional. "I was sick. He had been to Annie's room, and apparently she kicked the crap out him, in his groin."

"He was livid," Alex went on. "He told me he loved Annie, but that Annie hurt him real bad. He said he had come to my room to get my gun, and he was going to shoot her right then."

Jonathan could not believe what he was hearing. He could have sworn Toby was a harmless imbecile.

"I pleaded with him not to, but he took the gun and loaded it."

"Oh, Alex," Barbara cried in horror.

"Then he headed for the door," Alex recounted. "I jumped out of bed and begged him not to hurt Annie. I was eleven. I was scared to death. He told me there was one way that I could save Annie's life. He said since Annie wouldn't love him that I had to. And if I ever told anyone at all, he would take her into the woods and slash her throat."

"No," Jonathan muttered in pure disgust, "I let that man into my house."

"Remember the missing cat? Fido?" Alex asked them all.

"He took me out back and grabbed Fido. He got out his pocketknife and cut the cat's throat slowly. He made me watch it die. He said if I ever refused him, that's what he'd do to Annie."

No one could speak. Alex turned toward the fireplace, completely humiliated at the revelation he had just given. Megan stood up to continue the story.

"He gave himself to Toby over and over and over again so Toby wouldn't kill Annie," Megan added. "It wasn't until he was 16 that he made Toby stop."

"He came into my room one night and insisted on things I just couldn't bring myself to do anymore," Alex said as he turned back around. "I was expecting him. I threw him against the wall and put my 12-gauge to his forehead. It was fully loaded. I told him if he didn't promise me he'd never enter this house again, I would blow his head off. He laughed. I cocked the gun. He stopped laughing."

"I remember when he left," Jonathan said weakly. "I asked why he was going so early this time. He said my family didn't love him, and I tried to talk him into staying."

"I hate Annie because I went through all those years trying to protect her," Alex continued. "Every time he came to me, he reminded me of Fido and he reminded me of Annie. And he always said it was Annie's fault, because he really loved her, but she wouldn't love him back. If I ever were to deny him, he would take her into the woods and show her what happens to people who reject him."

No one knew quite what to say next. Barbara stood up and tried to hug Alex, but he backed away.

"Honey, it's not your fault," she told him.

"It's *my* fault," Jonathan said in confession. "Your mother always warned me about him. She had a bad feeling, but I refused to listen to her."

He stood and walked back around the rear of the couch, running his fingers through his hair and over his face in total frustration.

"This is not Annie's fault," Jonathan told Alex. "It's mine."

"I should have insisted," Barbara broke.

"You did," Jonathan said quickly. "I wouldn't listen. It's amazing, isn't it? I tried to protect my kids from all the evil that was out there in the world, all the while I let the worst kind into my house to chew them up and spit them out."

"Andie, why didn't you tell us?" Barbara asked her.

"I was afraid," Andie admitted. "He was a lunatic. He threatened to kill all of you! I was only 13! I was so relieved that he never tried anything again; I didn't want to remember it. In fact, I had hoped it was all forgotten."

"Why didn't you say anything, Angie?" Barbara asked her other daughter.

"Same reason," Angie told them. "His threats were pretty severe."

"Extremely," Jonathan agreed. "Alex, is that why you insisted we never have another pet?"

Alex nodded. He still felt too humiliated to even look up.

"The biggest reason Alex and I didn't marry for so long had nothing to do with money or a career," Megan told them. "He didn't think he could ever live with someone—intimately—after all that Toby had put him through. I loved him too much to give up. I knew we could work through it, and I thought we had until he decided to get revenge on Annie. When I found out that he had made the whole thing up on the tour. . . ."

She could not finish. She could only stare at Alex and wish that somehow everything could have been different from the start.

"I don't suppose you even want to consider pressing charges at this late date," Jonathan asked his son.

Alex only shook his head.

"I understand," Jonathan nodded. He sighed with almost a moan and began to pace slowly behind the couch. "Well, then, I think its time that we let healing begin. I need to start by saying that all of the blame *begins* with me. It doesn't *end* there, Alex. A lot of bad decisions were made in this, and it has snowballed into something that has become so large and out of control that it will be impossible to ever really end the blame game. However, you need to let go of blaming Annie for all of this. As I see it, there are no innocent people in this room except your mother. Andie, Angie, had you said something to begin with, it would have stopped there. Had Annie said something, it would have stopped. But Alex, had you said something, it would have stopped. He threatened you with the same things he did the others. You could have told us too."

"How do you tell someone that?" Alex cried. "How do you explain the humiliation and total frustration of being abused in the most unheard ways?"

"You told Megan?" Jonathan offered.

Alex looked at her, and for the first time in weeks, his expression was tender.

"Yes," he said faintly. "I did tell her. She convinced me that I could trust her, and I did."

"I never betrayed you, Alex," Megan said, her face wet with tears. "Not even here in front of your family thinking I had nothing left to lose. What you did to Annie was wrong. She didn't deserve that, and I told you that over and over and over again."

"I know," he nodded. "I know."

"I'm sorry, Alex," Angie said as she came over to him. "I wish like crazy that I had had enough courage to tell what had happened to me. What you went through was inexcusable. I should have said something."

"Me too," Andie said with tears. "It happened to me too, Alex. You weren't the only one. In fact, I struggled quite a bit with Doug over it when we talked about getting married."

"I had to convince her I didn't care," Doug clarified. "She wouldn't believe me for the longest time. She felt dirty and ashamed."

"But we got through it," Andie continued. "And you and Megan can work this out too. Don't let Toby keep ruining your life after all these years. You be a husband and a father to your own family."

Alex took another deep sigh and reached up to wipe the bitter tears that had managed to escape his hard façade. He could not explain the array of emotions that were working inside of him at the moment.

"I . . . I don't know what to say," he strangled out. "I was only 11. I was so scared. Even now, when I think about it . . ."

"Stop thinking about," Jonathan said as he came over to him. "No more. This nightmare is over and look what you've got at the end. Megan, come here."

Megan obeyed and walked over to Alex and Jonathan. Jonathan took her hand and placed it inside of Alex's.

"Step one in all of this is for you two to work things out. Angie and Andie will go to Bob and Kim's and pack your things, Megan. You two can stay in the garage apartment for the rest of the holidays."

Alex held tightly to Megan's hand. He still could not bring himself to look at anyone.

"Go on upstairs," Jonathan told them. "Talk this over. Take all afternoon or take all night or however long you need. We won't bother you, and when you feel like you can face the family again, we'll be here with open arms and hearts. And then as a family, we will take the next step by beginning to let all that's been broken over the years start to heal. Can we agree on this?"

Alex nodded slowly as he forced himself to look at Megan. She smiled hesitantly as she saw his eyes. He led her by the hand to the staircase, and together they walked up and went inside the apartment.

It was freezing in the garage room.

"Let me turn on the heat," Alex offered as he moved away.

"No," Megan pleaded as she grabbed his hand and turned him back toward her. "I don't care how cold it is. I need you to know that I love you, and that I want to be with you so badly I can hardly breathe."

He smiled as he pulled her close to him and held her tightly. For the first time since she had known Alex, he began to cry. She simply held him as the sobs began to pour from him. He cried longer than she had known anyone to cry. When he finally began to subside, she pulled back to look him in the eyes.

"Please tell me you still love me?" she pleaded as she reached up to touch his wet face. "And tell me you want this child."

He couldn't speak, but he nodded and tried to smile through his quivering lips. Megan felt a huge sense of release rush through her body, and for the first time in weeks, she felt as though life might still be worth living.

Alex bent down to kiss her gently, but she could not hold back. She wrapped her arms around him and let her passion get the most of her. As she let herself go, Alex immediately responded by picking her up in his arms and taking her to the bed. His only thought at the moment was thankfulness that his father had promised not to interrupt them until they came down from the room.

"Telephone for ye, Miss Annie," Mabel said cheerfully as she peeked inside the den where Annie and Stephen were decorating the tree.

"Thank you, Mabel," Stephen told her as he went to pick up the phone on the table next to the couch. "Here you go," he said as he handed it to Annie."

Annie took the phone and reached over to kiss Stephen quickly as she bounced past him to the couch.

"Hello," she said brightly.

"Hey, sweetheart," came her father's voice. "How's the weather?"

"White," she said with a big grin. "How's the weather down there?"

"Are you sitting down?"

"Yes," she replied guardedly. "What's going on?"

Stephen had long since stopped decorating the tree to join Annie on the couch. When she finally hung up after an emotional and drawn out conversation, she immediately fell into his arms on the couch and cried. He did not bother asking her what had happened because there would be no way she could talk at the moment. As horrible as the situation appeared to be, Stephen was glad that he was the one on this end offering the comfort.

When Annie finally could speak, she remained in his arms and laid out the whole story. As he heard it, his body boiled with emotion. His abuse as a child had been purely emotional. He could not imagine anyone going through what Alex had. When Annie finished, he held her tightly and began to pray aloud for Annie, Alex, and the entire Wright family. He poured out his heart for God to work a miracle in all of them.

"All those years he hated me because he thought it was my fault," Annie said in unbelief. "If only I had known."

"Don't you wish you could change the past sometimes?" Stephen asked wistfully.

"Yes," she nodded. "Desperately."

"But we can't," he sighed sadly. "However," he sat up and turned Annie's face toward him, "we can definitely shape the future."

She agreed, but did not know where he was going with his thoughts.

"I'm tired of my past," he confessed to her. "Shoot, I'm tired of my present. I'm tired of going in circles year after year, doing the same thing over and over."

"But you do it so well," she half-teased, ready to lighten the mood.

"But what does it matter if it has no meaning any more?" he asked her. "All I am doing with my life is fulfilling a contract. I am so sick of it. I want a change, Annie, a *big* change."

"You can't quit, Stephen," she tried to be the voice of reason in all the emotion.

"I know," he said as he took both of her hands in his, "but maybe if I didn't have to do it alone. Maybe if you would just consider joining me?"

"On what? The next album? The next tour?" she wondered.

"In life," he simply said.

She was confused.

"Marry me," he pleaded. "Just marry me, and then do everything with me. Get me through these last two albums, and then I will give myself to anything *you* want to do."

Annie's eyes grew wide, and she felt herself begin to grow faint again. Had he indeed just proposed? It couldn't be possible! She had hoped that perhaps this relationship would grow into marriage, but she had really imagined it too improbable. He stared at her with a look of longing and expectation. Surely, he did not expect an answer right away! How could she just decide on the spur of the moment if she wanted to marry him or not?

Annie-girl, there is nothing spur of the moment about this! You have been head over heels in love with him since you were 15! He just proposed; you had better tell him something.

"When?" she managed to squeak out.

"Wednesday," he said quickly.

"Which Wednesday?" she asked, still in a complete daze.

"Tomorrow Wednesday," he offered as he held her hands tighter.

"You want to get married tomorrow?"

"No, I want to get married right now," he smiled, "but I figure you probably need a day to do whatever it is you might need to do before tomorrow."

"My gosh," she said as she felt her face go flush and her consciousness begin to fade, "I think I'm going to pass out."

Stephen immediately laid her back on the couch and raised her feet up on a cushion as he asked, "Is that good or bad?"

"Tomorrow, huh?"

He looked down over her and smiled as he said, "Too ambitious of me? I guess I'm just so ready to have you here, forever. If you'll just agree to marry me, I'll try to be happy, regardless of when."

Annie smiled and closed her eyes as she felt the blood rush back into her head. She thought back to when her father had said goodbye at the terminal. He had told her not to be too conventional with her thinking. Is that what he meant? Had he known that this would happen?

"I need to call Daddy," she suddenly realized.

"I don't want to marry your Daddy," Stephen teased her.

She chuckled slightly as she opened her eyes to see his face. So handsome, so caring, so gentle, and genuinely in love with her. No, this had nothing to do with her father. Did she want to spend the rest of her life with this man? Did she?

"Yes," she answered herself aloud.

"Yes, I want to marry your Daddy?" he asked puzzled.

"Yes, I'll marry you—tomorrow."

"Yes!" he yelled as he jumped into the air and twisted his body in a circle. "Yes! Yes!"

He ran to the double doors, opened one, and yelled out, "Mabel! Leonard! She's going to marry me! Tomorrow!"

He ran back to the couch and knelt down beside her.

"Tell me again," he asked her. "Tell me you'll marry me."

"I will," she said cautiously, still feeling a little faint.

"You will what?"

"I will marry you?"

"Yes!" he yelled again. "And if you actually do pass out during the ceremony, I'll be right there to hold you up, until you say *I do!*"

"I feel so secure about it all, now," she giggled. "You're sure you want to marry me?"

He said nothing but instead bent down to kiss her. She put her arms around his neck and pulled his whole body closer to her. He laughed and pulled away to tell her, "You'd better not. I promised your father no hanky-panky until we were married."

"For crying out loud," she complained. "This is not hanky-panky. Angie did more than this in the balcony with Billy Marcum. Besides, you've got to get the blood back into my head before I really do pass out."

"Well, if you insist," he smiled as he kissed her again.

Chapter Twenty-Seven

"Good morning, beautiful. Happy Valentine's Day."

Annie knew that was Stephen's voice, but she was so tired and disoriented that she could not remember much of anything else.

Very sleepy. Where am I? Oh, Paris. Charity concert tomorrow night. Jet lag, again. Stephen! It's okay; we're married. Roses? I smell roses?

"Good morning," he said again in a singsong fashion.

Annie tried to open her eyes, but only one managed to make it. A red blur was swaying before her face. She closed her eye and then reopened; both eyes made it this time. When she finally focused, a single red rose was being waved in front of her eyes. She smiled at the thought and rolled over in her bed to face the blue eyes and blond curls lying beside her.

"Happy Valentine's Day," he said again.

"Just one rose?" she asked him. "Before we were married, you used to shower me with dozens at a time."

"Do you not know the significance of a single rose?" Stephen asked her.

"Until I met you, the only flower I had ever received was a corsage for my senior prom. That's it. Don't know much about the whole flower thing."

"Well, let me enlighten you," he said as he laid his head back and held the rose into the air. "A single red rose symbolizes true love."

"Well then, I accept your rose with a warm heart and a mutual return," she said taking the rose and leaning over to kiss his cheek gently.

"Are you awake now?" he wondered.

"Close. How do you manage to just get over the jet lag thing without being totally exhausted?"

"Years of experience. Now, how awake are you?"

"Awake enough! Why?"

He jumped up from the bed and began to rummage around in his luggage. He yelled and came back to the bed bearing a small gift. He sat down next to her and handed her the package.

"Oh, my," she said with a smile as she sat up in the bed. "Valentine's Day in Paris and a little present to boot. You are quite the romantic this morning, aren't you?"

"Well, it's not actually morning, if you really must know. It's around two in the afternoon."

"Really? What time is it in New York?"

"About eight."

"This is unnatural," she complained with a pout as she rubbed her sleepy eyes.

"Would you stop whining and open your gift," he said impatiently.

"Okay, okay," she agreed.

She carefully removed the white bow and then began to untape the shiny red paper. Once off, a small white box was revealed.

"How nice," she teased him. "Something practical?"

He rolled his eyes at her said, "Go on. Finish the job."

She removed the lid from the box and pulled out a small white velvet box.

Jewelry.

She looked over at the cross necklace he was wearing that she had given him at Christmas. He had put it on Christmas morning and had yet to take it off. No one had ever given him jewelry before, and he refused to buy it for himself, thinking it was vain and senseless to spend money on pure adornment if it held no sentimental attachment. His cross was extremely sentimental to him now.

Annie smiled expectantly as she slowly pulled open the top to the box. She gasped in awe at the beautiful diamond ring inside.

"Stephen," she whispered, "this is huge! My finger will fall off if I actually wear it."

"People keep asking us if we're really married. They can't see that tiny little band on your left hand. This," he said as he removed the ring from the box, "should stop all speculation."

"I should say so! You put it on me." She sat straight up and scooted beside him, holding out her left hand.

Stephen gently slid the large diamond over her finger and then leaned down to kiss her hand.

"There's more significance to this ring than you know," he told her. "I actually bought it here, in Paris, months ago."

"You're kidding? When we were here on the tour?"

"Yep," he nodded as he sat back on the bed and pulled her next to him, cradling her against his chest. "I was going to propose to you after the concert."

Annie shot up quickly and turned to face him.

"You actually had *this* ring with you that night?"

"In my pocket during the entire Paris concert. That's why I wanted to meet you afterward."

Annie shook her head sadly and admitted, "And Alex convinced me instead that your intentions were totally dishonorable."

"But we're not going there," he reminded her. "I just wanted you to know that this ring has been in the wings since then, waiting for the right time of its unveiling."

"You knew we'd be back in Paris for Valentine's Day," she smiled.

He nodded.

Annie lay back against his chest and relaxed for a moment. So much had happened to them since that November in Paris. After marrying in December, they decided to work on a Christmas album together, postponing Annie's future career by a year. They would record the album in the spring, release it in October, and do an abbreviated tour during November and December. That would leave Stephen with only one year more to fulfill his contract. So for now, he and Annie decided they would make the Christian album to honor the Lord with their gifts. Annie confessed to being uncomfortable with the glitz, the glamour, and even the sensuality that seemed to accompany her short time in pop music. As much as she loved the recognition, that persona was not who she was. While Stephen was completing his last album, Annie would release her first solo album, a collection of Christian songs she had written over the years.

"I sort of have a Valentine's gift for you," she said with a sigh.

"New pajamas?" he asked hopefully.

"What? You don't like my scrubs?" she said turning up to see his face.

"Well, I mean, there are other options for sleeping attire," he told her. "You don't have to throw the scrubs out completely, just change now and then, you know, spice things up."

"Like you need that," she giggled. "No new pajamas."

"Okay, what then?" he asked as he pulled her even closer.

"I think I'm pregnant."

"What?" he nearly yelled.

He pulled her away and slid in front of her to see her face.

"You *think?*" he asked.

"I'm not sure," she said awkwardly.

"Why do you *think* that?"

"I'm so hungry all the time," she began. "That's how Andie always got. Plus, well . . ."

"What?" he asked, his eyes growing very wide.

"I haven't had a period since we've been married. That's probably a good indication."

"Whoa," he said shaking his head. "I never thought about anything like that. I mean, I haven't lived with any women since my mother died."

"I've never been real regular with it," she explained, "so I didn't think anything about it either, but when I started wanting to eat everything in sight, well, I put two and two together."

Stephen slowly rose from the bed and ran his hand through his tangled hair as he began to pace slightly.

"Is this okay?" Annie wondered, not being able to read his reaction.

"Okay?" he said turning toward her. "It's . . . I don't even know how to describe it! I'm totally delirious. No, I'm not *delirious*. I'm more like . . . gosh, Annie . . . I'm . . . *what* am I?"

"I don't know," she said concerned. "Are you happy or sad?"

"Thrilled!" he called out. "I'm completely thrilled!"

He came down next to her and gently touched her tummy.

"How do we find out for sure?" he asked with excitement. "Do we need to see a doctor?"

"You can get a home testing kit," she told him.

"Let's order one up now!" he said jumping up.

"You can't order them up like food. You have to get them from the drug store."

"I'll call Jeff and send him out for one right away!"

"Alex!" Megan called as she stood at the top of the balcony in the Wright home. "Have you seen my black heels?"

Alex scratched his head and thought.

"No, honey!" he yelled back. "Did you wear them to church on Sunday?"

"I can't remember," she said shaking her head as she went back into the garage apartment to search further.

Alex walked into the kitchen where his mother was cooking something delicious.

"Evening, Moms," he said as he came to see what smelled so good.

"Where are you headed off to on this Valentine's Day?" she asked him.

"Riccatoni's," he smiled. "Megan feels like Italian."

"Are you packed for New York yet?"

"Just about," he smiled. "Stephen and Annie will be back on Saturday. We start recording on Monday."

"That's wonderful," she said as she reached up to gently caress his face. "I'm so glad things have worked out for all of you."

Alex nodded, slightly smiling. "The counseling has been good for me," he confessed. "I didn't want to talk about it, not at all, but it was a good thing. I'm thankful to be moving on."

"You have a lot to be thankful for," Barbara said with a loving smile. "A beautiful wife, a perfect job, a baby on the way . . ."

A bundle of fur burst into the kitchen interrupting Barbara's sentence.

"Hey, Rover," Alex grinned as he reached down and picked up the puppy. "How you doin', boy?"

The puppy barked and wiggled as he tried to lick Alex's face.

"What a cutie," Barbara remarked. "He'll probably destroy your apartment with all that energy he has."

"Who cares?" Alex laughed. "Let him at it!"

Megan walked into the kitchen dressed in a lovely red dress, complete with her black heels. She was barely showing, so the loose cut dress accentuated her still trim figure.

"Wow," said Alex in admiration, "you look beautiful."

"Why, thank you," she smiled back. "Put down the dog and get me some food, quick!"

Alex complied and waved to his mother as he and Megan left the kitchen. Barbara glanced down at the puppy that was staring at her with big, brown eyes, practically begging for a taste of whatever it was he smelled.

"Oh, all right," she said exasperated.

She reached into the pot and pulled out a squared cube of beef.

"Sit!" she commanded.

The dog immediately stood on his back legs with his paws out. She dropped the morsel into his mouth where he promptly gobbled it up and stood back on his paws hoping for another bite.

"No more," Barbara said firmly.

Suddenly the sound of laughter and pure rambunctiousness came bursting through the front door. The puppy forgot his present obsession and took off out the kitchen for some major puppy lovin'. Barbara smiled as the noise of grandchildren began to fill the previously serene house.

"Roefer!" yelled Ashley as the puppy greeted her excitedly.

Barbara gave the stroganoff another stir and went to the great room to greet her houseguests for the night.

"Where's my baby?" Barbara asked with her arms outstretched for the newborn little girl.

"Here she is, Mimi," Doug smiled as he handed the pink bundle to her. "Are you sure you're up to this? A whole night?"

"Of course!" Barbara exclaimed. "I raised four of my own, remember?"

"Yeah, but these are a little more on the wild side, wouldn't you say?"

"Are you kidding?" Barbara laughed. "You obviously didn't know Angie and Annie well as children!" She turned her attention to the infant. "Hello, baby Aimee. It's Mimi," Barbara cooed.

"Augh! Grrrr!" came Jonathan from the bedroom, complete with monster slippers and tattered robe.

The three older children squealed in delightful terror as he chased them around the room, individually scooping one after another up and tossing them above his head. The puppy was barking profusely as he ran around the room trying to decide which bit of the chaos he wanted to attack first. His decision was made when Ashley pulled him up into her arms and kissed his nose.

"Okay," Doug said cautiously, "I guess I'm leaving them with you."

"This is a wonderful Valentine's Day present, Doug," Barbara said as she rocked Aimee on her shoulder. "A whole night off from the kids. She should love you forever after this."

"I don't know," Doug said questionably. "She's worried about whether Aimee will take the bottle or not since she's only nursed her, and then Adam sneezed all afternoon. She says he doesn't have a fever yet, but . . ."

"Doug," Jonathan said firmly, "we can handle it."

"As for the nursing," Barbara said with raised eyebrows, "if she gets hungry, she'll eat. Andie will be more miserable than the baby by morning. Isn't that right, little boo-boo?" Barbara touched noses with the baby and went back to the kitchen.

"Have a wonderful evening," Jonathan told Doug as he shook his hand.

"It will mostly consist of letting her sleep, I imagine," Doug said. "I'm going to rent a wonderfully romantic movie and get some Chinese takeout. I'm hoping she'll fall asleep in the middle of it all and saw the logs until morning."

"You're a good man," Jonathan smiled.

"Yeah," Doug teased. "How did she get so lucky? Bye, kids! Daddy's going!"

He smiled with comfort because not a single child cared; they were thrilled to be spending the evening with Mimi and Gaga. He stopped by the video/music/pet food/tuxedo rental store for the most romantic movie he could find, and then dropped by the Chinese restaurant for some takeout.

Andie leaned back on the couch and picked up the remote control with one hand as she placed another piece of shrimp in her mouth with the chopsticks.

"Doug, go ahead and put the movie on," she told him as she stretched out. "I'm so sleepy I could drop right now."

Doug looked at her with a quizzical expression and asked, "Do you really think I'm going to relinquish control of the remote to you tonight?"

"Yes," she smiled as she pulled the remote close to her chest. "It's Valentine's Day."

"You're pushing it, you know?"

"It doesn't get much better than this," she sighed as she reached over into his plate with her chopsticks and picked up one of his shrimp.

She gently kissed his cheek before she placed the bite into her mouth. "This is the best Valentine's Day ever."

"You're kidding me, right? The best Valentine's day ever was our first one after we were married."

"The motorcycle on the Natchez Trace?" she said with wide eyes.

"Now *that* was a great Valentine's Day!"

"We could have been arrested for that, you know?"

"Yeah," he grinned. "I know."

"Well, things are a long cry now from what they were then. I mean, normally we would get all dressed up and go out to some fancy restaurant somewhere. Now, you come home and there's toys strewn all over the floor, school books piled on the furniture, and your wife is frumped out in an old sweat suit stained with spit up all over it. Between home schooling, the baby, the laundry, and the cooking, I don't even have time to remember how to spell my own name."

Andie glumly laid her head on Doug's shoulders and sighed.

"I wouldn't trade anything for what we have right now," he said gently.

"Really?" she asked as she looked up at him. "You really mean that?"

"Absolutely!" he said emphatically. "We had a great past! Two teenagers madly in love living off microwaved chicken fingers and tater tots."

"Just because we could!" Andie chuckled.

"Sure! And now we have this great present. Four kids, a messy house, very little sleep, but a ton of love and laughter. This won't last long, Andie. We'll blink our eyes tomorrow, and they'll be teenagers and then leaving home. I like the toys and the mess and the laughter. Shoot, I even love the crying! It all reminds me of how alive we are and what we have built together. You won't find one complaint from me."

"You're just being very sweet to me; that's all."

"Well, that too," he smiled as he tightened his arms around her. "We're building our future here too, Andie. This isn't the end, and I even love the way you look in that gorgeous navy sweat suit with spit up stains all over it."

"Hmmm," she smiled as she snuggled on his shoulder again. "You *are* just being nice. Put on the movie before I crash."

"Hey," Doug protested, "you *cannot* go to sleep on me during this movie. It was the sappiest thing I could find. If I have to watch it alone, I will be pure fodder to the guys at the site for the next month."

"Here," she said handing him the movie. "Put it on. I've got the remote."

Doug placed the video in the machine and came back to the couch. Andie curled up with her head in his lap and turned up the volume. She was out before the first scene even finished. He softly ran his hand down the back of her long wavy hair and smiled in admiration as his other hand picked up the remote. He turned off the movie and changed the television to the motorcycle channel.

"I haven't given up on the motorcycle again yet," he smiled. "I'll get you back on one eventually."

Angie came into her dorm room emotionally exhausted. She dropped her books onto the floor next to the desk, not even bothering to put them anywhere for the sake of order. Her room was a wreck anyway. She had taken too many hours again, but she would be finished with seminary at the end of April. Hopefully by then, the mission board would have found a way out of whatever the problem in appointing her seemed to be.

She grabbed a bottle of water from the small refrigerator and turned on the computer. *Maybe someone is online and feels like chatting for a while. I need to think about something other than the kings of Judah and Israel.*

As the computer dialed up her connection, she took down her ponytail and shook out her long hair. She was exhausted. Years of college, pre-med, medical school, internship, residency, and now seminary had just about taken their toll on her. She was 29, and she was still in school, and the promise of Padawin was looking dimmer with each month that passed.

She signed on to her instant messenger and checked to see if anyone she knew happened to be on line.

Unreal! Michael Collins is actually online! I didn't think this would ever happen!

She clicked his name and immediately typed in a *hello.*

DrAng: Hello!

farmboy: Angie?

DrAng: Yes! Is this Michael of Padawin?

farmboy: Yes! I can't believe we're actually chatting! Where are you?

DrAng: In my dorm. Can you believe that? I'm 29 and still in school. I was just bemoaning that fact.

farmboy: Hey, it's for a good cause . . . no! A GREAT cause! You're almost through. Hang in there.

DrAng: I'm trying.

farmboy: Any luck with the board?

DrAng: Do you really want to hear about all that during our first official chat?

farmboy: I guess not. Don't give up. I really believe that God wants you here. Things will happen. Remember, all things work out for the good.

DrAng: That's what my Dad keeps telling me.

farmboy: I'd like to meet your dad some day. He sounds like a great guy.

DrAng: He is. Moms is great too. Did you know today is Valentine's Day?

farmboy: No. I don't keep up much with holidays over here. We just celebrated Christmas here for the first time because I actually had enough Christians to warrant teaching them about it. Anyway, it's already the next morning here, so Valentine's Day has passed.

DrAng: So what did you get for Christmas?

farmboy: A monkey.

Angie laughed aloud when she read that.

DrAng: LOL . . . You did not!

farmboy: Yes I did! They thought it would keep me company. They wanted me to bring it in the house and let it sleep with me and the whole bit. I just couldn't.

DrAng: So, where is it?

farmboy: On the back deck tied to a rope. It's really a rather mean little thing.

DrAng: Save it for me. I want to see that when I get there.

farmboy: You'd better hurry, then. I have no intentions of keeping it around very long. It will "accidentally" get untied one day and run off to the jungle . . . I hope.

DrAng: LOL . . . I still think you're pulling my leg.

farmboy: I'm not that smart. Trust me, my sense of humor lacks a lot. Especially living over here. They do not get Western wit at all.

DrAng: Well, I do! In fact, I probably laugh more than I should. One of the professors here asked me if I took anything seriously. All I did was laugh aloud when he talked about David relieving himself in the cave. I couldn't help it! It reminded me of a Bible study back in youth group when my sister and I lost it during a study of David . . . that particular passage.

farmboy: There's nothing funny about that. Necessity calls, you know?

DrAng: What time is it there?

farmboy: 11:28 in the morning. You?

DrAng: Somewhere around 9:30 at night. I hope I adjust to time zones better than my sister.

farmboy: Does she travel much?

DrAng: She does lately. She's is Paris right now.

farmboy: Great place to be for Valentine's Day.

DrAng: Tell me about it. She's there with her new husband. I imagine it's a mighty awesome V'Day for the two of them.

farmboy: I guess so. So did you have a date tonight?

DrAng: Are you kidding? I'm not the ideal Valentine's date. As soon as my tour of duty is done here at the seminary, I'm heading out to the Pacific. It doesn't make for meaningful conversation.

farmboy: I think the monkey and I shared some dates together last night . . . you know, the fruit. That's as close as I've come to a date in nearly 12 years.

DrAng: You win the most pitiful prize award then. I have dated a little here and there.

farmboy: Potential missionaries don't make the best prospects unless you're blessed enough to find someone like-minded.

DrAng: Tell me about it!

farmboy: Oh, man! Kita, a little guy here in the village, just came in and said that the pen for the cows broke again. I've got to go.

DrAng: Duty calls. It was great to finally chat with you!

farmboy: Yes! I wonder what the possibilities are that our schedules will work out like this again. I seldom have free time in the morning like this.

DrAng: Well, at least I got to talk with a guy on Valentine's Day. Go get your cows.

farmboy: You hang in there, and don't give up. I've already told the villagers about Dr. Angie. If you don't come, they will be highly disappointed.

DrAng: Keep praying, then. Take care.

farmboy: Bye, Angie. I am praying.

DrAng: Me too. Bye, Michael.

Angie simply shut down the computer. Anything after talking with Michael would be a major letdown. She moved slowly to her bed and picked up her Old Testament textbook to try and memorize the kings of Israel and Judah, but her mind kept wandering to Padawin. She and Michael had exchanged e-mails for several months, but this was the first time they had ever been signed in online at the same time.

He was fun. I could work with that.

His e-mails had always been so serious, but his chatting took a lighter turn. She was glad. Perhaps he was like Annie—an e-mail was often nothing more than a report of her day, to the point and just the facts, please. In real life, however, she was a ball of fire.

Angie looked back at her text and read the name *Rehoboam.* This was not going to be a fun night.

If I actually refuse to learn these names, will I blow my whole missionary career? I mean, it's not like the bones of the body or the major organs. Who cares who begat whom?

She turned back to her book and forced herself to concentrate. Years of medical school had taught her that well.

Rehoboam. Jereboam. Abijah. Asa.

As Alex and Megan came in the front door, Jonathan immediately put his finger to his lips to keep them quiet. Megan tiptoed to the rocking recliner to get a peek at baby Aimee while Alex gently shut the door.

"She's so adorable," Megan exclaimed in a whisper. "Look at those little fingers."

"Where's the rest of the clan?" Alex asked them.

"On our bed," Jonathan told him.

Alex's eyes went wide in surprise.

"You let kids into the holy of holies?" he asked in unbelief.

"Why do my children keep calling my bedroom that?" Barbara wanted to know as she stopped rocking for the moment.

"Duh," Alex responded. "We couldn't even walk in there without knocking and identifying ourselves: name, birth date, and social security number."

"It worked, didn't it?" Jonathan grinned. "You knew your social security number. They're watching a movie. Ashley's already asleep."

"This one, however," Barbara smiled, "has not been so easy."

"She looks awfully content right now," Alex said as he peeked over his mother's shoulder at the sleeping bundle.

"She'll be awake again soon," Barbara told him. "She'll be hungry. She refuses to take a bottle."

"Good for her," Megan said. "I like a woman who knows what she wants."

"Let's see that attitude in a few months when yours comes along!" Jonathan laughed.

"Oh, we'll definitely move back here," Megan said quickly. "Then you guys can rock the little one when I'm exhausted."

"We'd be honored," Barbara smiled.

"Well, I *am* exhausted," Alex told them. "I'm ready for bed."

Alex and Megan started up the stairs as Barbara got up to put the baby down. Jonathan went to his bedroom and removed Ashley, taking her to a comfortable pallet on the great room floor. He walked the boys to the bathroom and then tucked them into the bunk beds in Andie's old room.

As he joined Barbara in their bed, he reached over and kissed her cheek.

"Happy Valentine's Day, sweetheart," He told her.

"I had forgotten," she laughed as she snuggled in comfortably. "Things are a little different now than they used to be, wouldn't you say?"

"Most definitely," Jonathan agreed. "Are you glad?"

"Are you kidding? I wouldn't change our lives for anything in the world. Beautiful grandchildren, wonderful in-laws, and a doctor heading to the mission field."

"If she behaves herself," Jonathan said grimly.

"Oh, don't be so pessimistic! Angie is a wonderful girl. God has a call on her life. She'll be on the mission field this time next year, you just watch."

"Do we know the same Angie?"

"Stop fussing and go to sleep. We probably only have a couple of hours before the angel awakes and we start the process all over again."

"*We?*"

"Just like when ours were little—if I get up so do you."

Jeff, Bull and Guy quickly guided Annie and Stephen through the balking crowd at the hotel to their limo. They both waved at the people as they ducked down to be seated. Jeff smacked the top twice, and the driver began to make his way slowly through the screaming mass.

"Just like old times," Annie smiled to Stephen.

"Hmmm," he sighed. "Not quite. This is a whole lot different than last time. We're married, we're expecting, and we get to *share* a dressing room."

"And we're not having to put on those silly *orange* costumes," she complained.

"What was your problem with that?" he asked. "They looked great on stage. You saw the videos."

"*Orange?*"

"You don't think the loud music will harm the baby, do you?" he asked suddenly in concern.

"Two pianos and microphones? I doubt it."

"Do you feel different?" he asked her as he took her hand and gently kissed the top of her head.

"I have felt different since the day I met you," she said meeting his eyes. "This is only more of the same."

"Good different?"

"The best."

At the concert hall, they left the limo to meet the screaming crowd. Annie deliberately waved her ring to the crowd that began to yell louder than before. Stephen took her hand and led her to the door. She waved once more as she entered the building.

Once in the dressing room, Annie found herself laughing as dozens of white roses were sitting everywhere.

"I was completely satisfied with the single red rose, you know?" she chuckled as she wrapped her arms around Stephen's neck and gazed into his blue eyes.

"But *I* wasn't," he admitted as he pulled her close.

"Will you spoil our baby as much as you spoil me?"

"Spoil?" he laughed. "You don't let me 'spoil' you! You insist on cooking, cleaning, and doing my laundry! Poor Mabel doesn't know what to do with herself!"

"I waited 27 years to dote on a man, and that's *exactly* what I intend to do."

A loud knock sounded on the door. "Ten minutes!" came a yell.

"Okay, let me get my tie on," Stephen said quickly as he grabbed the tie from his pocket.

Annie placed it around his collar and began to tie it to finish off the tuxedo. They were dressed in their most formal attire. Her flowing blue Tiffany gown just touched the floor allowing her to wear flat shoes incognito. As she straightened the tie, Stephen looked at her in pure adoration. When she finished, he leaned down slightly to kiss her.

"Down, boy," she teased. "We have a concert to do."

"I know, but you haven't put on your lipstick yet so I just couldn't resist."

Annie allowed him a kiss and then grudgingly went over to put on her bright lipstick.

"Did I ever tell you that you have the most beautiful, inviting, luscious lips in the entire world?"

"Did I ever tell you that *they* were my nemeses in life?"

"I thought that was Kelly McCall?"

Annie smiled as she dabbed her lips with a tissue.

"Must you always be so cantankerous?" she asked as she turned around ready to go.

"Me?" he nearly exclaimed. "I'm cantankerous?"

"Don't look so surprised," she told him as she ran her hand down his cheek on her way to the door. "I would have never married you if you were some passive person. Too boring."

They waited in the wings of the plush hall. The murmurings of the audience had been stilled as the speaker spoke of the importance of the charity function. Stephen knew enough French to loosely interpret what was being said for Annie.

"He's now talking about us," Stephen told her. "He says they have been honored to have me here every year for this benefit function. He says this year is extra special because my sexy wife is with me."

"He said that? Sexy?" she asked in unbelief.

"Okay, no," he confessed. "I added that part. He did say 'lovely,' however."

Annie nodded and smiled.

"Get ready," he told her. "When he announces our names, go on out. You first."

"No," she said quickly. "You first."

"No," he countered, "your piano is on the right. You should go out first."

"We'll hold hands going out," she offered another alternative, "and step in front of the pianos. You then lead me to mine."

The announcer said, "Stephen and Annie Williams!"

The crowd applauded enthusiastically.

"Go!" he told her.

"After you," she merely grinned, refusing to budge.

"You'll pay for this," he said as he stepped out, taking her hand and leading her behind him.

They went to the front of the pianos and bowed gracefully, waving and smiling for the crowd. Stephen then led her to her piano and patiently waited for her to be seated. He bowed politely to her, and then took his own seat opposite stage.

As the performance drew on, the crowd was pleased with the exceptional musicianship shown that evening. Annie enjoyed this more than any of the concerts on the tour the previous fall. She and Stephen excelled at their very best, using only two acoustic pianos. There were no drums, no guitars, and no other instruments except for their baby grands—hers white, his black.

When it came time for the final song, as usual, Annie began the prelude to *Autumn Sunset.* Just as on tour, she began the first verse by herself.

Early November, gaze out my window
Watching the leaves barely hanging on
Pour me some coffee, pick up a novel
Ready to spend another evening alone

Never thought it would be this way
I simply played it safe
And somehow I never gave my heart away.

She looked over to see Stephen smiling at her before he and his piano joined her on the chorus.

So while I'm waiting for someone to love me
Someone who knows me through and through
I'll watch the Autumn Sunset from my single room apartment
And hope and pray that dreams can still come true
And long to hear the words, "I love you."

As the song went on, Annie and Stephen sang to each other across the pianos. He winked, she smiled, and they flirted to the very end. When the last note hung in the air and the tone finally faded, Stephen stood up and went across to Annie. He offered her hand and pulled her gracefully to her feet. They stood in front of the pianos once again and bowed to the crowd that was now on its feet. Stephen looked over to Annie and gave her a gentle kiss in front of everyone. The crowd simply went wild at this.

Stephen leaned over, breathed in the scent of her hair, and whispered to her, "Dreams still can come true."

She leaned back and said, "Tell me about it, city boy."

They bowed again, and the speaker returned with a bouquet of red roses for Annie. She accepted them with another gracious bow and waved in appreciation to the audience. As they left the stage, the cheers continued.

Later that night, as Annie lay awake still jumbled between jet lag and confused hours, she listened to Stephen's rhythmic breathing. She carefully rolled over in bed so she could see him without awakening him. She gently reached up and touched his soft curls.

Dreams most definitely can still come true, she thought to herself. *Most definitely.*

Contact author Daphne C. Murrell
or order more copies of this book at

&

TATE PUBLISHING, LLC

127 East Trade Center Terrace
Mustang, Oklahoma 73064

(888) 361 - 9473

Tate Publishing, LLC

www.tatepublishing.com